S0-EJU-683

STEDMAN WRIGHT

American playboy who gambles
with his life even more recklessly
than with his money.

THEADORA BOULTON

London supermodel whose
beauty makes her the object of
every man's desire—no matter
how dangerous.

ROLLO ROCKFORD

English viscount whose celebrated
charm runs out when he stands
accused of treason and murder.

**A world of fabulous illusion and
deadly reality, where one
international secret controls the
fate of all...**

SMOKE

GEOFFREY LEEDS

WARNER BOOKS

A Warner Communications Company

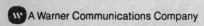

"When I first set out to see the world I thought it existed only in the places I was going to. I was in danger of becoming a series of deferred destinations. Now I know that travel, that 'in-between,' is the time when one lives. I am going to try to turn all my destinations into part of one journey, the long journey from beginning to the end...."

—Anthony Adverse

Contents

Prologue
A Philadelphia Story

1

It was one of those cloying muggy days that come unexpectedly to the City in early spring. The racquets court on the top floor of the Club was not air-conditioned; its cavernous dimensions and many skylights made any effort to reverse the effects of the sun foolhardy.

The two men dressed in whites on the black slate court had been pushing themselves to the limits of their endurance for over an hour. From the spectator's gallery, they appeared to move with ease between the crimson lines, but it was the majestic proportions of the chamber that magically slowed the pace and imparted an effortless grace to their movements belying the 125 M.P.H. speed of the small, rock-hard ball. Loss of concentration could easily mean the loss of an eye, a hazard from which those in the unprotected gallery were not immune, as the pitted bruises in its mahogany benches bore witness.

Stedman Wright had broken the French gut on four of the special long-shafted, small-faced racquets. This was not unusual in tournament play, but it gave his good friend and opponent, Wiley Travis, a strong clue that something was seriously bothering Steddy. The game over, Wiley asked Steddy frankly what was eating him.

"I've got to go to Philadelphia. Suki's marrying my cousin Harry tonight."

Wiley was shocked. Steddy had been living with Suki

for over two years until a few weeks ago, when they'd had a fight, but they had fought often.

"Jesus, she's got balls. What are you going to do about it?"

Steddy shrugged. "Dance at the bitch's wedding, I guess."

Wiley offered him another game, but Steddy said he had to get moving. Later, in the showers, they conversed loudly over the partitions and the noise of the running water. Steddy's deep anger and resentment came more and more to the surface as Wiley tried to placate him with the usual clichés friends employ when trying to rationalize the irrational.

"It's better this happened now. You might have done something really stupid—like marry her yourself."

Oblivious, Steddy bellowed, "God damned whoring cunt!" and punched his fist through the glass partition. The shower ran red with blood.

Calmer now, his initial anger surfaced and expended, Steddy sat in the paneled dressing room sipping a cold Bass Ale from a chilled crockery mug while Charley, the old squash pro, bandaged and taped his injured hand. Wiley sat nearby, his legs sprawled over the arms of a big leather chair.

"You won't be able to drive very well with that hand. Want me to run you down to Philadelphia?"

"No thanks, Wiley. I'm taking the Metroliner anyway."

"Well, at least you had the good sense not to tear up your sporting hand."

"Why? You looking for a handicap?" Steddy smiled for the first time that day.

At thirty-six, Stedman Wright could no longer be referred to as an eligible young man—a bachelor, a club man, a champion athlete, or a sportsman perhaps, but although the older generation liked him well enough, they thought him too worldly, too self-centered, and not "settled" enough to consider him a serious candidate for their daughters.

He was six-foot-two-inches tall and had inherited his mother's dark auburn hair and ease of carriage and his father's eyes, which were a startlingly deep emerald green.

He was well tailored, but anything he wore on his lanky frame took on a casual mid-Atlantic elegance. He seemed unaware of the impression he made, and this quality, coupled with a boyish, devil-may-care attitude about life, made him well liked by his men friends and irresistible to most women and girls.

As the train jerked through the depressing landscape of chemical plants and oil refineries that dot the drab gray Jersey marshes, Steddy sipped a brandy and soda in the comfortable seat of the first-class passenger car. The hypnotic monotony of the bleak scenery gave way to reflection, and reflection to brooding. He had just lost the only girl who had mattered to him in a long time, but the worst part was the realization that she never really could have cared for him, or how could she be marrying his wealthy cousin so cold-bloodedly just three weeks after they had broken up?

The break had been over the usual thing: why couldn't he do something serious like other people? All he did was play games; when would he grow up? She loathed the life-style that had become his routine since leaving college. He rose late, usually walked to the club unless he was late for a game, played racquets, swam, and then enjoyed a late, leisurely lunch. Afterward, he would play bridge or towie, depending upon who was available. Around four-thirty he normally played court tennis or another game of racquets, then at six or six-thirty, he would descend to the main hall, where he earned his "funny money" playing in the high-stakes backgammon chouette until eight-thirty, when, if there were no specific plans, he would go back to his flat at the hotel, have a nap, bathe, and if they could still find a restaurant open, take Suki to dinner.

More often than not he would play backgammon after dinner until the wee hours of the morning, when, around four AM, he would find time for Suki and wend his way home reeking of Havana cigars and brandy.

He could have lived well enough, if not brilliantly, on the income from his trusts, but gambling held an irresistible love-hate attraction for him. It was a particularly vicious cycle. When he won, he won big but usually had a hard time collecting. When he lost, he lost big, and true to the code he had set for himself, he settled his accounts on the spot. The squeeze was ulcer-making, as it was oddly important to him never to show outwardly that he cared. His close friends knew how much winning meant to him because they all came from the same mold, lived by the same code, and rarely gave any quarter. At important racquets matches, his opponents often accused him of gamesmanship when he fled the court to throw up or joked about what he had done the night before, but his friends knew that it came from the underlying tension that is always present in a true competitor no matter how cavalier his superficial aspect.

His mother's car collected him at the station. Earl, the chauffeur and general factotum, who had taught Steddy everything he knew about cards, dice, and street fighting, told him that his "duds" were in the car and that his mother was already at the club doing the place cards.

Presuming Steddy would be late as usual, she wanted him to change at the club instead of at the house.

Steddy shrugged and slumped into the front seat of the old Chrysler, bracing his knees up against the dashboard. The cared-for country smell of the automobile brought on a flood of feelings—unidentifiable but warm and reassuring. Earl got in beside him, tossed his cap in the back seat, started the motor, and then, with one hand on the wheel maneuvering the lumbering vehicle into the stream of traffic, drew a squashed pack of Camels from the shirt pocket under his jacket and lighted one.

"Do you want to talk about it, son?"

"You know more about it than I do. I didn't know the bitch was even seeing him until I heard about the wedding last week; ain't life grand?"

"I meant the hand. Who'd you have a run-in with?"

"It was with a *what*. A shower partition, to be precise."

"Jesus, son, she's not worth it, never was. You never gave two shits for her until now."

"Don't tell me you're on her side?"

"Hell, no. Nice piece of ass, but I never could stand her. You're better off without her. Maybe now you'll meet someone decent."

"For two and a half years everyone told me how great she was. Now, all of a sudden, no one can stand her."

"You never asked me."

Steddy grunted and changed the subject.

"Is Two here?" (Steddy was the third Wright, his father, the second.)

"No, your father's still in Florida."

"The bastard's never here when Mother needs him."

They drove on in silence. Steddy closed his eyes as the dusk turned to evening. His father had never been around; he had never really known him. Earl had always been the closest thing to a father he had ever known.

Steddy was dozing when the exploding noise of gravel under the fat, old-fashioned whitewall tires signaled their arrival at the club. He sat up in the car and pushed his fingers through his hair. Earl, eyes still front, put his hand on Steddy's knee and said, "Now try to take it easy tonight, Sted."

Steddy reached over with his good hand and put it for a moment on top of Earl's.

"Yeah, sure. Thanks, Earl."

Steddy wondered what would happen to the world when it ran out of Earls. Men who did their jobs and then some. He had a soft-spoken brand of wisdom that made everything seem so simple, seen through his eyes.

He smiled, remembering how as a little boy he had wanted his mother to marry Earl. He had thought it a wonderful idea and had told them so repeatedly to their indulgent laughter. Earl had never married, and Steddy often noted how the two of them, Earl and his mother, had a quiet sort of way of communicating—like an old married couple, with Earl anticipating her at every turn. He wondered for the first time in his adult life how deep that understanding went. He hoped for his mother's sake that she wasn't really as alone as she seemed, or as he felt when he stepped from the car and walked into the club.

2

The locker room where Steddy was changing into his dinner clothes still held a sprinkling of golfers and tennis players. One or two came over to Steddy to congratulate him on his mother's horse winning the Preakness the previous Saturday. Georgianna Wright had inherited her father's racing stable, and instead of selling it as everyone had expected, she had thrown herself into its management with a vengeance. The results had surprised the racing world, but not Steddy. He had never known his mother to attempt anything that she wasn't sure she could do well, which was perhaps why she indulged Steddy his backgammon, as he was the best—even if he did lose too much from time to time.

He had ordered a bottle of champagne before getting into the shower and was now methodically drinking it as he dressed. His cousin Tom, the bridegroom's brother, whom Steddy had always beaten at every game the club offered, approached him, and seeing the champagne bottle, asked him snidely "What are *you* celebrating?"

"Getting rid of a French cunt," Stedman replied calmly.

The fight that ensued was short-lived, but as Steddy stepped out onto the terrace, where cocktails were being served before dinner, he noted absently that his already bandaged hand was beginning to seep blood from the blow he had landed.

One of Georgianna Wright's eyebrows was slightly raised as she greeted her son—he sensed that she was secretly amused. Her family were New Yorkers, and after forty years of living in Philadelphia, she still thought of the locals as a bunch of pompous hicks. The Philadelphians, to their credit, recognized quality when they saw it, and that, coupled with her husband's family's position in the city, caused them to look to her as an arbiter of fashion and correct form. They also knew that her shoulder was the only objective one they could bring their troubles to without having them broadcast up and down the Main Line.

Stedman's aunt and uncle had been killed in a small plane in Canada three years before, and although Georgianna Wright didn't much like the children, she had automatically assumed the role of surrogate parent, hosting her niece's debut and now Harry's wedding. The loss of their parents had meant that his cousins had inherited at a very young age, and Steddy concluded that this was at the bottom of Suki's decision to marry Harry.

Suki came over to Steddy and greeted him as though they were brother and sister and had never meant anything more to each other. She linked her arm in his, and maneuvering him away from the receiving line, said, "We must talk." When he didn't respond, she went on. "Darling, you knew I couldn't go on like that forever—you'll never grow up." Her almond-shaped eyes squinted into slits, and he wondered how he could ever have thought them beautiful. "I've told you a hundred times that I simply can't live without security, but you wouldn't change. Harry loves me—oh, I'll never want him the way I want you, but . . . ."

Her voice faded into the background chatter. Steddy stood quite still for a moment without expression or comment, numbed by hearing from her own lips that she was in fact marrying Harry for his money. Finally, he turned from her as though she had never been there and strode to the bar.

Aunt Edith took his arm and steered him from the bar, but not before he had got both of them a glass of champagne. She wasn't really his aunt but his mother's oldest and closest friend, ever since they had been at school in Florence together as girls. She was the daughter of an

English duke and had married a Scottish earl, who had been killed at El Alamein during the war.

Steddy adored her and sometimes thought she cared more for him than she did for her own two boys. The eldest, Jock, had inherited the title when her husband died. He was essentially a farmer who spent his life running the estates and making arcane speeches on insects in the House of Lords. That wasn't so bad, but what was anathema to her— was the fact that he hated shooting and all sport even to the point that he left Scotland when the grouse season began. Peregrin, the younger son, had become a forty-year-old hippie, in a state of delayed development, and frittered away his time racing from one guru to the next one who became fashionable, be he in Bangladesh or Los Angeles. Neither of her sons gave her any joy.

He smiled, remembering how she had sneaked him his first champagne cocktail at a party in her hotel suite in New York when he was fourteen. Ever since then their relationship had been one of contemporaries, even though she was more than twice his age. They would lunch whenever they found themselves in the same city, which could just as easily be Rome or Lausanne as London or New York, and they exchanged confidences—he about the problems he was having with his latest girl friend and she about how boring it was to have to go out with creaky old men. Though she was well into her seventies, she was still a handsome woman of timeless elegance, who retained a giggle of girlish mischief. Once when she was visiting with them in Philadelphia, an old bag at the club had told her she looked marvelous and then bitchily asked if she'd had her face lifted. Edith's answer, in the days when such things were kept secret, had been: "If your dress is wrinkled, you have it pressed, don't you?"

Her opening remark brought Steddy from his reverie.

"Now you're not going to misbehave are you, dear boy? Your mother's quite concerned."

"Don't worry, Edith—they deserve each other as far as I'm concerned. But what are you doing here? Surely you didn't come all this way to see those two insects get married?"

"Certainly not. I don't care for either of them any more than you do. I was over having a little "tuck" at Boston General, and your mother asked me down for a few days—I don't think this little event was even in the works when she asked me. It's all rather sudden, isn't it?" she said with a mischievous twinkle in her eye.

"Now, Edith, don't *you* be naughty. You know very well that 'sudden' is the understatement of the year!"

The dinner gong was sounding, and a dapper white-haired gentleman with a crimson carnation in the lapel of his dinner jacket approached to take Edith to her table. She winked slyly at Steddy, who was eyeing her beau, and said, "Now don't you do anything I wouldn't do."

"That certainly leaves me a lot of leeway!" he parried, smiling with affection.

3

The dinner for two hundred fifty was in the Trophy Room, a vaulted Tudor affair with paintings and animal heads climbing the walls in no apparent order until they disappeared in the dusty darkness made by the shadows of the heavy crossbeams.

Steddy, already slightly pissed, found that he was seated at an orphans' table made up of obscure relatives and anonymous faces on the outer fringes of the gathering, but, happily, near the service bar. Dinner passed without incident—Steddy talked to no one. The others accepted his silence and spoke behind him or across him as he sipped from a second bottle of Cristal that he had sequestered from the bar and made quite clear to everyone was his and his alone.

Dessert over, the last toasts from the corners of the room were petering out when Steddy drew himself erect and banged a spoon on his glass for silence until he broke it.

All eyes were on him with the possible exception of Suki's and his mother's. Gripping a giant torpedo-shaped Monte Cristo number two Havana in the same hand as his champagne glass and speaking with the surprising clarity and semblance of sobriety that someone very drunk can occasionally command with the aid of luck and a surge of adrenaline, he began, "I would like to drink to Suki's family in Paris, none of whom are with us this evening and all of whom have been sorely neglected in the toasts so far this evening."

A tremendous wave of applause and table thumping followed, prompted not so much by sentiment as by collective relief that Steddy hadn't said anything to embarrass anyone.

Stedman waited politely and then tapped another glass to indicate that he had not yet finished. The last sporadic applause died, and Steddy continued.

"I especially would like to drink to Suki's guardian— one of the finest, most hospitable women in Paris, whom it has been my pleasure to have known for many years."

Everyone was beaming at him, not noticing the dark cloud that was passing over Suki's face. Steddy continued:

"In fact, it was Suki's aunt, with her heart of gold, who introduced me to the bride some two and a half years ago in Paris. Ladies and gentlemen, I ask you to raise your glasses . . ."

A great scraping of chairs ensued as the men stood, glasses held high.

". . . and drink to Madame Claude, who runs the best hook shop in Europe."

There was a momentary burst of applause until what he had said dawned on the celebrants. As the clapping stalled and died like an overprimed outboard motor, Suki could be heard screaming as she fled the hall in the deadly embarrassed silence that followed.

"You cocksucker!"

Part 1
A Time Aloft

4

In spite of twenty-four hours of abstemious behavior since the fiasco in Philadelphia, Stedman was still feeling very rough around the edges. By some miracle he had made the Concorde check-in at JFK with an hour to kill, and after obtaining his seat assignment, was told with a Gallic shrug that the air conditioning in the Club 2000 wasn't working. He went into the terminal and headed for the first bar in sight, a pseudo-English pub beyond the check-in where, although the ancient oak beams were made of Styrofoam and the barman was from the Bronx, at least the Bass Ale was the real thing and was served authentically, if accidentally, warm.

The pub was cool and mercifully empty. Stedman drained the pilsner glass and ordered a bullshot. He rationalized his behavior at the wedding for the fourteenth time and was halfway through his second bullshot when the flight was called. He paid the bill and sipped on the remainder of his drink while waiting for the change. He didn't give a shit about embarrassing Suki, but his mother was a different story—he was mortified, especially as she had been so unbelievably understanding, without any recriminations. It was she who had suggested that he get away to Europe for a while, and when he had confessed that he was broke, she had bankrolled him with the proviso that, if he had to gamble, he stick to backgammon. He was smiling at the way mother and son understood one another when the barman interrupted his thoughts to tell him that his flight had been called for the second time.

A surprisingly matronly Air France stewardess showed him to the aisle seat he'd selected, and with that relaxed, drowsy feeling that comes with knowing that the earthbound tether is about to be shorn, he settled down low in his chair and closed his eyes.

He wasn't sure whether it was her perfume—something between Mitsouko and patchouli—or her throaty, lived-in voice that he was first aware of. When he opened his eyes, he found her arched over him. She was as tall as he was, and in the cramped fighter-plane fuselage of the Concorde, she had to bend in two in order to get over him to reach the window seat at his right. Her chestnut hair was thick and very long and completely enveloped his face as she tried to pass. He rose too quickly from his chair to help her and banged his head on the cabin's overhead. She chuckled throatily, and two dimples appeared high on the corners of her tanned cheeks.

"Wouldn't you prefer the window?" she said, back in the aisle again—still laughing after her unsuccessful attempt.

"No, thanks. My legs don't fit unless I stick them in the aisle."

She giggled, looking down at her own long legs, and then they both laughed. She handed him an enormous duffle that she called her "bag," and while he grappled with it in his hunched stance, she hung a Nikon around his neck. Thus free of encumbrances, she gracefully slid by him into her seat. The stewardess tried to relieve him of his burdens, but the girl insisted upon keeping everything with her, and somehow they managed to stow it all around them. Stedman good-humoredly feigned annoyance when she told the stewardess, "We'll keep them with us, thank you," as though it were a *fait accompli* that they were traveling together.

The "No Smoking" light went out, and when she saw that Steddy was having difficulty reaching for the lighter in his trouser pocket, she lit his cigarette for him. It occurred to Steddy then and there that he had never met a girl as beautiful who had remained so totally devoid of guile.

When the steward offered them champagne, she asked for hers on the rocks, and Stedman—who had always scoffed at people who did that to good champagne—inexplicably ordered his the same way. Before they had finished the first glass, they were already whispering remarks about their neighbors and laughing conspiratorially. Steddy had felt a hundred years old when he boarded the plane—now he felt like a boy of twenty on his way to Europe for the first time. Her enthusiasm was infectious; even the aircraft held a sudden interest as he explained to her that the dial on the forward bulkhead would register when their airspeed hit Mach I, and again when they reached Mach II.

"Oh! We have to celebrate my first time at Mach II," she said.

"I'll order some more champagne." He reached for the bell.

"No, no, wait a minute, I've got some terrific coke someone gave me as a going-away present, and I have no intention of taking it through French customs."

"I've never had cocaine," Steddy said sullenly, but she swept right over his change of mood.

"Good, now we'll both have a first to celebrate. Have you got a hundred-dollar bill?"

"Will five hundred francs do?" Steddy asked, still not altogether pleased with the turn of events.

"Oh, perfect. It doesn't really matter, but as it's your first time, it should be special."

Without the least effort to conceal it, she took a tiny vial and a mirror from the duffle, and after adjusting the air vents in the overhead to point in the opposite direction, proceeded without a qualm to spoon out the white crystals onto the mirror in full view of anyone who cared to look. *Steddy* didn't know where to look, but for some reason he was more anxious lest she notice his discomfort. He felt so silly the first time he tried the coke—bent over her lap with a five-hundred-franc note rolled up in his nose—that he laughed and blew a considerable amount of the stuff all over the place. She had to demonstrate how it was done and in so doing was able to transform an awkward act into something sensual and even erotic.

They skipped lunch and had more champagne and just the caviar instead. Steddy was a new man; he felt totally rejuvenated, and for the first time in ten years, only the second time in his life—unbelievably—he was sure he was in love.

She was laughing, and he was nibbling on her ear when the chime ended what seemed the shortest flight of his life. He was suddenly afraid of losing her.

"You can have dinner tonight, can't you?" he asked.

"I'd love to. In fact, I'm beginning to get hungry."

"Where are you staying?"

"With my mother and stepfather at the Plaza-Athénée."

With growing relief and trying not to overplay his hand, Steddy asked, "Then you're not with anyone?"

She laughed, understanding the question but choosing to ignore the point.

"Technically, no. They don't get in from London until tomorrow."

"Well, let's see, we won't get into town until about eight, so I'll drop you at the Plaza, go to my place and change, and pick you up at nine-thirty."

"Make it ten in the bar. I want to wash my hair."

Steddy dropped her at the Plaza and told the driver to take him on to the Ritz. She had hardly left the cab when doubts started to creep into his thoughts—she was too good to be true, something would go wrong, maybe she was married. He didn't think so, but girls like that don't just fall into your lap as she had. He started to panic when he realized that he didn't even know her name. What if she wasn't there? How would he find her? Maybe she wasn't even staying at the Plaza.

He stepped from the shower, and taking a heavy pull on a martini, walked over to the window and looked out on the Place Vendôme. Funny, he didn't remember ordering the drink or, on reflection, even checking in, for that matter.

Stedman reached the bar at the Plaza at nine-thirty and spent the longest forty minutes he could remember—sipping from a bottle of Cristal, trying not to drink too much but nervously not knowing what else to do. The last thing he wanted to be was drunk.

It was her perfume that told him she was standing behind him. He spun around on the stool, and for the first time since dancing class days, felt all thumbs. As it was so late, he suggested dinner upstairs at Castel's. She agreed on the condition that they go dancing afterward. He had thought of Castel's because there was a nightclub downstairs. He knew that if he could just get her in his arms, even if only on a dance floor, all his anxiety would fade and everything would be all right.

5

Stedman awoke with a start and a weight across his stomach. She was sprawled across him talking on the phone, which had rung on his side of the bed. When she had finished, she kissed him good morning. She wore no makeup, and the steady sea-blue gaze of her eyes under thick, straight, mannish eyebrows met his with delight and humor.

"Guess what, darling? Mummy and Nubie aren't coming till this evening, so we've got the whole day to ourselves. They said I could use their box at Longchamp, so if you feel like it, we can have lunch at the track."

He kissed her again to shut her up.

"And good morning to you," he said, kissing the corners of her mouth. "Now don't you think it would be a good idea if we start the day by introducing ourselves at this late stage of our acquaintance?"

"What a spoilsport you are—it's so intriguing having a mystery lover. And besides, you might have a perfectly terrible name, and that would be awful."

They kissed again, and passion was beginning to steal the place of humor, when there was a knock at the door. She pushed him away, sat up in bed, and pulling the sheets around her, said, "*Entrez.*"

"What the hell is that?"

"It means 'come in.'"

"I know that. I mean who is . . ."

The room-service waiter picked his way across the obstacle course of discarded clothing without raising one Gallic eyebrow.

She whispered mischievously, "I rang while you were kissing me."

They ordered an enormous breakfast, and when the waiter had left, Steddy stood formally, but still quite naked, at the foot of the bed.

"It has been a pleasure meeting you. May I introduce myself—my name is Stedman Wright."

She held out her hand with equal formality.

"I'm Theadora Boulton. Delighted."

They fell together on the bed, laughing at first, and then made beautiful, slow, morning love until the waiter arrived. Steddy ordered a bottle of champagne to go with breakfast, and they sat cross-legged on the bed eating from the table, guzzling champagne, and chatting as though they had breakfasted together for years. Then Thea said, "Your name sounds familiar. Should I know it?"

"I was just going to say the same thing about you, although I know I've never met you before—some things one doesn't forget."

"Do you know my stepfather, Nubar Harkonian?"

"I should have realized when you said 'Nubie' before, but really he was the furthest thing from my mind."

"Where do you know him from?"

"The Clermont in London. We're backgammon cronies. I support myself on his losses whenever I'm there, although, to be quite fair, he regularly skins me at bridge."

"Now I remember. He calls you Steddy, doesn't he?"

"Everybody does."

"He likes you. He says you're the only true sporting gentleman of the younger generation. You play racquets or squash or something as well, don't you?"

"Yes to all of the above. And you must be that stepdaughter he's always trying to palm off on me."

"Oh, really?"

"Yes, something about a rock star in L.A., as I recall."

"You see, I told you we shouldn't have introduced ourselves."

"Never mind, no more talk. I'm going home to change and then stop at the club for a second to get some money, then why don't we take them up on their offer and have some lunch at the track?"

"Okay. Nubie said I could use the car as long as it picks them up at the airport at seven, so while you're gone I'll have my bath and pick you up—at the Travelers, I presume?"

"How did you know?"

"It's predictable, at least now that I know who you are, but don't get in a game or we'll be too late for lunch."

"I don't work on Sundays. Today is entirely yours."

Later, at the bar of the Travelers, Steddy ran into Wiley Travis.

"What the hell are you doing here?"

"I might well ask you the same thing, but I already heard the 'Philadelphia Story,' which is how everyone's already referring to that little stunt you pulled."

"Christ, I'd already forgotten."

"I can assure you, you're the only person who has."

"Then let's drop it. How long will you be here?"

"I'm leaving tonight—don't you remember? I told you I was going to Germany on business?"

"Oh, yeah, I forgot. Anyway, how's the action around here?"

"If you mean are there any backgammon pigeons, I can tell you there's nary a one—they're all en route to Harkonian's *schloss* for his tournament."

"Is that now?"

"I'm surprised you didn't get the nod. I thought he was a pal of yours."

"I didn't expect to be in Europe. I imagine he'll ask me if I call and let him know I'm here." Steddy continued on his way to the door, "Will you surface anywhere after Deutschland?"

"I'll walk you out. I'll be in London for ten days starting next week."

They reached the street, where the big navy blue and

cream Harkonian Rolls was just pulling to the curb of the Champs-Elysées in front of the club. The door popped open before the chauffeur had come to a complete stop, and Thea leaned out to kiss Steddy, who then turned to Wiley and said, "Sorry we can't drop you, but we're late for the races."

They lunched at the track and ran into far too many people that both of them knew and didn't want to talk to, so they called it a day and went back to Steddy's suite at the Ritz, where they lingered in bed under the Ritz's pink sheets while twilight descended on the Place Vendôme. When the floodlights bathed Napoleon's column outside the window, Thea said that she had to get back to change for dinner with her mother and Nubar.

"I'm sorry we can't be alone, but I haven't seen Mummy in almost a year. Do you mind terribly?"

"Not if you promise to come straight here after dinner."

"Oh, no, I meant do you mind terribly having to have dinner with them? You absolutely have to come."

Nubar grinned all through dinner at Lasserre and occasionally guffawed and slapped his wife, Elizabeth, on the thigh, so amused was he that the two of them had met on their own after he had tried for so many years to promote a liaison. Nevertheless, Steddy could tell he was a bit miffed when, after getting a high sign from Thea, he refused Nubar's invitation to play backgammon at the hotel, on the excuse that he had promised to take her dancing. He did, however, accept Nubar's invitation to the tournament at his *schloss* in Austria, starting on Wednesday.

Steddy intended that they would part company with Thea's parents at the door of the restaurant and go straight back to the Ritz, but Nubar insisted on dropping them at Régine's in his car. Thea protested that Régine's was too noisy and too much of a hassle, so Steddy suggested Raspoutine as an alternative.

"It's a White Russian clip joint, but the music's as authentic as the vodka is at twenty bucks a shot," he said with little enthusiasm.

"Do they have Gypsies?"

"Oh, yes, they're wonderful," Elizabeth Harkonian

piped in. "If we didn't have to leave for Austria so early tomorrow morning, I'd come with you," she said, nudging Nubar in the ribs.

"Don't get any ideas about delaying our flight—as it is, some of your guests may have already arrived, before we get there."

"My guests?" Elizabeth said archly.

"All right, my guests. But you know very well you enjoy it every year in spite of the fuss you make, my dear." And then, turning to Thea and Steddy: "And don't you two stay out all night and get to the airport late, or you'll find yourselves without a lift!"

When the car had pulled away from the curb, Steddy said to Thea, "We don't really have to go in now that they've gone . . ."

"But I'd like to. I love Gypsies, and I've never been to a Russian nightclub—it sounds fabulous."

They negotiated the three flights of red carpeted stairs to the basement until they reached the bar at the far wall of the bottom landing. The balalaika music and the Gypsies' mournful cries, only faintly audible from the stairway, now obliterated any effort at conversation. Steddy tried to ask Thea if she wanted to have one drink at the bar, but not hearing him, she followed the maitre d' down the three remaining steps into the large, multi-vaulted main cellar, to a small table on the edge of the dance floor, lighted, as were all the tables, by a single silver candlestick with a fringed red silk shade. The Gypsies were seated in a semicircle formed by their chairs at the center of the dance floor. The dark-skinned female lead had oiled and plaited jet-black hair, wore a garnet velvet dress, and had hundreds of gold chains and medals about her neck and wrists. She was just finishing the solo part of "Or chichornia," and as Steddy and Thea took their seats, the rest of the group stood and joined her for the staccato refrain that rapidly mounted in tempo. Steddy was caught up by the music, and when the captain leaned his head over to hear Steddy's order, instead of asking for a bottle of Cristal as he had planned, Steddy just said "Moscovscaya"—the Russian vodka he preferred. When the small bottle arrived at the table encased in a thick ice overcoat, Thea raised an eyebrow and looked at him with a slightly "We are not amused" expression. He poured out the frozen, clear liquid into the small glass in front of her and shouted over the din, "You wanted to go Russian tonight—that's not something you can do by half measures!"

She started to sip from the glass, but his hand restrained hers, and pointing at himself to indicate that she should follow his example, he raised his glass and knocked it back with one quick snap of the wrist. Thea picked up her glass but hesitated for a moment, until Steddy leaned over and whispered in her ear.

"If you'd rather sip it through a rolled-up five-hundred-franc note, I'll understand, but I'm not sure my friends will," he said, nodding in the direction of the Gypsies, who were now singing on their feet and approaching the table.

Thea smiled and without moving her lips said, "You know, you're a regular little shit." And with that, she downed the glass and held it out to be refilled.

Before he could do anything about her glass, the Gypsies were upon them for the last cries of their song, and then fell all over Steddy as he stood to applaud and greet them. Each of them embraced him in a bear hug as he introduced them to Thea in a mixture of French and English until they realized they had stopped the show. Natasha, in heavily accented English, said, "Now we will play your favorite." The lead balalaika player began the delicate opening strains of "Two Guitars" that would become a sad ballad with Natasha singing until it built into the inevitable frenzied crescendo of the whole troop.

Natasha sat at the table for a moment when they had finished, and the others stood around them while Steddy poured them each a glass of vodka. When the regular orchestra began to play for dancing, they left, promising to return after the next set.

"You must have spent a million dollars here over the years to get that kind of attention," Thea said.

"Not really, but about ten years ago they had a Russian Fortnight at Annabel's in London—redecorated the whole place and everything—and imported Natasha and her troop to entertain for the entire two weeks. We used to take them home with us every night, and they'd play until eight or nine in the morning.''

"Who was your little comrade then?" Thea asked, sipping her vodka.

Ignoring her question, Steddy said, "Why don't we dance? Isn't that what you wanted to do?"

"A tango?" Thea said incredulously.

"Why not? Haven't you heard I do a mean tango?"

"I think I'm more interested in hearing about your *last* tango in Paris."

Steddy was already standing. Taking her hand, he pulled out her chair and swept her onto the dance floor. Spinning her and forcing her to lie back dramatically over his arm, he drew her to him and into the pulsing rhythm of the music. He had intended to satirize the steps of the dance to teach her a lesson, but Thea was light as a feather in his arms and responded to the sense of his body without the need for exaggerated commands. Her tall, lithe frame fit into his as though he were the mold she was cast from, so much so that after a few passes across the floor, the other dancers made room for them—some couples even stopped to watch. When the music ended, they were both surprised by the applause from the crowd that had gathered without their realizing it. They started toward their table, but the clapping continued until the orchestra began playing another tango—"Orchids in the Moonlight." Steddy bowed his head to Thea in invitation, and she nodded acceptance.

This time they both became lost in the music and its sensual cadence. Their eyes were closed, and the erotic aura of Thea's perfume caused Steddy's nostrils to flare involuntarily as he pocketed her earring and nibbled on her earlobe. The vodka had done its work and freed them of inhibitions until, perspiring profusely and almost panting, Steddy realized that they had to get out of there right away.

He had to drag Thea away finally, but not before the leader of the orchestra had presented her with a cassette of his music and the old woman who sold flowers had given her a bouquet of all the gardenias she had left in her basket. After paying and tipping everyone and his uncle, Steddy had to have the concierge at the Ritz pay the cab driver. The lights in the lobby and in the corridors were already dimmed as they made their way through them to his apartment. Thea was humming the tango; clinging to each other, they reached his door by its measured steps. They kissed just inside, and Thea began undoing his black silk bow tie.

"God, even your tie's soaking wet!"

"I haven't danced like that in years—I'd better take a shower." And then crushing her in his arms with a force that seemed to fill him, he tried to dance her toward the bathroom.

"You go ahead," she said, pulling away but kissing him gently. "I might join you in a minute..."

When he turned off the water of the shower, the strains of the tango that had been echoing in his head actually seemed to be drifting through the partially opened door to the bedroom—Thea had found the cassette player he traveled with and was playing the tape from the nightclub. He turned off the light in the bathroom and stepped over the threshold into a room very different from the one he had left five minutes before. Thea had draped her flowered pink silk shawl over the bedside lamp, bathing the room in a soft dappled-rose light. The scent of gardenias was everywhere— she had rubbed the petals into the sheets—and the violins played "Orchids in the Moonlight" as though they had never left Raspoutine. He drew her to him and gave himself over completely to her and the world of scent, sound, and magical light that she had created.

6

By the time they surfaced, they were too late to ride with the Harkonians to the airport but managed somehow—with the help of three pots of black coffee and the Ritz's conscientious concierge—to stop at the Plaza for Thea's things and reach the private section of Le Bourget on their own. One of Nubar's agents spotted them and waved the driver onto the field, where the white Mystere 20 could be seen gleaming on the apron as they approached. Evidently the Harkonians had not yet arrived, as the crew was standing in loose formation at the foot of the access stair. Thea explained to Steddy that the black, crimson and gold stripes on the crew's uniforms, as well as those on the aircraft's tail assembly, were her mother's by right, and that, they were descending from the banners of her Austrian forebearers dating back to the Crusades. Nubar's middle European origins had always been something of a mystery, and Steddy suspected that this was the reason he had so greedily adopted and preserved the symbols and trappings of his wife's ancient heritage. He had spent a fortune restoring her family *schloss* in Austria to its pre-war glory, although Thea said she was sure that it had never approached anything like its present grandeur in its entire history.

Thea greeted the crew in her naturally friendly manner, and they were chatting at the foot of the stair when a truck from Fauchon pulled up and men in surgically immaculate white coats proceeded to unload large, exotically marked wooden cases that Steddy learned contained hundreds of pounds of fresh caviar, truffles, pâté, and champagne. "Quite a shopping list for a five-day weekend!" he mused out loud. "How many people are coming?"

"I think about sixty, unless they overcrowd the house."

"Anybody fun?"

"Well, certainly your gang from London. But I'm sure you'll know everyone and have to introduce me. After all, it is a backgammon tournament."

"Don't knock it. That's how I pay my rent."

"But the prize is only a gold bar."

"It's not the prize money. That's the least of it. The big money's in the private games and the side bets."

"Will I see you at all, or will I have to enter the tournament in order to get to play games with you?"

"You know you're the best game in town. All you have to do is touch me with your little finger to get my undivided attention."

The navy and cream Rolls swept onto the field followed by a Bentley station car and approached the private jet with the slow ceremony of a state occasion. The automobiles came to a halt as though overcome by inertia; the driver of the Rolls smartly snapped open the passenger door precisely at the foot of the stair. Nubar was the first out, and then he handed down Thea's mother, Elizabeth. It was evident by his manner that she was his most prized possession. She, in turn, appeared to delight almost girlishly in the court he paid her—although Steddy had noticed her wince with disdain the night before when Nubar had repeatedly slapped her on the thigh. Her features were more delicate than Thea's, and while tall, she was small-boned and looked European. Thea had obviously inherited a lot of her lanky, uncomplicated beauty from her Yankee father.

Turning to Stedman, Nubar said, "Look who I found at the club."

Viscount Rollo Rockford stepped from the car. He was storybook tall, dark, and handsome, or as half the girls in Europe called him simply: talk, dark, and *hands*. His complexion was too dark to be pure English and was a throw-to his Spanish grandee great-grandmother. A silky black, casually drooping mustache set off his coloring and added a satanic tinge to his overall appearance.

Steddy was genuinely happy to see him, and after greeting him warmly, introduced him to Thea.

"Dearest, this is Rollo Rockford, or as he's better known, Roll-em Rockford."

'Oh, I'm sure I would have known him without an introduction. He's a legend."

Rollo flashed a brilliant smile. "I'm flattered, but I can't return the compliment, as Nubie has, until this moment, carefully avoided making any mention to me of your existence."

Nubar laughed. "It seems safe enough now, as it appears Steddy has her well in hand."

"Where's your bride?" Steddy asked.

Rollo's face darkened visibly. "She's in the country, at Blyden with my father and the children."

Elizabeth Harkonian, sensing the tension, broke in.

"Come, let's have a glass of champagne while they finish loading. The heat is stifling."

As they climbed the gangway, Thea whispered into Steddy's ear, "That was a rotten thing to do. You know he hates her."

"Just defining the territory, darling," he answered, grinning.

Stedman did know that Rollo hated his wife; who didn't? Rollo had married far beneath him, despite the violent opposition of his family, but his father, the Earl Blyden, had done a complete about-face when the children were born and now worshipped Rollo's wife and his grandsons, to the total exclusion of Rollo.

The old earl and Rollo's wife loathed his gambling, and when, the previous year, Rollo had won one hundred eighty thousand dollars at the casino in Deauville and actually left the casino and gone home, his wife greeted him sourly.

"And how much did you lose *tonight?*"

"But I won, darling—one hundred eighty thousand dollars!"

"Did they pay you?" she hissed.

"Well, no, I took their marker. Didn't feel like waiting for a check."

"Well, you march right back there this minute and get one."

He went back to the casino, and while waiting for the check to be drawn, looked in at the now almost empty baccarat table. Forty minutes later he left without the check, leaving his marker behind for an additional two hundred thousand dollars. She *left* him and moved in with his father at Blyden.

Stedman knew that the loss had broken Rollo utterly but assumed, as did everyone, that Nubar had been bankrolling him ever since. Nubar liked Rollo enormously, but more important, he was impressed with Rollo's family and the fact that he would one day be one of England's premier earls.

The interior of the *Flying Cloud*, as Nubar had christened the aircraft, smelled and looked like the inside of a Bentley Continental. Walls, chairs, and settees were upholstered in tobacco-colored glove leather. The tables were made of burled walnut veneers trimmed with polished nickel, and the deep leather steamer chairs appeared to be so heavy that Stedman wondered how the aircraft was able to gain its element.

As they took their seats, the chief steward—now in a crisp white jacket—poured champagne into enormous Baccarat balloon glasses that were arranged on a silver tray with a bowl of scarlet and white carnations. In fact, everything—coasters, napkins, matches, even the cigarettes—was imprinted with the plane's name and colors.

Harkonian touched the side of one of the tables, and the spring-loaded top flipped, revealing a backgammon board on the other side.

Stedman threw his head back and laughed. "Christ, we've been conned. It's a flying casino."

"Beware of Harkonians bearing bloody gifts," Rollo echoed.

Nubar smiled. "Well, I've got to make this little toy support itself somehow. Would you gentlemen care for a brief chouette before lunch?"

Before anyone could answer, the captain entered the main cabin.

"Baron Harkonian, sir. Whenever you are ready, we have been cleared for takeoff."

"Carry on, Captain."

Elizabeth turned to Nubar. "Now, there will be no gambling during takeoff, and lunch is being served as soon as we're level."

As the aircraft taxied to the runway, an assistant steward distributed menu cards. Steddy marveled that each one was printed with the date, a tiny map showing the course they would take to Salzburg, and the flying time of one hour twenty minutes. The menu itself was printed, but the name of the plane and its colors were engraved on the creamy, stiff, gold-bevel-edged cards.

They lunched at a commodious table and were given cold lobster to start, then medallion of veal, and a frozen soufflé Rothschild for dessert. To keep things simple, champagne was served throughout the meal.

They had just finished their first cups of coffee, poured from a perfectly simple but rare Georgian pot, when the captain announced they would be landing in a few minutes. Rollo toasted the captain with his Armagnac and said that it had been the most pleasant flight he had ever had.

The touchdown was imperceptible, and only the throaty roar of the reversed engines indicated that they were on the ground and that the flight was over.

7

The approach road up to the *schloss* seemed familiar to Steddy, but only because it reminded him of the documentary newsreels he had seen of wartime Mercedes-Benz and similar looking Horchs speeding up the steep incline at Berchtesgaden to a rendezvous at Hitler's "Eagle's Nest." The path was so narrow that the gatekeeper had to telephone up to the *schloss* to assure the way was clear before passing the ubiquitous Harkonian Rolls onto the almost vertical road up to the house through the densely forested fir trees.

Stedman's ears popped halfway up, and he was still distracted trying to clear them when the automobile reached level ground at the summit. The panorama before him was not at all what he had expected. Instead of a large house clutching a rocky promontory, a broad, open plateau extending for at least a mile, surrounded by near and distant Alpine peaks, spread before him in all directions. In the middle was a great, black, serpentine glacial lake that reflected the puffy white clouds as in a black mirror. The *schloss* was on a gentle rise beyond the lake, and as the car entered the main *allée* that led on a straight axis to the entry court, a black, red, and gold standard broke from a flagstaff on the principal turret. It would have been very difficult not to have been impressed; even Rollo, whose family house, Blyden, was one of the grandest in England, gaped. Gardeners and gamekeepers in traditional alpine uniforms uncovered their heads as the Rolls swept by them through the deep blue-gray gravel.

At the entry, the butler and at least forty in staff were lined up in review. Stepping from the car, Stedman felt as though he had slipped through a time warp into the Edwardian era.

Elizabeth Harkonian asked Thea to show Stedman to his room, which, it turned out, was reached by means of a tiny, round, blue-silk-lined elevator that rose inside one of the corner turrets. On the small stone landing, Thea pushed open a low oak door into a pie-shaped room with stone walls and a high, vaulted, wood-beamed ceiling. The bed was an austere Napoleonic campaign bed covered in red velvet with a vicuña throw. The rug and chairs were vicuña as well, and a fire burned in the grate.

"The bed isn't much, but the rug looks terrific. What are you doing the rest of the afternoon?"

"I'm free for a little while before I have to help Mother, but I have a better idea."

Stedman looked downcast as Thea turned from him and walked over to two large doors at one side of the room.

"Will you help me push these apart? They haven't been opened in years."

"If you're sure you wouldn't rather stay here."

Beyond the doors was a tented room that contained the most enormous bed Stedman had ever seen.

"I thought you might enjoy seeing my room before you got any ideas."

8

Stedman lay in bed transfixed as he watched Theadora dress. It was all so unreal. Only a week ago he had been in Philadelphia, totally demoralized, and now he was high in the Austrian Alps with a girl who in a few days had become an inextricable part of him.

She stood in front of a picture window that had been hewn from the stone walls of the turret. Beyond her he could clearly see the snow-capped Alpine peaks. She stopped to step into her chemise, and the profile of her body made him shudder. He understood all at once, and for the first time, what it meant to love someone so much it hurt. Still, he was afraid to show too much or attempt to express what he felt for fear of suffocating her. He felt clumsy and boorish in the company of her delicate grace. She bent over and kissed him. A curtain of auburn hair closed out reality. Her perfume had become for him a Pavlovian aphrodisiac. She gently broke loose from his arms.

"Darling, I must go. I promised Mother I'd help her. Come down when you're dressed, and we'll put you to work."

She slid through the door, and then still holding it, poked her head back inside. Her eyes sparkled with the reflected mountain light.

"I love you, you know."

Without waiting for a reply, she was gone, the door clicking shut behind her.

Stedman was still in bed reflecting on Thea's exit when the ring of the telephone from the room next door jarred him from his reverie. It was Nubar asking Steddy to join him in his study for tea. Steddy said he'd be right down, knowing full well that with Rollo out riding and none of the other guests due until the following day, it was backgammon—not tea—Nubar had in mind.

He was actually on his second cup of tea before the fact that he was ten points behind roused him sufficiently to concentrate on the play. They continued for an hour or more, and by the time his hostess interrupted and told them it was time to get dressed for dinner, he was well ahead. Entering the circular lift, he was rather pleased with himself, for he could now start the tournament with $5,000 more to play with than he'd had when he arrived.

The doors between their rooms were still open, and as he neared them, her smell enveloped him. He whistled, and she called to him from behind an alcove, where he found her soaking in a sunken marble tub that was big enough to accommodate an entire Japanese family. She splashed him until he undressed, and as he sank into the warm scented water, he began to wonder if with her he might not be able to accept happiness.

The next morning, Stedman and Thea went riding after breakfast. They road in the park that extended for about a mile and a half behind the *schloss* to the edge of the plateau. It was like being in a Disney production of *Heidi*, suspended among the mountain peaks with nothing to mar the nature of the surroundings or the perfection of the day.

When they returned, the drive at the front of the *schloss* looked like a motor show; elegant automobiles of every conceivable mark and color were splashed about the gravel forecourt like a metallic bouquet. Brigades of servants descended on them like vultures, picking them of their contents and leaving them for the grooms to drive round to the garages to make room for the new arrivals that streamed up the mountain road.

Taking in the sight, Steddy and Thea were about to turn and ride off again, but a groom was already at the bridles of their horses, and Nubar had spotted them.

"Steddy, come over, won't you? There's someone I'd like you to meet."

Thea was already looking dejected.

"Well, I guess now I won't be seeing you for three days and nights."

"Don't be silly, darling, but I do have to try to earn enough to keep you in the style to which I am so rapidly becoming accustomed."

The baronial hall was full of guests milling about the central table, where name cards with room assignments were lined up in alphabetical order. Elizabeth Harkonian was threading her way through the crowd with a footman carrying a tray of glasses and a bottle of champagne in her train. Steddy knew about fifty percent of the people and was standing with Thea on the edge of the crowd, pointing out to her anyone he thought she might find interesting, when Elizabeth reached them.

"Now, one glass of champagne and then off you go to change out of those riding things for lunch. I want to get this horde seated before they get lost all over the house, and I'll need both of you to help me round them up." Stedman was about to refuse the champagne, but after another look at the crowd, he gulped down a glass, and taking Thea by the hand, said, "Come on, darling. There's a small matter I'd like to take care of before lunch."

"You said it, I didn't," she teased.

9

The toast Stedman gave that night at dinner was a far cry from the last one he had delivered in Philadelphia, and a good deal less startling. The guests were in high spirits, and the toasting continued in a jovial vein until at last Nubar rose, welcomed his guests, and commenced the Calcutta—the auction to sell the players in the tournament. It was generally assumed that Steddy would fetch the highest price in the bidding, but when an Arab that nobody seemed to know paid twelve thousand pounds for Rollo—two thousand pounds more than Steddy had brought—it came as a surprise and started the whole room buzzing. Thea whispered to Steddy that Rollo had asked Nubar to invite the fellow on his guarantee, as a personal favor.

The tournament was scheduled to begin the following day after lunch and would last for two days, with playing time limited to the hours between lunch and dinner, leaving plenty of time for private high-stakes games in the evening.

After a polite glass of champagne with the ladies, Stedman joined the chouette already in progress in the study, with Rollo; the Arab, Omar; Jack Pilkington, an English film producer; and, of course, Nubar. After about an hour's play, Rollo had won a few games as part of the chouette but had lost two eight games in the box and was behind six thousand pounds. He suggested raising the stakes to a thousand pounds a point with automatic doubles—an astro-

40

nomical amount. Steddy, Nubar, and Omar stayed in, but Pilkington dropped. Rollo was in the box with Steddy playing for Nubar and Omar.

The game opened with two automatic doubles—the sort of game Rollo liked, a chance to recoup his losses and take a big lead in one grand stroke. He went immediately into a back game—his favorite position—establishing Steddy's one and three points. Steddy offered him the cube at eight. Rollo was one of the best back players on the circuit; Steddy never doubted that he'd accept. Rollo rolled everything he needed then, and had closed his own board but for a blot on his six point. He tossed the dice and picked off one of Steddy's men on his seven point and slapped it on the bar. Steddy couldn't get in. Rollo grinned and slid the cube back to him with the sixteen showing. Steddy polled his partners. He wanted to take. Nubar liked backing long shots, so he was in. Omar accepted without expression. Steddy surmised that if Omar was really bankrolling Rollo, it wouldn't end up costing him a penny more however it came out. Steddy took the cube and nodded his acceptance. Rollo rolled double sixes, the worst possible combination. He couldn't cover, and he couldn't remove the blot from his six point. Steddy rolled double sixes and took out Rollo's man with his from the bar. In spite of controlling two points in Steddy's board, Rollo's next toss didn't get him in. Steddy redoubled to sixteen. It was taken, and Steddy's previous roll became the start of a streak as he continued to throw fives and sixes turn after turn. The game became a rout as Rollo fled for home to avoid the triple game. As it was, he lost a double, thirty-two points to each of them. It was late, and they all agreed to continue again the following night after dinner. Rollo's losses were a hundred two thousand pounds for the evening.

It didn't surprise Stedman that Rollo wasn't the least perturbed at the turn of events—he was a master at maintaining his English cool. But knowing his financial straits, Steddy was now sure that staking Rollo must have been the price Omar had had to pay for admission to the select gathering. Steddy didn't care. He was up thirty-four thousand pounds, with every chance of getting paid for a change.

Later, in bed, Thea, who had been one of the silent spectators, said that seeing him play the last game was the first time she'd really grasped the excitement of high-stakes play. Steddy said, "I hope I can keep it up so we can really paint the town in London."

"You didn't invite me to London."

"The tournament at the Clermont is in two weeks. You will come, won't you?"

"Of course I will, but you don't have to impress me, you know. I live on a ranch at home."

Stedman replied with sarcastic humor, "I can just imagine."

By the time the dinner gong rang the next evening, Stedman had advanced to the finals of the tournament by beating a Greek shipping tycoon in three straight games. Rollo had also reached the finals after an easy win over Nubar; thus the match for the gold ingot, scheduled for the next day after lunch, would be between Stedman and Rollo.

When Stedman and Thea came down for dinner, the decibel level of the sixty guests having cocktails in the main salon seemed twice as high and more frantic than on the previous evening.

"They're making side bets on tomorrow's game," Steddy explained to Thea. "Excuse me, darling, while I try to pick up some of the action."

Stedman left Thea at her mother's side and threaded his way through the crowd. He was only about halfway across the room when Omar clasped his shoulder.

"Who are you backing tomorrow?" It was a fair question—players often laid off bets against themselves in a tournament.

"Rollo's under pressure, but I'm feeling lucky."

Omar's eyes narrowed. "I think you're the better player, but on the other hand, I think Rollo's due for a winning streak, and judging from his easy win over Harkonian, he may have hit it."

The Arab's voice had a shrill, whining pitch. Steddy responded to his probing.

"Well, I'm always delighted to back the man I believe in. What did you have in mind?"

"Perhaps you'd like to make a small sporting wager?" Omar grinned, showing his noticeably small teeth. "Say ten thousand?"

"I was thinking more in terms of twenty-five," Steddy parried.

Omar's sardonic smile didn't change, but when Thea came over to take Steddy's arm in to dinner, and it became clear to him that Steddy had no intention of waiting for his answer, he quickly said, "Done," before even acknowledging Thea's presence. Stedman was still smiling as they walked into the dining room.

"You look positively delighted with yourself. What did you do to that poor Arab?"

"Let's hope he's anything but poor. I just accepted a wager on tomorrow's game."

"Who did you back?" she teased.

"Me, whod'ya think?"

"Oh, I don't know, I just wondered. I've often heard Nubar talking about laying off bets. Isn't that the clever thing to do?" she replied, the picture of innocence.

"Not when you're hot, darling, and I've never been as hot as I've been since I met you."

"That's sweet, but just how hot have I made you?"

Stedman's hand under the table, which had been gently resting on her knee, started to slide up under the cool chiffon of her dress.

"Not that kind of hot!" she said, smiling over clenched teeth. "I mean, how much did you bet?"

"Twenty-five thousand."

"Twenty-five thousand dollars!" she said, truly shocked.

"No, darling—pounds."

Concern was written over Thea's face.

"Dearest, I hope you're not doing this for me. I really don't care about the money, and I'd feel dreadful if it was my fault that you lost so much—I don't think I could face you."

Stedman's expression softened. He took her hand.

"Darling, this is the way I would have played whether

I'd met you or not. The only difference is that now, because of the way I feel about you, this has all become a game—it's the first time I think I've ever seen it in perspective. Probably because up until now, I've never had anything or anyone else that mattered enough for me to make the comparison. Oh, I still care about winning; in fact, I want to win more than ever. But if I lose, it won't really matter. I don't know if you can understand this because I'm not sure that I do myself, but that's why—for the first time in my life—I'm absolutely sure that I will win.''

Thea kissed him on the ear and whispered, "Every day I think it can't be possible to be this much in love, and then you say something like that and I love you more.''

10

The library where Steddy, Nubar, and Rollo gathered unhurriedly after dinner had once been the billiards room. The original green silk damask hangings still covered the walls, but along them, interspersed between crowded trophies of stag and boar, new mahogany bookcases filled with colored calf and morocco bindings now soared to the ceiling. The old billiards lamp with its large pleated silk shades still served as the room's chandelier and hung directly over the backgammon table that was already prepared for the next day's final—spotlighting it in contrast to the shadowy recesses around the room.

While the combatants fixed themselves brandies and selected cigars, the other guests drifted in by twos and threes. They sensed that a mortal blow was about to be dealt and that tonight's private game, rather than the next day's final, would be the more exciting. It was the scent of blood that had drawn them—but respectfully they stayed apart, and in spite of their numbers, did not crowd the players or disturb the hushed sanctity of the stately room.

The players moved into the circle of light and took their seats. They each threw a die to determine who would hold the box first. The staccato clatter of the dice on the ivory playing surface stilled the whispered chatter and brought the room to attention. Not one of the fifty-seven remaining guests was absent.

Steddy took the box, accepted an early double, and won the first game and four points. The next game, with Rollo opposing him, opened with one automatic, then, with one man on the bar, Steddy accepted a double. He came in with double fives, took one of their men off, and closed his board. Rollo eventually got in and home, and they were in a race to bear off. A timely pair of threes gave Steddy the eight game—another sixteen thousand pounds. The next game he lost a two, and the box passed to Nubar, who quickly won a double and a single, then lost a two.

When Rollo took over the box he was already down a hundred two thousand pounds from the night before and five thousand pounds more so far this evening. He took a double game off Steddy and another double off Nubar, and then dropped a sixteen when Nubar tried to double him to thirty-two.

Stedman's dice were hot—Nubar quickly conceded a single to him, and he retook the box and opened with two automatics. He was up eleven points, so he accepted Rollo's early double to eight and beavered to sixteen. Then Rollo, true to form, worked his way into a back position and took out two of Steddy's men when he only had seven left to bear off. Rollo doubled to thirty-two. Steddy didn't get in on his next turn, and when Rollo rolled, he was able to shut Steddy out. One of Steddy's men came in when Rollo cleared four men off the six point with double sixes, then with two men on the five point and three men on the four, they rolled double fives, leaving a blot behind on the four point. Steddy rolled double fours, knocked their man out, and headed for home. Rollo was in and out again with double fives, passing Steddy on the way. The spectators had drawn closer to the table and could contain themselves no longer. When Steddy rolled double sixes, they gasped. Rollo's next roll left him with one man on the two point and one on the one point. It was Steddy's roll. He had one man on the one point and one man on the five. He looked Rollo in the eye, picked up the doubling die, turned it to sixty-four, and with three fingers extended, calmly pushed it toward his opponents.

This was the game played at its best—on the edge, using guts and the doubling die when luck wasn't enough.

If Nubar dropped—and Steddy was banking that he would—Steddy had hedged a possible loss of sixty-four with a win of thirty-two and increased his possible winnings from sixty-four to ninety-six thousand pounds for the game.

Everyone in the room knew they were witnessing a game that, whatever the outcome, would be replayed all over Europe and the States for years to come. The room was hushed, so no one missed Nubar's quiet reply to the challenge.

"Drop."

Equally quietly, Rollo's answer was, "Roll-'em."

A roll of five and one would have been adequate, but Stedman threw a pair of sixes, consistent with his performance the whole evening.

It was Thea who broke the tense stillness that followed.

The applause started when, in a burst of enthusiasm, she ran to Steddy and hugged him—even Rollo had got up from his seat and clapped him on the back in what Steddy knew to be a genuine act of good-sportsmanship. Rollo had just lost sixty-four thousand pounds on one toss of the dice.

"Just like the cinema, it was your bloody cavalry to the rescue as usual!" he roared, in a good-natured attempt at bravado.

"And lucky for the poor Yank, too!" Steddy countered, smiling. "I was sure all evening that Rockford's marines were just waiting up your sleeve to take the day."

Nubar saw to it that everyone had a full glass of champagne—even the servants had stopped circulating during the last twenty minutes of play—and a round of toasting commenced.

Later, when they were alone, Thea told Steddy that an unsmiling Omar had put down his glass untouched and left the room.

The final of the tournament the next day was pure anticlimax. Rollo had been so soundly beaten that even though he tried to put up a good front, his heart clearly wasn't in it.

Stedman took him in straight games and afterward

accepted the solid gold brick worth twenty-five thousand pounds that Nubar ceremoniously presented to him as the traditional first prize of the tournament. The check for ten thousand pounds that Rollo received was little consolation.

Directly after the presentation, in front of the full complement of guests, Omar walked up to Steddy and handed him a check for twenty-five thousand pounds drawn on an obscure but solvent London bank, covering his side bet on the outcome of the tournament, and then, with something of a flourish and a total lack of discretion, he handed Steddy a second check covering Rollo's losses. Now everyone knew for a fact what had up to then been only speculation.

Stedman was deeply embarrassed for his friend and went straight to Rollo and offered to take his marker. Rollo turned him down flat.

"Take his check, old boy. He owes me that and more."

Unpleasantness aside, Steddy was over the moon. In four days he had cleared two hundred two thousand pounds.

That night in bed, Stedman said to Thea, "Darling, I'm feeling very rich, and we've got a week before we have to be in London for the Clermont. Where would you like to go? Anywhere in the world." Steddy had never been able to say that to anyone ever before, and the thought exhilarated him.

She replied, "I'd just like to be alone with you. I feel as though I've been living with a soldier who commutes from the front."

"How about Marrakesh? There wouldn't be anyone there at this time of year."

"I couldn't stand another hotel. After all, this place might as well be one. I want to make breakfast and dinner—that sort of thing."

"I know someone with a house in Jamaica that I can use if they're not there . . . but it's full of servants, and once word got out on the bush telegraph that we were there, we'd be swamped with people."

"Don't worry about it, darling. It doesn't really matter. I just thought . . ."

"I've got it! Do you have any woollies with you?"

· "Alone is one thing, but don't you think the North Pole is going too far?"

"No, no joke. A friend of my mother's—she's like an aunt to me—has one of the most beautiful places in Scotland. It's remote, and she has a few cottages that she lets friends use. They're quite a way from the castle, and she never goes up herself until August. She's always asking me to stay. I'm sure it would be all right, and it'll be fabulous now. A little cold, but you'll have your wish—there won't be anyone around for miles and miles of the grandest country you've ever seen."

"Oh, Steddy, can we leave tomorrow? Nubar and Mummy are staying on for a few days, but I'm sure they'll let us use the plane just to go to Scotland."

"I'll have to call her first, but we could make an early start and call her from the plane. . . . I assume there's a phone on the plane?"

"Natch."

"Somehow I find it awfully difficult to give any credence to that country-girl image you keep promoting, when you seem to adapt so easily to your present surroundings."

"If we fly commercial, we'll lose the whole day changing planes in Vienna. Anyway, just get me to the Highlands and buy me a pair of walking shoes, and I'll make an impression on you that you won't soon forget."

"Darling, you've done that already—now it's my turn to make an impression on you."

11

It was almost midnight when the train pulled into King's Cross Station. During the six days they spent in Scotland, they became so in tune with the simplicity of their surroundings that they preferred the gentle reentry to civilization provided by a six-hour train ride to the inevitable hassle of dealing with airports. Even so, they were grateful to see the big car from Claridge's, which helped immeasurably to cushion the shock.

The lights in the lobby had already been dimmed when Steddy and Thea arrived. Steddy was glad it was late, as there was less chance of running into anybody—if only for one more day.

He was signing the register when, from behind him, he heard: "Where the hell have you been?"

He turned and faced one of the few people in the world that he could have been happy to see at that moment—Wiley Travis.

"Wiley, old boy, it's great to see you. You met Thea in Paris."

Wiley, who was in dinner clothes, clicked the heels of his patent leather shoes, and bending from the waist, said, "You S.O.B., you know very well there was no way you were going to introduce me in Paris." Then, turning to Thea: "I am happy to meet you at last. No thanks to this bum."

Thea was amused and liked Wiley at once. He had strikingly blond hair with darker eyebrows and even, Arrow-collar good looks. She could tell he was at once sophisticated but still the sort of American who could live abroad forever without becoming Europeanized.

"Come on," Wiley said. "Let me buy you both one for the ditch. I want to hear about your Austrian coup from the horse's mouth."

Thea turned to Stedman.

"Not me, darling, but you go on. I've got to wash that train out of my hair."

"Okay, I won't be long."

As Thea stepped into the lift, Stedman and Wiley went into the hall and took a table opposite two Arabs—the room's only other occupants. Wiley ordered a stinger, so Steddy had the same.

"Jesus H. Christ, Steddy, you really pulled one off. Everyone in London's talking about it. I just had dinner at the Ashtons', and you were the sole topic of conversation. I'm so bored with hearing the story, I left early. I even heard about it in Munich."

"There were a lot of Germans at the *schloss*."

"Come off it. What's the real poop? Rollo, of course, still hasn't recovered. I gather he's been losing badly at roulette, and that wife of his is giving him no end of shit about Austria."

"Fuck that. It's not my fault. I told him he didn't have to pay me right away, but he insisted that I keep the Arab's check."

"What Arab?"

"Some guy called Omar that Rollo had in tow. I didn't really want to take his check because he made such a bloody show of giving it to me to cover Rollo. Everyone saw it—he made sure of that. I'm surprised you didn't hear about that, too."

"Not a word, but I have heard about the Arab—none too appealing from what I gather. People seem to think he's a little sinister."

"Well, I hope to hell his check clears. Come on,

here're the drinks, let's change the subject. Tell me what and who you've been up to?"

"Not so fast. Where the hell have you been? Everybody's been asking me how to get hold of you. George even called me from Paris."

"I'm not telling you where I've been. It was so perfect that just talking about it would be an intrusion."

"The man's in love!"

"I admit it unabashedly."

"I'm glad for you, after all the shit Suki put you through."

"Suki who?"

"You lucky son of a bitch. Is she as great as she is beautiful?"

"Every bit of it. She is—no shit—the only woman I've ever really loved."

"Have you set the date?"

"I haven't even asked her. I don't want to crowd her."

"The woman who feels crowded by a proposal hasn't been born yet."

"She's different, but maybe you're right. We think so much alike, I sort of took it for granted that she knew how I felt. Listen, I'm bushed, but let's have lunch tomorrow. I really want the two of you to get to know each other—say, one o'clock at Wilton's?"

"Okay with me, but if you're getting married, I'm buying—even if you are the man who broke the bank at Monte Carlo, by way of the Austrian Alps."

12

The following evening was the kickoff dinner and Calcutta at the Clermont for the London gambling club's annual backgammon tournament. Stedman and Thea sat with Rollo, his wife, Nubar and Elizabeth, and Wiley, who was with the English girl he had brought to lunch that afternoon. Stedman fetched the highest price in the auction, even though for once he didn't buy part of himself, but he did buy a piece of Rollo to make sure he went for a respectable amount. Jackie, Rollo's wife, bitched all through dinner about his gambling, his drinking, and his friends—evidently caring very little that most of them happened to be at the table. Stedman had yet to see Thea display a temper or act rudely, but he was sure that if he didn't get her away, she'd punch Jackie in the nose.

The minute the auction was over, Stedman got up and announced he was taking Thea downstairs to Annabel's for a dance. They ran into some friends they had in common from New York and sat with them for about an hour, when the page from the Clermont appeared, sent by Wiley to get Stedman. Steddy said he'd be up as soon as he finished his drink, but the fellow said he had better come straight away.

"What is it, John—is anything the matter?" Steddy asked.

"It's Lord and Lady Rockford, sir. They're having a terrific row at the roulette table."

Steddy rose from the table and excused himself from the others. Thea asked him, "What is it, darling?"

"Evidently Rollo and Jackie are brawling. I'd better go up and try to get them out of here. Why don't you stay? I won't be too long; I've become something of an expert at breaking up their knock-down drag-outs."

"No, I'll come with you. That bitch was trying to castrate him all through dinner."

They went through the small door that connected with the hall of the Clermont. From the bottom of the spiral stair, the Rockfords could be heard clearly, shouting at each other. It was like *Who's Afraid of Virginia Woolf?* No marriage could survive the things they were yelling at each other in public. Halfway up the stair, Stedman could see Rollo's face—it was crimson from drink and anger. His hair—always plastered to his head like patent leather—was rumpled into devil's horns, and his eyes were wild and bloodshot. He was literally foaming at the mouth. The sight of him made Stedman's stomach go clammy, so that he didn't even feel Thea's fingernails dig into his palm.

Jackie, whose face couldn't have been more than an inch from the exploding locomotive that was Rollo's, was as cool as a cucumber—not a hair out of place. She answered his shouts in her high, shrill, phony aristocratic voice, which only angered him more. Stedman was sure that Rollo would either have a heart attack or burst a blood vessel.

As they climbed closer to the appalling scene, Stedman spotted Wiley, his face white and pinched, crowded in the front row of the semicircle of spectators that had formed along the railing. They reached the landing and were threading their way through the crowd when Steddy heard Jackie shriek gratingly, "You bastard—you gamble because you can't get it up. You can't screw me, so you think you can prove something by trying to screw the house and your friends."

Rollo's face went from red to black. He raised his joined fists in the air as if to strike her. Steddy found himself wishing that he would. The moment froze in suspended animation. Then, with a great gasp of air rushing from his lungs, Rollo smashed two fists into her chest with all his strength. Jackie shot over the banister without making a sound except for a hideous thud when she landed on the marble floor of the foyer below. Stedman was struck dumb for a second, overcome by an irrational mixture of emotions—horror and elation. Then his adrenaline flowed, and an automatic response to events took over. He was the first to break for the stair and reach her side. Her head had caught the last step, and though he had never seen a broken neck before, it was clear from the exaggerated angle of her head what had killed her. He wouldn't have known how to properly feel for a pulse, but it didn't matter. There was a mass of keening from above, and when he looked up, he saw Rollo standing behind him, visibly shaking and quite pale now.

"Dead?" Rollo asked.

"I'm afraid so, as far as I can tell."

Without another word, Rollo strode past him into the hall and out the front door to the street. Steddy followed, but by the time he reached the stoop, Rollo had already put his navy blue Aston Martin into gear and was accelerating out of Berkeley Square.

13

The next morning, the police arrived at Steddy's suite at about the same time as the morning tabloids. There is very little that the British press enjoys exploiting more than the fall from grace of a peer of the realm. They were already labeling what Steddy considered an accident as out-and-out murder. Stedman's name, along with Nubar's, Wiley's, and half a dozen others, was splashed all over the front pages in a very unflattering light. They were generally represented as dissolute gamblers and "idle sports."

The inspector from Scotland Yard whom Stedman found waiting in the sitting room was polite enough but more than a little peeved that Steddy and Thea had left the scene of the "crime." Steddy replied that he wasn't aware a crime had been committed, as what he had witnessed had surely been an accident. But the inspector only repeated that had they remained until the police arrived, it would have been easier to determine the facts of the incident. He informed Steddy that there was to be an inquiry conducted at the Clermont that afternoon at four and that he and Thea would be required to attend.

Wiley called as the inspector was leaving and suggested that they meet for lunch.

"I hear the hotel's swarming with reporters. Why don't you come up to me and we'll eat here?" Steddy replied.

Wiley looked shaken when he arrived. He tossed an

extra edition of the paper over to Steddy. The headline read: ROLL-EM ROCKFORD CRAPS OUT. Rollo's Aston Martin had been found in a remote area by the Dover cliffs, the implication being that he had thrown himself into the sea. A search had begun, but so far they hadn't come up with anything. The paper, quoting so-called reliable sources, said that Rollo had been heavily in debt from gambling and that that, combined with his hand in his wife's death, could have been a motive for suicide. It went on to say that the police had not rejected the possibility that the positioning of the car had been a purposeful ruse and that Rockford was still in England or had fled to the Continent.

"The fool," Steddy said. "Now that he's run, he looks as guilty as hell."

"That becomes academic if he is in fact at the bottom of the Channel."

"I don't think he's the type to do that at all. On the other hand, I've never seen him in the state he was in last night. If I'd only been able to catch him at the door, it could have all been cleared up then and there. He was justified in striking her. The fact that she fell over the banister was an accident."

"But surely he must have realized that, Steddy," Thea said.

"I'm not so sure, darling. He was very drunk, you know, and then it's not as if he wasn't provoked—I think he wanted to kill her when he struck her. I don't think he meant for her to go over the railing, but I do think that in a moment of uncontrollable rage, he very much wanted her dead."

"So then he might have killed himself when he realized what he had done," Thea speculated.

"No, I don't think so. Even if he did drive to Dover with that in mind, I'm sure that by the time he was halfway there, he would have figured out some sort of scheme. He'd need help, but I can't think who he'd turn to. Certainly not his father—the way Blyden felt about Jackie, he probably would have turned him in. I just hope for his sake that whatever he might have planned last night, he'll reconsider it in the cold light of day and come back to stand at the inquiry."

"He might have called Nubie. He often turned to him when he was in trouble or for advice. You two order lunch while I call Mummy and see if she's heard anything."

It was half an hour before Thea came back into the sitting room.

"Any news?" Stedman asked.

"No, we were just talking about the whole thing. Mummy hasn't seen Nubar all day. He went out before she was up. She's been trying to reach him, though, to let him know about the inquiry."

"Didn't he say where he was going so early on a Saturday morning?"

"No. He just left word that he'd be back sometime after lunch."

"Sounds to me as though old Nubar has already got things well in hand," Wiley said.

"I only hope you're right," Stedman mused, more to himself than to anyone in particular.

14

Omar was at the inquiry, although Steddy didn't recall seeing him at the Clermont dinner. He walked back across Berkeley Square to Claridge's with Thea and Steddy afterward, and managed to wheedle an invitation to come up to their suite. It was eight o'clock when they got back and nine before Wiley returned from dropping off his girl friend, who knew nothing but had felt very important when the police requested her presence as well. They decided to order dinner in the suite.

It became clear during the proceedings—although nothing specific was said—that the police were investigating a murder. The late editions confirmed that the general consensus was that Rollo was still alive and still in England.

They all tried to avoid the subject that had been rehashed at the Clermont for the last four hours, but dinner was passed in speculation.

At about ten-thirty, Thea's mother called to ask her to spend the night at the house in Belgrave. Nubar had been called out of town on an emergency, to negotiate a labor dispute before a strike developed, and the servants were already down in the country for the weekend—unaware that it had been canceled. Thea agreed to go as soon as she'd finished dinner.

"Nubar didn't say anything about leaving town at the inquiry," Wiley said.

"Mummy said it came up at the last minute or they would have gone to the country. I know he makes it look easy, but you don't run an empire like his without problems all the time. He just doesn't go on about them."

"He was out early this morning, too. Wasn't he?"

"What are you driving at, Wiley?"

"Well, it just seems to me that if Rollo was going to call anyone, it probably would be Nubar. Who else does he know who has two jet planes, houses, and agents all over the world—and most likely a vault full of cash?"

"If he had called Nubar, I'm sure he would have made him go straight to the police—accompanied by the best attorney in London. Don't you agree, darling?" Thea was beginning to get annoyed with Wiley.

"All I know for sure is that Nubie values his British passport more than anything in the world—I'm sure he wouldn't do anything to jeopardize it."

Omar, who hadn't said a word all evening, now added his two cents.

"Sometimes the very rich think themselves above the law."

"Do you feel that way?" Stedman asked sharply.

"Oh, where I come from, I'm not very rich. In fact, I'm considered rather middle class."

Steddy was warming to the subject and was about to ask Omar just where he *did* come from when Thea interrupted and said that she had better leave. Steddy walked her to the lift. It was the first time that they had been separated since they had met. They both realized it at the same time and felt foolish making so much of it.

"They say absence makes the heart grow fonder."

"It's not possible," she replied simply.

"Will you call me from your room when you get to bed—no matter how late it is?"

"Yes, darling—and we can leave the line open all night."

Before Steddy could say anything, the doors of the elevator opened and someone got out, so she had no choice but to get in. She waved forlornly, and the door closed. They hadn't even kissed.

Steddy was already beginning to feel blue by the time he had walked the half mile of corridor back to his suite. He almost relished the fact that he could feel that way. It hadn't been so long ago that he had been incapable of feeling anything. The thought cheered him a little.

There was a bottle of Martell Cordon Bleu on the chimney with the manager's card leaned against it. So far it had remained unopened. Steddy peeled off the seal and drew the cork.

"Who'll join me in a brandy?"

"I'd be delighted, if you'll join me in a few games of backgammon," Omar replied.

"Great idea. You in, Wiley?"

"No thanks, Sted—not at your stakes. But I will have a brandy, and then I'm for bed. It's been a long day."

"Oh, hell, I haven't got a board."

"I have one in my room. We could play there if you like."

"Thanks, Omar, but I'm expecting a call. Why don't you get it, or ring down and ask the hall porter to fetch it and bring it up?"

Omar left to get his board while Steddy and Wiley sipped their drinks.

"He's not really such a bad fellow," Stedman said.

"I suppose not, but he gives me the creeps."

"You're just not used to being around Arabs—they're all like that a bit. They're just completely different from us. You'd seem just as strange dressed up in Arab gear sitting in Sharjah or Abu Dhabi or wherever it is he comes from."

"That's just it, Steddy. He's never said where he comes from—never talks about what he does or anything. He never talks at all, for that matter, but he sure does listen. He didn't volunteer a word about Rollo all through dinner, even though we all know he's been bankrolling him for months."

"So what? Maybe he's just shy. It's not easy to be around a bunch of old friends gassing and inject your own two cents every five minutes."

"All I know is that he gives me the creeps and I'd be very careful what I say around him if I were you."

At that moment, Omar let himself in. He had left the door on the latch and was carrying two matching attaché cases.

"Why two boards—superstitious?"

"Not at all, my dear fellow. One contains money. I like to settle my gambling obligations with cash—although tonight I feel lucky and don't think I'll need any."

"Well, if that's the case, I hope you won't be offended if I have to give you a check."

"Not at all. It's just that where I come from, we always play with cash. That way, we can't play for more than we have with us and there are no problems later."

"That's very sensible. However, if we had to do that here, no one would ever play at all. But why don't I limit myself to what you have on you?"

"That would be one hundred thousand pounds sterling."

Wiley whistled softly and interjected: "And I thought this was going to be high stakes! Good night, fellows—I don't even want to watch this."

Stedman drained his glass and poured out another.

"You sure you won't stay and watch the fun?"

"No way, José. I'll see you tomorrow and buy you lunch. You'll probably need a free meal. Good night, Omar."

Steddy refilled Omar's glass from the now almost empty bottle. He noticed that Omar had brought an identical bottle back from his room.

"I see we are both recipients of the manager's largess," Steddy said.

"Except the card on mine was addressed to the man who must have been in my room before."

They played two or three games when the phone rang, and Steddy, knowing it would be Thea, shut the door as he went into the bedroom to take the call.

"Darling, I miss you terribly."

"So do I, darling. I've got Mother in bed, and it just occurred to me—I don't know why you didn't come, too. I mean, she wouldn't have minded—in fact, it would have made a lot more sense to have a man in the house if anything happened. Now it's too late, because she's already set the bloody alarm system and I don't know how to turn it off—I think you can only do it from her bedroom."

"Yeah, and I'm playing backgammon with Omar anyway."

"That's not very flattering. I thought you'd be miserable and missing me."

"I am, darling." He hiccuped.

"You're drunk! I leave you for two hours, and the wheels fall off. I know those Arabs. I'll just bet he's got three or four bunnies from the Playboy Club on their way over right now—you bastard."

"Wouldn't that be fun? Pussy de Lapin à L'Arab."

"Oh, darling, you really are loaded. How is it possible in two hours?"

"Sheer misery. It heightens the effect."

"Listen, darling, try to take care of yourself. Get rid of Omar and get into bed—and no monkey business. I'll be back first thing in the morning, as soon as Mummy turns off the alarm."

"Nag, nag, nag. So this is what married life is going to be like. I have a good mind to withdraw my proposal."

"I wasn't aware that you had."

"Had what?"

"Proposed."

"Oh . . . in that case, will you marry me? Please, darling—see how miserable I am without you?"

"Ask me tomorrow when you're sober, and don't think I won't remind you. Now get rid of Omar and *go to bed!*"

"If you think I'm drunk, you should see him. When last seen, he was drinking straight from the bottle."

"I can't believe it. You're all like children. Where's Wiley?"

"He left hours ago."

"He's the only one with any sense. I'm hanging up now, so say good-bye and please go to bed."

"Good night, dearest—I love you. Do you remember that first night at the—"

"Now I mean it. I love you, but good night."

Steddy felt drunkenly forlorn. He couldn't tell if Thea had been really angry or only amused and teasing. A pull at his brandy didn't clear up the quandary, but he realized that he'd left Omar alone for rather a long time.

He found Omar passed out in a wing chair and tried to awaken him without the slightest success, so, in a drunkenly protective way, he lifted Omar's feet onto a chair and tucked him in with a blanket from the bedroom.

Steddy poured himself another drink and then, seeing the diminutive Arab wrapped up like a Cherokee, became convulsed with laughter at the realization that the Prophet had obviously known what he was doing when he forbade Arabs alcohol. Still chuckling, he managed to get himself back to the bedroom and take off his clothes. He was asleep before his head hit the pillow.

The telephone's ring that awakened him sounded like a freight train running through his room. It was, in fact, Thea, and it was nine AM. She was calling to say that her mother wasn't up yet, so though dressed, she still couldn't get out of the house. Thea made no comment about his behavior the night before, but she did say that the phone had rung "at least twenty times" before he had picked up.

Stedman rang down for a pot of black coffee, and then, remembering that Omar was probably still there, added another pot to the order. He opened the door to the sitting room and through the curtained gloom was able to discern Omar's legs still stretched out on the chair as he had left him. "My God, is he going to be stiff," he thought to himself, and decided to let him sleep a bit longer while he showered.

He had just put on a white shirt and the glen plaid trousers of an old tweed suit when he heard room service knock at the door of the other room. The waiter came in while Steddy signed the bill. When he had left, Steddy poured a cup of coffee from the tray, walked to the window, and drew the curtains, flooding the room with light. Turning to Omar, he said, "Come on, Sleeping Beauty, wake up. It's coffee time."

The appalling sight that the daylight revealed caused Stedman to drop the steaming cup into Omar's lap. It didn't matter—he couldn't feel it. The entire back of his head was missing. Stedman was paralyzed. It wasn't until he had finished drinking a second cup of coffee that he realized he had walked over to the couch, sat down, and poured it.

From the couch, he could see Omar's face. He was slumped as if dozing, with eyes closed, still wrapped up in the blanket as Stedman had left him only hours before. The only noticeable difference in his appearance was a small black spot on the bridge of his nose.

There was a pungent odor in the room that mingled with the wholesome aroma of the coffee. He had smelled it before in the bullrings of Spain. It made him gag and feel weak in the stomach. At bullfights he had attributed the queasiness to the heat, the dust, the cheap cigars, and the sweat, but now he recognized it as the smell of blood and guts and brains and death, and he knew he would never mistake the odor again.

He was beginning to wonder who to call when the phone rang. It was the hall porter.

"Chief Inspector Allsloe and two detectives from Scotland Yard to see you, sir. Shall I send them up?"

"I'm just in the shower. Ask them to wait fifteen minutes and then send them up, would you?"

Stedman replaced the receiver and immediately regretted what he had just said. Why hadn't he simply said he was just about to call them? He knew the answer—Allsloe would never have believed him. Steddy knew Allsloe didn't like him from his run-in with him at the inquiry. The inspector had made it plain that he thought the lot of them to be a bunch of degenerates, and foreigners to boot. He had almost blamed Steddy flat out for not stopping Rollo from leaving.

Steddy imagined the headlines: ROCKFORD'S PALS SHOOT IT OUT IN WEST END HOTEL. It had been so easy for Steddy to be objective about what Rollo should have done— stay and face the police. Now the shoe was on the other foot, and Steddy knew he had to get away and get away quickly—but how?

He ran to the wardrobe, tore the jacket of his dinner suit from its hanger and then fumbled at tying a black bow tie around the collar of his white shirt. From the bed he tore the top sheet, trembling fiercely all the while. He folded it twice and wrapped it around his waist, covering his plaid trousers like an apron. With the jacket on, he looked a fairly convincing waiter.

There was a knock at the door.

Steddy was beginning to panic. The trembling had developed into racking shakes, and the sound of his heartbeat almost drowned out the knock when it came a second time.

Now they would find him like this, and nothing he could ever say or do would convince them he wasn't the killer. Irrationally he ran to the window, seeking a way to escape, and looked down hopelessly at the traffic six floors below. An idea came to him, wrested from his desperation and fueled by adrenaline. In one step he was at Omar's side, and with the strength of a terrified madman, he picked him up bodily, still swathed in the blanket, and without breaking stride, heaved him from the window as far as he could into the rush-hour traffic on Davies Street. He didn't stop to see the havoc that resulted, but took up the breakfast tray that was still on the coffee table and opened the door. Holding the coffee pot, he gestured hysterically at the startled men in the hall, screaming in broken English.

"The window . . . the window . . . I try to stop him . . ."

They were already past him like a shot, straining to see out the gaping window, blinded by the billowing glass curtain and then tearing it from its rod. Stedman could hear the horns and screeching brakes, and before he realized it, they were past him again and on their way to the elevator and the stairs. Steddy tried to pull himself together. They'll be back soon, he told himself. Get out of the apron, get your passport and some money . . . money! He only had twenty pounds cash—not enough for anything—shit! He switched jackets for the one that matched his trousers, tore the bow tie from his neck, and stuffed a tie from the wardrobe into his pocket. As he ran for the door, his eye caught the second of Omar's attaché cases—it had been hidden before by Omar's body and the blanket. Steddy plucked it up without opening it and ran from the room and down the stairs that led to the lobby. He slowed his pace on the last flight, where it became the grand stair that spilled into the middle of the main lobby. His caution was unnecessary—everyone in the building had rushed out the side door into Davies Street to see and add to the commotion. Steddy strode out the unattended front door into Brook Street, and without looking back, walked the two blocks to Bond Street feeling a thousand imagined eyes at his back. At the corner he hailed a cab.

"Where to, guv?"

"Uh, uh, the zoo, please."

Part II
Hop Scotch

15

Why had he picked the London Zoo? He'd never even been there. Hell, one place was as good as another to collect his thoughts and call Thea. God, Thea, what would she think? Serious doubts began to invade the disengaging hatches of his brain that had been battened down for action—why the hell had he run? Fear must have paralyzed his reason, and now as it returned, he could see nothing to justify what he had done. How could he go back and face the music after heaving Omar's corpse out the window? It was disturbingly macabre, and the thought of it made him shiver. Men had hanged on much less damning evidence.

He distracted himself by opening Omar's briefcase, vaguely remembering that he had said it had money in it—there was nothing vague about the neat piles of banded twenty- and fifty-pound notes that filled it to the top. Now it came back to him—Omar had said he had a hundred thousand pounds with him, but somehow it hadn't registered before. There was a notebook as well—a small brown paper one, the kind that fits into a breast pocket. Steddy flipped through it—there was a lot of writing, but it was all in Arabic; at least he assumed it was.

The cab pulled up at the zoo. The driver was not at all happy to make change for a twenty-pound note. "That was my first mistake as a fugitive," Steddy thought. It wouldn't

71

take Scotland Yard very long to trace him now. He would have to move away from there on the double, at least as soon as he had called Thea—if he could still catch her at home, and he prayed that he would.

She answered the phone, but he forgot to push the coin into the box to complete the circuit. Damn! When he rang back, the line was busy. He was still so shaken that he dialed three wrong numbers before it finally started to ring again. Ten times and still no bloody answer. He was sure he had the wrong number again but was afraid to hang up for fear it was the right one. He was about to slam down the receiver and try again when a voice answered. It wasn't Thea's.

"Double three, double one."

"Could I speak to Miss Theadora, please?"

"I think she's just gone out. May I take a message, sir?"

"It's terribly urgent. Could you try to catch her?"

"Well, I'll look out the window if you'll wait a moment."

Steddy was apoplectic. If he missed her now, he'd never get her, as they would surely be watching her. Damn the waiting. He had to put another coin in the callbox. He heard footsteps coming to the phone.

"Well, I hope it's important, sir—I had to call her back all the way from the corner."

"I assure you it's very important."

Thea was breathless and curt when she took the phone, but her tone softened when she realized it was Steddy.

"Couldn't it wait five minutes? I had one foot in the cab."

"Darling, I'm afraid it's very important, and I don't have much time."

Thea sensed from his voice that something was wrong.

"What is it, darling?"

"Thea, Omar was murdered in my suite last night when I was asleep."

"Oh, my God, you poor thing . . . who did it?"

"That's just it, I haven't any idea, but I think someone set me up on purpose, and I'm afraid I bolted."

"But why, darling? They couldn't possibly accuse you."

"I'm afraid the evidence was rather convincing, and then everything I've done since has only made things look much worse."

"What did you do?"

"Darling, there just isn't time now. Please don't ask any questions and just listen. I've got a lot to tell you and very little time. I've got to get out of town fast and—"

"But where will you go?"

"I don't know, dearest, but what's important now is that they'll be watching you, so we have to figure out some way of communicating that they won't be able to trace."

"Please go to the police, Steddy—look what happened to Rollo because he panicked."

"It's out of the question."

"But listen—"

"It's too late for buts. You'll understand when you read about it in the papers. That's why I have to be able to call you and tell you what really happened."

"Darling, don't do this to me. You must tell me what has—"

"You're wasting time. I may have only a matter of minutes. Now just listen. Okay?"

"Okay, but—"

"Tomorrow, I want you to go to the Savoy and have a drink in the American Bar, as though you are waiting for someone. Don't arrive a minute before six—I don't want them to have time to trace the call or anything."

"Will you meet me then?"

"No, dearest, but I'll call you there at five minutes past and—"

"But what if there's some reason you can't? Oh, Steddy, what do I do if they're following me, or questioning me, and I can't get away?"

"Listen, Thea, you've got to stay calm. You'll be my only way of communicating with the rest of the world. I may not be able to get to a phone on time—we have to plan now for every possible fuckup.''

"Steddy, don't do this, please . . ."

"When I call tomorrow, the first thing I'll tell you is where and when I'll call the next day. That'll be safe; they won't be able to trace it that quickly.''

"And if you don't call, or I'm not there?''

"Then we have to have a backup, some restaurant or something.''

"How about San Lorenzo? It's always crowded.''

"That's fine, but only if we haven't connected—then you go there at noon the following day. Got it?''

"I think so, but, darling, this is all so unnecessary. You didn't do anything, so why should you run? You're not English—you'll stick out like a sore thumb, and you won't even know where to go. They'll catch you right away, and then you really will look guilty.''

"Listen, I know my chances aren't great, but if I went to the police now, they'd throw me in jail, and I couldn't stand that. I've just got to buy some time. Maybe it will all just straighten itself out.''

"If you insist, then I'm coming with you. I'm so worried—''

"Don't worry, I'm not going to get hurt. If they catch me, I have no intention of doing anything stupid—I'll go with them like a lamb. Now I've got to go, darling, they may have traced my taxi by now. And please, darling, try not to worry—I love you so much.''

"I love you, too. Be careful and—Oh, wait! Steddy, is it Claridge's at six tomorrow?''

"No, dearest, the Savoy . . .'' And then: "At *five past*,'' he screamed into the phone, but the money ran out, and the line went dead.

Next to the telephone booth was a kiosk that sold candy and postcards and things for tourists. Steddy bought an A to Z map of London and a small guide to Great Britain. He didn't know what to do next, but he did know that he had to get away from the zoo and that the map would help him get out of the area without taking another traceable taxi.

He knew that he couldn't stay in London and didn't even entertain the thought of appearing at one of the railroad stations or airports.

The map showed that Luton was the first major town on the rail line to the north, and he could get there by Greenline Bus. The nearest bus stop looked about half a mile away from where he was, so after buying a supply of candy bars and biscuits, he set out for it at a good clip. The military surplus store that he passed on the way had an anorak in the window. He bought it as well as some trousers, underwear, hiking boots, and a money belt that caught his eye. He wore the anorak and stuffed everything else into a navy-issue duffel bag.

Steddy was lucky—it took only five minutes for the bus to come, although it seemed like hours. He got off at Hampstead, took off the anorak, hid it in the duffel, and put on the black knit tie that he'd brought in his pocket. He was sure it wasn't very professional, but it might put them off the scent and gain him some valuable time. Whatever he might have gained was probably lost when the bus took over twenty minutes to get to Hampstead—the church's clock tower read ten forty-five. He couldn't believe it; it seemed as if a week had passed since the telephone had awakened him. Now, in a little under two hours, he had become a fugitive on the run, and he didn't even know where he was running to. Steddy was amused that at least half of the thought cheered him—if he didn't know where he was going, Scotland Yard certainly didn't either.

On the bus, he studied the small map of Great Britain in the guidebook. When he spotted Scotland, he realized that it had been in the back of his mind ever since he had realized that he couldn't risk leaving the British Isles. Probably because he had just been there with Thea he thought of it as a refuge, a place where you could get lost and become part of the scenery as they had done. But then, no one had been *hunting* them. An American on his own, with no reason to be there, would be very noticeable. Aberdeen and the North Sea caught his eye. He had just read a big piece in *Time* about North Sea oil, and how the Scots resented the American drillers on leave from the offshore rigs, turning Aberdeen into their private playpen/pigpen. It could be just the right place for him. He'd be just another ugly American amidst hundreds of drillers, marine biologists, helicopter pilots, and service personnel. Absolutely perfect. Now all he had to do was get there in one piece.

The bus trip to Luton took about forty-five minutes, and Steddy was able to find the station without having to ask directions. He had determined from the map that the safest way for him to go north was to take a train to York, where it looked as if he could change to a direct line to Edinburgh and there catch a train to Inverness—the end of the line.

From the timetable he picked up at Luton he learned that in order to get to York he had to change at Sheffield. The train for Sheffield left at eleven-thirty—in fifteen minutes. He had just enough time to buy his ticket and a backpack and sleeping bag that he had seen in the window of a shop nearby. He hoped that combined with his anorak and boots, they would make him less conspicuous. He was still stuffing everything he had bought earlier into the backpack when the train arrived. The two-and-a-half-hour ride was uneventful, and he made the connection without a hitch. He would arrive at York in time to catch the 4:01 train to Edinburgh.

Steddy was lucky and found an empty compartment, but before the train pulled out, a mother and son took two seats opposite him. He buried his nose in the Scottish guidebook he had purchased and tried to concentrate on reading it, but the compartment was very hot, and in spite of his tension and fear, he had to fight to keep his eyelids open.

A policeman had him by the shoulders and was shaking him—when he opened his eyes, he saw it was the conductor, who was trying to wake him up. The train had stopped, and when he looked around, he saw they were in a glass-covered station.

"This is the end of the line, unless you've a mind to spend the rest of the night in the shed, you'd best be on your way."

"Where are we?" Steddy asked.

"Newcastle. We've been here for twenty minutes."

Steddy gathered his things and left the train. The station clock read 4:45. There was a train to Edinburgh at 5:08, but he'd lost fifteen minutes checking the schedule and now had only eight minutes to buy a ticket and board it. How stupid he had been. He had tried to go unnoticed, and now, if asked, the conductor was certain to remember him.

The train was on time, and Steddy found a compartment with only an elderly lady in it. Too late, he noticed that the overhead racks were full of gear. He started to leave, but the lady told him sweetly to take a seat as there was one left. There was nothing he could do then but comply. He was just stowing his backpack when four young men dressed in hiking clothes entered the compartment and shut the door behind them. Steddy could tell they were Americans before they said hello, and by the time the train left the station, he knew just about everything there was to know about them, short of whether or not they still had their wisdom teeth. Within ten minutes they were pumping him about where he was from in the States and where he was going in Scotland and wasn't it a coincidence that they were all going hiking.

It hadn't occurred to Stedman that he would need an alias, so when they introduced themselves, he was hard put to come up with a name—Wiley's was the best he could manage on short notice. It turned out that all four of them were from Colorado and were in the army, stationed together in Germany. They were on a two-week furlough and were bound for Scotland to climb Ben Nevis and hike through the Grampians.

Steddy told them that he taught marine biology at Rutgers University and that the college had sponsored his trip to study plankton in Loch Ness. "Plankton" was the only scientific-sounding marine biological word he knew. They kidded him about the Loch Ness monster, and Steddy allowed that he hoped to get a glimpse of it. Fortunately they were too excited about their own trip to ask him any searching questions about his.

They had bought a lot of cold chicken and pork pies and beer at the station and insisted that he share it with them. After his second beer, Steddy found to his surprise that he was enjoying himself—wishing that he really was on his way to climb Ben Nevis with them and not a fugitive on the run from Scotland Yard.

The trip to Edinburgh took just under two hours, which meant they would arrive at seven PM, just missing the last train to Inverness. The hikers already had the address of a hostel where they could spend the night. When they asked Steddy where he was going to stay, he said the hostel sounded like a good idea.

16

Chief Inspector Allsloe was not amused. His office on the tenth floor of the New Scotland Yard, though the biggest in the facility, was crowded. Fourteen men of the Yard of varying ranks surrounded his desk, to the extent that some of them were backed up against the sixteenth-of-an-inch simulated Tudor paneling that covered the walls.

Allsloe had never before been seen by his fellows with a loosened tie and an unsprung collar. He was one of the few men in London who still wore separate collars—not through any desire to be eccentric or for that matter smart, but rather because he parsimoniously wore the same shirt three times during a given week, limiting himself to two fresh collars.

He had a wife and a char and once a week a laundress, but still persisted in maintaining himself like a first former from a bygone era. He hadn't been to the best schools, nor had he been to the worst. Neither middle-class nor upper-class, he was simply middle-aged. He was in that second-son limbo—uncomfortably bright for his allotted station, he had nonetheless perservered and found in the service his own dusty niche, having reached that sleepy cerebral level at the Yard where he was normally only called upon to judge the work of others.

There wasn't a man in the room who didn't know this, yet they all sensed with the Rockford case an awakening in him, a change from passive to active. There was no doubt in their minds that this was to be very much his show. Few of those present had ever seen him in action, but the legend of his past work—like a tangible thing in the room with them—brought a stillness to the gathering that was far from the norm for an average briefing.

Allsloe possessed all the theatrical accoutrements one would expect from a brainy, pedantic civil servant or an arcane professor of history: the worn, lovat-green tweed jacket, the fuming meerschaum, and the noble but battered brown fedora. In his right hand, he constantly clicked and rolled two glass marbles—a habit that had earned him the nickname "Queeg" (though Allsloe had shattered many an immy long before Wouk took pen to paper). The hand that held them had a rumpled, chalky, scholastic look that was in harmony with his general visage. In contrast, his startlingly red eyebrows popped out as though they were surprised by the dull, colorless eyes that they framed.

As his annoyance grew, the modulation of his voice did not change; only the more urgent clicking of the crystal balls in his wizened paw signaled his mood.

"When I briefed you all six days ago, I told you only what I felt you needed to know, fully confident that you would be able to perform the tasks assigned to you.

"You will notice, dispersed among you, a number of unfamiliar faces."

No one looked around—they had already marked the strangers.

"These gentlemen are from another branch of government service and will, for the time being, be monitoring our briefings anonymously."

The marbles were now resounding with a high-pitched ping, until one fell to the carpet and rolled under the ornate Victorian desk.

"Till now I did not deem it prudent to brief you further than was necessitated by the scope of your duties with regard to the surveillance of Stedman Wright and the Arab known as Omar. You were all aware that this work pertained to the Rockford case, but you did not know until now—and I might add, until each of you signed the Official Secrets

Act ten minutes ago—that this case also involves the nation's security.

"Other than saying that I have been selected to head the joint team composed of ourselves here at the Yard and MI5, I can only add that a grave matter of national and, I dare say, international security is at stake."

Murmurings filled the room.

Allsloe's vacant gaze scanned the suddenly taut, nervous faces.

"Any one of you not wishing to involve himself further in this investigation may leave the room and remand himself into custody, at full pay, for the duration of the investigation."

Frozen but steady stares returned his, as he fixed on each of them individually.

"I said this was to be a joint operation. Allow me to elaborate. Some time ago, it came to our attention that our brothers in the secret branch sought to eliminate a certain Arab. We occasionally learn by chance what the secret chaps are up to, and normally we don't interfere. However, in this case, an unusual opportunity seemed to present itself, and we were able, through channels, to convince the ministers involved that a collaboration of the two services in this particular operation would be in the best interests of the country."

Everyone in the stuffy, overcrowded room knew of the special relationship Allsloe had enjoyed with the last four or five occupants of Number Ten and thought of him as a British backstage version of America's high-profile J. Edgar Hoover.

"Could one of you please find the marble I just dropped?"

The sudden request recaptured their attention and brought everyone in the vicinity of his desk to his knees.

He left them to it for a minute or so and then abruptly told them to let it go. It took a moment for them to settle down, as no one had wanted to abandon the search unsuccessfully.

"Now, I'd like you to imagine that the lost marble is Lord Rockford."

No one dared question his hypothesis with so much as a raised eyebrow.

"He has rolled, if you'll pardon the pun, from sight, and just as the transparent marble takes on the color of the carpet and is rendered almost invisible, so too is Rockford capable of becoming invisible against the multicolored carpet of these British Isles he knows so well. Especially as they are scattered with the dwellings of influential friends who are all too willing to hide him.

"The fall of the marble was silent and unobserved, making the finding of it much more difficult—we don't even know in what direction to begin to look. Rockford's disappearance was also unobserved, and anyone who might have any information is unwilling to come forward—they don't believe he has committed a crime. I believe he is still in this country, but his chances of escape by private aircraft or boat increase dramatically with every day that passes."

A blond inspector in the front row tentatively raised his hand.

"How do we start, sir? I mean, do we have any leads or anything at all to go on? Oh, and how does Stedman Wright fit in?"

"I told you of a combined operation with our clandestine brethren. This was launched the very night of the Clermont murder, which is why I was not able to brief you to the extent that I would have wanted. Let us hope that this excessive caution over security has not cost us the entire operation." He fixed the head liaison officer from M15 with an accusing stare and continued.

"Stedman Wright is our one possible direct thread to Rockford—a thread that we took a great deal of trouble to spin. I cannot emphasize too strongly the importance of finding him and keeping him under constant surveillance before he slips through the looking glass as well."

Allsloe paused, allowing what he had said to sink in, watching their faces from beneath his red brows for their reactions. Then, slowly raising his right hand above his head, he held out the second glass marble between his thumb and index finger. It was red, and he displayed it as if it were a gem of great price.

"You will remember that the first marble you were unable to retrieve for me I referred to as Lord Rockford." Everyone nodded to signify that he did. "Well, this one is Mr. Stedman Wright, American."

The marble tumbled from his fingers in much the same way the first had, except that this time twenty-eight eyes followed its slight, silent bounce and gentle roll under the desk.

"Now, do you think one of you could retrieve Mr. Wright for me?"

Holbrook, the blond chap who had spoken before and was closest to the desk, was first to his knees and in a moment had the marble in his hand. He did not immediately rise, however, but took a minute to scan the vicinity where he had located it and was rewarded by finding the Rockford marble, transparent and almost invisible, behind a foot of the desk. Holbrook stood and handed them to Allsloe. The significance of the click of the two crystal balls, once again united, was not lost on the others.

"Am I correct, sir, in thinking that we eliminated the Arab in order to set up Wright so that he would lead us to Lord Rockford, and that now that Wright's given us the slip, we're back to square one?"

"Essentially, yes. Although Rockford is far from the most important bag in this particular shooting match."

"How so?" Holbrook queried.

"There are others involved—foreign agents that we know about and perhaps some that we do not, as well as the possibility of some very highly placed individuals in this country. We're not at all sure how deep this thing goes.

"As far as Wright's giving us the slip—that remains to be seen. He certainly didn't slip away quietly or unobserved. We should be able to get a line on him fairly soon through standard police work." He glared again at the man from M15 and continued, "Remember, he's not the transparent marble that can fade into the woodwork as Rockford did. He's the colored one—an American who will stand out and be remembered by anyone he comes in contact with the moment he opens his mouth.

"We do have a few leads, though. We know that, as

with Rockford, Nubar Harkonian is his most influential friend in England—someone he might naturally turn to for help. He's also carrying on an open and serious affair with Harkonian's stepdaughter and is bound to try to contact her. He can't have much money on him. As far as we know, he never carries more than a couple of hundred pounds—and if he tries to cash a check or use a credit card, we have circulated his picture and description to all the usual sources with strict instructions to notify us. He left the hotel with only the clothes on his back, which we should have a description of from a cabbie or a busman very soon.

"Unfortunately, tossing that Arab out of the window was an extremely effective diversion—no one at Claridge's saw him leave the building. It causes some problems for us. We had hoped to set him running without any undue public attention—don't want some high-minded British subject doing his duty and turning him in. So far, the press is playing ball with us and is trying to make the Arab's death look like a suicide, but I don't know how long we can hold them. You all know what they're like.

"Are there any questions so far?"

17

Thea was very nervous. Not wanting to be too early or too late, she had nevertheless arrived at the Savoy five minutes before the appointed hour. She paced the lobby, trying to detect whether she had been followed and worrying over the discrepancy between the time on her watch and that of the clock on the wall, when it occurred to her that Steddy's watch might be five minutes fast and she already might have missed his call. She hurried into the bar.

What with the London season still in full swing, the small bar was packed, and there wasn't a table to be had. Only by flirting with two men standing at the bar was she allowed to put an elbow between them. Most of the crowd were Americans from the midwest talking animatedly about the tennis, or the racing, or the theater, or the prices, or a mixture of everything at once. When one of the men bought her a bullshot, she was too distraught even to thank him, but she did tell the barman she was expecting a call. The phone rang on two occasions, but both times the cashier spoke briefly and replaced the receiver. What if someone else got a call first? She felt like screaming.

The third call was Stedman. He wouldn't tell her where he was.

"But I'm so worried. There's been nothing in the papers except a small piece on the second page about an accidental fall from a window at a West End hotel. They didn't even say it was Claridge's or mention your name.''

She raced on, not letting him get a word in.

''No one from the police has even called me, and I'm sure I'm not being followed. Maybe they really think it was an accident.''

''Don't you believe it, sweetheart. That's what they want you to think so you'll relax your guard and lead them to me.''

''But they might not even think you were there. You could have been out.''

''Sure. I answered the phone when you called and spoke to the hall porter when he announced the cops.''

''But—''

''And besides that, they will have found out by now from the autopsy that half his head was blown off and he was dead on arrival when he hit Davies Street.''

''Oh, darling, I've got to see you. I can't make any sense talking to you this way—I have to whisper; I'm standing at the end of the bar leaning over, and the place is jammed.''

''Listen, they're probably tracing the call by now, or at the very least listening in on the line. I've got to go. Goody-bye, darling, I love you.''

''Oh, Stedman, I'm so afraid.''

''Don't be. Just remember, I didn't do anything—it's just got to sort itself out. Now good-bye, darling.''

Thea was about to hand the receiver back to the barman when she heard Steddy scream on the line: ''Oh, shit! I forgot. Did you have lunch at the Connaught?''

''With whom?'' she replied, totally nonplussed.

''The Connaught!'' he screamed with frustration.

''What . . Oh, God, yes, *the Connaught!*''

Steddy realized that she had at last understood where and at what time they would liaise the following day and gingerly replaced the receiver as though it had suddenly become very hot but was too delicate—or dangerous—to drop.

Thea finally grasped his meaning, but as she passed the phone back to the barman, she wasn't sure whether Stedman had said lunch or dinner—meaning whether he would call at one in the afternoon or at six in the evening. Tears welled in her eyes and made them glisten as though sightless. She went back to where she had left her bag, and the man who had paid for her bullshot asked, "If he can't make it, perhaps you'd like to join us for dinner?"

The tears rolled freely down her cheeks in big gouts. She smiled through them as though they had surprised her by falling out of a blue tropical sky, thanked him for the drink, and left.

As her cab pulled out of the Savoy's courtyard, she thought she noticed someone she had seen in the bar jump into the passenger seat of a black car parked in front of the theater, and then pull into the traffic behind them.

18

Stedman stepped from the stale, reeking callbox and made his way through the beer-brown haze to the bar of the seedy pub. The fear that the call might have been traced made him want to run, but he gritted his teeth and ordered a pint of lager from the landlady, resigned to awaiting the time and charges for the call. When his beer arrived, he hunched over it to avoid being drawn into the boisterous conversation of the American oilmen who seemed to be everywhere.

He had left the train at Edinburgh with the hikers, finding their hail-fellow-well-met attitude both refreshing and somehow reassuring. Their excitement was infectious, and Steddy was quick to realize that their company provided him an excellent cover. They went straight to the youth hostel and left their gear (Steddy was happy he had transferred Omar's funds to the money belt on the train). And then the boys insisted he come with them to the pub next door, where in the hour left to them before closing, they got bombed on beer and swore eternal friendship.

Steddy felt dreadful the next morning and was shocked he had behaved so sophomorically with the entire police force of Great Britain after him.

They parted at the hostel, promised to meet again, and five minutes later he was at the station. But he missed the first train and was forced to wait over two hours for the next one—to wait and be noticed he thought morosely.

He could hardly credit the number of stupid, amateurish mistakes he had made in the last twenty-four hours. Then again, he thought, I am an amateur at this—thank God! The thought didn't comfort him. In fact, he had prided himself all his life on retaining his amateur status in everything he had ever done—probably from some unformed fear of becoming a professional anything.

When he'd been offered a chance to go on the professional tennis circuit and had declined, Suki had said he was afraid of making a commitment because he was afraid of failure, but it wasn't that. He didn't look down on athletes who played for pay; he just didn't want to be one of them and felt it would somehow tarnish and confuse his motives.

Wiley—one of the few friends who understood what he suffered after sustaining a big loss, especially a gambling loss—once asked him if it was possible that people like him and Rollo didn't sometimes subconsciously precipitate spectacular losses in order to publicly reaffirm their cherished, devil-may-care, we're-here-for-the-sport-not-for-the-money attitude. Stedman had never replied.

As he analyzed his predicament, he argued that this was nothing more than a new amateur event. True, he was pitted against unknown professionals with no pro in his corner this time to train and guide him; nevertheless, it could be foolishly argued that he had been presented with an extremely rare sporting opportunity. After all, in the end he was innocent.

The loud clanging of the telephone behind the bar roused him from his reverie. As the landlady approached, he downed what was left of the beer and reached for his change.

"That'll be eighty P, dearie."

Steddy thanked her, pushed the change across the bar, and exited into the street to hurry the few dank, rotting blocks to the hotel/flophouse where he had secured a bare cubicle with an iron bed.

19

Inspector Holbrook knocked and entered Chief Allsloe's room at the Yard.

"Well, Holbrook, what's happened?"

"Miss Boulton led us a bit of a chase all over town and ended up at the Savoy, where she hung around in the lobby for a bit, seemed nervous about the time—Jones and McHenry were sure he was going to show. Then she went into the bar, where two chaps bought her a drink."

Allsloe cocked a crimson eyebrow.

"No, sir, the men checked them out. She didn't know them, but she did take a call at the bar."

"Did they get a trace or monitor it?"

" 'Fraid there wasn't time for that either. She was on the call for less than two minutes."

"They questioned the barman?"

"Yes, sir. She gave him her correct name and said she was expecting a call."

"Was it a man on the line?"

"Yes, the barman was sure of that, but he didn't recall whether it sounded local or long distance. All the noise in the bar, you know."

"It had to be him. He must be still in the country—if he'd been calling from abroad, the fellow would have noticed and remembered. What did she do then?"

"She left right away; went by cab straight to Claridge's

and met Wright's friend Wiley Travis in the hall. Do you think she could have been talking to Travis on the phone, sir? Possibly they were to have met originally at the Savoy.''

"I suppose it's possible, but it's easy enough to check out.''

"Sir?''

"Get through to Claridge's and find out if he made any calls to the Savoy. You have the precise time, I presume?''

"Certainly, sir.''

"Well, if he called, they would have had to charge him; there'd be a chit.''

Holbrook started toward the door.

"And, Holbrook.''

"Yes, sir.''

"If you can't determine that Travis made the call, I want a man on permanent duty at the Savoy switchboard and one in the lobby.''

"Yes, sir.''

"And make arrangements with the G.P.O. for a rapid trace from the Savoy and Claridge's as well.''

"Claridge's is already in place, sir, but I'll see to the Savoy right away.''

"And, Holbrook.''

"Sir?''

"Is she still at Claridge's with Travis?''

"No, sir. They went by foot to Mark's Club in Hill Street. 'Fraid we can't get in there, sir, without making a fuss, so Jones and McHenry are staying with it outside.''

"Quite right. Those two flatfoots in Mark's Club would really set the cat among the pigeons.''

The heavy oak-paneled door clicked shut on its polished brass hasp. Allsloe wondered if he had underestimated his man. The plan had been that they would throw a scare into Wright and leave him an opportunity to escape—a controlled operation. But Wright's unexpected, ruthless reaction had taken them completely by surprise and made a botch-up of the scenario. Allsloe had had his men stationed all over the ground floor of the hotel; every means of egress had been covered. He really couldn't blame them for leaving their posts to a man when the body had splattered all over

Davies Street. Then it had taken fifteen minutes or more for them to identify the corpse. They had known there was a body in the suite—they should have noticed that it was gone.

No, Wright's irrational, or perhaps very clever, behavior had simply bowled them over. God save us from amateurs he thought, or could this American really be something more than a dissolute, drunken gambler? The file they had compiled showed him to be an athlete. That didn't really go with the drinking, but there it was. No military service other than a private troop for privileged boys, not even any business training. Nothing, in effect, to indicate that he would be prepared to handle this sort of situation. Yet it was now over thirty hours since he had disappeared, and all they were sure of was that he had gone to the zoo and bought a map of greater London—then nothing. Allsloe had no misguided affection for Stedman Wright, but he did hope the Yard would get back on his track before the PLO did—for Wright's sake.

20

Thea asked for Wiley on the house phone in the small booth by the main entrance of Claridge's.

"Well, home at last, eh? I've been calling you for two days. I was sure that the two of you had pulled a disappearing act on me."

"Wiley, I'm downstairs."

"Where's Steddy?"

"Could you please come down?"

He sensed a tremor in her voice.

"Sure. I'll be right down—get a table in the hall."

That son of a bitch, he thought as he replaced the receiver. One night on his own and he's already screwed up. *La plus ça change . . .*

He had sensed that she was upset, but her pallor surprised him. She was always so vibrant, so vital, it was almost impossible to imagine her going to pieces. She wasn't at all the sort he would have expected to weep on "the best friend's" shoulder. She had too much pride or style or class or whatever you call it.

Thea got up when she saw him, and he found himself returning her hug with the strength that she seemed to need to draw from him. His cheek was wet from hers when they drew apart.

"Thea. What's happened?"

"How much do you know?"

"Only that I haven't been able to reach either of you since yesterday. I thought you'd gone off again to be on your own someplace."

"What did the operators say when you rang the suite?"

"No answer, no answer, no answer, when they were polite. Usually they just left me on the line ringing an empty room. I even asked the manager Mr. Bentley."

"What did he say?"

"Oh, just that he'd had no instructions from Steddy. You know they're used to him taking off for a few days or even a week without saying anything."

"Wiley, will you order us a stiff drink, please."

"Okay, Thea, but listen, I'm sure he's all right. You know, he was quite drunk the other night when I left. He could easily have gone off with Omar—they're probably holed up playing backgammon in Antibes or something like that. It wouldn't be the first time."

"Then you don't know about Omar?"

The waiter, dressed in formal livery—jacket, silk stockings, pumps, and satin breeches—unchanged for over a hundred years, did not notice the queer aspect Wiley's expression had taken when he arrived to take their order. If he had, he wouldn't have let on.

"Could you let us have two Gordon's martinis, very cold, straight up with a twist of lemon, please," he said without consulting Thea.

"Right away, sir."

The Gypsy orchestra started playing "Fascination." The clock had stopped many decades in the past at seven PM.

A little less sure of his ground now, Wiley asked, "Now what about Omar? He checked out yesterday."

"He certainly did!" Thea laughed nervously.

"What's so funny about that? They told me he'd checked out, when I tried him yesterday to see if he knew what had happened to Steddy. That's why I thought they might have gone off on a toot together."

"He checked out all right—right out the sixth-floor window."

Tears started to roll from her sea-blue eyes, and her

strong, straight brows seemed especially severe against her pale, pinched face. Wiley realized he was seeing Thea at the age of eleven or twelve, momentarily stripped of all sophistication.

"Thea, get hold of yourself, the drinks are coming." Wiley cringed at public displays of emotion, under any circumstances.

They drank for a bit in silence, while Thea pulled herself together. After a time, she calmed and her color returned. Wiley ordered two more drinks.

"Theadora. Do you know where Steddy is?" Wiley had inherited his father's habit of addressing people by their full Christian names to bring them to their senses when they were, in his opinion, "out of control."

"No, I don't, damn it—not exactly, that is—I did just talk to him."

"So he's all right."

"I think so."

"Hell, Thea, I can't help if you don't tell me what's going on."

"Wiley, could we go someplace less public to talk? We may be being watched."

"Come on, Thea, don't you think you're being just the slightest bit melodramatic?"

"You'll understand when I tell you everything. Please, just trust me until then."

"Okay, listen," he said, gulping down the last of his second martini and rising from the table, "you stay here and finish your drink while I go upstairs and call Alexandra—"

"Oh, Wiley, I'd forgotten you had a girl here. I didn't mean to mess up your evening."

Wiley rolled his eyes.

"Don't worry, I can always meet her later. She'll understand . . . I hope."

Thea smiled wanly, and Wiley raced on before she could change her mind.

"Is Mark's okay with you? We can walk over, and it's a club, so no spooks can get in unless they're members."

"Fine."

They cut across Berkeley Square on foot in the now-warm evening. Neither of them spoke. Wiley knew that she would talk when she was ready. He was mystified by her behavior and wondered if she hadn't perhaps gone over the top.

He opened the unmarked door of the discreet townhouse for her and signed the register in the entry. They climbed the small circular stair to the tiny bar at the top of the first landing, and Wiley steered her to the end of the bar, to a chintz-cushioned window seat that was just big enough to accommodate them. Thea asked for a daiquiri, and Wiley had one, too. The waiter brought them with the menus. The atmosphere had a comforting effect on Thea. It was more like a cozy Edwardian residence than a club.

An hour and a half and two daiquiris later, they still hadn't ordered, but now it was Wiley who was ashen, while Thea was flushed from relating her story.

The only evidence she could show him was the small shred of newsprint torn from the second page of the *Daily Mail,* but Wiley knew before reading the report, which named no names, that Thea was telling the truth—at least the truth as she knew it.

"It's all really too fantastic, but I believe you—only don't get annoyed if you catch me looking for traces of blood on the pavement on our way back to the hotel."

"God, Wiley, I'm so relieved. There isn't anyone else I can talk to."

They agreed not to talk on the phone about anything to do with Steddy, so Thea suggested that they meet the next day for lunch and said she would collect him at the hotel at noon. That would give them plenty of time to walk the few blocks to the Connaught for the one o'clock telephone rendezvous with Steddy—if, in fact, it was at one o'clock and not at six; she still wasn't sure.

21

Steddy awakened in his dreary box-stall room without any idea of the time of day. He never wore a watch, and the constant gray light of the northern summer morning gave no hint of the hour. He lay in bed smoking, staring at the distant, peeling ceiling and the unlighted bare bulb suspended from it—thinking.

It had been about forty-eight hours since he had stepped into Brook Street and taken a cab to the zoo, and up until this moment, all of his waking hours had been absorbed in struggling to maintain his freedom—but to what end? He had argued with Thea that he was running to gain time—but for what? Maybe she had been right; perhaps he should have stayed. Why should they think he had killed Omar? He hardly knew him. On the other hand, it was obvious that the inspector from the Yard had a pretty low opinion of him, and he probably would have assumed they had argued while gambling. Not a bad motive, but then where was the gun? But there could have been a gun somewhere in the suite for all he knew—he certainly hadn't even thought to look for one, but if someone had wanted to make it look as though he had killed Omar, there would have to have been a gun.

Someone had tried to make it look as though he had killed Omar!

That was the crux of the whole thing. The thought that he was being set up had crossed his mind before, but this was the first time it had taken root. It couldn't have been a fluke or a freak coincidence—he had been deliberately set up, but by whom, and where was the motive?

It hadn't been robbery—the hundred thousand pounds wrapped around his waist proved that. But the money had been hidden by the blanket that covered Omar's legs—he wouldn't have noticed it himself had he not removed the obstruction, as it were.

No, it must have been deliberate. But why?

Then there was the police showing up like that out of the blue. Why would they have come unless someone had deliberately tipped them off? Or had they simply come to ask more questions about Rollo? Certainly not at that hour of the morning. After all, he was just an innocent bystander in the Rockford affair . . . Rollo again! And why hadn't anything been released to the papers yet? They surely knew by now that Omar hadn't died from the fall.

No, it was all too fishy. Either they knew Stedman hadn't done it, or they were sure that he had and wanted him to relax and assume that they thought him innocent.

Omar, of course, was still the big question mark. No one even remembered his last name. They had all accepted him at face value on Rollo's introduction. Rollo again; it all seemed to have everything to do with Rollo—the son of a bitch, or poor devil, depending on who was feeling sorry for whom. But why was Steddy being dragged into it—whatever "it" was?

Stedman got up and poked his head out the window to get an idea of the time. The Granite City was looking pretty gray and run-down in this part of town, and it was obvious from the name of the pub across the street that he had picked the right neighborhood. It wasn't called the Bonnie Prince Charles, or the Caledonian, but rather, in bold red, white, and blue letters, the sign above the door read: "Yankee Go Home Saloon."

He had read how irritated the Aberdeeners were over the invasion of their picturesque city by swarms of red-neck American oil riggers, and he wondered how the plate-glass window of this particular establishment had survived their onslaught.

The big clock in the tower tolled eight-thirty—time to get moving. He pulled on his trousers and shirt, grabbed the single, threadbare towel from the night stand, and padded barefoot down the hall to the door marked "Bath."

It certainly was the American neighborhood. If there ever had been a bath, it had been replaced by two shower stalls—decidedly un-British—and a Rube Goldberg toilet with shiny brass pipes of enormous dimensions that led to a varnished mahogany water tank near the ceiling.

Undressing, Steddy found there were no hooks for his clothes. The floor was awash, so he hung his shirt, followed by his money belt and trousers, on the fulcrum of the toilet's pull chain.

It was the first wash he'd had in almost three days, and he was beginning to enjoy it when a red-haired, embarrassingly fair-skinned, bearded Incredible Hulk of a man came in. Incongruously, he was shod in Korean rubber flip-flops and barely joined about his extraordinary girth was a terrycloth wraparound. The giant grunted by way of acknowledging Steddy's presence. Steddy grunted back and began to rinse the soap out of his hair. A minute or two later there was a terrific banging and clattering that penetrated the noise of the shower and made him jump so that he crashed his head into the low-mounted showerhead. He heard the man grumble, "Oh, shit," and then the shower next to his joined the cacophony.

When Steddy finished, he saw the cause of the commotion—his clothes had fallen when the clod had pulled the chain of the WC, and now, money belt on top, they lay sodden across the loo. "Thanks a lot, fella," Steddy muttered angrily.

"Anytime, asshole," was the brusque retort.

He dressed quickly in the rumpled but dry things from his duffel, descended the impossibly canted stairs that reeked of frying fat, and managed to avoid alerting the landlady, who invariably poked her pincurled head out the door of her small front room when anyone passed. He wanted no part of the breakfast she offered, preferring the Buttery at the station, where he could at least read the London papers. That was where he headed after stopping to buy a black plastic digital watch at a Pakistani shop that had signs in French and the Scandinavian languages in the window.

There wasn't a word about him, or Omar for that matter, in any of the papers, but there were a few items about Rollo—mostly a rehash of stuff about his ancient family heritage, his gambling, and his girl friends. His wife had been interred at the family crypt in a private service.

As if anyone would have gone if they could have! Steddy thought. How ironic. If Rollo had married someone decent, I'd probably be lolling in the sun somewhere with Thea at this very moment.

It pleased him to be able to vent his anger at her, rather than on his friend Rollo.

Holbrook had rung Wiley at seven-thirty that morning to make an appointment for Allsloe to see him at nine. Wiley had had precious little sleep—only about two hours.

He had returned to his room the night before in a very agitated state over Thea's revelations. So much so that he had drunk half of the bottle of Black Label he kept in his room while rolling the problem around in his mind. Finally, at two in the morning—eight in the evening in the States— he had decided to put in a call to his boss. However, the number he had asked the Claridge night operator to get wasn't that of Skinner, Hart & Crowley, but a private number in Washington, D.C., that rang directly through to a switchboard across the Potomac, in Arlington, Virginia. Wiley had left his name with the telephonist, poured himself another drink, and settled down for what was to prove a long wait for a call back.

22

It was the same damn thing! The rain. In England or in Scotland, it was always the rain. At this particular moment, the rain was responsible for all the crossed telephone lines and short tempers that were making it impossible for Steddy to complete his call to London. Under normal circumstances he would have been furious and raised a royal stink, but as things were, he couldn't afford to draw further attention to himself. It was bad enough to have to make the call from a pub in the first place.

Steddy was in the Yankee Go Home Saloon—a totally Americanized saloon bar that had been virtually taken over by the red-neck mothers presently residing in the North Sea, forty miles off the coast. On the day of the big anti-Yank demonstration, the old Scottish pub had sported a big "Yankee Go Home" banner across its front windowpanes, precipitating a genuine old-fashioned wild-West fisticuffs. The landlord and the American foreman were the last two men on their feet. A twenty-dollar gold piece was tossed to settle the dispute, and the rest was history. The Yankee Go Home became the only totally American saloon east of the Lizard, and the banner was eventually replaced with a carved and gilded red, white, and blue sign that had an elaborate coat-of-arms made up of crossed cowboy boots, an oil rig, and an armadillo with a bald eagle on its back wearing a cowboy hat. The atmosphere was very "y'all," and to Stedman's amazement, though the place still looked very much the Scot's pub, down to the tartan rug, the dress and accents were unquestionably American southwest, and they actually had Coors on tap.

Even though it was a weekday afternoon, the Yankee Go Home was crowded with tough-looking customers, including the red-haired hulk from the boardinghouse, who was holding forth at one end of the bar.

Steddy was across the room in an alcove, adding cigarette butt after butt to an already overflowing tin ashtray on the shelf in front of him. The call to the Connaught finally came through. The crisp, familiar tones of the hotel operator's voice—like a direct connection to normality—made him feel even more distant and remote. He asked the bartender for Thea, and while he waited, heard conversation and laughter and a cocktail shaker in the background. It was like being lonely and miserable in boot camp on a rainy Sunday and getting a call from the family, who are all having a wonderful time around the pool. Then Thea was on the line, and the resonance of her voice made the cords in the pit of his stomach go all sloppy, like loose guitar strings. She sounded a million miles away—so foreign, yet so familiar. For a moment, he felt a terrible resentment that almost bordered on hate. The shock of the strength of his emotion deafened him to the meaning of what she was saying. He was mesmerized by the sound of her voice, trying to match it with the memory, staring blindly at the black and red numbers on the dial of the telephone as though it were a Rosetta stone that would bring clarity to the meaningless palaver that she was spouting about newspaper headlines and murder.

The surprise of hearing Wiley's voice brought him up short and back to reality.

"Damn it, Steddy, listen to me. I've got to see you. I may be able to help, but we have to sit down face to face and talk it out."

"Shit, Wiley, what can you do? I don't need a pep talk. This isn't an A-team squash meet, and I'm not turning myself in, so don't waste you breath, and if you want to buy an exclusive on the publishing rights, you'll just have to wait till the hero gets the girl in the last chapter and everyone goes to the seashore.''

"Cut the crap, Steddy. I don't want you to turn yourself in. I've got friends who can help, but you've got to let me talk to you."

"So talk."

"Not here and not now—it's got to be face to face."

"No can do, Wiley."

"Listen, pardner, don't say no. Just promise me you'll call tomorrow—I'll know more then, and maybe you'll listen to me."

"Hey, pal, I need all the help I can get, but I can't risk anyone knowing where I am—they're probably trying to trace the call right now."

"Will you promise to call tomorrow? Please, Steddy."

"Thea will know where and when."

"Okay then."

"Put her on."

Thea grabbed the receiver as though it were a ratline to the last lifeboat on the *Titanic*.

"Darling, I'm in physical pain—you've got to let me meet you. If I were with you, I could stand it somehow."

Steddy looked down at the digital face of his newly acquired Japanese watch.

"Sweetheart, it's been almost three minutes. Are you dining with David tomorrow?"

"David . . . . ? Oh, *David*, well, I think so," she said, recovering quickly, "but I haven't heard from him yet. I did say I'd meet him in the boss's suite around seven, so I guess it's still on."

Steddy understood her right away. "The boss," was the nickname that Thea alone called her father, Grover Boulton. He kept a suite year round at the Dorchester—the hotel the *D* in "David" had stood for. She had offered it to Steddy when they had first come back from Scotland, but the odd proprietary feelings he had where she was concerned had made him decline.

"Well, give him my best, darling. You can't know how much I love you."

"Me, too," Thea said, feeling inadequate and at a loss for words.

The phone clicked loudly, crackled, and went into the grating continuous rattle of a British dial tone.

"That's really the jackpot! They were on the phone for over three minutes in a public bar, and you didn't get a trace? I simply can't believe it."

Allsloe was pink with rage.

"I put two men on foot and two in a mobile unit on both the girl and Travis, and they manage to carry on a three-minute conversation in public with the most wanted man in the British Isles, under your very noses—it really is the limit."

Holbrook tried to stare into the eyes of the portrait of one of Allsloe's predecessors that hung on the paneled wall directly behind him, in a vain attempt to appear to be bravely facing the music, but he found no solace in the cold glare that the picture returned. Glumly he allowed his gaze to bypass his chief's as it descended once again to his large, brown, unpolished shoes.

"Well, sir, they just strolled over to the Connaught from Claridge's— even stopped first in that little wine bar on Mount Street, next to the butcher, but it was full up, so it really seemed as if they were only going to have lunch.

"They had just ordered a drink when the barman went right up to her—he must have known her—and called her to the telephone. It didn't seem at all planned."

"Listen, Holbrook, these people are obviously not the silly asses we took them for. He's the bloody devil incarnate.

"From now on, the minute that girl walks into a hotel, I want a man on the switchboard and the G.P.O. notified immediately. Have you got that?"

"Yes, sir, but really there was no way we could have—"

"*Stop*. From now on, be it hotel, restaurant, bed and breakfast, or brothel, get through to the G.P.O. on the double. Even if she goes into Harrods! They think they're diabolically smart, but they're really just smart alecks, and we'll get them, but only if we're on top of them every minute.''

Holbrook nodded his agreement but didn't reply for fear that anything he said would bring on another diatribe. He was deeply ashamed of the report he had made—but then, their behavior was so erratic and bizarre, he just didn't know what else his men could have done. He departed with his tail between his legs—bested by amateurs, and Americans to boot.

23

The lifeline was severed again—at least for another twenty-four hours. Being alone in a crowd took on a new meaning for Steddy as he stepped mentally from Thea's side at the Connaught's bar into the Klondike gold-rush atmosphere of the saloon. He was feeling bloody-minded, desperately needed the company of his fellow man, the release of drinking with the boys. Instead of cowering off in a corner to wait for the time and charges, he went straight up to the bar, found a spot he could get an arm through, and ordered a shot of Black Jack with a Coors chaser. He hadn't had one of those combinations since the summer when, at eighteen, he had been sent by his father to work as a gofer for one of his friend's oil exploratory companies outside Tulsa. The taste was welcome and familiar, and because he was tight as an overwound cheap alarm clock, the pungent liquor almost instantly made the muscles of his neck and shoulders as relaxed as if he'd just had a two-hour massage.

When he ordered the third set up, he realized that he didn't remember ordering the second and could only tell that he had from the shotglasses lined up in front of him. A tattooed and bearded giant with extraordinary plumage in the band of his Stetson insisted on buying him a fourth, and by the fifth, Steddy was buying drinks for at least six of the drillers at the bar and realized from their conversation that he must have told them he was a stringer for *Newsweek*, doing a story on the local effects of the American invasion of Aberdeen.

The landlady gave him the charges on his London call, which prompted a few questions from his new best friends, so he told them he had met a stewardess from London on the plane on the way over and that he was hoping to see her on the way back before he left. The conversation rapidly turned to the available local talent, and finally to comparisons between the kilted Scottish lasses and the tight-jeaned honeys of the Southwest. Downing another neat shot of bourbon, Steddy toasted the cowgirls and swore that no one on earth could compare with them, although he allowed he had been in Aberdeen only a few days and had no way of forming a firsthand opinion.

By unanimous acclaim, it was decided that this was a situation that could not go unremedied for another minute, and with a great many whoops, yeehas, and yahoos, bills were settled, numerous full bottles of Black Jack found their way across the bar, and almost the entire company (including the hulk from the boardinghouse, Steddy noticed through a bourbon haze) exited into the street with Steddy leading them, singing another chorus of "Up Against the Wall You Red-Necked Mother" at the top of his lungs. They headed down toward the docks, to a destination unknown to him, but frankly he didn't care. He was happy, trusted, and loved.

Wiley left Thea after lunch, on the excuse that he had some errands to run, but promised to have a drink with her later so that they could make plans to meet for Steddy's call the next evening—without being followed. She walked him to the corner of Grosvenor Square, where he left her to cut across the park in the center of the sedate Georgian enclave, past the black-bronze statue of FDR to the modern, misplaced American Embassy that no amount of time could mellow.

He entered the building at the side through a glass door marked "Visa Department," and when he identified himself to the girl on duty, she directed him behind the counter to a lift down the hall. The marine guard posted there punched out a three-number code in the wall unit by the door that allowed him access to the security area of the lower basement.

Wiley knew from experience that the CIA didn't burn agents unnecessarily. He had never even met one—that is, aside from Pete Register, who had recruited him at Princeton, and, of course, the men who were processed and briefed with him for six weeks at "the Farm" in Virginia, when he had first joined up some fifteen years ago.

One never, never met a field operative. After all, Wiley wasn't one of the Agency's "spooks," as they were often called in some of the books he published. His sole role was to absorb information and contribute to the daily stew of worldwide intelligence/gossip, which he assumed nobody ever read or paid any attention to.

Another marine guard was stationed outside the lift when the doors opened at the lower level, and with only the word "sir," he escorted Wiley down an unpainted Sheetrock corridor to a gray metal door. A similar security unit with buttons was mounted on the wall to the left of the knob, but the guard didn't use it—instead he rapped discreetly three times with his white-gloved hand, turned smartly, and quick-marched back to his post. Wiley waited for a response to the knock, but it wasn't until the sound of the retreating marine's footsteps was almost inaudible that the door finally opened.

The room was carpeted, but the color was indiscernible, as the ceiling was devoid of the harsh fluorescent tubes that dominated the outer corridors. There was, in fact, very little light in the room at all, just two old-fashioned tin-shaded gooseneck lamps on the military-issue metal desk at the far side of the room. In front of the desk stood two similar green-gray steel and vinyl armchairs.

A disembodied Camel-smoker's voice came to him from behind the door.

"Good afternoon, Mr. Travis. Thank you for coming in."

"How do you do," Wiley said, turning toward the voice.

A second voice came from the darkness beyond the lights on the desk.

"Don't turn around, Mr. Travis, if you don't mind. Just come over here and take a chair and make yourself comfortable."

Wiley did as he was told, even though he did find the ritual a bit melodramatic. As he took his seat, he heard a light tread along the periphery of the room—the chap behind the door was joining his colleague.

The fellow hidden by the light must have seen Wiley smirk.

"Forgive us, Mr. Travis, if these precautions seem obsessive, but you will appreciate that it takes many years and a great deal of money to place undercover and deep-cover agents in the field, and it would be irresponsible to expose their identities, even within the "family," unless it was absolutely necessary."

"Burn them, you mean?"

"I see some of the Company's terminology hasn't escaped you."

"Most of it I've learned from reading the galleys of some of the books we publish. I never really took much of it too seriously."

Wiley could hear the other man sitting down.

"Well now, to get down to cases, you seem to have got your control back at base pretty excited over this Stedman Wright business."

"I just told him what I knew and asked if there wasn't some way we could help him."

"State is the agency that goes to the aid of American tourists who get in trouble abroad—why didn't you go to them?"

"Steddy's a really good friend of mine, and I thought that Pete . . . er, my control might be able to get to someone here in British Intelligence who could intervene."

"It seems that there are other circumstances involved here. Perhaps we should start at the beginning."

"Well, I ran into Steddy in Paris about eight weeks ago at the Travelers Club—"

"Was that the first time you'd ever met him?"

"I've just told you, he's my best friend—I've known him all my life."

"Well, then, let's start again *there*—if you don't mind."
Wiley heard a tape recorder being restarted.

Wiley's nameless, faceless interrogators were very thorough. He was there for over two hours, during which time they left the room periodically by a second door to confer, he supposed, or to consult with someone else. They seemed reasonably satisfied that his account of Steddy's patriotism, politics, and moral fiber tallied with the report that had probably been flashed to them from Washington, although they accepted it somewhat grudgingly, as Steddy's life-style didn't appear to be something they entirely approved of.

The Camel-voiced fellow re-entered the room and sat down.

"Do you think you could get him to call you at a secure phone here at the embassy?"

"I really doubt it. He was adamant that he wouldn't take a chance on anyone tracing his call."

"We can guarantee that the call won't be traced. The number we'll give him is an automatic collect-charges acceptance line in Washington—it connects directly into the government Audibon system. The call is then scrambled and rerouted via satellite directly to the descrambler unit in the ambassador's office."

"Who should I say wants to talk to him?"

"Well, don't say 'CIA' over a land line, whatever you do."

"I'll have to say something, or I won't be able to get him to do it."

"Just say that you're a friend of the ambassador's and that it's the only way you can have a truly secure conversation with him—and that you think you can help him."

"Can I?"

"That will depend largely on your friend."

"Do you think you might at least tell me what this is all about? He's my best friend, and I'd like to know what I'm getting him into."

"That's not quite right. He may already have got himself into a highly sensitive situation, and I can assure you that it is not made any easier by the fact that the host country is our closest ally.''

"Wouldn't the British cooperate if you just told their people what this is all about?''

"Mr. Travis, you have a great deal to learn about intelligence operations—even between allied nations—and this is neither the time nor the place for an introductory course.''

"But for Christ's sake, I'll have to say something. What the hell has he done?''

"We hope nothing, in which case this whole thing can be straightened out fairly easily. That's why you're not cleared at this time to know any more than you absolutely need to.''

"Do you mean that the whole thing could be nothing and we could just bring him in?''

"We sincerely hope so, but I don't want you to get the wrong idea, because it's vital that you impress upon him the urgency of calling in. I *will* say just this—if he is involved in any way, he could be fooling with at least three of the most dangerous foreign operatives that this agency has ever monitored.''

"Good God, but how? I know Steddy's never been mixed up in anything like that in his life.''

"Does he know you're with the Company?''

"Of course not.''

"Well, if your positions were reversed, I'm sure he'd swear that there was no way you could be involved with the CIA.''

"Are you suggesting he's an agent of a foreign power?''

"Probably not. It could simply be a matter of being in the wrong place at the wrong time—or having the wrong friends—or it could be an attempt to make a quick buck.''

"He'd never do that.''

"I don't think there's any point in further speculation.''

The nicotine-stained fingers that were attached to the Camel-smoke voice slid a small white pad across the bare linoleum top of the desk.

"The top number's for you to reach me when you've

set up the call, and the bottom one in Washington is for him to use.''

"Who do I ask for when I call?"

"Just tell them your name; that'll get me. Oh, and by the way, I'm putting a man on you and on the Boulton girl—just in case.''

"Just in case of what, for God's sake?"

"If any of those guys I mentioned are looking for your friend. You two would be the best place to start.''

24

It was seven when Wiley arrived at the Harkonians' cream-colored Georgian mansion off Belgrave Square. Thea came to the door in answer to his tug on the big brass bell pull. He was struck anew by the sheer simplicity of her beauty.

Her hair was long and liquid as though floating in water. She wore a man's pink shirt with the tails knotted at the waist—there was a monogram over her left breast that Wiley knew was Stedman's without the need or desire for confirmation. Her feet were bare, and her blue jeans looked as if they'd ridden a lot of fence somewhere out west. Yet in spite of her outfit, she was surprisingly at home among the elegantly gowned eighteenth-century ladies in the full-length Gainsboroughs that graced the walls of the hexagonal black and white marble entry hall; if anything, there was a wistfulness of expression and a common acceptance of position that belied the radical difference of their costumes.

"Let's go into the study. I've got the news on."

Although his interest in pictures was limited to British sporting paintings—primarily Munnings at that—he couldn't help but be impressed by the Van Gogh that completely dominated the small, well-proportioned room. He had seen it before, of course, in virtually every art-history book he had ever looked at—or for that matter published—but the collection that it came from had never been identified, and he had just assumed that it was in a museum somewhere.

It was the portrait of a peasant woman seated in profile, rigidly at attention as if posing for a tintype. Her face was brutally mannish, starkly set off by reddish-brown hair gathered in a knot at the top of her head. In contrast to her dour visage, the colors were electric—the background a brilliant emerald green, her dress an equally bright royal blue, and crisply folded about her shoulders was a warm yellow flowered shawl that she clenched at her bosom in both her gnarled hands.

The walls of the room were the same impossible yellow-ocher of the shawl and glowed with a depth of sheen that is achieved only after twenty or thirty coats of hand-rubbed lacquer. Two couches flanked the picture and the chimney; they were really armless, overstuffed divans covered in deep royal-blue velvet with heavy, straight corded tassels that brushed the floor and made them seem to float.

When he looked down from the picture, Thea was casually sprawled on one of the tufted sofas in a nest of rumpled newspapers. The television was turned on behind her with the sound off, and a telephone was perched precariously on a fat yellow silk cushion at her elbow.

She looked up and caught Wiley just as he realized that his mouth was open.

"She affects everybody like that the first time."

"Gosh," was the most sophisticated comment Wiley could muster.

"She's so powerful, isn't she?" Thea said.

"It's just that she's so much more alive than any of the reproductions I've ever seen."

"Nubie has a few other great things scattered about. I'll show you around after the news is over, if you like?"

"I'd love it, but it will have to wait. We've got a lot to talk about."

Thea was immediately alert.

"Have you found anything out?"

Wiley knew he would have to tread very cautiously where Thea was concerned; she didn't miss a thing, and he had been put on notice by the men at the embassy to tell her as little as he had to.

"A little."

Thea now sat up with her legs crossed under her.

He started slowly.

"Well, I went to see a pal of mine at the embassy after I left you today, and he thinks Steddy could be accidentally involved in something pretty serious."

"But like what? Do they think he murdered Omar?"

"No, no, nothing like that. It's just that the murder did happen in his suite, and he could have inadvertently got involved with some rough customers."

"You mean like the Mafia or something like that?"

"No, I don't think so. They really wouldn't tell me very much, because it may all be some sort of a nasty coincidence—in which case there isn't a thing to worry about."

"Oh, what a relief. I know he wouldn't be purposely involved with people like that."

"Well, it isn't quite as simple as that."

"What do you mean?" Concern raised ridges on her forehead and crinkled her eyebrows.

"It's those other types, you see. They may think he is involved in the murder or even something worse."

"But what could be worse?"

"I don't know. They wouldn't tell me. It's on a need-to-know basis."

"But what on earth could it be? Except for that one night, I've been with him constantly since he arrived in England—or even in Europe for that matter."

"Thea, they just wouldn't say any more, and that's a good sign because it means that they really don't think he's involved. They just don't want us to know about something when the mere knowing would land us all in hot water."

"Not very reassuring. And anyway, why are the Americans involved? Are they working with Scotland Yard?"

"No, and we're not to tell the British that we've even talked with them."

"But none of this makes any sense. Who did you talk to anyway . . . ?"

"Hold on, Thea." She was getting away from him. "They really do want to help, and I think that if we can establish that Steddy's not involved, they can fix the whole thing with the British."

Thea started to interrupt again. Her avid mind was racing to questions and conclusions that Wiley was anxious to avoid.

"Listen, Thea, this is what they want us to do."

He told her about the special satellite hookup.

"Do you think we can get him to call? You heard how he is."

"It'll be perfectly safe, and we'll be able to talk openly for as long as we like. The embassy boys can ask their questions, and maybe then we can put an end to this. We've simply got to convince him when he calls tomorrow. It's the only way he's ever going to get out of this. He can't just hole up somewhere forever—he probably doesn't even have any money. And what if the British police get hold of him? Just look at that headline"—Wiley pointed to the newspaper that had fallen to the floor: WRIGHT DONE HIM WRONG— "They've already convicted him."

"I know. It's a nightmare."

"Listen, we can't afford to start keening. Let's try to keep ourselves occupied with practical things that could help him. For the moment, we're the only lifeline he's got."

"What can we do?"

"First off, we've got to make a plan for tomorrow— we've got to get ourselves into that suite at the Dorchester without being followed."

"Are we sure we really are being followed? Aside from that one car that seemed to be following me from the Savoy, I haven't noticed a thing. Have you?"

"No, but there's something I forgot to tell you."

"Ugh." She clenched her fists.

"The boys at the embassy have assigned each of us a watchdog for the duration."

"You mean like Secret Service?"

"Sort of, but I think they're a little more secret than that."

"But why? We're Americans—don't they trust us?"

"It isn't that at all. It's just that if there is anything to this, they think that the men who'd be after Steddy could try to get to him through us."

"Oh, Christ," she said, pressing her hands over her eyes and then down through her hair. "But then shouldn't we be glad to have them around—if only for protection?"

"I think it's only fair to Steddy that until he agrees to go along with them, we play the game by his rules."

"Okay, but how do we manage it?"

"Normally I'd say we should split up and divide them, but in this case, we know for a fact that there's at least one man following each of us, and you can be sure they're good. Scotland Yard probably has a man on each of us, too—at least we should assume they do—so that makes four; I can't begin to speculate about the others, and there isn't much point in trying, but I do think we have a better chance of being sure we've lost them if we stick together, four eyes being better than two and all that. Also, if we're apart, there's a greater likelihood that one of us wouldn't shake all of them, and that would blow the whole show."

"You mean me," she said accusingly.

"No, no, but at least if we're together and we know we haven't pulled it off, well, then, we can be quick on the phone and set up the next rendezvous. Whatd'ya think?"

"The logic's sound." Thea looked at him as though she were seeing him for the first time. "Wiley, you don't seem the type—how do you know so much about this sort of thing?"

"Oh, I guess just from reading the bad spy books we publish. But listen, we've got to come up with a place that we can lead them to and lose them. Any ideas? My knowledge of London is pretty much limited to hotels, restaurants, and theaters."

"You mean someplace where we could go in one door and out the other, sort of?"

"That's the idea, but it would have to be really fast before they caught on and no place obvious like a hotel that runs through a street—they'd be sure to cover both entrances."

Thea looked pensive.

"You know, a few years ago there was a reception for

the Queen's Jubilee. Well, I was at the hairdresser—it was pretty late, I remember, because it was almost impossible to get an appointment what with all the royals in town and—''

"Thea, do get to the point."

"Well, anyway, I hate that sort of thing, but I was in London, and Mummy insisted that I go—she'd bought me a dress in Paris especially and said my hair had to be just so—you know, up, with flowers and jewels, ich! I don't honestly think I've been to a hairdresser since."

"Thea!"

"Well, Grace and Caroline were there, too, and there must have been a hundred newspapermen and photogaphers in front of the door—I had to really fight my way through them to get in . . ."

"Um hum." Wiley was beginning to get annoyed.

"So anyway, I was finished at the same time they were, and as we were about to leave, the lady downstairs told them—Grace and Caroline, I mean—that she had sent someone to tell their driver to go around to the mews entrance at the back."

Wiley's interest picked up markedly.

"Grace was very grateful, and I asked the woman if I could leave that way, too—you know, the press were so rabid, they really didn't care who you were, they just pulled you to pieces until they found out. . . . Anyway, we went out into the mews. The big Roller was already there with flags flying, and there wasn't a soul around, and they were very sweet and gave me a lift home."

"Where is this place?" Wiley asked, his interest now fully primed.

"On South Audley Street, right at the top of Mount Street. You must have seen it—it's the place with the striped, tenty sort of canopy on spears. You couldn't have missed it."

"Sure, I know the place you mean, only I always thought it was a bakery."

"I suppose in a way it is."

Wiley ignored her attempt at humor. "It could be perfect. How long does it take you to have your hair done?"

"Gee, I don't know anymore."

"Come on, be serious—this is important."

"Anywhere between an hour or two, depending on what you have done."

"You mean if you asked for one sort of thing, it might take an hour, but if you were going to a ball, it could take two?"

"Listen, I know some people who spend the whole day—three times a week. They have the works, a facial and a manicure and then—"

"Hey, hold it. Timing this thing is critical. Do you realize that it's less than a minute's walk from that mews to the Dorchester?"

"Why do you think I brought it up?" She looked at Wiley as though he were a dope and made him feel like a chastened two-year-old.

25

The pain. Only a shattering scream can attempt to convey and give form to real pain in a way in which others can grasp the full extent of its presence..

The pain was everywhere. His eyes felt as if someone had carefully placed a baseball over each one and proceeded to smash them one at a time with a sledge hammer.

Stedman wasn't sure which had surfaced first, the pain or consciousness. Probably it had been consciousness of the pain. It was daytime, he knew. The light was too bright for him to open his eyes—any attempt made them run water down the sides of his face that formed wet pools in his ears. That was how he discovered that it was agony to turn his head as well. He tried to raise it in an effort to drain the irritating water from the wells of his ears but succeeded only in passing out.

When he came to again, the pain was still there, and he knew better than to move a muscle. He just lay there trying to remember, trying to concentrate over the pain.

Thea was the first image to break through. He had talked to her from a bar, but where? The taste of bourbon still strong in his mouth brought it back—the Yankee Go Home—he remembered the men he'd been drinking with. But the pain—this couldn't be simply a hangover, not in a million years. He tried to peep open one eye, but the sharp needles of light exploded inside his head and mercifully knocked him out again.

When he awoke again, the pain seemed to ebb and flow from mild to excruciating, like an afternoon tide in the Mediterranean, gently lapping at the edges of his sanity. Not knowing where he was and the fear of where he might be were responsible for about eighty percent of the sweat he was swimming in. It was the fear of the unknown that finally overcame his fear of the pain, and he opened one eye.

The first thing he focused on was that bloody bare light bulb suspended from the ceiling, glaring at him. He averted his eyes—the general illumination from the window seemed softer than it had before. He was enormously relieved to find himself in his room. From the condition of his body, he had been sure that he would discover himself in Scotland Yard's worst security cell or, during the wilder flights of his tortured imagination, in a dungeon in the Tower of London.

The pain hadn't dissipated, but he was able to manage a move or two. He was literally punching through the pain, desperate to know what day it was, horrified that he might have blown the whole telephone arrangement with Thea and broken the chain—his physical and emotional lifeline.

Crossing his arm over to read his watch made him curse the Japanese technology that required that a button be pushed in order to read the date. He had to repeat the painful exercise over and over until he was able to comprehend the AM, PM, and day sufficiently to determine that it had been less than twenty-four hours since he had last spoken to her.

His eyes closed to conserve strength, he tried to figure out how much time there was before the next telephone rendezvous by running their last conversation over and over in his mind until—fragment by fragment—it came back to him. He recalled talking to Wiley but wasn't absolutely sure he hadn't dreamed it. There was no time for further reflection— if his watch wasn't as bruised as his body, he had less than two hours to make it to a phone.

Getting to the mirror to determine the extent of his

injuries became his primary goal, and the way he felt, two hours might just be sufficient time to accomplish the trek across the room.

First, legs over the side of the bed—oh, God, the pain—then, thanks to the cheap iron bed, he was able to pull himself slowly upright, using the bars at its head. His ribs felt cracked—he knew the feeling from both snow and water skiing—and his eyes felt as if they had been carefully sanded with a fine grade paper, just to remove the top layer of tissue.

Upright, holding to the bars so that his knuckles were white from the pressure, he almost fainted again. He was sick to his stomach and painfully swallowed like mad, trying not to retch. The cold sweat that ensued in the now shaded room made him shiver. As he stood there shaking, he sensed almost more than saw the familiar square-shaped bottle of Jack Daniels at the side of his bed. That was when he knew for sure he didn't have any kind of king-sized hangover. Somehow, seeing the poison made him realize the relatively minor role it had played in the drama that his body was staging.

He snatched at the bottle and managed to hang on to it. It was unopened, and cracking the export seal that surrounded the top required a supreme effort. When he did get it open, he took the first sustenance he had had in probably twenty-four hours. It hurt to swallow, and the bourbon burned fiercely going down, but in the hurt there was help.

He felt like collapsing but realized that the trip back up would be far worse than the trip down, so he clenched his gut and waited for it to pass so that he could have another pull from the bottle.

There was a large, old-fashioned jug full of water on the bed table, and in spite of the pain that each gulp brought to his ribs, he greedily swallowed half of it. The next fifteen minutes seemed like hours as he alternated pulls from the jug and the bottle. He could move a bit now through the miracle of alcohol. A few more swallows and he could stand without holding on. His eyes were still mostly closed, but his hands were now free to clutch the two sources of his returning strength. He knew there was no way he could get drunk—the pain would never let him.

Snatches of memory came back to him. There was the wee lass in the upstairs parlor of the whorehouse, except that she hadn't turned out to be wee or a lass, but an old pro imported from Zurich. He remembered now sitting with her on a black Victorian horsehair settee; she was trying to put a condom on him the way cheap hookers will before giving a blow job. His attention had been occupied elsewhere, in playing with and slurping on her big, pendulous Swiss tits. Still, every time she succeeded in getting the rubber on, he had whipped it off with a flourish and thrown it over his shoulder, leering with drunken disdain. He had spent more than his share of time in hook shops the world over, and after consuming at least a bottle of Black Jack, he was in no mood to be trifled with.

It was the soreness in his crotch from all the plucking that was bringing back the memory. He recalled that the unpopular game had gone on through a series of erections and deflations until he had got as bored as the girl had already looked when he first arrived. He had given her a twenty-pound note from his money belt, told her to go fuck herself, and headed downstairs.

The money belt—oh, shit, where was it? How big a fool could one man be?

That was when he remembered the Incredible Hulk from the boardinghouse coming for him in the alley. He had been too drunk even to take a stab at defending himself. He must have been beaten almost senseless, and from the feel of his ribs, kicked after he had gone down. But before he'd blacked out, he remembered seeing a shadowy figure creeping soundlessly through the haze of the alley, and then the Hulk had crumpled on top of him.

Steddy took another big swig from the bourbon and the last of the water. Eyes open—streaming, but open—he took in the totality of the room at last. His clothes were neatly folded over the chair. (How had he managed that?) With a stab of pain, he threw them to the floor. No money belt.

He looked under the bed, and as he bent over, the

pressure in his head increased like a depth charge fast approaching detonation.

Another pull at the bottle—no water now, but none necessary. He could actually stagger to the mirror and was amazed by what he saw. There wasn't a mark on him. He was red here and there, but there was no blood—no bruises. He must have been worked over by a real pro. On the sides of his chest, where there wasn't any hair, he could see some inflammation and swelling, and when he gingerly pressed on his ribs, he could tell they were, at the very least, fractured. There was no doubt about it, he'd been royally rolled.

Steddy smiled a crooked smile at himself in the mirror—happy to see his teeth were still intact—and remembered Warren Beatty's line in *Bonnie and Clyde* when, after chopping his toe off to get out of prison, he learned he'd been pardoned minutes before: "Ain't life grand?"

After another slug from the bottle, he threw himself across the bed in his first moment of hopelessness and despair since the whole mess had begun.

He found the money belt intact under his pillow.

Steddy allowed himself a few minutes to ponder the series of things that made no sense: his clothes piled neatly on a chair, the unopened bottle, the money and the diary still there, the shadowy figure in the alley, who must have been the good samaritan who had got him home—none of it made any sense. Who was his benefactor and why had he done so much for him? And if he had gone to so much trouble, why hadn't he taken him to a hospital? (Thank God he hadn't, or Steddy would have awakened in a police station.) And how had the man known where he lived? He'd been careful not to tell any of the men he'd been drinking with where he was staying.

There was no time to analyze it further. He only had an hour to get to a phone and call Thea.

26

It was six-fifteen when Wiley crossed South Audley Street and took the few paces that would bring him to the tented canopy that marked the entrance to René of Mayfair.

He knew he was being followed. He had spotted two cars that he was sure of, although they were not the same two that he thought he'd seen earlier in the day.

He'd met Thea for lunch at Fortnum's Fountain, and keeping to the plan they had carefully developed the night before, they went upstairs afterward, where Wiley sat affecting a bored countenance—without too much difficulty—while Thea modeled one evening gown after another. At three-fifteen he made a big show of looking at his watch and saying she'd be late for the hairdresser. She quickly opted for the first dress she had tried on, and they left the shop in a hurry and hopped into a cab on Jermyn Street. Wiley dropped her off at René's, paid the driver, and then walked the few blocks back to Claridge's, where he napped restlessly until it was time to change into black tie and fetch her.

Wiley walked back to South Audley Street in a fine English summer rain. He took his time, ostensibly looking at antiques in the numerous shops that lined both sides of Mount Street—he was really trying to mark, reflected in the polished showroom glass, the two cars he was sure were following him and the two men on foot on opposite sides of the street, who he didn't think were out for a stroll. As he pulled open the glass door of René's, he wasn't sure but he thought he saw in it, behind him, a signal of recognition pass between one of the men who had followed him and a man stationed on the corner across the street from the shop. Probably one of Thea's watchdogs, he thought to himself as he entered the hairdressing salon.

She wasn't down yet, but then he was ten minutes early. He asked for her at the desk, and the girl rang upstairs and told someone in French that there was a gentleman waiting for Mademoiselle Boulton, *la fille de la Baronne Harkonian.*

He cooled his heels walking around the reception area looking at the dramatic photos of painfully thin girls modeling the latest hairstyles.

At exactly six-thirty, the door of the small lift opened, and Thea stepped out—at least he thought it was her. Only her height and the fact that she walked straight to him and kissed him confirmed her identity.

She was ethereal in a diaphanous Grecian, off-the-shoulder, sea-green chiffon dress that barely dusted the floor. Her hair was up and was the main contributor to the dramatic change in her appearance. It was braided and intertwined with tiny pale green orchids and two lacey diamond clips that must have had each stone mounted on a separate spring, the way they shimmered so at the slightest movement of her head.

The play had started, and they both knew their lines.

"Hello, darling. Did I keep you waiting long?"

"Not a bit, in fact you're right on time. I was a little early."

Then, for the benefit of the staff: "We've got plenty of time now to get down to Kent and still make it to the Johnstons' for cocktails before the Stricklands'."

"Let me just sign the bill, and we can leave."

Thea went to the counter, signed the bill, said *bon soir,* and taking Wiley's arm, started for the door. Then, stopping as though she had remembered something, she turned back to the desk and said: "*Mademoiselle,* I wonder if we could go out through the mews? I left my car parked there, and with the weather outside—well, the less slogging about in the foggy, foggy dew, the better the chances of your fabulous coiffure arriving at the ball in one piece.''

The Gallically effusive compliment served to allay any question of complying with *mademoiselle's* wishes.

"*Mais, bien sur, m'selle!*"

They followed her through a small stockroom, where a door was unlocked, and after thanking her profusely in her native tongue, the door was gently closed behind them, leaving them alone in the silent, damp cul-de-sac.

In spite of the crowds in Aberdeen station at quarter-to-six that evening, Steddy was the sole occupant of the long mahogany bench opposite the telephone exchange.

Dressing had been an agony but nothing compared to negotiating the three flights of stairs at the boardinghouse. On impulse, he'd stuffed his few possessions into the duffel and taken them with him, spooked that someone he didn't know knew where he was.

Communicating his destination to the cab driver had been an unexpected trial—when he tried to use his voice for the first time in twenty-four hours, he found it didn't work, and only after endless throat clearing had he been able to utter, "Station." He wondered what Thea would think when she heard him, and if he could even carry on a conversation.

With one eye on the clock, he began to flip through the evening paper. At first the caption at the bottom of page three hardly held his attention; he was looking for an update on his own story. Then something made him turn back and study the headline more carefully: DEAD MAN FOUND IN DOCKS ALLEY STILL UNIDENTIFIED

His physical senses grasped the story before his brain did, then cold sweat materialized on his neck and spine, and his stomach developed that queasy, back-to-school feeling. From the description of the corpse, it had to be the Hulk from his rooming house.

The body had been discovered at eight-thirty that morning—the time of death was fixed at approximately one AM. What really got to him was that the cause of death, "originally assumed to have been a heart attack," had been ruled by the coroner to be death by misadventure when the autopsy uncovered a bloodless wound at the base of the skull that penetrated five inches into the cortex. Death had been instantaneous, they said, and the weapon would have resembled an ice pick in both strength and length, but the track it had left was as fine as that of a hypodermic needle.

The sound of the old town clock striking seven brought Steddy out of a state of mental arrest. He had been sitting staring sightlessly at the clock on the wall when the alarming toll zoomed it into sharp focus. Seven o'clock! He hadn't even placed the call to Thea!

Incapable of running, he shuffled as quickly as he could across the aisle to the telephone office—a man was ahead of him. Steddy reached past him for a scrap of paper and a pencil, and carefully wrote the London area code and the number of the Dorchester. Blessedly, by the time he had finished, the man was departing for a booth, but the girl behind the counter was the only attendant, and she was busy getting his number.

He stood there with the paper quivering between his fingers, his mind still locked like the overheated gears of a formula one racing machine. He had been present at the scene of two murders in less than ten days, the country was being scoured for him as the prime suspect in the first one, and now it wouldn't be long before they placed him at the second. He was nearly ready to give himself up and face the music before something else happened—but what else could happen? he asked himself.

The attendant's voice came to him from a great distance.

"If you want this call, sir, please go to cabinet number two."

Steddy looked at her as though she were mad.

"That's cabinet two, sir. You do speak English?"

Steddy looked down at his hand and saw that the bit of paper was no longer there. When he noticed it was in hers, he understood, and like a sleepwalker, made his way to the booth.

He lit a Players while he waited for the connection. The rough smoke clawed at his throat, and when it reached his stomach, he had a flash of nausea. It passed and left him a little high.

"Thea?" Steddy croaked to the girl's voice on the line.

"This is the Dorchester, sir. May I help you?"

"Miss—I mean Mr. Boulton's apartment please."

"Putting you through."

The line had hardly rung.

"Steddy?" And when there was no immediate reply: "Steddy, isn't that you?"

Hearing her voice that had come to mean so much to him made something like a sob well up in his throat and join with the smoke to render him speechless. He just kept nodding his head—yes, yes, it's me, come and get me and never...

"Wiley, I hear breathing, but no one says anything. Steddy? Steddy?"

Wiley took the phone from her hand.

"Hello, hello? Is anybody there?"

The sound of Wiley's voice brought Steddy to attention.

"Is that you, Wiley?" he rasped.

"It's me." And hearing Steddy's voice: "But is that really you?"

"Don't be an asshole."

"That's you all right. What the hell's the matter with you?"

Thea pulled at the receiver.

"All right, all right, Thea wants to talk to you, but stay on the line. I've got to talk to you, and we've gone to a great deal of trouble to make sure that the phone's not tapped, so don't worry about the time. Okay?"

"Wiley, I don't give a shit anymore. If they're listening, I'll tell them where I am right now and save them the trouble of tracing it."

"Just don't do anything until I talk to you. Promise."

"Okay, okay, just let me talk to Thea."

"Darling, what's the matter?"

"Just a bad cold." He lied, all of a sudden feeling silly—the sound of her voice made him want to be strong.

"But it sounds terrible. Where are you? Please let me

come. You can tell me now, darling; I swear there is absolutely no one on this line.''

''Thea, darling, you know I can't tell you; it wouldn't be fair. What could you do, ring me up to say good night, or come to meet me and become an accessory after they've followed you to me? Try to be sensible, darling. You must know I need you just as much, especially now. You're all I've got—and only for three minutes a day.''

''But that's just it, Steddy. Wiley thinks he can fix it.''

''How do you mean?''

''Well, he's been with the ambassador and all sorts of big shots at the embassy, and, well, I'll let you talk to him, but don't hang up when you finish.''

''Darling, the only reason I'll talk to Wiley is if it might mean that there's a chance we'll be together again sooner . . . I love you.''

''Oh, darling, and I love you. Now here's Wiley, and listen to what he has to say and do exactly what he tells you,'' she said, nodding the phone at Wiley. ''In case you've forgotten, he's a really good friend of yours.''

Wiley took the phone.

''Steddy, what Thea said about the embassy and all is essentially true, but first—''

''I knew there'd be a 'but.' ''

''Now hold your horses. Simply put—if you haven't done anything, you've got no problem.''

''Listen, kid, I certainly know I haven't done anything, and you fucking well ought to know that, too, for Christ's sake . . .''

Steddy started coughing from the strain of yelling, and Wiley had to repeat himself.

''Let me finish, will you? Jesus, you'll never change. Now will you please hear me out?''

''Okay, okay.''

''Okay, it's like this. No one in our government thinks seriously that you had anything to do with that murder—''

''So then what's the problem?''

''The only problem is that there are other factors.''

''Such as?''

''*Will* you hold on?''

"Shoot."

"Evidently Omar was mixed up in something pretty high level and secret, and he wasn't alone in it, because three other governments besides our own are involved in it, too."

"What is 'it'?"

"Listen, who do you think I am, J. Edgar Hoover? That's just the point. They don't want any of us to know what it is, which is why they're worried that you could have got yourself involved, either by accident or by design. Now don't get huffy—they don't think you're a spy or anything. They just want to know what you know, if anything."

"Wilcy, there's been another murder. I don't think it's related, but it sure has me spooked."

"Jesus Christ, Steddy, are you shitting me?"

"The only shitting I'm doing is in my pants—I'm scared to death."

"Where did it happen?"

"Well, I was bombed leaving this cheap local whorehouse —hey, don't say anything to Thea—and I got jumped by this brute who was staying in the same boarding house I was. I'm certain he saw my money belt, so the motive is pretty damn clear and—"

"Where did you get a money belt? Thea said you hardly had any money at all."

"Ya, well, Omar had quite a lot on him, and I didn't figure he'd mind in the condition he was in when I last saw him."

"So it was self-defense—the guy who jumped you, I mean?"

"Wiley, I didn't lay a hand on him. I was so drunk, I could barely stand."

"Shit, Steddy. Can't you at least try to stay sober? You're in enough trouble!"

"Shut up, Wiley. Not in front of Thea."

"Okay, so who killed him?"

"Well, he gave me a pretty good beating..."

"So that's why you sound so lousy."

"Yeah, and all I remember before I passed out—listen, it was very misty, so all I remember was this sort of shadow of a man behind the big guy who was beating up on me. Then, all of a sudden, the big guy collapsed on top of me without a whimper. I think that's how my ribs got broken.''

"So the guy behind sandbagged him, and he didn't wake up.''

"*No no,* it's definitely murder. It's all over the papers. He was punctured in the brain by some sort of super-thin stiletto; they didn't even notice the puncture until the autopsy—there wasn't any blood.

"You noticed that there wasn't any blood when you came to?''

"That's the weird thing that's really got me spooked. I came to in my own bed feeling as though I'd gone a few rounds with King Kong, but other than that, my clothes were all neatly piled by my bed—and I know I couldn't have done that—my money belt was still there—which really fucks up the motive—and even the bottle of bourbon I had with me was on the night table. I tell you, I can't figure it out. It's really got me going.''

"How much was in the money belt?''

"The better part of a hundred thousand pounds and Omar's diary. I just don't get it.''

"You have Omar's diary?''

"Well, it looks like a diary or an agenda or something—shit! It's probably his betting book, for all I know.''

"Didn't you read it?''

"It's in Arabic—I think.''

"Wiley, let me talk to him. What's all this about?'' Thea interrupted.

"Hold on, Thea. This is very serious.'' And then into the phone: "Now listen, Steddy, I want you to take this telephone number down now, in case we get cut off or anything. It's very important—have you got a pencil?''

"No, but—''

"Get one!''

Steddy reached out of the booth, painfully stretching on the receiver and its cord, and grabbed a pencil and a slip of paper from the counter. The girl was reading a magazine and didn't even notice.

"Okay, I've got one.''

"Now, whatever you do, don't lose this number. I don't care if you have to have it tattooed on your backside, don't forget it."

Wiley dictated the number in Washington to Steddy.

"Okay, now, when they answer at that number, if you say my first name, they'll accept the charges, no questions asked, from anywhere in the world. Your call will be switched by secure tie-line to a location in Virginia, where it will be simultaneously scrambled and transmitted by satellite to the safe phone on the ambassador's desk here in London. At four PM tomorrow, I will answer that phone, and you had better be on the other end of it. And listen, if you get into anything you can't handle before then, you can still ring the number and a duty officer or the ambassador will pick up. You can talk to them as you would to me—minus the X-rated crap," Wiley quipped, and then immediately became serious again. "Is that crystal clear?"

"Sounds a little CIA to me, old boy."

"Steddy, I don't give a shit what it sounds like to you. You do it!"

"If I'm still a free agent."

"Steddy, you've got to give me time to talk to these guys—you don't have any idea what you've gotten yourself into, and believe it or not, I don't either. But I'll promise you one thing. I'm going to go over there right now and find out."

"But if you think it was Omar's diary they were after, why didn't they just take it?"

"I don't have any of the answers, Steddy. I'm sorry, I know that doesn't help. All I do know is that you're possibly in the company of some of the most dangerous agents in this hemisphere, and it appears that one of them has taken a shine to you."

"A sort of fallen guardian angel," Steddy said without mirth.

"He may be the best protection you have until we talk tomorrow. Now be good, and for God's sake, stay sober!"

"Not in front of Thea, you shit!"

"Here she is."

27

The big meeting room adjacent to the chief inspector's working office was being used to accommodate the additional staff now included since the first briefing. Subsequent meetings—since they had lost their quarry on the first day—had been strained, but today the mood was hopeful. Stedman Wright had at last been traced to an Aberdeen brothel, where a Swiss prostitute had positively identified him from a picture (reaffirming Allsloe's contention of Wright's total dissolution), placing him at the scene of another murder—this time not staged—precisely at the hour the coroner adjudged to be the time of death.

Things hadn't been so cheery the night before, when it was discovered that Wiley and Thea had given them the slip at the hairdresser's, but no one was mentioning that in light of the new developments.

The combined operations meeting had been in session for over an hour filled with interdepartmental back-slapping when Allsloe, who had only recently come in, asked Major Lowson of M15 if he would care to add anything on behalf of his department.

Lowson, whose physical stature and bearing singled him out as the archetypical Guard's officer, wore a double-breasted gray chalk-stripe suit, stood six-foot-six inches, had a decidedly receding chin and disdainfully pursed lips, and had never observed anything or anybody except down the full length of his nose. He rose from his chair.

"As regards the actual murder, our branch is quite familiar with the perpetrator's particular—how do the Americans put it? MO?"

His tone was more than slightly condescending, and one could easily tell that he was both uncomfortable and unhappy speaking openly about secrets his department had carefully garnered in front of a room full of men he so clearly dismissed as clods. Nevertheless, he had been ordered to collaborate, so he went on.

"There can be little doubt that the execution was performed by Chelak."

The room was silent. The name meant nothing to most of those present. Allsloe, not wanting to ask and trying to maintain his dignity and control of the combined ops group said, "Major, I wonder if you would mind elucidating on Mr. Chelak for the benefit of those present who are not already acquainted with his activities?"

Lowson, still standing, clasped his hands behind his back and automatically came to parade rest.

"Quite simply put, Chelak is the most effective and, I hasten to add, the most dangerous agent the Israelis have."

Allsloe's red brows arched, and his eyes took on an unaccustomed sparkle.

"It's the wound you see," Lowson went on. "He invariably strikes the victim from behind in precisely the same spot with exactly the same weapon. We could, and we will, match a cross section of the wound from the Aberdeen corpse with a dozen X rays in our files, but it isn't really necessary to make a positive ID."

Holbrook, Allsloe's assistant, broke in.

"What is it he uses?"

"No one's ever survived to tell us for sure, but we've had it on pretty good authority that it's a platinum surgical pin. The sort they nail aging aristocrats' broken bones together with."

The room filled with the buzz of conversation until the

voice of another of Allsloe's men was heard above the rest.

"But what have the Israelis to do with all this?"

Allsloe cleared his throat loudly and interjected, "I think I had better answer that one, Major. Thank you."

Lowson took his seat.

"I will now tell you what, up to this minute, only the prime minister, the major, and his chief, as my opposite number, have been aware of. The Israelis have everything to do with this operation."

He paused, waiting for the room to quiet, and then continued.

"Till today, for reasons of strictest security, I have been compelled to keep this information on a need-to-know basis. Now, largely due to the good major's swift and astute identification of the killer as an Israeli agent, all that has changed. It seems the Israelis have got the jump on us, and we will have to double our efforts to locate Wright.

"Essentially, the game hasn't changed. It will simply be played out at a faster pace. If the Israeli is as clever as the major says he is, he will not wish to impede Wright from leading him to our common goal. We must, however, get there first without their knowing it."

"But, sir, aren't we allied with the Israelis?" the same fellow asked.

"When it comes to military secrets, politics very often takes a back seat. For a while we even wondered whether Wright might not be an American agent, but nothing in M15's records or, for that matter, in his background, points to that."

"Do you mean, sir, we're up against the Americans as well?"

"No, surely not against them; in fact, as far as we know, they aren't aware of this opportunity—and we'd like to keep it that way."

A number of hands were raised, but Allsloe, with the gesture of a conjuror, caused them to disappear.

"Hold your questions for the moment, and let me tell you what you need to know. We must get on with this. The Aberdeen chief of police was flown down here on a military aircraft and has been waiting outside for almost an hour.

"It all goes back to Lord Rockford. Some time ago, he befriended one of the military attachés at the Israeli Embassy here. It was not an altogether unlikely liaison—the man was a drinker, a womanizer, and a gambler. In other words, a perfect companion for 'Roll-Em' Rockford. They met at a weekend party and continued to meet and play backgammon in the Israeli's flat, quite regularly—Special Branch keeps tabs on embassy personnel in London as a fairly standard operation. Round about the same time, Military Intelligence picked up a rumor of a new Israeli Strategic Military Plan for the Middle East. Their previous contingency plan for war—which we were fully briefed on by the Americans—was just that, a contingency plan—planned retaliation to every possible action their neighbors might take.

"Recent developments have only bolstered M15's suspicions that the original plan has been superceded, that a new plan does exist—a plan whereby the Israelis are preparing to initiate aggressive action. The mere possibility of such a thing has made Whitehall very nervous—very nervous indeed, especially as the top-level feelers we've put out to the Americans make us sure that they haven't the foggiest notion that the new plan exists. They can be very naive at times you know—which is why it became vital for us to get hold of the plan. This attaché chap at the Israeli Embassy seemed to be just the weak link M15 needed.

"From then on, after reviewing his file and doubling the surveillance detailed to him, everything pointed to Rockford as the logical lever to acquire the plan. One: he was seconded to Intelligence when he did his national service with the army and had a reasonably high security clearance. And two: As you know, his family has an ancient and illustrious history of military service and loyalty to the crown. Anyway, Rockford loved intrigue, everything was a game to him—or should I say 'is'? Well, he went for the idea like a shot and before long had the fellow so deeply in debt playing backgammon that when Rockford threatened him with exposure if he didn't pay up, well, he knew how desperate Rockford really was, so he believed the threat and would have done anything to prevent the scandal from ruining his career. Rockford meanwhile was making regular reports to his control at M15. One day he reported that the chap had agreed to get hold of the document and turn it over to him in settlement of the debt. Rockford had rationalized it to him by convincing him that as we're all allies, it didn't make any difference anyway. The next thing we knew, the fellow had made a trip home and back—presumably to fetch the plan. Well, the day after he returned, Rockford said the man was spooked and wouldn't do it.

"It wasn't too much later that first the Israeli and then Rockford disappeared.

"That's it in a nutshell, except that we think Rockford has the documents, and knowing their value, has decided to peddle them to the highest bidder to cover his own debts—which would explain why Omar, a known Palestinian agent, was spending so much time with him, and how the Syrians and the Russians seem to have got wind of the existence of the plan as well. He may have disappeared because he had a change of heart or got scared—we can only speculate—but the plan is still out there somewhere and most probably in his hands, or the Israeli's and everyone else wouldn't still be looking for him."

Allsloe started to gather his notes, preparing to go on to his next meeting.

"Wasn't Rockford a buddy of Harkonian—as in Harkonian Industries?"

"Yes. Harkonian may be mixed up in this somehow. He could be hiding Rockford out of friendship, or he could even be the agent for the sale of the documents. He's one of the few people in Britain who could field a play that requires the kind of contacts and resources that this operation does. But let me add that apart from his friendship with Rockford, we don't have a thing. I raised the question of investigating his involvement at the last ministerial conference and got shot down for my trouble the minute I named him as a suspect. He's a personal friend of at least two members of the government, and they won't hear a word said against him or even authorize me to put any pressure on him without my first producing hard factual evidence of his involvement.''

''But how can you produce anything without launching a full-scale—?''

''There's many a way to skin a cat, and our recruitment of another of his protégés, one Mr. Stedman Wright—albeit unbeknownst to him—will hopefully provide us with all the hard evidence we need.

''Now, gentlemen, if there are any further questions, I'm sure that Major Lowson will be happy to provide whatever information he feels is appropriate and germane to your duties. I really must see our colleague from Aberdeen. I've kept him far too long.''

With that he swooped up his notes, and like a harried Oxford don, hurried from the room.

Eight hours earlier, at eleven PM Washington time, Pete Register arrived at the White House for a hastily summoned ASAP meeting with the President's chief of staff. The routine report he had filed on his conversation with Wiley Travis had for some reason set alarm bells going in the upper echelons of government, and as he negotiated the newly installed anti-terrorist concrete barricades that now blocked the entrance, he wondered just what kind of a mess Wiley had tumbled into. He had known the man he was going to meet both socially and professionally for many years, but nothing in their terse, one-sided conversation had allayed his fears that something was very, very wrong.

The guard inside the door of the small white reception pavilion checked the picture on his credentials and then his name against the clipboard roster. When he matched the name, he carefully double-checked Register's face, returned the identity card, and courteously waved him through. As always, there was a hum of activity about the place, and as he followed the page down the ramp that led to the executive offices, he noted that a number of them were in use. But this was not unusual; in fact, it was reassuring—not crisis frenzy, just people quietly and efficiently going about their work like the night shift in a hospital.

''How the hell are you, Pete?'' He was greeted through

the open office door by the White House chief of staff. "It's been a dog's age, but this job doesn't leave much time for socializing." The tall, smiling man stood in his shirtsleeves. Stacks of documents, folders, and newspapers were piled all around him, covering the floor, couch, and chairs, leaving only his desk curiously devoid of clutter. "Here, let me make some room for you," he said, picking up two fat stacks of papers in his enormous hands and carefully placing them crosswise on top of two other piles on the floor. "The President says that if I don't get this place cleaned up by next week, I'm fired." He grinned, confident of his indispensability.

"I don't imagine you called me in to help you?" Register said wryly.

"If only you could. I've got four secretaries out there, and even they can't help—I've got to go through this shit myself."

Register gingerly picked his way through the path of papers and took the seat that had been cleared for him. His friend sat on the corner of the desk.

"I'm sorry to get you out at this hour, Pete, but the President is vitally interested in the report you made this afternoon about your operative in London—"

"The President!" Register interrupted. "Since when has he started reading routine Agency interoffice memos?"

"He hasn't. It was brought to his attention by the director."

"But why's he interested in a spoiled kid who's got himself in a jam? I was going to turn the whole thing over to Geoff Mitchell at State."

"You haven't, have you?" Concern furrowed the chief of staff's brow.

"No, not yet. I didn't think it would hurt to let him stew for a few days. What's this all about?"

"He may be a spoiled brat—we don't have anything on him yet—but apart from that, he appears to have got himself involved on the inside of a situation that we've been desperate to get a line on. We've called in your man Travis; he's being interviewed in London as we speak. It seems things have already escalated considerably."

"What do you mean *you* called in my man? Who called in *my* man, and why wasn't I aware of it?" Register's anger colored his face a deep crimson.

"Keep your shirt on. The President ordered it, and the director arranged it with your own people. We couldn't reach you, and the boss wanted immediate action taken. The reason you're here is because the President wants me to take charge of this operation personally, and the director's given me permission to assign you to head up the field operation—after all, you recruited Travis, didn't you?"

"Yes, but . . . what operation? What the hell is this all about? Travis isn't really an operative, he's a feeder, a listening post, that's all. If this is really something serious, he couldn't possibly handle it."

"That's why there's an air force jet warmed up and waiting for you at Andrews. You can be in London in three hours."

Register put his hands in his jacket pockets, slid down in the chair, and crossed his legs. "Don't you think you'd better tell me what this is all about?"

He took Register patiently through the convoluted social connections of Steddy and Rockford, and of Rockford and the Israeli military attaché, pointing out how Steddy was clearly involved in some way, as the man found dead in his rooms at Claridge's was a known Palestinian agent. Then, referring to the flimsy of a telex, he told Register that Steddy had been rescued in Aberdeen by Israel's top field operative.

"Who was it?" Register asked.

"I don't know. You'll be fully briefed when you get to London."

"What exactly is the significance of the Israeli documents that's got the President so het up?"

"For some time now, we've been aware that the Israelis have formulated a new strategic plan for the Middle East. It was your people who first got wind of it a couple of months ago, but since then they haven't come up with a thing. State's useless—don't believe Israel would do anything major without consulting us, is all they say—you know what the gentlemen over there are like. When did the Israelis ever

consult us except to ask for more? is what I say.'' Register
grunted agreement. ''And up until this afternoon, we haven't
had a single lead. The President's vehement on the subject;
he's in the middle of some delicate, top-level negotiations
with the Saudis, and Hussein and is damned if he'll get
caught with his pants down if they pull any more surprise
monkey business like when they took out the Iraqi atomic
plant with our planes and our missiles. Every time they do
something like that without telling us, the Arabs scream
bloody murder and won't even talk to us for six months at
the very least, and then we have to start from scratch with
an agenda that's twice as long as the one we were halfway
through. It's political dynamite, but he can't go on negotiating in the dark.''

''I understand the problem, but do you seriously expect
a rank amateur with no more experience than a six-week
field course he took fifteen years ago, and a spoiled brat
who's never done a lick of work in his life, to solve this for
you without the whole thing blowing up in your face?''

The chief of staff's smile was replaced by a serious
expression of sincerity that did little to mask the underlying
threat of his words. ''No, I don't. The President and I are
counting on you to bring this operation to a fruitful and
expeditious close.''

''You realize, of course, that I haven't operated in the
field for more than twenty years.''

''Listen, we don't expect you to get your hands dirty—
just orchestrate from the wings. You'll have everything we
can bring to bear at your disposal. All you have to do is pull
the strings.''

''You make it all sound so easy, when even under the
best conditions—''

''Don't get me wrong. I know it's a tough assignment,
and we don't expect miracles.''

''That's what you're asking for . . . and what about
the British, are they aware we'll be operating on their
turf?''

''I thought I'd made it clear that this operation carries
the highest priority.''

''You mean they don't know.''

"That's right. They know the document exists but not that we have any idea that they do. And that's the way it's got to stay or the plan won't be of any use to anyone. The British are just trying to prove that they still have a say in the way the world turns, but they don't, not really, and their service is riddled with leaks—how the hell do you think we found out about this? If they get hold of the document, within five minutes it won't be worth the paper it's printed on—to them or anyone else."

"I guess there's nothing more to say. I'd better go home and get my toothbrush," Register said wearily.

"There's an air force car and driver waiting for you outside. He'll take you by your house on the way to Andrews. Don't worry about your car. We'll take care of it for you."

Now, eight hours later, only the Brooks Brothers suits differentiated the cast of characters assembled in the American ambassador's office in Grosvenor Square from the men meeting at the same time in Allsloe's office across London at Scotland Yard.

The ambassador was not present. He couldn't be a party to a covert operation on British soil, and in any case, his security clearance wasn't high enough to attend Wiley's briefing.

The night before, when Thea and Wiley finished talking to Steddy, they sat for an hour over large whiskeys, planning what to do next.

Thea was adamant that she would go to the embassy the following day when Steddy called. What she had gleaned from Wiley's side of the conversation alone had been enough to make her realize that Steddy was in mortal danger, and Wiley could say nothing to mollify her concern.

She wasn't a woman's liber simply because she didn't expect to be treated as a woman where serious issues were involved. She asserted that she'd never got in the way and, moreover, that if it hadn't been for her plan, they never would have given the slip to the men following them. Wiley had to agree but said that once they went back to their respective abodes, they'd never lose the tail again, and that if they were both seen going in and out of the embassy, by the British or whomever, it would complicate matters and make it more difficult for the Americans to help them.

Thea would not be put off.

"In that case, why don't we both stay here?"

"You mean at the Dorchester?"

"Why not? No one knows where we are; there's a closet full of Pop's clothes that will probably fit you better than your own, and I've worn his girlfriend's stuff before at the ranch. Anyway, it would only be for a day or two at the most."

Wiley ran over the possibilities in his mind. Once again, seemingly without trying or being fully aware of its importance, Thea had come up with the perfect solution. From what Steddy had told him on the phone, it looked as though he was up to his neck in this business—CIA business— and that meant that the less either of them was seen going in and out of the embassy, the better. On the other hand, if they stayed where they were, he could brief his contact that evening by telephone without its being bugged, and then they could both go to the embassy tomorrow at four without being followed. After that, who knows—they could probably set up some means of making contact without having to go to the embassy, or maybe by then the whole thing would be settled.

At eight-thirty he called the number that his contact had given him and was surprised to recognize the Camel smoker's voice answering on the first ring.

Not wanting to say much in front of Thea, he simply reported that there had been another murder and that they had better get together so he could fill him in before the four PM call the next day.

The fellow seemed very agitated and asked Wiley where he was.

"I'm at the Dorchester in Thea's father's apartment talking on his private line, but there's no need to worry, we gave everyone the slip."

"You think you're pretty clever, I suppose."

"Well, actually . . ."

"Listen, shithead, two of those men you gave the slip

to were mine, and they're not very happy; and in case you can't tell from the tone of my voice, neither am I."

"Listen, whoever you are, in case you don't know it, I don't get paid to do this, so you can—"

"Can it. Is the girl with you?"

"Yes."

"Okay. You're about to find out who I am, or at least what I look like. Call me back in fifteen minutes."

There was a click, and the connection was terminated. Thea wanted to know what had transpired. Wiley answered, "He wants to meet me."

"When, tonight?"

"I guess so."

"Who was that, the ambassador?"

"No, just one of his assistants."

They met at Cunningham's Oyster Bar in Curzon Street, but as it had moved across the road since Wiley had last been there, he was a few minutes late for the nine-thirty rendezvous.

Instead of the supremely elegant bottle-green velvet womb shining with polished brass and candles that he remembered, like so many other places, it had obviously changed hands, and he was surprised to enter a bright, pedestrian restaurant, minus the famed Oyster Bar. It was understandably not very crowded, and he had no trouble locating his man, who, according to plan, was engrossed in a copy of the pink London *Financial Times*.

They greeted one another as friends would who had only parted at the club a few hours earlier, and then, once Wiley was seated: "You're late."

"You didn't happen to mention the place had moved."

"That was ten years ago."

The man was lanky, with sandy hair that might or might not have been shot with gray. His age could have been anywhere between forty-two and fifty-two, and the smoker's voice had a slight Texas softness to it. He dressed as though he either had been educated in the East or had been in London long enough to find a decent tailor.

"Those men were there for your protection. Don't ever pull a stunt like that again."

"I had to have a chance to talk to Steddy long enough to convince him to call in tomorrow. He would have hung up in three minutes if I hadn't been able to swear to him that we hadn't been tailed. As it turns out, it was lucky I did—he gave me quite an earful."

Tex didn't look convinced or impressed. The waiter came, and Wiley realized that he had hardly eaten all day, so, a little mischievously, knowing that Tex just wanted to get on with the business at hand, he ordered a cold lobster and half a bottle of Bollinger. Tex was gritting his teeth but ordered a spritzer for himself.

Obviously a reformed drinker, Wiley thought.

The waiter left them, and Tex—for that was the name Wiley had assigned him when he hadn't given his name and probably never would—said, "You're a real prize. Jesus! How the hell do we get people like you?"

"I know you won't take it personally if I remind you that we managed to lose two of your best bloodhounds this evening—how the hell do you get people like them?"

They were off to a good start.

Wiley related verbatim his conversation with Steddy.

Tex said nothing until Wiley mentioned the way Steddy had described the murder weapon.

"So he's in Aberdeen," Tex said pensively.

"What makes you think so? He didn't tell me where I was."

Then, as if talking to himself, not looking at Wiley at all, he said,"We had a flash about that earlier today."

"Why a flash? Steddy said it was in all the local papers."

Tex looked at Wiley as though he were a child and said, "We don't read 'all the local papers.' You'd better just sit tight here for a minute. I've gotta go out and make a call."

Without further explanation, he got up and left the restaurant.

The waiter came and asked Wiley if he wanted the bill. Wiley told him he was a guest and that his friend would be right back.

Tex paid the bill when he returned, though not very graciously. When the waiter brought the change, he asked for a receipt and then hustled Wiley out the door and into a small, nondescript automobile that smelled of wet dog. They drove in silence (Wiley figured there was no point in asking where they were going), eventually parking in Knightsbridge. From there, it was just a short walk in the now more insistent rain to a narrow house at the back of Brompton Square. It had been converted into flats, and they had to climb three flights of stairs before reaching their destination.

It was typical of all dreary service flats—Wiley had taken enough of them before his company had agreed to spring for the tab at Claridge's. The walls were a color that made it impossible to tell if they hadn't been painted in twenty years or if whoever had had the bad taste to select the furniture had actually chosen the paint as well. The focal point of the sitting room was the chimney, which was walled up and had an electric fire planted in it. The rug felt damp underfoot and smelled.

Two nameless men of different sizes were waiting there. When Wiley walked in, one went into the next room and shut the door. Wiley was then asked to repeat, word for word, his conversation with Steddy. When he finished, the two men exchanged places, and he was told to repeat the whole thing over again.

He never questioned them or complained. Only once did he depart from the script to ask if he could call Thea to tell her he was all right. Permission was not granted, but they told him they would get a message to her.

They kept him all night, frequently leaving the room to confer or make calls, always in tones too low for Wiley to overhear.

At first light, a greasy plate of ham and eggs was brought to him from some beanery next door in Knightsbridge. He left it untouched until noon, when he gingerly picked at the ham.

At about twelve-thirty, they took him to the embassy. He and Tex entered with the rest of the lunchtime crowds through the visa entrance at the side. He was allowed to shower and shave in the marines' locker room in the basement, given a bologna sandwich in the staff cafeteria, and then left to cool his heels until two-thirty, when he was escorted up to the ambassador's office, only to be greeted by Pete Register, the man who had recruited him for the CIA at Princeton, and whom it seemed he had just talked to on the phone in Virginia.

"Hope you weren't waiting long. I got here as fast as the air force could manage."

What followed was essentially the same briefing that Allsloe and Lowson were giving their men across town at virtually the same moment.

28

Steddy headed for the small chemist's shop near the entrance to the station, by the kiosk where he had bought cigarettes. There were four boxes of Veganin on the counter by the register. He took them all, hoping the codeine would bring him some relief from the gnawing pain, and as an afterthought, he asked the clerk for an elastic bandage, hoping that if he taped his ribs it might be easier to walk.

The men's room was miles away—he wanted to get some of those Veganin down where they could do some good. It was full of people when he got there, so he locked himself in the nearest stall and collapsed onto the seat, using loo paper to mop at the perspiration that was pouring from his brow, neck, and underarms.

When he had cooled down, he tried to swallow one of the tablets, but without water it started to dissolve in his throat and made him gag and sweat all over again. He could hear loud conversation outside the stall; people were still coming and going. So he pulled himself up, hung his duffel on the hook behind the door, and began the painful process of taking off his shirt. It was difficult not to cry out; the jabs of pain were so intense as he wrestled with the sleeves. He seemed to be getting stiffer. Maybe the booze is wearing off, he thought as he unwrapped the bandage and began to wind the first turn tightly around his chest, under his arms. He had to lean against the marble wall of the stall to recover between each rotation. The cold marble was a relief against his sopping, pounding head. It could have taken fifteen minutes or an hour to complete the operation. By the time he fastened the clip at the end of the bandage, time had become irrelevant and the elastic was soaked through. The thought of using the cubicle for the purpose it was intended crossed his mind, but the mere idea of sitting down and standing up again dissuaded him, until he remembered from his youth his mother always saying, "You never know when you'll have a another chance." He really didn't know when he'd have another chance, so for once mindful of good advice, he unhitched his trousers and sank to the seat.

Mother—good God! The thought made him momentarily forget even the pain. She must be frantic. He had to get word to her right away, but how? He couldn't call her directly—the way Wiley had painted the picture, even her phone could be tapped. Aunt Edith—why hadn't he thought of her before? She was right here in Scotland, or she certainly should be by now; the shooting season was due to start any day. It seemed light-years since he and Thea had escaped to her house after Nubar's tournament. Edith could relay a message to Philadelphia, but she was such a good sport that it wouldn't be fair to get her involved in all this, even though she'd adore the intrigue. During the war, she had told him, that by staying awake while her daughter (who worked in Churchill's war room) talked in her sleep, she had been the first civilian in Britain to know the time and place of the invasion. This was right up her alley, but hell, Wiley could use that tricky phone of his and get word to Philadelphia. Enough people had been dragged into this mess as it was.

Steddy stood up, fastened his trousers, and then peered into the loo to see if he'd sustained any internal injuries. But the only thing of note, which made him chuckle, was the name of the manufacturer: Thomas Crapper.

The washroom was deserted now, so he ran the cold water, and using his hands as a cup, managed to swallow four Veganin. The cool water felt so good on his face that he doused his whole head and combed his hair. Looking in the mirror, he was amazed to see that none of the beating or the pain showed in his face. It almost wasn't fair, but drawing attention, and sympathy to himself was something he didn't need.

As he skulked from the men's room back into the bustle of the station, it occurred to him that he had no place to go. It was well after eight-thirty, and he couldn't spend the night there—airports and train stations were the first places the police looked for a fugitive.

Maybe it was because he'd been thinking about Edith and his mother or the phone call with Thea and Wiley, but he suddenly realized that he just didn't feel like a fugitive. He'd allowed this thing to get the better of him. After all, he was someone who belonged somewhere. He hadn't committed a crime.

There was a pub winking at him across the mall, and he strode toward it as best he could. At the threshold, he remembered his "fallen guardian angel" and paused to look back over his shoulder. There was no one there, but the hackles stood out rigid on his neck.

The saloon was a dreary station pub, and the people who patronized it were dreary station people, all browns and grays. Steddy sat at the bar and waited for the synergism of the alcohol and codeine to work its wonders.

Gazing into the grimy mirror of the back bar, he found it impossible to conceive that any of the pedestrian types reflected there could be his fallen angel. Of course, he had no idea what to look for. He didn't even know the man's nationality or anything about him. Well, that wasn't quite true, he did know one thing: whoever he was, he had to be extremely lithe and athletic to have done what he did with such ease and accuracy. He had to be strong, too—he'd got Steddy home and up three flights of stairs, which was no easy feat with a hundred-eighty-five pound dead weight.

Of course, he must have had an accomplice, Steddy thought. But how could he have fingered me, how could he have picked up my trail so easily when even Scotland Yard hasn't been able to? And what the hell does he want from me? He doesn't want to harm me, or he would have already, and he can't want anything I've got, or he would have taken it. Maybe that's it, maybe he found out I don't have what he wants, and he's gone and left me, left me with my bottle of bourbon as a token of farewell.

Certainly it was a possibility, wasn't it? That he wasn't being followed anymore?

The alcohol and the drug were beginning to have their effect. He was feeling a bit floaty and euphoric—even rather pleasant, but still he tried to untangle his thoughts.

But Wiley said that this man would follow me if he could, and Wiley knows that I don't know the first thing about this business. And then he said that the fallen angel could be the best protection I could have.... What the hell...?

Steddy's mind was getting muddled. The stilling of the pain was accompanied by a dulling of the brain. He had no facts, ergo he could reach no conclusions. Well, he thought, if he's the only protection I've got, here's to him.

He raised his glass to offer a mock toast over his left shoulder and found himself looking into a grinning, vaguely familiar face.

29

Fear of recognition and a hundred other fears blurred through his mind in a fraction of a second before Steddy realized that the smiling, uncomplicated face in front of him was friend, not foe—but he couldn't place him.

It wasn't until he noticed the trio in the background and realized that they were calling him Wiley that he remembered them as his companions from the train, the hikers he'd spent the night with in Edinburgh. He couldn't recall ever being so happy to see anyone in his whole life—he felt as though the marines had landed.

"Hell, we never thought we'd run into you again," Bill said.

"Yeah, sport. Did you see that monster?" another interjected.

"Monster?" Steddy drew a blank. The only monster he'd seen was safely in the Aberdeen morgue.

"Loch Ness. The monster?"

It came back to him—he had told them he was a marine biologist. "No, 'fraid not, but it really is good to see you—*all* of you! How was your climb, and what are you doing here?"

"Fantastic! The mountain's unbelievable. Of course, by the time we got to the top, the weather was so bad we couldn't see a thing and almost froze our nuts off, but it was really worth it."

"Didn't you just get in on the train?"

"Hell, no. We've been camping along the Spey, and then we got onto something called the Whiskey Trail. Ever heard of it?"

"No, but if there is one, it would have to be in Scotland!"

"It's wild. Seventy miles of the best drinking ever—and all marked with signposts," Tom said.

"How do you mean?"

"Well, just about all the malt distilleries in Scotland are clustered in this one area, I think it's because of the water in the Spey. Ever heard of Glenfiddich and Glenlivet?"

"I see you got an education as well as a snoot full. 'Tis Glenfiddich that I hold in me hand," Steddy said, raising his glass with a flourish. "You'd better all have one."

"We'd better stick to beer," Bill interrupted. "We spent so much money on malt whiskey to bring back to the base that we're just about broke."

"Don't be silly. It's on me. After all, this is a celebration—a reunion. Besides, I can't swear that I remember much about that night in Edinburgh, but I don't think you guys let me pay for a thing."

"Well, thanks a lot."

Steddy ordered the drinks.

"Anyway, you wouldn't believe it, all these distilleries let you drink as much as you want free. It was really terrific—no kidding. Of course, each one had a shop, and we bought a lot, so I guess it works out, but I swear every time we tasted the malt at a new distillery, it was better than the last."

"I'm not surprised," Steddy said, laughing for the first time in ages. They were so full of enthusiasm, it would have been impossible not to climb aboard their high.

"Don't tell me that with all that whiskey in you, you walked all the way to Aberdeen?"

"Nah, Tom here sprained his ankle in a gully, so we took the train from Elgin and here we are, just in time for a drink!"

"Well, Tom, that makes two of us," Steddy prevaricated. "I had a nasty fall down a river bank, so I'm a bit battered, too."

"Are you coming or going?" Tom asked.

"Just got in from Inverness," Steddy said, not liking to lie to these decent fellows.

"Where are you going to stay?" asked Bill, who was obviously the spokesman.

"No idea."

"Well, you're sure welcome to stay with us. We heard about this great beach with a campsite south of town—lots of action with French and Scandinavian chicks, unless the guy who told us was a bullshitter."

Steddy felt as though the silent prayer he didn't remember offering had been answered.

"That'd be great, but I haven't got any camping gear—just a sleeping bag."

"Hell, we've got two big tents—U.S. Government issue—and all the whiskey you could drink in a year. What else d'ya need?"

"Frankly, I can't think of a thing. I'd love to."

"Fantastic." They all whooped and slapped him painfully on the back. Steddy ordered another round, and they drank together to the camaraderie of the road.

"The only problem," Steddy said, "is how are we gonna get there? I'm as bad as Tom when it comes to walking—if not worse."

"We thought we'd hitch a ride," Bill said. "It's not supposed to be too far, but it's definitely too far to walk on a bum ankle."

"I'll tell you what," Steddy said, "we could rent a car." And then, hushing their objections; "Don't worry about the money, I don't have to pay for it anyway. The university will, that's part of the deal."

'Well, in that case—"

Steddy cut Bill off. "There is one problem."

"What's that?" Bill asked.

"When I fell in the river, I lost all my papers—driver's license, credit cards, the works."

Their faces all hung in unison.

"But I do have plenty of cash, so if one of you has a driver's license, I can give you the cash for the deposit."

"That's no problem. I've rented cars before over here with my military license. As long as you've got the cash, there's a place right over there." Bill pointed outside, across the mall from the pub.

Steddy had been fiddling with the money belt inside his shirt, his hand covered by his parka, so that when he pulled out a bundle of notes and counted out the money, it appeared to have come from an inside pocket. He handed it to Bill.

"Better take two hundred fifty pounds, just in case."

"By God, you may never see me again." Bill grinned, fanning himself with the wad.

"Listen, Bill, if you'll organize that—and be sure to get the biggest one they have 'cause I can hardly bend—we'll order your dinner for you while you're doing it. All on the old alma mater, you understand."

"I'm beginning to feel like an alumnus."

They gorged themselves on Aberdeen sausage, a hearty meat roll made of minced beef and ham, which Steddy had been virtually living on for the past week, and washed it down with bumpers of thick, dark beer and raucous conversation. Bill had no trouble renting a comfortable Rover, and as darkness comes late in the northern summer, it was still light when they piled into the car in the parking lot behind the station.

The rental agent had marked a map for Bill, so he had little trouble finding the coast road, where they turned south along the shore in the lazy, lingering dusk.

The first two campsites they reached were full, and as they continued south, the warm gold of the late evening sky gradually colored the clouds and stretches of sand with the full spectrum from rose to violet.

Throughout the drive Steddy painfully twisted his neck around to see if they were being followed, but the continual bends in the road made ideal hiding places for a pursuer, and with the sky so bright, there was no chance of sighting the telltale cut of a headlight's beam.

Eventually, in the gathering gloom, they spotted the

glow of camp fires, and this time there was a place for them.

The camp was populated almost exclusively by Finns, and as Steddy and Tom—the invalids—built a fire and Bill and the others erected the two ungainly khaki tents, their neighbors approached to welcome them, tall and golden in the flickering firelight, conjuring up ghosts of their Viking ancestors, invaders of those very beaches a thousand years before.

Of those who came by, three girls and a tall, gangly, storklike boy lingered by the fire until the work on the tents was done. Bill broke out a bottle of his precious malt and invited them to join in round the fire. The boy accepted for them—he was the only one who spoke English and happily turned out to be the younger brother of one of the girls. They had brought a bottle of aquavit, but Bill wouldn't hear of it, making the boy literally translate: "When in Rome . . ." which totally confused the issue and left them all rolling with laughter. Things got even sillier when they discovered that the statuesque redhead next to Bill was Danish and had some difficulty communicating with her own companions, although not, it appeared as the evening progressed, with Bill.

The girl sitting between Tom and Steddy had unbelievable legs that never quit. Her name was Kirsten, and she was staggeringly beautiful, with long, straight, white-blonde hair and the ice-blue eyes of a Siberian wolfhound mellowed by the setting of her browned-butter tan—the signals Steddy got from her transcended the language barrier.

She saw that Steddy was in pain and by gesture offered to massage his neck. Steddy took pains to explain that it was still too tender so as not to hurt her feelings, and when she understood, she captivated him with a smile that caused the corners of her mouth to crinkle up and two tiny white dimples to materialize at either side.

The group continued to pass the bottle, but the effect ceased to be exuberant. The hypnotic flicker of the fire, the silence, but for its crackle, the faint glow in the distant sky, and the magnificence of the Viking girls were archetypical symbols that united to release ancient memories—tantalizingly beyond the grasp of consciousness—memories that bestowed a mystical timelessness to the night.

Steddy never noticed when the brother and sister left, nor did he see Tom leave after Bill and the Danish girl drifted off. They were alone on the planet. No words were spoken, but the thoughts that flowed through their eyes sealed a covenant of nature. She stood and extended her hand to Steddy, who took it, rose to her side, and followed her into the darkness beyond the perimeter of the fire's light.

The smallness of her fit the palm of his hand like the warm, trusting head of a tiny animal. She held his beaten body to her with a healing tenderness that, in helping him, seemed to fulfill some basic need in her. For a long time the familiarity of their intimacy was enough.

When it came, the transition from warmth to passion was as imperceptible as the faint wisp of smoke that precedes spontaneous combustion. There was no change of tempo to warn them, but a languorously unfolding Karmic fusion that grew in intensity until it overwhelmed them and left them wasted and bewildered.

That they had no common language saved them from attempting to analyze the ferocious force that had possessed them until sleep released their troubled spirits.

30

By the time they surfaced, the entire compound seemed to be lunching under awnings extended from their campers or at tables set up alongside their tents. The August sun was warm, and the note that Steddy found pinned to Bill's tent said that they'd decided to take advantage of the rare opportunity and were across the road on the beach. When Steddy and Kirsten found them, they were sprawled like so much flotsam washed up on a shore of khaki army blankets. Bill raised himself up on his elbows, not wanting to disturb the lovely Danish redhead, who was apparently asleep, using his washboard midsection for a pillow.

"Well, we were just about to send out the reserves to see if you were still in the land of the living," Bill said good-naturedly. "You missed breakfast, but you didn't miss much."

"That's okay. I've got to go to town to make a phone call, and we can pick something up then," Steddy said, looking at his watch. It was almost two o'clock, and he'd promised Wiley and Thea that he'd call them at four.

Bill and the others made room for him on the blankets, while Kirsten untied her knotted shirt to reveal that like the other girls in the group, no bra line marred the uniformity of the tan over her full but nubile breasts.

Steddy leaned over and asked Bill if he had the keys to

the car with him, and Bill replied, "What's up? If it's important I can drive you."

"No, I've just got to call a girl in London—I told her I'd be there today—she's a stewardess I met on the way over."

"Listen, as far as I'm concerned, it's your car, but what if you get picked up without a license? Maybe I'd better drive you."

"I didn't think of that, but I don't want to ruin your day. This is probably the best weather you've had since you've been here."

"No sweat."

"No, really . . . but if you lend me your license, I probably won't have to use it, and we have pretty much the same vital statistics."

"Sure, that's okay. Just don't do anything that'll land me in the stockade. I've only got six months to go in this man's army, and I'd like to keep it that way."

The Scandinavians had finished their lunch, and the seashore was filling up with uninhibited Finns, Swedes, and Danes frolicking in the surf *au naturel*. Steddy's limited wardrobe no longer seemed to be a problem, as the only thing the men had on was bathing caps. Sweltering in the heat, he made up his mind that it was no time for misplaced modesty. Kirsten helped him strip off his shirt and began gently to unwrap the elastic bandage that covered his entire torso.

"Holy Christ!" Bill exclaimed, after a low whistle.

"Why not? Everyone else is bare-assed," Steddy remarked, undoing his trousers.

"No, man, it's not that, but look at yourself! Shit, you really did have a bad fall. Have you seen a doctor?"

Steddy looked down, examining himself. He had turned every color of the rainbow.

"No, it's just bruises and a few cracked ribs. A dip in the ocean is just what the doctor ordered."

When Kirsten finished ministering to Steddy, she removed her own cutoffs to reveal a shocking-pink postage-stamp bikini bottom that didn't appear to have a back to it. They made quite a couple, walking down to the water's edge—Steddy hobbling like an old man with his outrageous technicolor bruises and mushroom-white, never-seen-by-the-sun backside, one arm around the naked waist of Kirsten, the leggy bronzed goddess. He wondered how the Scandinavian men managed to remain oblivious to the smorgasbord of bared beauties that surrounded them and was grateful when finally the icy water lapped at his waist.

It was too cold to stay in very long unless you were a Scandinavian or a masochist. Steddy was soon numb from the waist down and now had no further qualms about leaving the water. The Scandinavians seemed to thrive on the cold, and he came to the conclusion that as their veins ran with ice water, it mattered very little to them what state of dress they were in.

They dried each other with a big towel that Tom lent them and put their clothes on, preparing to go to town.

"Why don't I get a big steak and some vino in town, and we can have a real piss-up dinner tonight," he said to everyone.

"Great idea!" Tom answered enthusiastically.

Then they young Swedish boy, the brother of the girl who now seemed to be with Tom, said, "That would be a wonderful farewell party for us, no?"

"Are you leaving?" Steddy asked.

"Ya."

"All of you?" he asked again.

"Ya, ya, tomorrow morning."

"Kirsten, too?"

"Ya, Kirsten, too," the boy said, smiling in the sunshine like a snapshot of a forgotten summer.

Steddy, now frowning and using his hands to mimic the wings of a plane, asked Kirsten if she was really leaving the next day. She understood and nodded her head yes.

"Well, in that case, we'd better make it a proper gala. Have you got something we can cook the steaks on, Bill?" he said, feigning enthusiasm but really depressed at the thought of her leaving.

"Don't worry about a thing. You get the food and leave the cooking to the army."

At three-fifteen, they rounded a low hill and descended to where the foot of a magnificent valley spilled into the sea and formed the town of Stonehaven, nestled around a horseshoe cove that was full of sailboats and fishing craft. It was farther than some of the towns they had driven through the night before, but Steddy didn't want to run the risk of calling from a small fishing village that might have only one telephone with no privacy, and the map the rental agent had given Bill showed that Stonehaven was the nearest big town.

Throughout the silent fifteen-minute ride with Kirsten's arm around him, Steddy tried to analyze the powerful sense of loss he felt at the news of her leaving.

Here he was on his way to telephone Thea, who represented a depth of feeling and emotion on his part that a month ago he wouldn't have thought himself capable of, and yet the fact that he was drawn so forcefully to this delightful creature only seemed strange when looked at through the magnifying glass of guilt—and he was beginning to feel guilty that he didn't feel guilty—what he had with Kirsten seemed so natural.

With Thea, there was so much in common, so much humor, that even their lovemaking had always been punctuated by laughter and a joy of discovery, whereas with Kirsten, there was a oneness and a sexual power that was like nothing he had ever known. He didn't feel as though he was being disloyal to Thea, because he felt as though he had always known Kirsten and that he always would—like a wonderful dream that's totally lost with morning, the sense of wonder stays, and one knows that left unforced, it will one day return, only to be forgotten again until its next appearance.

The sight of a red telephone kiosk by the port brought him from his reverie. He parked the car by the quay, and looking at his watch, decided there was time to do some shopping before making the call. The first place they went into was a sporting goods store, and Steddy decided to take advantage of the opportunity to pick up some badly needed provisions. He purchased a sturdy pair of hunter-green corduroy trousers, a few shirts, and an oilskin slicker with a hood. He tried to get Kirsten to pick something out, but she wouldn't, so he got her three microscopic polka-dot bikinis in assorted colors. They went next door into a small market and ordered a giant Aberdeen Angus porterhouse steak. When he noticed that it was quarter to four, he gave Kirsten a fistful of money, pointed at the bins of wine, and made signs to her that he would be outside in the telephone.

He got in the booth and realized that there was still a good ten minutes before he had to call. Worried that someone would come along and need the phone just at the wrong moment, he picked up the receiver and pretended to talk into it to forestall anyone who might come along until it was time.

Unlike public phones in town, an operator came on the line and asked him for the number he wanted. In a totally reflex action, he found himself asking her for directory inquiry for Perthshire. When he realized what he had done, he told himself that it wouldn't be a bad idea to have Edith's number handy, just in case. Then, when the operator asked him if he would like to be connected, he thought, well, I'll just ring and see who answers. It was an enormous place, and she rarely ever answered the phone herself, but this time she did.

"Edith? What are you doing answering the phone?" he asked idiotically.

"You mean you rang me and you didn't want to talk to me?"

"Well, yes—I mean no, I mean . . ."

"Where are you, Steddy?" she said imperiously, as though addressing a child who's stayed out beyond his curfew. "We've all been dreadfully worried."

"Edith, are you alone?"

"Blissfully so. I've had a house full of people, who, thank God, left this morning. I can't imagine why I answered the phone; I've taken to my bed with a boiled chicken and left strict orders not to be disturbed." Then, exasperated: "Now"—she took a deep breath—"where are you?"

"I'm not far, but I don't think we should talk on the telephone. Someone may be listening."

"On my telephone? Don't be an ass. Why would anyone listen in on my telephone?"

"Because they're looking for me, or haven't you been reading the papers?"

"Of course I have. And your poor mother..."

"Have you spoken to her?"

"Of course I have. She's worried sick. How could you do it?"

"But I didn't do it," he answered wearily.

"I never thought that you did, but how could you not call your mother? She's been on to the White House, the ambassador, and every senator and congressman she knows. She's simply frantic—she's even called some Democrats."

"It isn't a game, you know. I was framed, and I'm trying to figure out why. None of it makes any sense."

"I'm afraid for once I agree with your mother—you've been running around with the wrong people."

"Edith, please. Don't you start to lecture me."

"All right, but you had better come straight here before you get into any more trouble. And then I can call Georgianna and at least put her mind at ease."

"Don't do that, whatever you do. A friend of mine is going to call her through a direct line from the embassy in about half an hour."

"Is everything all right then?"

"No, nothing's all right."

"Well, then, you had better come here until it is."

"But I can't get you involved."

"Well that would be the first time. Now just you listen to me Stedman"—her tone was commanding—"we can hide you in the old keep if it comes to that, and—" Stedman started to interrupt. "Hush, I say! Now, we can hide you in the old keep—heavens, they hid dozens of Catholics there in the sixteenth century, and no one ever found them—and you'll be very comfortable. Harry's father had it all done up in the nineties as a hideaway from his wife and her parties. It hasn't been used since long before the war, and I doubt if any of the servants, except Karesin and Cook, know that it exists. So what do you say to that? Eh?"

"I don't know what to say."

"Well, then, that's settled."

"But how would I get in without everyone seeing me?"

"That's easy. I'll send Karesin in to Scone to pick you up. As long as it's after ten in the evening, when everyone's gone to bed, no one will see you."

"But, Edith, I really—"

"There'll be no buts about it," she said emphatically. "This is what we'll do. Karesin goes down to the pub in town occasionally for a pint, the one in the square; well, I'll let him take the big car tonight, so you can't miss it. Just hop in the back and wait for him .Can you be here between ten and ten-thirty?"

"I can't, it's not possible, it's already . . . Oh, *my* God! It's already after four—I'm late for my call."

"All right then, we'll see you tomorrow night. Same arrangements. Now do try to stay out of trouble."

There was a click on the line. She'd rung off before Steddy could say another word.

Getting on to the overseas operator went surprisingly quickly, and when the number answered in Washington and the operator said she had a collect call from Wiley, the charges were accepted immediately.

Steddy glanced nervously at the big clock on the corner through the glass panes of the kiosk—it was nearly ten past. He lit a cigarette and prayed that Wiley would still be by the phone. He heard it ring once and then: "Steddy?"

"Yes, Wiley, it's me. Sorry I'm a little late, but it couldn't be helped."

"No sweat. Now listen, Steddy. I've been here all night being briefed, and an associate of mine has just been flown in from Washington on a jet fighter plane to take charge here—which will give you an idea of how seriously we're all taking this thing. I've known him since Princeton, and I'd trust him with my life. I want you to trust him, too, Steddy."

"You sound like a doctor introducing a terminal patient to the surgeon."

"That would be a pretty fair analogy, except that in this case the patient isn't terminal."

"Glad to hear it," Steddy said, sounding unconvinced.

"Now trust me, Steddy. I'm not walking away from this, but Pete's in charge, and he'd like to brief you personally—that's his name, Pete, Pete Register. Now I'm going to put him on the phone, and I want you to listen to him, and when he's through, I'll come back on the line and answer any questions you have. Then I'll get Thea for you. She's in the outer office now, but we don't think she should be in on this phase of . . . well, Pete will brief you on all that."

"Listen, Wiley, there's one thing you've got to promise me that you'll do the minute we're through."

"If I can do it, you've got it."

"Call my mother on that fancy phone of yours and tell her I'm all right."

"I can't do that officially, but—"

"Wiley, cut the crap. I wasn't born yesterday. I know you're CIA or something, but just you remember that we go back a lot longer than you and Uncle Sam. So call her. Call her unofficially, just as my friend, and tell her that I'm okay and that we're in touch and not to worry. If you won't do that, I'm hanging up right now."

"Steddy, I didn't mean that I wouldn't call her. Of course I will. I just meant that I can't make any statements on behalf of the government. But don't worry, I was going to call her anyway, after I talked to you. She's been calling the ambassador every day."

"Okay, Wiley. Now what's this guy's name you're putting on the phone, and exactly who the hell is he?"

When Wiley left the Dorchester to rendezvous with "Tex," Thea undressed, put on one of her father's pajama tops, and got into bed to watch television and wait for him. She was rather pleased with herself for the way she had orchestrated their escape and felt more at ease after speaking to Steddy.

A little after midnight—she knew the time because the BBC had just signed off for the night—she became concerned that Wiley hadn't returned, and leafing through old issues of the *Tatler* and *Queen* only added to her nervousness. At one AM, she poured herself some wine. At one-thirty, a disembodied voice on the telephone informed her that her "friend" was with friends and would see her the next day at four. He told her to go to the main entrance and ask the receptionist for her friend, and with that the connection was terminated before she could ask, "The main entrance of what?"

After that she tried to sleep but couldn't. She hadn't had any dinner, and it was too late to call room service. All there was in the fridge was a tin of pâté, which eventually she ate with a spoon.

The next day, tired and irritable and unable to wait any longer, she left for the embassy at two-thirty in a cab, even though it was less than a five-minute walk. The receptionist at the main entrance sent her straight up to the ambassador's office, where she was greeted by his secretary and told to have a seat in the outer office. She asked for Wiley periodically and was told that she would simply have to be patient.

At four-thirty the door to the ambassador's office opened, and Wiley poked his head out and told Thea to hurry in if she wanted to talk to Steddy—as though *she* had been late, she thought as she brushed past him.

The room was standard embassy stuff—light blue walls, bright green carpet, and red leather chairs. A silver-haired gentleman, who Thea assumed was the ambassador, rose from his chair behind the desk and proffered the red handpiece of the telephone to her. Wiley pushed an armchair behind her, and as she sank into it, she began to speak.

"Steddy, dearest, is it all over?"

"Not quite, darling, I'm afraid."

"You sound so subdued, so serious, what's the matter?"

"I'm not really sure yet." And then, trying to be cheerful: "I think Wiley's friends seem to have everything in hand, but it's still going to take a little time."

"But, darling, if it's just a question of time, we can wait together."

"It isn't quite that simple. It wouldn't be safe for a bit."

"What you mean is, they haven't done a thing!" she said, rapidly flushing with anger.

"Dearest, talk to *them* about that; let's not waste the time we have arguing."

"But I can't take this another minute. Not knowing anything, being followed, wondering if you're all right. Steddy, if I can't be with you, I'm going home and try to forget you. I mean it, darling."

Her threat broke his resolve.

"Darling, I'm being selfish doing this, and I know it's wrong, but I'm going to tell you how to get here. Now keep it to yourself, or they won't let you out of their sight. In about two days, I'll be staying where we went after Austria. Okay so far?"·

"Yes, darling, but how long will it take?" Thea disguised her exuberance and made it sound like despair.

"That's good, darling. You'd better wait three days before you come, until you're absolutely certain that no one's following you. Remember, you and I are the only ones who know where we were after Austria, so don't let on."

"Yes, darling, but why can't you hide in London?"

"Remember, no matter who you lost yesterday, you've got them back on your tail as of now."

"I know, but what will I do without you?"

She was doing a good job convincing the listeners in the room that she was being persuaded by Steddy to be patient and wait.

"Maybe the best thing to do would be to start as soon as possible. Lay a false trail somehow. Have you got your passport with you?"

"Of course I do, darling. Don't you know it already?"

"Okay, then maybe you should fly to Paris or Copenhagen and work your way back, but be sure, darling, that you want to do this. Remember, it's no game—I'll be miserable without you, but I'll sleep better if I know that you're safe in London."

"Darling, you know I'll be there. Just say when you're going to call."

Wiley and Register were getting nervous keeping Steddy on the line for such a long time. Register was not at all pleased with the job that he'd been forced to accept—running a top-security, highly dangerous operation with two amateurs and a girl—ridiculous. And he wasn't that far removed from amateur standing himself, not having worked in the field in over twenty-five years, but there didn't seem to be any other way to handle it except giving up, and the decision to go for it had already been made on a much higher level—the highest, he assumed, as they were operating within the borders of America's oldest ally without its knowledge.

What worried him the most was the unknown quantum—Stedman Wright.

He'd read Wright's dossier, of course, and Wiley had sworn up and down in his behalf, but he still had no sense of the man. Even after Register had talked to him and briefed him with as much information as he dared, Stedman hadn't given him an answer. He hadn't agreed to cooperate. He said he'd let them know and wouldn't even tell them where he was—wouldn't even tell Wiley, his best friend. How could they work like that?

Still and all, Wright was in their camp, and if anyone had a shot at locating Rockford and the plan, it had to be him. The Israelis were no better off, or they wouldn't be shadowing him.

Thea's voice interrupted his thoughts.

"Thank you for letting me use your phone, Mr. Ambassador."

Wiley cut in.

"Thea, I'm sorry, but we didn't have time before—this is a friend of mine from Washington, Mr. Register." And turning to Pete: "May I present Miss Boulton."

They exchanged greetings, and then Thea opened with: "Now, I would like to know just exactly who the hell you are and what you're really doing for Steddy?"

31

Steddy broke the connection with his finger but kept the receiver to his ear and continued to act as though he were engrossed in conversation. He could see Kirsten, not fifteen yards away, sitting on the hood of the car with her face to the sun, and needed a moment to gather his thoughts and compose himself.

Register's briefing had been too much for him to digest all at once, except for one bit of news that had burned through the mists that fogged his thoughts with the bite of a surgical laser—Chelak.

The shadow—his fallen guardian angel—now had a name, which made him more tangible; he had a reputation, which made him more frightening; but worst of all, he had no face. Register could give him no description, no clue at all to help him spot the man.

Slowly pivoting in the booth, Steddy scanned the landscape for this phantom. The people he saw in the streets were mostly local types: fishermen, shopkeepers, and housewives; the tourists were all still at play in or on the sea. No one except perhaps himself looked in the least bit out of place, but then why should this man—a master of subterfuge—look out of place, and how could Steddy hope to succeed in singling him out when evidently no one else had ever been able to?

He could no longer allow himself the luxury of assuming Chelak wasn't there, not after what Register had told him. And now that he was committed to meeting Thea at Edith's, he had to be damn sure that no one followed him there. But how would he know for sure that he had lost him when he wasn't even sure he was there at all? No, if one tenth of what Register had told him about Chelak was true, he would have to assume that he was there. Hadn't the man already killed to insure that Steddy survived until he led him to Rockford? The only possible edge that Steddy had was that Chelak probably didn't know that Steddy knew he was following him. Maybe somehow he could take advantage of that and make it work in his favor. . . .

Enough! He wasn't going to think about it now. If he was out there, then he already knew where Steddy was staying. No, there was nothing he could do now, and Kirsten was leaving in the morning—there would be time enough then.

He replaced the receiver, stepped from the shade of the booth into the sun, and walked to the car, where a smiling Kirsten awaited him.

They could see the GIs and the girls were still on the beach as they passed on the way to the camp, where they parked and unloaded the provisions. Kirsten took the salad things she had bought with her when they crossed the road, and when Steddy lay down on the blanket next to his sleeping friends, she continued on to the shore to wash them in the ocean.

He crossed his arms under his head and closed his eyes. The heat, held by the sand, penetrated the blanket and his shirt and eased the pain in the muscles of his back. Dozing, he wondered whether Chelak ever slept. Could he slip away in the middle of the night, or did the Israeli keep a constant vigil? He must surely have a car, but would he use it if Steddy left in the black of night on foot, and give away his presence, or would he abandon it and take to the road after him? How can I guess what this man will do? he thought. He was getting a headache from trying to figure out how to lose a man who might not be there, how to solve the problem without the main piece of the puzzle. Bill woke up and mercifully broke his muddled train of thought.

"So you're back. Have any trouble with the car?"

"Not a bit."

Then, looking around and seeing that Kirsten was by the sea: "Get hold of your girl?"

"Who?" Steddy looked puzzled. Surely he hadn't drunkenly told them about Thea?

"The stew in London." And when Steddy didn't spark: "The one you met on the plane on the way over."

"Oh, sure. She's expecting me tomorrow night."

"That's perfect 'cause we've got to leave tomorrow, too. We can all drive to the airport together and turn in the car."

"That'd be great," Steddy said, realizing that this was just one more problem, as he had no intention of going back to Aberdeen and didn't know how he would explain it to them. Changing the subject, he said, "We got one hell of a steak for dinner, and Kirsten's washing the salad. I hope you guys can really deliver the grill, or we'll be shit out of luck."

"Hey, don't worry about a thing. But maybe we should get started setting it up. C'mon, Tom, we've got work to do."

Steddy went with them to keep his mind occupied and his thoughts from dwelling on Chelak. Tom found an old refrigerator rack that someone had abandoned, and with the two cinder blocks left from levelling a departed camper, that Bill had already put aside, they had a fairly professional grill.

They busied themselves gathering wood while the girls helped Kirsten invent a dressing from their shared belongings and mix the salad in an enormous plastic garbage bag.

Steddy got a kick out of the way they behaved when they saw the size of the porterhouse steak; they were like kids ogling their first banana split.

"Geez, it's the biggest, fattest damn T-Bone I've ever seen anywhere!" Tom said, with the others chorusing his opinion.

"Well, we are in the home of the Aberdeen Angus,

you know, and apart from being the granddaddy of our herds out West, it's considered by some to be the finest beef in the world.''

As the steak cooked over the driftwood fire, Steddy borrowed Bill's army knife and drew the corks from the eight bottles of Margaux he'd bought in town. Nothing's too good for these chaps, he thought, as he started to hand them out one to a customer, when Bill stopped him and said, "Hey, let's save that for the steak. This is our last night together, and I think it only fitting that we share a dram from the country that brought us together, as an aperitif, before so fine a dinner as our host has provided.''

Everyone agreed.

Bill could be quite eloquent when he wanted to.

With that a bottle of malt whiskey appeared from Bill's bottomless duffel of booze, and after he had poured a drop in the sand, "for those who passed before," it was duly handed from mouth to mouth, and even though Steddy was busy turning the steak and rolling the potatoes on the grill to keep them from burning, he was not allowed to miss his turn.

As if measured by a master, the bottle of whiskey was finished precisely as the steak was taken from the fire. It was carved with a commando gravity knife, honed razor-sharp, and consumed from a rainbow of plastic plates. It was unquestionably the finest steak any of them could recall ever having eaten. Steddy toasted Kirsten and her crew in English on the delicacy of her salad, and Kirsten kissed him and toasted him back in Finnish. There seemed to be no language barrier; they all chatted away in their native tongues with the presumption that what they said was understood, and somehow it was.

As the light faded from the sky, the debris of bone and bottle disappeared into the pit that Bill's men had dug and was covered over with sand. Kirsten and the girls had gone off to clean the plates and now returned with the bottle of aquavit they had offered the night before. This time no one turned it down, and as they settled in around the fire, she found a place in the crook of Steddy's arm and he toasted her again for contributing the aquavit, "in lieu of port."

"That was one hell of a dinner," Bill said, passing the aquavit to Steddy.

"Best I can remember in a long time," Steddy agreed.

Though the ladies didn't retire, the fact that not one of them spoke English had the same effect, and as is customary with gentlemen the world over after a fine dinner with fine drink, the conversation quickly deteriorated to the telling of the filthiest jokes they knew. They howled and hooted with laughter until tears rolled down their cheeks, and the girls were caught up in the hypophrenia—even people from nearby camps drifted by to see what was going on, but the circle of comrades was to remain unbroken that night. There was a fraternity about them that precluded interruption.

The wave of hysteria subsided into silence, as so often happens. Some of the men and girls had already drifted off to their tents, and in the blaze of the moon and stars, Steddy could clearly see that the few who remained were dozing. Kirsten stirred on his shoulder and whispered in his ear what he took to mean that she was going to prepare for bed. He held up the last of the aquavit to say that he would be along in a minute, and when she left, all but Bill followed her. Steddy took a swig from the bottle and laid his head back on the duffel, staring at the extraordinary show in the heavens, when Bill surprised him by reaching over and taking the bottle from his hand—he had thought he was asleep. Bill drank deeply and then spoke very softly.

"Who are you really, Wiley?"

The question didn't startle Steddy. He had even forgotten that they knew him as Wiley. He was totally relaxed and at peace for the first time in weeks, and he was tired of lying. He was tired of the whole thing and felt that to lie any further to these men he had grown so close to in so short a time would break the bond of their newfound friendship and the ancient trust of the camp fire. These things were important and took precedence.

He didn't hesitate.

"My name is Stedman Wright. What gave me away?"

"Oh, a lot of different things. Is it serious—the trouble you're in?" he asked matter-of-factly, still gazing up at the stars.

"It's the worst trouble I've ever been in."

"Would it help to talk about it?"

"It would if I could, but I can't really. Even though I've accidently become the lead character in this show, it isn't my secret to tell. Plus it's not anything I'd want to hang around your neck."

"Are the cops after you?"

"I guess I can tell you some of it, the part that's in the newspapers anyway. You'd have read it yourself if you hadn't been on top of a mountain."

Steddy told Bill how it had all begun, how he'd been framed and how he was being pursued by the police and others.

Bill's face registered belief and genuine concern.

"Why don't you just turn yourself in at the embassy in London?"

"There's more to it than that. A friend of mine's been in touch with them—that's who I went into town to call— and they want me to play along with it, continue like this. I can't say any more about that, and you wouldn't want to know, but you see, they know I'm innocent, but they've asked me to be a sort of Judas goat and stick with it."

"Are you going to?"

"I haven't decided. I told them I'd let them know— you see, there's a girl involved, and I don't want her exposed to anything like what happened in Aberdeen."

"You mean you hadn't just arrived there when we ran into you?"

"No, I was getting the hell out—you guys were a godsend."

Steddy then told him about the murder in the alley of the whorehouse and—without identifying Chelak—about the man who had saved him and was, even now, pursuing him.

"So that's how you got beaten up; I knew that didn't happen in a fall the minute I saw the bruises. That was one of the things that tipped me off."

"Well, anyway, that's where I'm at now."

"Do you think you'll go along with the people at the embassy?"

"All I know is that I'm not going to make up my mind until I lose this guy and see Thea—that's my girl."

"Is she in on this, too?"

"I'm afraid she is by association, whether I like it or not, and I'm not going to decide anything until I'm sure she's safe. I'm supposed to meet her in a few days, but I can't with this guy on my tail—if in fact he is, but I've got to assume that he is. I don't have any other choice."

"Maybe we can help you with that."

"Hell, you don't need this, and anyway I think it would be better just now if the other guys didn't know. Not that I don't trust them, but with a thing like this, more is definitely not better."

"They won't have to know. I'll give them some story. Don't worry, they'll go along with me."

Steddy knew that what he said was the truth. In spite of his calm, quiet ways, Bill was a born leader.

"If there was only some way we could draw him off with the car and leave you behind. That way, by the time we got to the airport in Aberdeen and he realized that you weren't with us, you could be well away from here. You could even keep my driver's license if it would help; I could just report it lost when I got back and—"

"Shit, I'm sorry, I forgot to give it back to you," Steddy interrupted, reaching into his trouser pocket.

"No sweat."

"I hope you don't think—"

Bill cut Steddy off.

"Fuck that. Let's try to think of a way we can make this work."

They lay back again, as if the stars held the solution. And perhaps they did; after a while Steddy said, "A friend of mine once told me a story about being alone with an old native guide out in the bush in Kenya. They—"

"Is this just a story, or something to do with our problem?"

Steddy couldn't help but like the way he had said "*our* problem."

"No, no, it could be the answer," he replied.

"So what happened?"

"Well, the guide spotted a swarm of tsetse flies coming their way. Peter—that's my friend—said he thought it was just a dark cloud, until he realized how fast it was moving. Evidently, when there are that many of them swarming, the bites will kill you, so they buried themselves in the mud of a river bank and used a hollow reed to breathe through."

Steddy finished and waited for Bill's reaction.

"How does it apply?"

"Well, maybe I could bury myself until you've drawn him off with the car. See what I mean?"

"Yeah, you could use one of those big reeds we've been lighting the fire with."

"That's what made me think of it, but how could we pull it off and be sure that he hadn't seen us do it? I've got to be sure that he falls for it; otherwise I'll never know if he's behind me or not."

"I'll tell you what we could do," Bill said after a while, leaning forward on his elbows. "We could dig a shallow trench inside the tent and bury you in it just before we took it down. If we changed clothes, what with all the confusion of breaking camp and loading the car, well, if he is watching, he won't be close enough to tell whether it's you or me, and he won't be counting us because he won't expect one of us to disappear into thin air."

"That's perfect, but we'd have to play it out until the very last minute—we'd have to dig the hole way ahead of time so I could make a lot of trips out to the car and really make sure he knew what I was wearing, and then you'd have to become a quick-change artist so he doesn't notice anything fishy."

"I think we could pull it off," Bill said. "But are you sure you can take it that long—being buried for fifteen or twenty minutes? You don't get claustrophobic, do you?"

"Do I have any choice?"

Kirsten's tent smelled of musk and verbena from the scented oil that burned in the lantern on the ground by her mat. She was lying on her side, reading. Her white-blonde hair spilled from between her fingers and fell to the pages of the book like a fountain. The primitive light washed her sun-oiled breast with the golden glow of a Gauguin nude; only the brilliant blue of her eyes interrupted the sensually muted monochromes of the tent's interior.

When he unzipped the tent flap, she seemed startled by the intrusion and hurriedly covered her nakedness. Perhaps she was blinded by the light and couldn't see that it was he beyond the lantern, or perhaps she could see something in his eyes that frightened her, something that even he was unaware of. Whatever it was, seeing the fear in her eyes triggered a primal reflex and unleashed a demon within him from its bonds of civilized behavior. Probably the weeks of tension made him vulnerable to suggestion and no doubt the strong drink by the open camp fire had inflamed him, but standing there, towering over her trembling body, evoked a fantasy that invaded and captured his weakened ego. She was his captive Viking queen and he, her lord and master, a Norse berserker bruised from battle, returning for his prize.

He took her brutally as if by right. She fought him with a strength that approached his but could not equal it. She tore at him fiercely until that, too, became part of what he was taking from her and was all that she could withhold from him, but she realized it too late, and it was over as quickly as it had begun, leaving him spent and unconscious at her side, so that she could barely believe what had passed.

They parted the next morning after breakfast. Steddy still couldn't deal with or fully remember what had happened. He had never employed fantasies to summon passion, so he was unprepared for the force, so alien to his nature, that had overcome him the night before when he had pulled back the flap of Kirsten's tent. He had awakened in the middle of the night with a terrible thirst, to hear her sobbing softly beside him, and only then had a sense of what he had done come back to him. He had no common language to tell her how sorry and ashamed he was, and she had rejected the hand he laid on her head. Only when his own tears of genuine grief and frustration fell on her shoulder had she warmed to him, and they had clung to each other in the dark, like children who had carried a joke too far, and cried themselves to sleep.

Now they walked arm in arm along the edge of the sea to get away from the others and say their wordless good-bye. They had shared laughter and tears and a tender, healing passion without ever conversing, yet he knew that she was committed to someone, be it husband or lover, and he was equally sure that she knew he wasn't free. They were like former lovers who meet after ten years and pick up where they left off, knowing full well that they will have to part in the end until chance throws them together again. What they had shared was their sacred secret that demanded no reaffirmation. They didn't even know each other's names or addresses, but oddly, even that re-enforced their unspoken bond.

They returned to the road and the car, where her friends were waiting. Steddy handed her into the back seat of the little red Volvo, piled high with equipment, and kissed her tenderly through the window. As it drove away, he stared unblinkingly after it until the ice blue of her eyes vanished against the morning sky and his teared from the wind.

32

It was barely seven in the evening when they called down to room service and ordered supper. Neither Wiley nor Thea had eaten or slept very much in the last twenty-four hours, and they were both tired and hungry.

Thea went through and took a bath the moment she had finished ordering and returned just as the food was being wheeled in, wearing the top of a pair of her father's pajamas that hung down to her knees. They ate in silence with the television news on in the background, each absorbed by his own thoughts, grateful not to have to converse. Wiley was trying to digest everything he had learned at the briefing, a lot of which Thea wasn't privy to, while Thea planned her escape to Scotland and debated what she would say in a note to Wiley so his feelings wouldn't be hurt for not being included. She didn't like not telling Wiley, but she knew he was under strict orders not to let her out of his sight, and Steddy had been very clear that she wasn't to let anyone know where she was going.

After dinner they watched television for a while, each silently guarding his own secrets, until Thea said she was going to turn in.

"Me, too. I'm exhausted. Have you got an extra pillow and a blanket?" Wiley asked.

Thea went into the bedroom and returned with the

bottom half of the pajamas she had on, and tossed them over to him.

"Here, put these on and come to bed inside. It's a big bed, and we're both adults."

Wiley protested and said that the couch would be fine, but Thea pointed at the spindly wood-framed sofa and said, "Don't be silly, Wiley, that thing's too small for you. You wouldn't get a minute's sleep."

He acquiesced when she made him feel silly not to and went into the bathroom to shower. He had had a brandy after dinner, and after the shower, he felt relaxed and refreshed. When he opened the door to the bedroom, the lights were out and Thea was already asleep. He left the door open a crack to leave him enough light to negotiate his way to the far side of the bed. He got in gingerly not to disturb her and occupied the extreme edge of the bed so as not to disturb himself, for being in bed with Thea, enveloped by the sensual yet woodsy aroma of her perfume, he found was very disturbing.

He lay there for what seemed hours, hands clasped behind his head, waiting for sleep to rescue him from his wildly wandering imagination. "Yes," he thought grimly, "we *are* both adults."

Thea moved into him like a gentle breeze on a sultry, calm night. Her head nuzzled against his chest, and her long silky hair fell over his belly like a mist. He was sure that she was still sleeping and was afraid to breathe lest she awaken and spoil his fantasy. The silence gradually became oppressive. His arm, as if acting of its own will, reached round and held her to him. Eventually she stirred and raised her enormous eyes, which seemed coal-black in the light that seeped from the bathroom door. He arched over her and kissed her with a soul-borne passion that he hadn't thought he was capable of, and at that moment, in a lightning flash of realization, he knew that he had loved her since the day he had first seen her with Steddy outside the club in Paris. In the same split second, he knew that the kiss she returned was a sister's kiss, devoid of the passion that surged through him. His hopes had been trampled in the same instant they had bloomed. Thea reached up, took his head between her hands, and kissed him tenderly on the forehead. As she turned on her side, away from him, she said, "Good night, Wiley. See you in the morning."

Wiley lay there for a while with every cell in his body feeling like an individual hand reaching out across the bed to the source of the warmth beside him. He waited like that until he was sure she was asleep and then crept into the sitting room to pour himself a very stiff drink and settle down for the night on the uncomfortable, but welcome, sofa.

33

"The grave," as Bill insisted on calling it, had been dug, and although it was considerably shallower than the real thing, it still gave Steddy the willies when Bill and Tom and the others joked about it. Steddy had no idea what Bill had told them, but whatever it was, they seemed satisfied and went about their work, digging, etc., as though they were participating in just another college prank.

Steddy and Bill drove into Stonehaven right after Kirsten left, to book Bill's and his pal's airline reservations back to Frankfurt. They had decided the night before by the camp fire that the best time to make the switch was at dusk when visibility was the poorest. When it turned out that the last connecting flight was at four in the afternoon, Steddy insisted on paying the hotel bill for the night they would have to spend in Aberdeen.

They brought some cold cuts and beer back to the camp and spent the rest of the day lolling about on the beach until, at about five in the afternoon, great thunderheads drew up on the distant horizon like warships forming a line of battle.

Steddy pulled the car up near the side of the tent, ostensibly to facilitate the loading, but really so that their comings and goings would be at least partially sheltered from the view afforded by the high, craggy hills that surrounded the cove where they were camped.

At about eight o'clock, the car was loaded, and all that remained to be done was to strike the tent. Due to the threatening clouds, an especially dark dusk had fallen early for that time of year. They said their good-byes, and while Bill got undressed, Steddy took one last load to the car for the benefit of anyone who might be watching. The second he got back inside the tent, he tore his clothes off, tossing each article at Bill as he removed it, then he put on the things he had bought in Stonehaven and wrapped himself up well in the rubberized poncho, tying the hood securely around his face. He said good-bye to Bill once again—Tom and the others were already outside pulling up the tent staves—and then lay down like a mummy in the shallow trench. Bill tucked the poncho tightly around him and then covered him with a plastic ground sheet. He started methodically covering Steddy with sand at the feet, smoothing it as he went along, until he reached his neck.

"Well, so long, fella. You be careful, ya hear?"

"If I make it through this, I can make it through anything," Steddy said, beginning to have second thoughts. And then more cheerfully: "Now don't forget to call the number I gave you when you get stateside and leave an address so I can reach you."

"Will do. This is one story I want to hear the end of—and from the horse's mouth, not on television!"

With that, Bill placed the bottoms of the three large reeds they had tested into Steddy's mouth and covered the remaining exposed part of his face with his handkerchief. When he had finished tamping the sand around Steddy's head and smoothed the residual over the whole area, it was impossible to tell that anyone was buried there.

As Bill finished, the sides of the tent started collapsing in on him, and he called out to Steddy, "Wiggle the reeds if you can breathe all right."

They jerked reassuringly.

"Well, *adiós, amigo. Hasta la vista.*"

With that, he and Tom pulled out the two remaining collapsible tent poles and loaded them into the car.

They left quickly, so that even in the shadows of the gathering clouds, they would not be long observed.

Time did not fly swiftly withal for Steddy. From the very beginning of his interment, his jaw began to ache from grasping the reeds, and soon it was all he could do to fight the onslaught of claustrophobia. Under the circumstances, it was difficult to maintain even shallow breathing, when the capacity of the reeds was so small, and he had to continually battle the little gremlin of panic in his head that kept telling him to sit up and breathe before he suffocated.

He tried to follow Bill's advice and count out the minutes in military fashion—one one-hundred, two one-hundred, etc.—but kept losing his place when panic over-rode logic, even for a second. It seemed like days since he'd heard the car's motor start and the noise that the bite of its tires transmitted through the sand. He tried to sing in his mind to have some handle of the time that was passing, but he couldn't think of a song to save his life. He reasoned with himself that all he had to do was sit up if things got really bad and he'd be able to breathe, but he knew in his heart that that was not truly an alternative, not now that Thea was already on her way to meet him. He couldn't put her in harm's way by leading Chelak to her. . . . Thea—how long ago it seemed since they had been together. Would what he'd had with her seem frivolous after what he'd been through—after what he'd been through with Kirsten? Kirsten, to whom he'd never said a word. It was all so confusing. Could he really love anyone, or was he a . . .

All of a sudden, he became aware of a sort of intermittent sound, nothing he could put his finger on, but it seemed to be growing louder and more regular. It might be a car driving toward him, or worse, over him. He was ready to use any excuse to break from his confinement, and this seemed like a good one, when a great roar of thunder made him realize that it was rain he was hearing. The handkerchief that covered his face became damp and confirmed it.

Water seeped into the hood of his poncho, into his ears, and trickled down his nose, making him want to sneeze. He began to panic again—it felt as if he were drowning. He counted to twenty-five, promising himself that that would be long enough, then, when he reached it, he started over again, counting as quickly as he could and then going on to fifty and starting again. The noise of the storm was now very loud, and in a flash of black humor he thought how lucky he was to have his poncho on, when suddenly he felt a pressure on his feet. It increased and then changed position to his knees. Someone was walking on top of him.

It couldn't be one of the campers out for a stroll in the storm that raged above him, and anyone just arriving would wait in his car until it had passed.

The weight was now firmly planted on the middle of his chest, making his breathing that much more difficult. He was terrified that whoever it was would feel the rise and fall of his lungs under his feet. The reeds rammed violently into his cheek—he could taste blood in his mouth—then, as if it had never been there, the weight was gone.

34

As the brown Bentley barreled north at a steady seventy miles per hour, Thea relaxed and enjoyed the first real peace and tranquillity she had had in a very long time. It was her father's car, and as he wouldn't have radios or tape decks in his automobiles, she was forced to ride alone with her thoughts and had consciously decided to make good use of the opportunity.

She left the hotel at about four in the morning, wearing a big greatcoat of her father's with one of his old snap-brim Lock hats pulled down over her face. She took a circuitous route from the Dorchester, using taxi, underground, and foot, until, sure that she hadn't been followed, she circled back to the enormous underground garage that lay beneath Hyde Park, opposite the hotel. Taking the old Bentley Continental had not been a problem—all she needed were the keys and they were in her pocket—but finding the car among the thousands of others when she didn't know where to look had been another story and had taken the better part of an hour to accomplish.

After more roundabout driving in the empty early-dawn streets, she decided that she had not been observed, and totally contrary to Steddy's instructions, worked the car up to the Edgeware Road and finally onto the A1, where she pointed the flying *B* on the bonnet northward—to Steddy and to Scotland.

* * *

She tried to think when she had last been a free agent; the answer didn't come to her right away, and it suddenly seemed important to remember. Directing the powerful motor to take her wherever she willed re-awakened dim memories of freedom, and she needed to know where along the way that freedom had been lost.

She was sixteen when her parents divorced and had gone to live with her mother and Nubar in London, where they put her into the last real finishing school to survive a bygone era. It was a far cry from Foxcroft, the Eastern Establishment boarding school where her life had been ruled by the bugle and revolved around military drill and horsemanship, but the discipline she learned there saw her through, and she survived the starchy post-war English food and cold baths without a whimper. When she learned that she was to be presented at Court and make her bow to the Queen, that was the last straw. She flatly refused. Not yet eighteen and still a tomboy, she didn't want to make her bow to a society that she neither understood nor wanted to be a part of. There had been fits and fights until Nubar and Elizabeth finally got their way.

Elizabeth tried to get her into the swing of it and took her to Balenciaga in Paris, where she bought her almost the entire collection—minus the wedding dress—although she would have liked to have had a reason to order it as well. That was when Thea first began to realize that she wasn't all that unattractive.

Cristobal Balenciaga personally asked her to model his clothes at a charity fashion gala at Versailles. That launched her. She had always compared herself to the fragile, petite beauty of her mother and found herself wanting. Her five-foot-eleven frame she thought skinny and maladroit; her long, liquid, dark chestnut hair, formless; her eyebrows, too thick; and her size nine-and-a-half feet, out of the question; but she had been critically analyzing the parts individually without ever seeing the whole. Balenciaga and Alexandre the hairdresser had no such prejudice.

She stopped the show and stole it. For the rest of their stay, she was lionized by Parisian society and the press;

paparazzi waited outside both entrances of the Ritz to record her comings and goings, and just when she thought she had escaped them, invariably a restaurant owner or shopkeeper would telephone her whereabouts so that they were waiting for her when she left.

Eileen Ford, the head of the model agency, saw her picture on some contact sheets that a photographer from French *Vogue* showed her in New York and cabled London to offer her a job if she ever wanted to work as a model in New York. The timing was propitious. The cable arrived during another tearful session with Nubar and her mother, who wanted her to make her New York debut in the fall. She decided to go along with them, just to get there so that she could accept the Ford proposal to stay on and work. It was the first totally independent thing she had ever done, and now, as she sped north on the A1, she wondered if it hadn't been the last.

New York was fun then. She soon had her own apartment for the first time in her life and decorated it herself with things that *she* liked. She worked very hard at modeling, which she thought basically mindless, but she did enjoy the trips all over the world that went with it and the novel feeling that she was master of her own fate.

It was that wonderful moment in life when it seems that the piper will never have to be paid. She had a date every night and could easily be in El Morocco or Le Club until four in the morning without showing or feeling the slightest fatigue at an eight AM sitting the following day. The photographers and editors loved her. She was an original, always at ease and full of humor, as though unaware of her striking beauty and the effect it had on them. She quickly learned what they wanted, though, and was able to step into different roles and attitudes as if play acting in the nursery. It was a game to her. She was having fun, enjoying the attention, and it was just that buoyancy, which she was able to project through the lens and into print, that made her so in demand.

Most of the men she went out with were either clubmen she knew through the family, who came from the same mold, or fags that she met at work, so when she met Phillip

Wilmette, the acerbic New York theater critic, she found herself swept into a different world, his world, where she felt she was learning something and growing every day. She was accepted into his circle as a celebrity in her own right and was politely allowed occasionally to contribute to the incestuous conversation of the writers, actors, and journalists. Eventually she moved in with him.

She gave up modeling, spent more time at home, and soon after found out that he was temperamental and boorish. He slowly weaned her off her friends to the point where she saw very few of them, and then only for lunch. It was two years before she realized that she had become little more than a servant and left him.

In the ensuing years, she had lived with other men, but as she sped through the green English countryside, she realized that she had always melted into their lives, adopted their friends, their likes and dislikes, as though she had no personality of her own. She was never aware that her beauty and her social standing imbued anyone in her company with a presence and prestige that made her a highly desirable addition to any man's collection. Ambitious men fell in love with *their* idea of her as an object, their projection of her, rather than ever seeking her individuality.

Steddy had made no such demands on her. He was socially at ease wherever he went and seemed to like to be with her because he truly enjoyed her company. He was a man of her own class, and at the same time a bit of a bounder. She liked that quality in him; he wouldn't allow himself to become blasé and seemed to *try* to stay on the edge of propriety. She adored him, she adored his sense of humor and everything else about him, but was she really in love with him? It had all been so easy. They were happy doing the same things and seeing the same people—their affair had been like a vacation for both of them, at least until all the recent trouble. But would what they had together survive the dailiness of marriage?

He had mentioned marriage, and even though he'd been drunk, it had started her thinking seriously about it for the first time. No, she answered herself, dailiness could never become a real part of Steddy's life. She couldn't even imagine it. But didn't that, in and of itself, realistically eliminate the possibility of any kind of a basis for marriage, and was marriage what she really wanted anyway?

She felt that she needed Steddy desperately, but was it him that she needed or just someone, or was she being overly cautious for the first time in her life, when she didn't have to be? And then, she thought, if she was truly in love with Steddy, why had she led Wiley on last night? She admitted to herself that she had done it on purpose, knowing that he was in love with her—not a very kind thing to do if she had no feelings for him. Of course, he is cute and very handsome; I just wanted to see if there was any emotion lurking behind that sternly loyal, best-friend mask, she rationalized.

Well, one thing was sure. Right now, Steddy needed her, and that would have to be enough for the time being. She would play out the hand.

35

Finally it was fear that calmed Steddy. Not the illogical, panicked fear of claustrophobia, but the very real terror that the murderous Chelak might have been standing on top of him only moments before.

If he was in fact there, could he possibly have noticed Steddy's absence from the passengers crowded into the departing automobile? In an attempt to focus his thoughts, Steddy tried to analyze the chances in a rational way. It worked for a time, but the crazed monkey in his mind kept surfacing, telling him that he was an ostrich with his head buried in the sand. All the while, the rain had washed away the rest of his covering, leaving him lying there, exposed for all who passed to see. He continued to do battle with his own wits until he could stand it no longer. Then, his decision to get up made, he counted to one hundred as Bill had taught him, with deliberate, torturous slowness.

At one hundred, he sat up as quickly as the encumbrances of sand and poncho would allow. The reeds fell from his mouth before he could get his arms up and took a bit more of the tender inside of it with them. It was still raining hard, and the force of it peeled the sand-weighted handkerchief from his face. All was blackness. Even the muted glow from the three or four remaining tents was perceived as though through ten fathoms of water. His eyes didn't need to adjust to the dark, but the landscape was more somber than the brilliant flashes of color that fear had been projecting on the wall of his entombed mind.

A car approached, surreally silent along the meandering course of the shore road, its motor stilled by the rain's pelting wall of noise. A strobe flash of its headlights as it rounded a bend showed him that his legs were still buried and had not been exposed by the force of the water. He stood and retrieved his duffel from where it had lain under his feet. The rain seemed to be coming from all directions like a six-nozzle shower, and breathing was almost as difficult as it had been through the reeds. But the weight was lifted from his mind, and he stood rejoicing, holding his arms heavenward as though beseeching the deity, while the water washed the caked-on sand from the slick surface of his poncho. He raised the duffel to his shoulder, hobbled through the darkness and sand to the road, and set out down it to the south with nothing but the occasional faint glow from the well worn dividing line to guide him.

Although his entombment had seemed like hours, he was sure he would discover that the real time elapsed was only ten or fifteen minutes. But when he looked at the glowing red read-out of his watch, he was well pleased to learn that he had been down forty-five minutes and had actually exceeded the limit he had set by a good margin for safety—he hoped!

Only one vehicle passed him in the hour and a half that it took him to reach Stonehaven. After he had flattened himself against a rocky outcropping where the road had been cut from the side of the hill, it turned out to be nothing more than an ancient flatbed truck.

It was ten-thirty when he began the descent to the brightly lighted cove. The rain had abated, and the moon began to glimmer through the shredding wisps of cloud. He waited at the edge of town until the loud, boozy voices of the last people to leave the pub had ceased to echo in the empty, wet streets. His shoes had not been designed with the idea of being buried and exhumed, and their squeals of rebellion were magnified by the silence of the buildings whose shadows absorbed Steddy's own as he made his way along the quay.

The red telephone kiosk was ahead of him. It made him think of Edith, and he realized that at that very moment Karesin was waiting for him outside the pub in Scone. Steddy was afraid to call her. The kiosk was as bright as a beacon, and his whole plan depended on getting through Stonehaven unnoticed. Stonehaven would be the first place Chelak would check when he realized that Steddy wasn't in the car when it got to Aberdeen, and he didn't want him picking up his trail so easily, if he could help it.

On the other hand, if he didn't call Edith, she'd get worried, and then there was no telling what she might do, including the very real possibility of alerting the whole country as to where he was heading.

Steddy entered the booth, uncradled the receiver, and waited for the operator to come on the line. While he gave her the number, he used his cap to unscrew the bulb above him. Edith answered the phone on the first ring.

"Aunt Edith, it's me."

"Haven't you found Karesin? I've been waiting up for you."

"No, I'm afraid I haven't made it that far yet."

"Well, how long will you be? He won't wait all night, you know."

"I'm still fifty or sixty miles away. I can't possibly make it before tomorrow."

"Well, how long will it take you to drive here?"

"I don't have a car."

"Then how are you planning to get here?"

"It seems that I'll have to make it on foot."

"That's perfectly ridiculous—it will take you weeks!"

"I can't risk renting a car."

"Well, then, stay put and I'll send Karesin to fetch you in the morning."

"It won't do, Edith. I've got to be out of this neighborhood before morning and—"

"Well, then, we'll fix a place for tomorrow where you can meet. Where shall it be?"

Steddy wanted to avoid drawing any attention to himself, but the prospect of a sixty-mile hike in wet clothes was becoming less and less appealing, and it was also true that the sooner he got off the road, the less exposure he'd have.

"Are you still there?"

"Yes, Edith, I just have to get a map out. Hang on."

He pulled the car-rental map out from under his poncho, and with trepidation, tightened the light bulb in order to see. He was momentarily blinded and felt as though he were on display in a department store window.

"There's a town on the A94 called Brechin. Looks about twenty miles from here, which would put it about forty miles from you. I could make it there by about four in the afternoon."

"All right, let me get a pencil. All right now, what's it called, Blechin?"

"No, it's Brechin, *B-r-e-c-h-i-n!*"

"All right, Steddy, see you tomorrow."

"But wait, Edith—"

"Yes?"

"How will we find each other? I don't know the town."

"Well, it can't be very big as I've never heard of it. I'll just tell him to park in the town center; that's always marked. You won't miss him."

"Well, then, you'd better tell him that I'll signal him somehow to follow me until we get someplace where there aren't too many people."

"All right, Steddy, now *good night* . . . and be sure you're there on time; Karesin will have been waiting for you half the night in Scone and won't be very happy about it. You really should have called earlier; you know, he's not as young as he once was."

As he left the booth, Steddy could picture her perfectly, sitting up in that enormous bed of hers under a satin coverlet with her hair wrapped up in a turban and a book or tray across her knees. He knew there would have been little point in explaining that he would have called but he'd been buried under a foot of wet sand at the time.

Spotting Karesin was easy. He was leaning against one of the big P-100 headlights of the forest-green Rolls, wearing a beat-up pair of tweed plus fours and a khaki shirt, open at the neck. His white hair glistened in the sun as if competing with the brilliant shine of the Rolls's metal and body work. The car was a custom-made long-bodied tourer that would have turned heads in Berkeley Square; in Brechin, it dominated the center of town and might as well have landed from outer space for all the curiosity it generated.

Steddy elbowed his way through the admiring throng of children and automobile buffs until he caught Karesin's alert and twinkling eye and by cocking his head, indicated the direction of the road that led down the steep hill out of town.

The big car lumbered past him on a curve and then sped down the open road until it disappeared round a bend. They had their reunion just beyond, where there was a lay-by near a copse wood. Karesin was pretending to tinker with the motor when Steddy came abreast of him.

"Couldn't you find anything bigger in the garage?" Steddy greeted him.

"Coulda done, but I though this'un would do for you," Karesin was quick to reply.

"Guess you didn't think you'd see me again so soon." (Steddy had seen a lot of Karesin, when he'd been up with Thea.)

"Tell you true, I did nae think on it at all," he said, all the while his eyes smiling. "And I'll thank you to keep your appointments in future. I had to drink in the pub till after closing last night." The smile round his eyes crept down to the corners of his mouth.

"That must have been a real hardship for you," Steddy replied, laughing.

Karesin looked him up and down, taking in his sunburned, unshaven face, mussed hair, and general dishevelment.

"You're a fair sight. What have you been up to then?"

"Got cold cocked in an Aberdeen whorehouse, haven't had a bath in four days, and just walked almost thirty miles in wet clothes," Steddy said, not expecting sympathy from his old friend and not getting any.

"Do you good—want a bit of toughening up, you do."

Then, with a degree of concern: "Hop in the back and lie down flat before somebody comes along."

"Did Thea arrive yet?" Steddy asked before getting in.

"Not before I left. Why, was she supposed to?"

"Yes, but I don't know when."

Steddy climbed into the Rolls's womblike passenger compartment. The smell of all those matched hides and rosewood was as reassuring as a first-class ticket home, and the carpet, as thick as Devonshire cream, was the softest thing he'd lain upon since leaving Claridge's. He opened the bar and took a swig of whiskey from one of the cut-crystal decanters. Karesin heard the click of the cabinet.

"Now don't you be drinkin' up all milady's whiskey. Here, take this. Cook sent it to you special," he said, passing a large basket over the divider. "But don't eat and drink it all up, 'cause you'll have to stay in the car until after ten when everyone's gone to bed, and there'll be no more when that's done. And mind you don't make a mess back there; I just got through sweeping it out."

The hamper Karesin gave Steddy looked like something out of "Little Red Riding Hood." It was wicker, and inside it, wrapped in a red and white checked table cloth, were three big sandwiches—one of beef, one of ham, and one of cheese—all on thick-cut homemade oatmeal bread and slathered with butter from the dairy, accompanied by two pints of beer, an orange, and his favorite chocolate cake. He offered Karesin a sandwich and a beer, but he said he'd already eaten, so Steddy, who was famished, combined the ham and the cheese and wolfed it down, interspersed with shots of whiskey from Edith's decanter, with beer as a chaser.

The alcohol and a full belly soon had their effect, and with the sun's warmth through the big plate-glass windows, the comfort of the carpet under him, and the gentle sway of the three-ton vehicle, he was sound asleep before they had gone ten miles.

A strong beam of light awakened Steddy from a dreamless sleep that had evolved into a torpor. He had no idea where he was at first, but then the smell of the car and

Karesin's less than dulcet but familiar voice emanating from a point in the blackness behind the flashlight dispelled his initial fright.

"Come on, get out of there, sleeping beauty," Karesin intoned in a hoarse drill-sergeant version of a stage whisper.

"Where are we, Karesin?"

"I'm at Castle Lynde, but I think you're still at the feather ball. Now wake up and get out of there—and keep your trap shut so we don't wake anyone up."

Steddy followed the puddle of light in a trance, still punchy with sleep. He could sense rather than see the cavernous dimensions of the carriage house that had been his favorite place to play when visiting as a boy. They made their way past ghostly silhouettes of tarpaulin-covered motorcars, some so tall that a big man could get into the back wearing a top hat without stooping. These represented a history of the Lynde family's love affair with the automobile since its inception.

Steddy would have tripped on the crosspiece of the small door that was cut out of the garage's big double doors if Karesin hadn't caught him. He heard a muffled oath, and then the light was extinguished. They were out in the chill Scottish night with just enough light from the moon to guide them. The gravel of the drive gave way to a narrow stone path that cut through some hedges and then down three steps into what Steddy recognized as the kitchen and cut-flower garden at the back of the house. Suddenly they were in darkness again; he looked up to see the crenellated tower of the original castle's keep blocking the moon. Karesin held his arm and guided him up the broad balustered stone stair that led to the south terrace. They crossed it and went through an open French door into the vast paneled library, part of the Georgian wing added in the eighteenth century. The flashlight was on again, and its beam pierced the stately gloom as Steddy followed it through an endless number of sitting rooms and picture galleries. He was beginning to think they were going in circles, crazily passing through the same rooms like a dream sequence from a Fellini movie, when they crossed a broad stone saddle and entered the heart of the house—the great hall, part of the original fifteenth-century structure.

Steddy had his bearings now; the great hall was the main entrance of the house. They had come in from the most distant point at the back, working their way through generations of additions that the centuries had piled up against the ancient tower as memorials to the changing life-styles of the preceding earls and barons. The hall's lantern, the size of a small elevator cab, was extinguished for the night, and in the dimness of the sidelights, the epic staircase elled up to the first landing and slowly vanished above them like an invitation to a lost dimension.

He followed Karesin across the many carpets scattered over the stone floor, to a large Flemish tapestry that hung in a recess under the stair. Karesin pulled, hand over hand, on a cord behind it, and the tapestry drew to one side, revealing a small, very solid looking oak door. He opened it and flipped a switch, illuminating a steep spiral stair that descended into the bowels of the keep.

"You should be able to manage from here, sir," Karesin said, handing Steddy his duffel and indicating the stair. "And please turn off the stair light from the switch at the bottom."

Steddy, somewhat surprised at Karesin's abrupt dismissal, was crouched in order to clear the low door when Karesin stopped him.

"Welcome home, sir, and I'll see you tomorrow. Oh, and be sure to lock the door at the bottom behind you and don't open up for anyone, save me, Cook, and her ladyship."

"Where is Aunt Edith?" Steddy asked.

"Gone to bed, and she'll see you in the morning. Now get y'rself down there—y'll find it comfortable enough."

Steddy thought it odd that Karesin didn't show him to the room. All in all, the occasional gruffness of his manner was feigned, and he rarely missed the opportunity to indoctrinate a new arrival with the rules of the house or the peculiarities of a guestroom's plumbing—no matter how often one had stayed there before.

When he reached the bottom of the narrow stair, he turned the old iron ring handle and pushed open the heavy

door that was embedded in the side of the granite well. . . .
Karesin's odd behavior was instantly accounted for by the
pervasive scent of Mitsouko that made his pulse swell and
his ears ring, and inspired other Pavlovian manifestations.

Thea had arrived, and her scent proclaimed her occupa-
tion as strongly as if she had been standing at the door to
greet him.

Steddy threw his duffel into the room ahead of him,
and when there was no exclamation of welcome, he stepped
across the threshold. The apartment was not the cold, bare
dungeon he had expected, but rather, a warm and welcom-
ing hideaway. The stone walls were covered in a deep
scarlet felt, and the wall-to-wall carpet was a cheery tartan,
presumably the family's. The furnishings were simple and
unpretentious: a big brass bed with a furry vicuña cover, a
marble-topped dresser, a desk, and two small leather sofas;
but there was no sign of Thea other than the general
disorder that marked her presence and the lingering scent of
her perfume.

He was about to turn and reclimb the stair to get
Karesin and find her, when a door he hadn't noticed,
because it was covered with the same felt as the wall,
opened, and she stepped into the room with a towel wrapped
sarong-fashion under her arms and another that she was
using to dry her hair hiding her face.

Steddy's breathing stopped. He was frozen in place,
watching her as she stood outside the bathroom door, bent
over, rubbing her long hair between the folds of the towel.
She moved toward him unwittingly, still not aware of his
presence, humming the tango they had played over and over
again in Paris. When Steddy could no longer keep still, he
started to hum along with her, but it came out as a croak
that startled her. She threw her head back—they were inches
apart now, and Steddy was grinning at her surprised expression.

"You bastar—"

"Aren't you happy to see me?" Steddy asked, hugging
her tightly around the waist.

Thea held him off with both hands at his neck.

"And just how long have you been here?"

"About half an hour," Steddy lied, knowing how long it took her to wash her hair.

"Karesin was supposed to buzz me before he went to get you from the car." Her hands released his neck, but she turned her head and continued to talk while he kissed her behind the ear. "I wanted to surprise you."

"You did, darling, you did."

As they embraced, the towel fell from around her, and Steddy started to edge her toward the bed.

"That's far enough, buster," she said, grasping his ear firmly and pulling him painfully toward the bathroom. "You smell like a goat."

Still holding him by the ear, she made him take off his clothes and marched him into the shower. It was an old-fashioned one, a gazebolike structure made of fat brass pipes with nozzles pointing from every direction. He pulled her in after him in spite of her cries that she had just dried her hair, so she got back at him by scrubbing him from head to toe with a stiff Scottish bristle brush until his skin tingled—a process that, though he quailed, he thoroughly enjoyed. Then, when he wouldn't let her out, she gave him a proper welcome until the hot water ran out.

"I've always liked a cold finish after a hot shower, but that was a bit of a letdown," he quipped.

"Well, let's just see if we can't warm you up again."

They dried each other and climbed into the big metal bed. He reached for her, but she held him back, tenderly this time.

"Do you want to tell me about those bruises now?" she said, for the first time commenting on his technicolor torso that she had scrubbed in the shower.

"Not tonight, dearest, but you will be gentle with me, won't you?" He grinned.

36

Steddy was awakened by the insistent buzzing of the telephone's intercom. He located it on the bedside table but didn't pick it up. It continued to buzz.

"Pick it up, darling. It's either your aunt or Karesin."

"Hello?"

"Well, dear boy, I'm glad you decided to make it. All in one piece, I trust?"

"Yes, thank you, Edith." And then, looking at Thea: "Thank you for everything. Say, this is really swell down here—all the comforts of home, and I never knew it existed."

"That's just the point, no one does; and by the way, I'd like to keep it that way. It seems to come in handy once every hundred years or so."

"Don't worry, Edith, we'll keep your keep a secret." Steddy laughed.

"Good God, levity at this hour of the morning. How revolting. Now put on some clothes and come up here. Theadora will show you the way. I've had some breakfast sent up, and I'd like to have a look at you."

"Okay, we'll be right along." He replaced the receiver. "Come on, darling, rise and shine. Breakfast is ready, and Edith says you know the way."

As Steddy lay back in bed with his arms crossed behind his neck, waiting for Thea to finish in the bathroom, he wondered how he ever could have doubted the true depth of what they shared. In fact, their forced separation seemed to have brought them even closer together.

In the shower, Thea was musing over much the same thing when Steddy interrupted her thoughts.

"Hey, in there, hurry up—I'm starving."

Steddy followed Thea up the same stair he had descended the night before, and then up a further spiral he hadn't noticed. After opening another heavy oak door, she triggered a spring-loaded panel that was part of the decoration in an alcove between Lady Lynde's bedroom and boudoir. Thea motioned for him to stay quietly where he was while she went ahead into Edith's bedroom to make sure she was alone.

"Good morning, Theadora. Where's Stedman?"

Steddy heard her and crossed the threshold.

"You don't look nearly as bad as Karesin said," she noted after looking him over. "Why, you've even lost your casino pallor and got some color. I have to think this sort of thing agrees with you."

Steddy approached the substantial canopied bed and stretched across it to kiss the cheek she proffered. Her hair was still in a turban, but lipstick and powder, the only makeup she ever wore, were already neatly applied. In spite of the early hour, her aristocratic features, combined with the elegant cut of her frogged velvet bed jacket and her impeccably varnished, bejeweled fingers, imparted the air of a formal levee to the occasion, as opposed to just breakfast in bed.

"Theadora. You had best run down the hall to your room and muss the bed, or the servants will think it very queer that you didn't sleep there."

"All right, Lady Lynde."

"I thought we agreed that you'd call me Edith. After all, we are rather partners in crime, I suppose—thanks to this naughty fellow," she said, arching an eyebrow in Steddy's direction.

Thea left the room.

"You mean the staff know that Thea's staying here?"

"Well, of course they do. She arrived during the

middle of lunch, so what could I do? Anyway, what difference does it make? They could all see that she was quite alone when she came, and no one but cook and Karesin know that you're here.''

''I suppose as long as she wasn't followed, it really doesn't make any difference.''

''Now, Steddy, will you please stop playing Sherlock Holmes for a minute—or is it Professor Moriarty? I'm still not sure which role you're cast in—and explain to me exactly what *is* going on.''

Steddy sat down at the foot of her bed and patiently told his story, leaving out only a few of the gorier details and battling numerous interruptions, that is to say, the telephone constantly ringing and Edith having to ask him to backtrack in his account after each call.

Thea had re-entered the room and sat quietly beside him, only interrupting to clarify a point here and there about Wiley or the men at the embassy.

''We are going to have to call Wiley,'' Steddy thought out loud. ''He really stuck his neck out for me.'' Then, looking at Thea: ''Well, really for both of us, and it's not fair to leave him in the dark like this without even a word of thanks.''

''Well, I don't think you should call any of them. After all, why should you risk life and limb in this affair when it appears to have absolutely nothing to do with you?''

''I haven't said that I will help them, Aunt Edith, but I do owe Wiley at least the courtesy of telling him what I do decide.''

''Steddy, now you listen to me. After all, I feel somewhat responsible to your mother while you're under my roof and—''

''I don't think that I could help them, even if I wanted to.''

''Well, that's all the more reason to stay here where you're safe, until we can figure out a way of getting you out of here and back to America.''

''I can't spend the rest of my life in your dungeon, posh though it may be, now, can I?''

"Maybe I could though. . . ." Thea's voice trailed off pensively.

"Spend the rest of your life in a padded cell?" Steddy asked, amused and smiling incredulously.

"Don't be silly. Maybe I could help," she answered.

"Now *you're* being silly, my girl—" Edith jumped in but was promptly cut off by Steddy.

"Darling, you've done enough. I will not have you getting involved any deeper in this thing. It's far too dangerous. These people aren't fooling, and in any case, I'm the one in trouble and I doubt if I'm going to stick my neck out any further for those bastards—why the hell should you?"

"Steddy, as long as you're involved, I'm involved. As long as you're in prison, I'm in prison, and you know, darling, it wasn't all acting, what I said to you from the ambassador's office in London—I really have had it. If I can't be with you, I'll be without you, but for good."

"Is that a threat? Because if it is, God damn it, I consider the threat, the very real physical threat that hangs over me, and thereby you, if you're near me—of much greater consequence than anything—" Steddy was beginning to steam when Edith interrupted him.

"Children, children, be still! There can be no more question of Thea involving herself any further in this sordid business than of you carrying on with it," she said, glaring at Steddy. "You're as safe as houses right here, and here's where you'll stay until I can come to some arrangement with the authorities."

"Now, Edith, that is definitely out of the question! I don't intend to rot in an English jail until I'm sixty any more than I do in your keep—"

"That's just it, Steddy. We've got to try to find Rollo and make a deal. Don't you see? It's the only way to end this. They've got you in the middle, and they're not going to let you go until they're satisfied one way or another, and in spite of what you said, I think I *am* very much a part of this—and not just because I happen to love you."

"What do you mean?"

"If Rollo does have these documents and is being hidden somewhere. . ."

"Well?" Steddy coaxed her, perplexed.

"Well, if he is still alive, don't you see? There's only one person in all of England who could hide him . . ." She paused, her hands apart expressively, waiting for the realization to hit Steddy.

"Nubar," he said under his breath.

"Exactly. Now I've had quite enough for one morning," Edith said in what was for her a bellow. She came from the old school, and when she found that she was losing an argument, especially when she was confident that her adversary was in the wrong, she simply changed the subject.

"We'll discuss this further after lunch. Now I've got a lot to do, and you had better have your breakfast before it turns to ice."

She dismissed them, indicating the table that was laid in the window bay, opened her address book, and picked up the telephone.

During breakfast they sat head to head, quietly discussing the new possibilities Thea had raised, while across the room Edith bantered on the telephone.

"You know, I'm sure you're right. That's what Wiley said from the beginning. Remember, it was just after the inquest, back at the hotel. Omar was there, too," Steddy said.

"I remember, and I remember I got very chuffed when Wiley suggested Nubie might have had something to do with hiding Rollo. I said that if Rollo were still alive and went to Nubie, I was sure he'd get him the best lawyer in London and send him packing straight to the police to turn himself in."

"Well, it seems now that everybody is convinced he's still alive, and if that's the case . . ."

". . . that points a finger straight at Nubar," Thea continued for him, looking at Steddy with a hint of satisfaction over her deduction.

"Well, I can't just call him and accuse him, can I?"

"You could, but you wouldn't get very far. On the other hand, if I called him, he wouldn't be able to wriggle out quite so easily. I've got a few things on him that he wouldn't want my mother to know about. We've never discussed it, but he knows I know.''

"Thea, if he is involved in this, it's a lot more serious than a little back-room slap-and-tickle. If he's involved in this, I doubt that anything you could say would get it out of him.''

"You only see the suave, relaxed side of Nubie, but I assure you, beneath that well-dressed, portly aplomb lies a socially insecure, quivering mass of jelly who's terrified of my mother. If you know her, she's just the opposite— beneath her delicate poise lies a backbone of pure iron. She can be damn tough when she wants to be, and besides that, Nubar's terrified of anything that might ruin his social ambitions—he always pays the two dollars rather than risk a confrontation that might offend a potential steppingstone on the social ladder.''

"But, Thea, none of that could make any difference here. This is much too serious. He could go to jail if he helped Rollo.''

"Not Nubie. He'd produce banks of lawyers and psychiatrists and somehow come out smelling like a rose. He may be jelly when it comes to Mummy and an easy mark for his social pals, but he's a street fighter when he's cornered. No, you just let me handle Nubie.''

On reflection, Steddy realized that that must have been when he lost the ball. When he'd agreed to let her "handle Nubie," he handed over the helm of the course of events to Thea, and nothing had been the same since.

"Handling Nubie" meant calling him, and when Steddy told her that she couldn't call from the house or it would be traced right back to them, she said she would go to Scone after lunch and place the call from there through a third party—"a friend in Paris," she said. Her enthusiasm had railroaded him, and now he wondered how he had agreed to it.

He'd gone back down to lunch alone in the "dungeon," which, apart from providing the opportunity for a reunion with Margaret, the cook, was singularly boring. Thea had been forced to eat in the dining room with Edith and some of the local gentry for appearance's sake. She'd come down briefly afterward to say good-bye before setting out, and when he had objected again to her going at all, telling her that it was dangerous for her to be seen, she said that no one would be looking for her in Scotland, kissed him on the nose, and merrily went on her way.

That had been hours ago, and with every minute that passed, Steddy's cabin fever, after four nights in the open air, was getting worse.

At five-thirty, he was beginning to be concerned when she still hadn't returned. At six, she had been gone over three hours. Steddy put down the book he was reading and examined the intercom. The base had a row of small buttons next to corresponding but faded labels. He selected the top one and hoped it would access Edith's room. She answered.

"Oh, hello, Steddy! What is it?"

"Have you seen Thea?"

"No. Isn't she back from shopping yet? I assumed she was with you."

"No, I haven't seen her since she left."

"Well, it's only just six. I shouldn't be too worried. The shops are open until five, and it is a twenty-minute drive. I'd give her another half an hour; she might have taken a wrong turning."

"God damn it, I told her not to go, but she wouldn't listen."

"Give her half an hour more, and if she hasn't come by then, come up to my room, but buzz first in case I'm not alone."

"Okay, but I'm getting really worried."

Steddy replaced the receiver and began to pace out the diagonals of the room, his athletic stride cramped to a nervous shuffle by the confines of his quarters, like a young lion in a small, unfamiliar cage.

At six-thirty, he picked up the phone to buzz upstairs again, but there was someone already talking on the line.

". . . yes, I see, well, if you'll just drive into town and see if you can find her, Karesin. She's probably just lost her way, but she is well overdue, and we're getting rather concerned."

"Yes, milady."

"Hold on there, Karesin. I'm coming with you!" Steddy cut in.

"Stedman, you know it's rude to listen in on other people's conversations. Now put—"

"I just picked up the phone to ring you. Karesin, wait for me. I'll be right up."

"You'll do no such thing! Karesin, get along with you. Now, Stedman, you are not going to jeopardize everything we've accomplished, especially as there's every likelihood that Thea's had a flat or taken a wrong turn and will probably be home before Karesin. Now put down that phone and come upstairs where I can keep an eye on you."

He knew that she was right, but he resented it bitterly. Hadn't he said the exact same thing to Thea not four hours ago? If he hadn't indulged her, this never would have happened. As he mounted the stairs to Edith's apartment, he had to remind himself that nothing had happened. The thought was of little comfort.

"Allo. Qui?"

"Cristina! I don't believe it. It's Thea."

"Thee-zee, darling, how wonderful! Are you in Paris?"

"No. I'm calling from . . . well, no, I'm not."

"Then you must be coming. It's been ages."

"No, I'm not—not just now anyway. But I've been trying to ring you for hours. First there was no answer, and then it was constantly busy . . ."

"I was talking to Gerard—he's on assignment in New York. You won't believe it, but I just gave him your number out West. He's doing a cover story for—"

"Cristina, I'm sorry, but I don't have much time. I need you to do me a favor."

"Anything, if I can."

"Would you ring Nubar for me in London—it's very important—and tell him. . ."

"But where are you, darling?"

"That's not important, but there is a good reason I can't tell him myself, so if you wouldn't mind—"

"But are you in some kind of trouble? You know I'll do anything I can . . ."

"No, it's nothing serious. All I need you to do is call Nubar for me. Here, I'll give you the number in London. It's Belgravia—"

"I have your number in London, but what do you want me to say? He'll ask me where you are."

"He won't, because I want you to give him a message and hang up the moment you're sure he's understood it. Is that clear?"

"Yes, Thee-zee, but—"

"Just tell him that I said to be sure to go to the office at lunchtime tomorrow. I'll call him there at one o'clock. Oh! And be sure—"

"But, Thea, you are in trouble. Can't I—"

"Cristina, please. Just tell him to make sure he's not followed. All right?"

"Yes, of course, darling, but please, isn't there anything I can do?"

"No, just do as I say, and I'll be eternally grateful."

"All right, but will you call me again tomorrow? I'm very worried by all this."

"I'll try, but don't worry, it's nothing serious. I just have to talk to him on a phone when I'm sure no one else will be listening in."

"If you're sure, but please try to call me tomorrow. I'll call him right now, and I'll keep trying until I get him."

"Thanks a million, and please don't worry about me. I'll let you know how it all turns out."

"All right, darling, but, Thee-zee, please be careful."

"I will, and I'll talk to you very soon."

Thea broke the connection, left the booth, and went to the desk to pay for the call. It was already five-thirty— Steddy would be worried, but she didn't dare call him. She collected the coins from the counter and rushed from the hotel.

The change in the weather was dramatic. Only two and a half hours ago, she had driven into town from the castle under a glorious blue sky—that same sky was now black as night. As she gathered her cardigan around her shoulders against the chill, a clap of thunder exploded overhead, and rain started to fall—just a few drops at first, but each one would have filled a teacup. By the time she reached her father's car where she had parked it across the square, she was soaked to the skin.

The old automobile was still warm inside from the sun. Even so, at first it wouldn't fire, until she put aside her impatience and remembered to gently coax it to life, the way she had learned on the long drive north.

Thea picked her way carefully out of town. Even the piercing beams of the car's giant P-100 headlamps were of little help against the blinding rain. By the time she gained the narrow, stone-lined road that led into the valley, the rain had become so fierce that it was sheeting off the windscreen to the extent that she found she could see better with the wipers off. Her impatience got the better of her, and she pushed the heavy chrome stick shift into third and felt the big car surge forward. She knew Steddy was worried about her, but more than that, she was anxious to get back to him—anxious to prove to him what she could accomplish. How clever she had been to tell Nubar to go to the office, when no one listening in would know that that was how he always referred to the Clermont—his gambling club. Steddy would see that she was now a full partner with him in his troubles, no longer just a soothing voice on the other end of a telephone line.

As she piloted the car into the entrance of the valley, a flash of lightning bathed it in an eerie daylight, silhouetting the craggy stone peaks against the black sky and imparting a purple phosphorescence to the heather on the moors. The strobe flashes of lightning grew closer to the thunder until they occurred simultaneously. The storm was overhead. She began singing to herself but could barely hear her voice over its raging. As she pushed the car through a bend, expertly clipping the corner, the lightning revealed a gray sedan directly in her path, blocking the narrow gap between the stone walls that lined the road.

In the split second that fear and adrenaline stretch into a lifetime, she thought she saw a flashing light off to the side of the road, but she was only yards away, and there was nothing she could do. Her natural reaction was to jam the brake pedal to the floor, activating the powerful hydraulic servos. The car slued sideways and slammed broadside into the obstruction, virtually demolishing the lesser vehicle, dragging what was left of it for yards against the stoney embankment until the sparks created by their transit were doused by the rain, and darkness and the sounds of the storm were all that remained.

She never heard the footsteps on the gravel as they approached the wreck.

37

Wiley and Pete Register dined early at the Connaught Grill and went to a show to take their minds off things. The chain of command in Washington had "convinced" Register to stay on in London for the rest of the week and await developments. Register didn't have to "convince" Wiley to stay—Wiley was already deeply concerned about his friends' welfare, if a little confused as to his motives when it came to Thea. The circumstances of their last evening together at the Dorchester had become distorted in his mind over the last four days by wishful thinking, and now his handsome blond head was crowded with fantasies that were alien to the nature of his loyalty to Steddy.

The phone rang at about eleven, just as he was getting into bed. It was Steddy.

"Wiley, I'm sorry I didn't call you before this, but I've been trying to sort things out for myself and—"

"Damn it, Steddy, do you have any idea how many people have been sitting around in London waiting for word from you? And then Thea goes and pulls a disappearing act, too—makes me look like a real horse's ass and—"

"Wiley, hold it, please. Can you get up here right away?"

"Shit, Steddy, you've got to be kidding. First no word for days, and then you want me to meet you right away. I don't even know where you are."

"Thea's been kidnapped."

Steddy had spoken very quietly, but the impact of his words was not lost on Wiley, whose response was suddenly equally quiet, the quiet of a disciplined calm.

"Are you sure she was kidnapped, and if so, do you know who did it?"

"We've just had a note—it was Chelak."

"Where are you?"

"Your phone's probably tapped. I'll call you in fifteen minutes at the place where we had dinner after Wimbledon two years ago."

"Steddy, this is no time for—"

There was a click, and the connection was severed.

Wiley dressed quickly in the clothes he had just taken off and laid over the back of the chair by the desk. He was furious with Steddy for the way he casually took his compliance for granted, but his concern for Thea didn't allow him the luxury of even considering alternative action.

Steddy had been clever to recall that particular dinner, as it had been Wiley's birthday and Steddy had taken him to the men's final at Wimbledon and invited a group of friends to dinner at the Clermont afterward to celebrate. It had been a surprise, and Steddy knew that Wiley wasn't likely to forget where it had taken place.

The Clermont was the private gaming club over Annabel's where Rockford had knocked his wife down the stairs—in fact, where the whole damn mess of the last few weeks had started. Wiley reflected on this as he walked the few blocks down Davies Street to the club in Berkeley Square. He wasn't worried about being followed—as it was a private club, anyone on his tail would have to make a hell of a stink to get in, and hopefully by then he would have finished the call. More importantly, he really didn't give a damn anymore. As he entered the attractive Georgian house that was the club's premises, the porter at the desk greeted him.

"Good evening, Mr. Travis. We've just had a call for you. Let me just see if it's still on the line."

The girl who answered the phones confirmed that it was.

"Shall I ask who's calling?" she said politely.

"No, that's all right. I was expecting it."

Wiley walked to the booth at the end of the hall and picked up the receiver.

"Hello?"

"Okay, now pay attention, because I'm only going to say this once."

Wiley said nothing, but listened, resolved to the fact that the management of his actions, for the present, was no longer under his control.

"Take the seven-thirty morning express from King's Cross to Edinburgh—swear you won't tell anybody . . . *swear*."

"I swear."

"And make sure you're not followed. I don't care how you do it, but be damn sure."

"Okay."

"You get in at twelve thirty-four, and you'll be contacted at the station when the person who's picking you up is satisfied that you haven't been tailed. Thea's life depends on it. Please be careful."

Before Wiley could comment, the dial tone replaced Steddy's voice. He left the booth and headed for the front door. The porter interrupted his thoughts.

"Won't you be gaming with us this evening, sir?"

"No, I don't think so. But on second thought, I will go upstairs for a drink," Wiley said, shedding his raincoat.

He realized that he needed a few moments to collect his thoughts before launching himself headlong into he didn't know what. The small bar was empty.

"Good evening, sir. Whiskey and water?" the barman said attentively, glass in hand.

"Not tonight, Bruno, just a Coca Cola, please."

He would need to have his wits about him this night—and it promised to be a long one.

* * *

Steddy was sitting on a small satin boudoir chair pulled alongside Edith's bed. The telephone was still balanced on his knees.

"Do you really think it was wise to have called him Stedman? The note was very specific."

"I know, Aunt Edith, but I've got to have someone on my team whom I can trust and who knows something about this murdering maniac."

"I told you that I'd be happy to call old Moncrief. He was the head of Intelligence during the war; I'm sure he'd help."

"I'm sure he would," Steddy said to mollify her. "But the Americans are already deeply involved in this, so it wouldn't do any good having them against us at this point. And besides, at least they're not after me for murder."

"I just hope you're doing the right thing. After all, Thea's life is at stake. I've grown very fond of her, and I'd—"

"Damn it, Edith, I'm in love with her! Don't you see, this is the only way to do it. The Americans *know* what this man is after, and maybe even how to get hold of it for him. That's the only way we'll ever get Thea back. I've just got to play ball with them; there's no other way. At least with Wiley between me and them, I've got a chance to find out what they know and use it to get Thea back—damn the consequences! If I went to the British, I might end up in the slammer, and then how could I help her? This Chelak thinks that I'm the key to something he wants; that's why he took Thea. Only Wiley and his people know what it is that I'm supposed to know, so, you see, I really need him."

"Well, there's nothing more that either of us can do tonight, so you'd best get off to bed and get some rest. I'm sure you're going to need every bit of strength you can muster before this is over. I know I've had a bit more excitement than I bargained for, and I doubt if tomorrow will be any better."

Steddy warmed for a moment. Edith looked measurably older under the stark light that the bedside lamp threw into the shadowy recesses of her canopied bed. He bent over and kissed her on the cheek.

"I'm really sorry, Edith. I never wanted to get you involved in all this. I did try to warn you."

"Even if I'd believed you, I still would have done the same thing." And then, cheering up a bit: "Now, to bed wi' yee, as Cook would say, and try not to worry too much. This sort of thing just doesn't happen to nice people."

But Steddy was beginning to realize that either he wasn't too nice a person—or it did.

38

Karesin had no trouble spotting Wiley from the description Steddy had given him. His height, coupled with his ash-blond hair, made him tower over his fellow passengers and stand out like a beacon. He was also clearly an American, for though his clothes were Savile Row, he wore them casually, with the relaxed stance of a Gary Cooper.

On Stedman's orders, Karesin hung back to determine if anyone displayed more than a passing interest in Wiley. Although his only training in matters clandestine came from motion pictures, his inborn country suspicion helped him size up the various types loitering about the station, while Wiley, knowing that he would be watched, did his best to stay clear of crowds by casually wandering about looking into shop windows, studying the arrival and departure boards, buying a newspaper, and finally, out of frustration, when he felt that more than enough time had elapsed, going into the railway pub and ordering a pint of Pimm's with an extra measure of gin.

Karesin decided the coast was clear and made his move in the pub. He took a stool beside Wiley and ordered a lager. After a few sips and more than a few furtive glances about, he caught Wiley off guard by almost bellowing, in an untrained stage whisper, "Would you please follow me out, sir."

Wiley's surprise caused him to sputter a mouthful of Pimm's, but he recovered his equilibrium and indicated his assent by pushing some of his change on the bar toward the barman and pocketing the rest. Greatly relieved that his one line in the play had been delivered, Karesin calmly finished his beer before leading Wiley to the car park and the beat-up Land Rover that he had borrowed from the gamekeeper for the mission.

The ride to the castle took about an hour and a half and was conducted in sticky silence once Wiley realized that none of the answers to his questions would be forthcoming from the mute Karesin, who was busy watching the rearview mirror. In any case, Wiley was grateful for the opportunity to get some sleep after spending the entire night running around London until he finally found a car to take him up to Lincoln, where he could board the train north without worrying about being spotted by his own people.

He awoke just as they turned into the iron gates that pierced the ancient stone wall they had been following for many miles. The grounds of the park that flanked the drive had a studied air of benign neglect, as if the expanses of lawn surrounding the great old trees had been scythed by hand, allowing field flowers to sprout casually here and there. After a time, the flags flying from the high, crenellated top of the castle's keep emerged from behind the crown of the foothill they were climbing, until eventually, like the finale of a Broadway musical that rises from the center of the stage on a hidden elevator, the full structure loomed in front of them.

They crossed a lakelike moat and drove through the single narrow portal into the forecourt, where the dourness of the massive, worried gray stones was uncharacteristically relieved by geometric patterns of whitewashed flower boxes that overflowed with multicolored blooms.

A signal had evidently been sent ahead from the gatehouse, because the front door opened at their approach, and Wiley saw a tall, elegant lady in a periwinkle-blue afternoon dress standing at the threshold, flanked by a liveried footman. He stepped from the car, and she came forward to meet him, her arms extended in familiar greeting.

"Wiley, dear, I'm so glad you could come after all." And then, turning to the young footman at her right: "Edward, will you see to Mr. Travis's bags; he's in the Chinese Room."

Wiley was struck dumb—having never laid eyes on her in his life—when she held him round the shoulders and extended first her right and then her left cheek to be kissed, but dutifully he went along with it. Karesin brought the footman up short when he approached the Land Rover.

"There's been a mix-up with the bags, milady, but they'll be coming along later."

"Oh, dear, what a bore for you, Wiley; still, at least you've arrived in time for a well-deserved drink before lunch. But what am I thinking of? Karesin, I'm sure Mr. Travis would like to wash up after such a long time on the train. Will you show him the way? And Edward, would you fetch a drinks tray to the terrace and bring plenty of ice for our American guest."

With that she turned on her heels and disappeared into the depths of the house, leaving Wiley completely in the dark and once more in the hands of his silent warder. He followed the manservant across the great hall, up the stairs, and through Edith's bedroom, where Karesin activated the panel in the boudoir and motioned Wiley to precede him through it. Wiley stopped when he saw the steep stone stair that spiraled below him.

"Listen here, Karesin, or whatever your name is, I don't have to wash up, but I do have to get some answers out of you."

Karesin's expression registered not the slightest hint that he had even heard Wiley as he snapped the panel shut and swung the heavy inner oak door closed with a resounding clank that echoed eerily down the length of the stone stair.

"Now where's Mr. Wright? These schoolboy dramatics have gone on quite long enough."

Karesin stepped ahead of him and began to descend the stair.

"Just follow me, sir—you'll find the answer to all your questions at the bottom," he said ominously.

From behind, Wiley couldn't see the effort Karesin was exerting to keep from roaring with laughter.

Steddy had heard the door close and was waiting for them at the foot of the stair.

"God, I never thought I'd be so glad to see you," Wiley exclaimed, relief smoothing the wrinkles of concern from his face. "I was beginning to think I'd fallen in with the wrong crowd, imagining all sorts of things."

Steddy greeted him, smiling for the first time since Thea had disappeared.

"Don't tell me Karesin here's been giving you a hard time?"

"Why, sir, I was just following orders, doing like you said, keeping a sharp lookout and all that." He had stopped trying to control himself, and his beaming smile and twinkling eyes lighted up his whole face. Then he and Steddy started roaring with laughter, and try as he might, Wiley was unable to keep from joining in.

Steddy finally put a stop to the merriment.

"Enough of all this. We don't have much time, and there's a lot of ground to cover."

"Well, I'll leave you, sirs—just be sure to show the gentleman out through her ladyship's bedroom, and mind you're not more than twenty minutes. He's expected at lunch."

Steddy gave Karesin a military salute and said, "Yes, sir, Mr. Karesin. And by the way, thanks for everything."

Steddy then steered Wiley into his subterranean world and sat him down in one of the leather armchairs.

Well, there haven't been any new developments since I spoke to you, but here's the note that was given to the gatekeeper last night."

He handed Wiley a small, innocent-looking, pale-blue envelope that had typed on its face:

> Stedman Wright, Esq.
> C/O the Countess of Lynde
> Castle Lynde

"It would appear that your kidnapper has a copy of Debrett's."

"Wiley, I'm worried sick—you can't imagine. When I think that I put Thea in this terrible spot; if anything happens to her, I swear—"

"Calm down, Steddy, and let me have a look at that note."

While Wiley read the note, Steddy mixed them both a gin and tonic and handed one to him when he put down the sheet of blue paper. "Well, what do you think?" Steddy asked anxiously.

"It seems pretty straightforward, wouldn't you say? He wants the documents in exchange for Thea, and he's reminding you about Aberdeen so that you'll realize that if you don't play ball—the same thing will happen to her that happened to the man in the alley."

"But how does he know that I know anything about the papers? After all, I *didn't* know anything about them until your friend briefed me the other day, and that was on that trick phone of yours that, according to you, no one can tap."

"Well, it could have been tapped at your end."

"No way. I just stepped into a pay phone at the last minute—there wouldn't have been time."

"Listen, Steddy, I don't claim to be any expert, but there are all sorts of sophisticated devices that he could have used to listen in from quite a way away. Of course, that would only allow him to hear your side of the conversation."

"I wasn't doing much talking that day, just listening." And then pensively: "But he could have heard me agree to let Thea meet me and then have had someone follow her up here."

"That's a possibility, but if he was that close to you, he would have just followed you himself."

"Shit, no matter how you look at it, there's no one responsible for what happened to Thea but me."

"Let's not think about where to lay the blame. Let's just think about how to get her back, okay? Now, I think we have to assume that he doesn't think that you know what he wants or even exactly how to get it, or he would have taken you long ago and never bothered with Thea. He wants to force you to do his work for him and—"

"But do you think he'll honor the exchange?"

"Not if he can help it—at least not if she's seen him. But he may have used someone else to take her, in which case it wouldn't matter to him, as long as he gets what he wants. In any case, there are ways to make sure that both sides stick to the bargain—that's just a question of craft. The big thing here is, can you get your hands on the papers?"

"Wiley, be serious. How the hell would I know how to get hold of top-secret Israeli strategic war plans? I'd never even heard of them until a few days ago."

"Did you tell Thea about them?"

"Hell, no. I didn't have time. I hardly saw her, and then she was taken. Oh, Jesus!"

"Calm down, Steddy. Now, do you know where Rollo is?"

"Shit, Wiley, I swear to you that if I knew where that son-of-a-bitch was, I'd kill him myself if he isn't already dead. Christ, after what he's put us through . . ." And then, as if he'd just heard what Wiley said: "But you're *sure* that he's alive, aren't you?"

"No, not sure."

"But then, what the hell do we do if he is dead?"

"It wouldn't really change things much unless we could prove that he had the file with him when he went over the cliff."

"But that's impossible. The police never found his body."

"That's why we'd better just hope and pray that

he's still alive—and all my instincts tell me that he is.''

''I agree. He'd never kill himself, no matter how drunk he was—not as long as there was one roll left. But how can *I* find him if nobody else can?''

''It seems the British, the Americans, the Israelis, the Palestinians, and possibly even the Russians have every confidence in your ability to do just that. I even heard some talk about the Syrians.''

''But that's absurd. I don't have a fucking clue. You believe me, don't you?''

''I believe that you think you don't know where he is, but of course you haven't been trying to find him, have you? And that's what everyone was counting on.''

''What the fuck's that supposed to mean?''

''Look, Steddy, we're pretty sure that you were set up with that thing at Clardige's with Omar and all—''

''But for what? Don't tell me the fucking CIA did that to me?''

''No, no, calm down, it wasn't us—''

''So you admit you're CIA—God, I thought I knew you, and all the time you were a fucking spy and you never told me.''

''Steddy, I was working for *our* country. I wasn't spying on you, and anyway, I've never really been a spy, just an unpaid, glorified listening post.''

''Well, if the CIA didn't set me up, then who the fuck did?''

''We don't know, but it was probably the Israelis.''

''But shit, I don't know where Rollo is! Christ, what have I got Thea into?''

''You can't blame yourself, Steddy. You've been manipulated all along. The trouble is, you've been too resourceful.''

''What do you mean?''

''Well, the way we figure it is, when they set you up, they thought that as an American in England, on your own and running in the same crowd as Rollo, you'd probably run in the same direction. But you didn't, did you?''

"Isn't that a little farfetched—a hell of a long shot? I mean, what made them so sure I'd run at all? What if I'd just turned myself in?"

"They probably would have scared the shit out of you and allowed you to escape, with the same end result."

"God, it's all so Machiavellian. . . . Hey, wait a minute, Wiley. If that were the case, wouldn't it have to have been the Brits who set me up? Otherwise how could plan B ever have worked?"

"You've got a good point there, and believe me, no one has discounted the possibility that the British are capable of launching an operation like this. It just goes to show you how desperate everyone is to get their hands on this file."

"But where the hell did they think I was going to run to?"

"If they knew that, we wouldn't be sitting here right now. You'd probably be off in the sun someplace with Thea, and I'd be sweltering in New York, reading manuscripts and fighting my way to Long Island every Friday just to get drunk for two days and fight my way back to town in order to get my laundry done in time to start all over again."

"Stop it, Wiley! I just don't know what to do. Maybe if I met this guy and told him the truth—"

"Do that and you're both dead."

"So what do I do—give up?"

"Hell, no. Your Uncle Sam has a few ideas even if you don't."

"I can't take the chance. Oh, God, you didn't tell them about this, did you?"

"Steddy, I gave you my word."

"Forgive me, Wiley. I'm not myself."

"Steddy, can't you see that you have to throw in with us? Who else are you going to trust?"

"It's too risky Wiley. You read the note—they'd kill her

if they knew I had anything to do with the CIA. Don't you give a damn about her?''

''Of course I do, but I don't think you realize what's at stake here from the point of view of the various governments. You're not even a speck of dust in their eyes when it comes to something as hot as this. You've gotta have protection or they'll steamroll you.''

''But can't you see that that's just it? None of them—and that includes the CIA—gives a shit about Thea and me, and the only way I can even try to protect her is to hang on to as many cards as I can.''

''Steddy,'' Wiley said with renewed patience, ''alone you just don't have the means or resources to—''

''I've got the means, kiddo, but you've got to tell me what buttons to push—like for a start telling me what your CIA pals thought I would have done.''

The intercom interrupted them. It was Edith.

''Steddy, whatever can you be thinking, keeping Wiley with you so long? The servants will think he disappeared into thin air. Get him up here at once.''

''You've got to get back upstairs pronto, but first tell me what your theory about Rollo is.''

''Steddy, now it's my turn to think this one over. It's a pretty serious matter to go against the Company and take matters into my own hands. It's not like the movies, you know.''

''What's that supposed to mean?''

''Just that I'm going to think this one over before I decide what to do. I'll let you know after lunch.''

''Is that your final word?''

''My word will be final after I've had a chance to think it over. I'm not making any more spur-of-the-moment, rash decisions, and whether you believe it or not, I care a great deal about Thea and, yes, even you, what it comes down to that, and I won't let you bully me into doing something that in my best judgment will eventually prove harmful or even fatal to either one of you. I intend to think this one through.''

''Just promise you won't do anything until we talk again after lunch—that much you owe me.''

"Steddy, I'm not sure at this point that I owe you anything. But don't worry, I'll come back and tell you what I've decided."

A table was set under an awning on the broad terrace that overlooked the Italian garden. Conversation was at first something of a trial for both participants, as they had never met before and had to pretend, in front of the footman, that they were old friends. But it didn't take long for Edith to realize that as an old friend of Steddy's, Wiley had to know his mother, Georgianna, so she bombarded him with questions about her and Philadelphia until the subject was exhausted. She then switched expertly to what Wiley was up to these days, which led to an animated discussion of books, and then particularly of a book Wiley had recently published on the Mellon collection of British sporting paintings at Yale, which led to Wiley asking her how she thought the Scottish grouse-shooting season—which was to open in a few days—would be this year, and finally, over coffee, to a merry gossip about mutual shooting friends whom they found they had in common.

They not only appeared to be old chums to their audience, but by the time Wiley accepted her offer of a walk in the gardens, they both felt as if they had known each other forever. The pressure of the roles that they had had to play had forced them to compress into forty-five minutes associations that under normal circumstances would have taken months or even years to establish.

In the sunken garden, Edith asked him if he and Steddy had decided on a course of action.

"Actually, I've only just read the note."

"But surely the CIA intends to take some sort of immediate action?"

Wiley was shocked. After fifteen years of perfect cover, it suddenly seemed as if the whole world knew he was CIA.

His answer was tentative, but when Edith said that if the CIA didn't intend to do something, she certainly could call on old friends in British Intelligence from the war. He quickly cautioned her that any action of that sort could put Thea and Steddy into immediate jeopardy.

Wiley realized that Edith would be an important ally in convincing Steddy to do the right thing and told her as much.

"He's simply got to play ball with the CIA. To bring in anyone else at this point would prove fatal. And as *I'm* already involved, I really don't see what difference it can make."

"But as you said yourself, the note was quite specific. And of course we're all being watched, so any more people would—"

"That's just it. I am here. No one knows I have any connection with the CIA—that is, no one except you and Steddy. I don't think Thea ever knew, although she might have guessed. You see, I can act as an intermediary so that we'll have their full support without any obvious presence. It's really the only way."

Wiley realized as he was talking that he had made his decision and that he would have to make Steddy see it his way, for everyone's sake.

"Even if he were able to get hold of what this fellow wants without our help—which I very much doubt—the odds of his successfully completing the exchange without CIA backup are very slim. I don't think either of them would survive."

"You've convinced me, Wiley. Now let's go and convince him."

They went back to Edith's bedroom, where she locked the door behind them and called down to Steddy on the intercom to join them.

Edith reclined on a tufted satin sofa by the fireplace while the two men stood circling each other, arguing the merits of their opposing opinions. Steddy kept saying that he thought the CIA was composed of double-dyed idiots, if even half of the things he'd read in the papers were true, but Wiley kept hammering at the point that Steddy couldn't handle the operation on his own and that he'd be putting the responsibility for Thea's life on his own head if things didn't work out.

Steddy answered, "I'd still feel responsible for getting her into this no matter who was running the show."

That was when Wiley played the trump card he'd been holding back, not wanting to use it. He blamed Steddy for leading Chelak to Thea in the first place, reminding him that if he'd let the CIA take care of her in London and let them send someone up to Scotland to handle Chelak, she wouldn't be a captive at all.

Steddy shrank visibly when Wiley had finished and come to the realization that ninety percent of his belligerent behavior was due to the guilt that he felt—he wasn't being the least bit objective. At last he sat down on the sofa opposite Edith, defeated but not ready to give in entirely.

"Well, Steddy, do you agree that I can call Pete Register on the secure line and put him in the picture?"

"On one condition."

"And what's that?"

"That you, and you alone, are my direct contact with them, and that you agree to stay with me at all times and make no effort to contact them other than by mutual agreement."

"Don't you think that's going to hamstring them to the point that we might as well not have them?"

"No, I don't. But what I do think is that this bloody Israeli has eyes at every point of the compass. As you pointed out, I've had some very unpleasant brushes with him, and I will not take any more chances with Thea's life that one of your cronies might get spotted contacting you or vice versa. They can keep an eye on us from a safe distance—and I mean *safe*."

It was Wiley's turn to sit down. This was turning into more than he had bargained for. He had never worked in the field before, and while he had taken the basic field-operative training course and a refresher every year or so, he was not by any stretch of the imagination a seasoned agent. Other than using codes occasionally, he had never put anything he had learned to practical use, and now, if the Company agreed to Steddy's ultimatum, he would be pitted against one of the most ruthless, experienced operatives in the world.

Edith, smiling and having no idea what Wiley was letting himself in for if he went along with Steddy, said triumphantly: "Well, Wiley, wasn't that just what you wanted?"

"In spades, I'm afraid. In spades."

"Well, I'm glad that's settled. Now, you both had better get out of here. I've got a fitting in ten minutes."

As they descended the stone stairs to the keep, they mentally shed the dissension that had grown between them, so that by the time they reached the bottom, they were cleansed of it and once again members of the same team.

Steddy poured a drink off whiskey from the decanter on the sideboard and cocked the crystal tumbler at Wiley. Wiley didn't really feel like a drink just then, but he sensed the ritual and knew that it was an important unspoken gesture to the reaffirmation of their friendship. Steddy handed him the glass and poured himself another, then he flopped on the old leather chesterfield, suddenly feeling the full weight of the physical strain and emotional drain of the past weeks and relieved to have another shoulder to bear some of it.

"I guess if you're going to call them, Wiley, there's no time like the present. The phone's behind you, and don't worry about it being tapped. Edith told me that it was put in during the war for some secret stuff and there's no record of it. She doesn't even get a bill."

Wiley took a slug from the glass, put it down on a table, and went over and sat on the bed by the telephone. As he picked it up, he said, "Steddy, I know we're doing the right thing, but in any case, I want you to know that I give you my word not to do anything without you knowing about it first."

"Wiley, we're all in this together now—in every sense of the word. We are trusting each other with our lives.

You're on my side now, and I'm glad of it—it's been pretty lonely. Just don't trust them any more than you would normally, and we'll be okay."

Wiley dialed the direct codes for Washington, mulling over what Steddy had said. The full extent of their isolation hit him like a cold shower. He felt chilled to the bone and reached for his glass of whiskey.

Trained professionals exposed themselves to these sorts of risks every day for their country, but they did it by their own choice. Now he had been drawn into doing the same thing by a friend, with no way of extricating himself. But was he doing it for his country, or, in the final analysis, was he really doing it for himself, to fulfill the need to prove something basic, something that up until now he had just played at, all the while allowing himself to believe it was the real thing and imparted nobility and purpose to his otherwise pedestrian existence?

Wiley had the feeling that he was about to find the answer to a lot of questions he had avoided asking himself in the past, and he was afraid and thrilled at the same time by what he might discover.

The operator in Washington came on the line, and Wiley asked for himself, making use of the signal they had set up for Steddy that would raise the senior CIA man on duty at the embassy. He was more than a little surprised when Pete Register answered on the first ring.

"I knew you'd call, and it's about time, too. Where the hell are you? You know, these disappearing acts aren't making you very popular with the local chaps—and by the way, that goes double for me."

"Listen, Pete, I'm with Steddy, and there have been some new developments—"

"I asked you where you are."

"Steddy has agreed to play ball with us, but there are certain conditions."

"Do they include your not telling me where you are? Because if they do, I don't want to hear them."

"Pete, listen. Chelak has made his move, and Steddy's

just taking precautions, which might not be a bad idea in the long run.''

Register's interest was sparked. "Shoot."

Wiley started to speak, but then looked over to Steddy, whose eyes were riveted to him. He made a calming gesture with his hand as if to say, take it easy. I won't let the cat out of the bag unless he agrees.

"He'll go along with us, but only if I'm the only contact with you and then only by secure phone—no direct contact with you or any other agent."

"Do you agree to this?"

"Yes. It's the only way he'll go along with us, and in view of what's happened, I think he's right."

"First of all, are you just saying this for his benefit, and secondly, what has happened?"

Wiley looked Steddy directly in the eye and answered, "No, I'm not saying this for his benefit, and I cannot tell you what's happened until you agree to his terms—and I want your personal word of honor to me on that."

Register didn't hesitate for a second.

"You've got it, but I hope you have some small conception of what you're getting yourself into."

"I do, but I think you had better give your word to Steddy directly. I want him to accept it personally, then I'll brief you."

"Put him on."

Steddy didn't require the double assurance, and he told Wiley so, but Wiley insisted, so he took the receiver.

Register repeated himself to Steddy.

"Are you sure you really understand what you're getting yourself into without a lifeline? 'Cause in case Wiley hasn't told you, his experience has been limited to writing memoranda."

Steddy didn't reply.

"You still want my word of honor?"

"Yeah, and crossed fingers don't count."

Register ignored the sarcasm and gave Steddy his word. Steddy passed the phone back to Wiley, who covered the mouthpiece with one hand and asked Steddy if it was all right to go ahead. Steddy nodded in the affirmative.

"Chelak's taken Thea Boulton as ransom for the plans."

"Oh, that's just great. God damn it! You guys are really a bunch of amateur jerks. How the hell can I help you with a thing like this with my hands tied behind my back? Don't you realize that that girl's life is at stake? Put that moronic, punch-drunk playboy friend of yours back on the line. We can't go on like this for a second longer with that girl's life in danger."

The second note from Chelak arrived by the same means, shortly after they had finished briefing Register. He had raved and ranted, but Steddy had stuck to his guns, and Register had agreed in the end to play it their way as long as he was kept constantly informed of developments as they occurred.

The note instructed Steddy to go to the ruins of the original twelfth-century castle, which was about half a mile across the estate, atop a hill. The meeting was called for midnight.

"I don't think you should go alone," Wiley said.

"You read the note; it was very specific."

"Nevertheless, if I'm going to be of any use, I can't just sit around waiting to react, when and if you return."

"That's not very encouraging."

"Maybe not, but I think it would be a good idea to get him used to the fact that I'll be around helping you—right from the start."

"Yeah, maybe, but I don't know if it's a good idea at this first meeting. Seeing you might just scare him away."

"You can tell him that I'm your oldest friend and that as the police are after you, you'll need someone to do the leg work for you."

"That would make sense, but I still think it's risky to take a chance on blowing the first meeting."

"Steddy, you need a safety factor. These people are not averse to the use of torture to get information out of people.

If I'm there, or at least nearby, the chances of his trying to take you are at least marginally reduced.''

"Maybe if you came most of the way with me and then waited where I could signal you with a flashlight if I needed you.''

"That's a good idea, but let's make it that unless you signal me to stay where I am, within, say, five minutes, I'll come ahead. That way I'll know that you're all right.''

"Okay.''

"Do you know if there's a gun in this house?''

"I should think just about any kind you want. This is one of the finest shooting estates in Scotland.''

They asked Karesin for a revolver and two flashlights, and then Edith volunteered two walkie-talkies from the ones the gamekeepers used on the estate to keep in touch with each other.

"We may try to maintain the old ways here,'' she said, "but we don't live in the dark ages.''

With forty-five minutes to kill before leaving for the rendezvous, they returned to the discussion of Rollo, Nubar, and the file. It appeared from what Wiley said that the CIA had come to the same conclusion as Thea; that if Rollo was still alive, the only person who could possibly have helped him was Nubar.

"There are no two ways about it, Wiley. We'll have to get Nubar up here and put the screws on him to find out if he knows anything. The trouble is, how do we contact him? That's what Thea was trying to do when..." His voice broke off. "I'm sure his phone is tapped, and anyway, once we do reach him, how do we make it look normal for him to come up here without drawing attention to ourselves?''

"Contacting him should be no problem. That's something my people in London should be able to handle without much difficulty, but as for a reason for his coming...''

"I think I can provide an excellent excuse," Edith said. "Do you boys have any idea what the date is?''

They looked blankly at each other and then at Edith.

"Well, for your information, today is the tenth of August.''

The light of comprehension still did not dawn on their faces.

"Well, if today is the tenth, in two days it will be the twelfth . . ."

There was a pause, and then they both blurted out simultaneously, "The Glorious Twelfth!"

"Exactly. And in case you've forgotten, the opening of the grouse season on the twelfth of August is just about the biggest thing that happens in Scotland every summer. It wouldn't seem the least bit out of character for someone like this Nubar—at least as you've described him to me—to come for the opening of the season. In fact, if he's the sport that you say he is, it would be positively odd for him not to."

"Edith, you're a genius," Steddy exclaimed. "It's perfect. No one would think it the least bit out of character. But have you got an open gun?"

"Of course not. What do you think, three days before the most important shoot of the year? All my guns were invited and confirmed six months ago."

"But it would look odd if he came all the way up here and couldn't shoot," Wiley said pensively.

"I'll have to give up my gun, that's all. There have never been more than nine guns on this shoot, and I'm not about to change that. No, he can have my place, and I'll double-bank behind someone else. I've done it before, although never on the opening day."

"Gosh, Edith, that's a terrible sacrifice for you. I'd hate to ruin your day," Steddy said.

"It's settled now; don't give it another thought. Just be sure you can get him up here. A few of my guns are arriving tomorrow evening, so he can come as soon as you like. In fact, the sooner the better. I'd like to get to know him before everyone else arrives. Does he have a wife? Oh, of course he does—Thea's mother. Do you think he'll bring her? It would make a difference what room I put him in and with the table placement. I did them ages ago for all the meals—now, of course, I'll have to redo them. . . ."

Steddy grinned at Edith's priorities, knowing it was

just her way of hiding her excitement and the fact that she was enjoying herself tremendously.

"Wiley, we still have almost twenty minutes before we've got to go. Do you think there's enough time for you to get the ball rolling in London?"

"I don't see why not. But you do realize that we're going to have to come down on him pretty hard—about Thea and all—in order to convince him to drop everything and come."

"Of course you will, but the alternative is that if he doesn't come, we've lost the whole shooting match."

Wiley got up to go to the telephone, and Edith called after him, "Don't forget to have them find out if he's bringing his wife."

39

The moon was on the wane though still half full in the sky as Steddy and Wiley set out across the low hills to keep their rendezvous with Chelak. They made their way quietly, using the flashlights from time to time to expose the gullies and deep cuts along their route. Only then, as they trekked through the sopping wet, fragrant gorse, was Steddy struck with the realization that he would soon come face to face with the phantom who'd been tracking him so relentlessly for so long. The thought was oddly comforting. He didn't know why, he certainly didn't feel particularly brave or, for that matter, reckless. It was just that at last things were coming to a head; there was a plan, and he felt more in control of his actions. For a change he was orchestrating events instead of being manipulated.

He was grateful to have Wiley with him and couldn't imagine how he had ever thought he could have proceeded on his own. Just the simple matter of contacting Nubar would have presented insurmountable difficulties that he could never have broached alone without bringing half of Scotland Yard down on his head and putting Thea's life in greater danger than it already was.

They crossed a narrow horse trail and then climbed a steep rise that brought them to the ancient, rough-cut stone road that spiraled up the hill to the ruin. Steddy illuminated his watch—it was two minutes shy of midnight. Funny, he thought, midnight rendezvous were strictly out of dime novels, but maybe the dark was for his own protection. They'd told him that no one had ever seen Chelak's face and lived to tell about it. He turned to Wiley and said with a note of regret, "Well, pal, I guess this is where we part company."

"Okay, Bogey, but check that you've got your radio on standby." Wiley chuckled, surprised by his own levity.

Steddy checked it and said, "Right. Now, give me ten minutes to signal you with the flashlight—two flashes if you're to come up and one if you're to stay where you are."

"And if I don't get a signal after ten minutes, I'm coming up. Understood?"

"Yeah, and the radio's just in case something we haven't thought of happens."

"Good luck," Wiley whispered. "And for God's sake, stay calm and don't get excited."

40

At half past midnight, Edith was still sitting up in the library of the castle with Karesin to keep her company. Wiley had told her before leaving that he doubted Pete Register would call back before they returned, but if he did, just to say they were unavailable for the moment and would call back as soon as possible.

In any case, neither Edith nor Karesin had the least intention of going to bed before "the boys," as they referred to them, got back.

At five minutes to one, the telephone did ring, and although Karesin was the first to reach it, Edith exercised her prerogative and snatched the receiver from his hand. She stood up straight, raised the instrument to her ear, and in her most regal voice, which registered somewhere between Queen Mary's and Eleanor Roosevelt's, intoned: "Lady Lynde speaking. Who is that, please?"

There was a moment's silence, a throat readjusting itself after the unexpected salutation, and then: "Good evening. Could I speak with Wiley Travis, please?"

"Who is that speaking?"

Another pause.

"This is Peter Register, ma'am, and I hope I haven't disturbed you at this hour."

"How could you possibly disturb me when I'm staying up to see them safely home."

"*Them*, ma'am?"

"Wiley and Stedman, of course. Somebody has to look after their welfare, as it certainly doesn't appear that the CIA gives a hoot!"

Register couldn't believe his ears. How could Wiley have been so irresponsible as to confide in an old lady? He chose to ignore her remark.

"You say they're out, ma'am?"

"That's right. They're out there in the dark meeting that horrible Israeli who kidnapped Theadora—doing your job for you, I'll wager. I think it's simply dreadful that you spies find it necessary to involve decent young girls and boys in your nefarious goings-on. Why, in my day . . ."

Register had turned beet red and was steaming.

"Excuse me, ma'am, but I don't think this sort of talk is going to help any of us just now. How long ago did they leave?"

"Didn't they tell you what they were doing when they called you about Nubar Harkonian?"

At the mention of Nubar's name, Register became apoplectic.

"Madam, you'll forgive me, but I don't think any of these matters are appropriate for us to discuss. I do not know you, and you have not been cleared to have knowledge of this information."

"Not cleared? Not cleared? I like that." And then aside to Karesin: "Imagine the nerve of this puppy! Young man, I'll have you know—"

"Were you talking to someone else in the room, ma'am?"

"Certainly. My manservant, Karesin. I suppose you think that he's not cleared—you have a nerve. I'll have you know that I was given the highest security clearance in the kingdom by his majesty's government in 1940. Why, I even knew the date of the invasion before the King did. And as for Karesin, as for Karesin, his people have worked for my people for over three centuries and fought side by side for this country all over the world, and the only war we ever lost was for the colonies, which is evidently what's the matter with you. Not cleared, I like that! You could take a lesson or two when it comes to . . ."

Register's eyes had rolled back in his head; he succumbed totally to her onslaught. When at last she appeared to be running out of steam, he tried again.

"I think you can appreciate that we are not going to gain anything by continuing in this vein." He waited for another stream of invective, and when it didn't come, he continued. "Now, believe it or not, all of us here are vitally concerned with their safety"—he was thinking to himself that he could cheerfully shoot them if they were standing in front of him at that moment—"and will do everything we can to help and protect them, but they must consult us before going off half-cocked, or there's nothing whatsoever we can do."

"I agree with you absolutely, of course. After all, didn't I help Wiley convince Stedman to cooperate with you in the first place?"

"I didn't know that ma'am."

"Well, of course I did, and I must say I'm surprised that they didn't tell you about tonight's meeting, but they're both so worried about Theadora, and, well, you know, boys will be boys."

"Yes, ma'am." (He couldn't believe the about-face in her attitude. He decided that she was a lunatic.) "Now, when did they leave?"

"Well, the rendezvous was at twelve, and as it's about a fifteen-minute walk from the castle to where they were meeting, I'd say they left at about eleven forty-five, or thereabouts."

"So they've been gone for a little over an hour?"

"That's right. I'm frightfully worried, but still, what with coming and going, that's not so terribly long, do you think?"

"I don't know, but if they're not back by one-thirty—no matter what deal I made with them—I'm going to send in the marines."

"You'll forgive me for saying so, but don't you think that's what you should have done in the first place?"

"Would you please have Wiley call me the minute they get back."

"Certainly. Is there a special number you'd like him to call?"

Register was beyond anger.

"He has it. Thank you, Lady Lynde, and good night."

"Hold on a moment. What about the Harkonians?"

"Well, what about them?"

"Well, are they coming to my shoot or not?"

"Lady Lynde, this agency is not a social secretarial agency." And then, defeated: "But to answer your question, the baron will be arriving on his private jet at eight AM tomorrow morning. I hope that will be convenient."

"It couldn't be less convenient, but we all have to do our bit, don't we?"

"Yes, I guess we do."

"At least he'll be in time for the first drive, but you didn't tell me if the baroness is coming with him."

"The baroness?"

"Yes, Baroness Harkonian. I must know if she's coming—for the table placements and the rooms, don't you know."

"I'm afraid I don't know whether or not she's accompanying him."

"Well, do find out and get back to me, won't you?"

"I'll certainly do my best. Good-bye."

41

Steddy knew the ruin of the old castle well. He had played there as a child with Edith's children, and during the shooting season, if the weather was fine, a picnic was laid for the shoot lunch in the lee of the tallest stone wall, which had once been part of the original hall. As he carefully picked his way up the steeply winding road, he could see that wall looming above him, silhouetted against the sky-line like a snaggled tooth jutting from the soft, mossy ground.

When he gained the top of the tor, the structure came alive and took on its own eerie existence, resonating with a melancholy melody orchestrated by the wind and backlighted by the racing moon, which cast it in deep, undulating shadow one moment and then pitch-blackness the next.

He crossed a great worn stone that must once have been the threshold, and his flashlight's beam picked up the charred indentation of the hearth directly opposite. He advanced halfway toward it and then pivoted slowly, shining his light on the low, decaying walls that defined the perimeter.

The woodsy timbre of the voice when it came was so thoroughly in harmony with the windsong that Steddy was not startled by it. He merely continued to scan the ruin, now seeking the source of the disembodied words.

"You will not find me in the light of your torch. It will be better for you if you do not see me," the voice said in clear, distinct English without the slightest trace of any accent, although the use of the word "torch" instead of "flashlight" led Steddy to conclude that the man's training had been British.

"Before we discuss the business at hand, would you kindly tell me why you chose to disregard my request that you come alone?"

Steddy didn't like being put so quickly on the defensive.

"Let's just say he's my oldest friend in the world and likely to be concerned if I disappeared. I also thought that in case I get picked up by Scotland Yard, it would be a good idea for you to have somebody else to deal with so that we can get Thea back safely."

"I have no desire to do any harm to anybody."

"I don't know what it is you want. If it's money, I have quite a lot of cash—"

"I am well aware of how much cash you have, Mr. Wright. If I had wanted money, I would have taken it in Aberdeen. You forget that it is only thanks to me that you still have your cash—not to mention your life."

"So it is you I have to thank for that?"

"Don't mention it."

"I suppose I also have to thank you for the mess I'm in. Why did you murder Omar and make it look as though I'd done it?"

"Alas, that was not me, Mr. Wright. A very messy business, not at all my style. I think you will have to blame that one on your friends, the British. Not so civilized as they like one to think, are they, Mr. Wright?"

"But none of this makes any sense. Why would they do such a thing and make it look as though I had done it? And if you don't want money, what do you want? I don't understand any of this."

"Your friend, Lord Rockford, has what we all want."

"But he's dead."

"That is doubtful."

'If you don't want Wiley to come up, I'll have to signal him now. He may already be on his way."

"Then by all means do so, and take your time, Mr. Wright. We have plenty of time . . . tonight."

Steddy retraced his footsteps over the threshold to the edge of the track and signaled down in the general direction of the spot where he and Wiley had parted. There was no answering flash, so he signaled again and this time got a reply right away, but from much closer up the path than where he had left him. He'd already started up, Steddy thought as he turned back to the ruin, glad he had caught him in time.

"Oh, Mr. Wright." The voice seemed to be coming from the chimney. "If you will just shine your light to the right of where you are standing, you will find a snapshot that I'm sure will be of interest to you."

Steddy aimed the beam in the direction Chelak had indicated, and almost at once, the light picked up the glint of the photo against the dull, mossy stone. It was a Polaroid of Thea.

"When you get back, you will be able to compare the London *Times* that Miss Boulton is holding in the photograph with today's edition. You will find they are the same, but don't conclude that the photo was taken in London, or even England, for that matter—as you know, the *Times* is sold the same day all over Europe."

Steddy stared at the picture he held under the flashlight. How strange that the closer one is bound emotionally to someone, the more difficult it becomes to conjure up that person's features from memory, Steddy thought as he studied the snapshot of Thea sitting upright in a chair, her long hair untypically covering one side of her unsmiling face—how ironic it would be if this were to become the only image of her he would ever have.

"Come, come, Mr. Wright. Let's get on with this. The picture is yours to keep."

"But what will happen to Thea if Rockford *is* dead?"

"I have told you that Rockford is not dead. He contacted someone after the time that he was supposed to have thrown himself into the sea."

"Well, wouldn't whomever he contacted be better able to find him than me? I don't have the slightest idea where he is."

"I'm afraid that the only person we know he contacted

was the man you so blithely threw from the window of your hotel room, which should prove to you that I had nothing to do with his demise.''

"I have his notebook—it's in Arabic or something, but maybe it could tell you something."

"I had an opportunity to look that over in Aberdeen as well. There was nothing in it of any value, although Lord Rockford appears to have been in greater debt to him than I had supposed."

The sound of the wind through the ruin increased to a howl. Big drops of water began to fall. Steddy became impatient.

"Look here, the only thing I'm interested in is getting Thea back safely as soon as possible. Now suppose I'm able to locate Rockford—what then?"

"You have but to tell me where he is, and once we have recovered what is ours, Miss Boulton will be returned to you."

Here Wiley had coached Steddy very thoroughly, and Steddy was grateful that he was prepared.

"I'm afraid I couldn't agree to that. How could I be sure that you would return her once you had what you wanted? No, we would have to work out some sort of exchange."

"I commend you on your prudence, Mr. Wright. I am sure we could work something out provided you can obtain what we want."

Steddy was astonished by the civilized banter that this assassin was capable of.

"And what is it that you want? If Rockford is alive, I'm not going to turn him over to you so that you can do to him what you did to that man in Aberdeen."

"I told you, I have no interest in harming anyone. All we want is what is rightfully ours. Lord Rockford has certain documents in his possession that are the property of my government. They are in a yellow envelope and are sealed with sealing wax with identifying marks stamped into the seals. The seals must not be broken or Miss Boulton's life will be forfeit."

"But what if they are already broken?"

"I do not believe Lord Rockford would have done that, as their only value for sale would be lost if they were opened."

The rain was pelting Steddy in earnest now.

"Well, I'd better get to it, then," he said, wanting to bring the interview to a close. "How will I contact you when I learn something?"

"You cannot. I will contact you. We will meet here tomorrow night at the same time."

"But what if I discover something and have to leave to find him before then? I don't want you to think that I ran out on you."

"That would be most unwise—for Miss Boulton's sake."

"That's just what I meant. Will you be nearby the whole time?"

"I think you can appreciate that I have no intention of answering a question like that. But you will be watched, if that's what you mean."

"No, it's not that. It's these walkie-talkies." Stedman wrestled the unit from under his jacket and held it up by the flashlight. "The keepers use these on the estate; they have a very long range because there are booster antennas all over. I think they're good for about ten miles, and they're synthesized, so we can set them to work on whatever frequency you like."

"You are full of surprises, aren't you, Mr. Wright?"

"Just being prudent, as you said before. Wiley has the other one, and if you pick a frequency, I could leave this one here for you and match the setting on Wiley's."

Steddy stood in the driving rain for some minutes before Chelak answered.

"What frequency is it set on now?"

Steddy examined the digital readout of the synthesizer as Karesin had shown him.

"It's set at 440.050, for Wiley and me. We changed it from 440.025—that's the frequency the estate uses."

"Then leave it as it is and place it where you found the picture."

Steddy walked back to the wall and placed the transmitter under the stone shelf.

"Now, Mr. Wright, we will establish a rendezvous time—shall we say every two hours, starting at eight AM through one AM?"

"That will be fine with me, and if anything goes wrong with the radios, I'll be here at the same time tomorrow."

"Then good night, Mr. Wright."

Steddy stood there for a moment, but there was no further sound save the wind reclaiming the rain.

Part III
The Glorious Twelfth

42

It was precisely eight AM when the wheels of the
white Mystere 20 alighted on the tarmac of the small airstrip
outside Perth. The cabin door containing the stair opened as
the jet came to a halt. Karesin drove the lumbering old
Bentley shooting brake onto the apron and parked alongside
the aircraft. Nubar was out of the plane, with Elizabeth
hurrying to keep up with him, before the steward had a
chance to secure the stair.

Harkonian neither waited for Elizabeth nor acknowl-
edged Karesin, who held the Bentley's weather-beaten wooden
door for him as he climbed in—he was obviously in no
mood to display the courtesy people thought was second
nature to him. He sat in the back, fists clenched and face
like a thundercloud, oblivious to the activity around him as
Elizabeth entered the car and two small cases were placed in
the rear compartment by the steward. When the car had
gained the main road back to Scone, Karesin addressed him.

"Her ladyship's compliments, sir, and I was to tell you
that the party was gathering in the forecourt at nine-thirty."

"Party? Party? What party?" Harkonian appeared to
have been awakened from a dream, or perhaps a nightmare,
and the trace of an accent suddenly tinged his normally
flawless English.

"Why, the shooting party, sir," Karesin replied.

"Shooting party? Are you mad? I've come all the way

up here to see Mr. Wright on very urgent business." And then, genuinely confused: "Isn't that where you're taking us?"

"Yes, sir."

"Then what's all this about a shooting party? Is this some sort of a joke? Because if it is, you can turn—"

"No, sir, it's just that her ladyship thought it would be safer for you to meet during the shoot—what with all the guests about the castle."

Nubar was fuming. "This is preposterous, and who is this lady anyway?"

"Countess Lynde, sir, and I think it would be best if her ladyship explained everything to you when we get to the castle." Karesin's tone made it clear that as far as he was concerned the conversation had come to a close, and although Nubar grumbled and mumbled under his breath to Elizabeth, he had spent enough time in Scotland to know that he would get nothing further out of Karesin.

Edith was in the hall greeting arriving guests and directing them either to their rooms, if they were staying the night, or into the dining hall, where an enormous shoot breakfast had been laid. She was prepared for the Harkonians when they appeared, as she was getting quite used to treating perfect strangers as long-lost friends, and had no trouble recognizing them, in their fashionable town clothes in contrast to the comfortably worn country tweeds of her other "guns."

"My dears!" she exclaimed, walking forward to meet them as they entered the hall. "I'm so glad you could make it. It's been an age," she said, kissing Elizabeth on both cheeks. "Let me take you to your rooms so you can get changed."

Noting their puzzled expressions and to avoid any embarrassing questions, she took hold of Elizabeth's elbow with a force that was surprising in a woman of her stature and directed her in a no-nonsense manner toward the stair—presenting them to a royal duke and a newspaper tycoon along the way.

"I can't think why you've stayed away so long," she could still be heard cooing as they ascended the great stair.

The sense of the castle and the position that his hostess appeared to command in the social order of things tended to oil the troubled waters of Nubar's temper, for though he loomed large in the power structure of Europe's financial capitals and moved with ease among a glamorous circle of friends, he was still a snob, and shooting at the elbow of a royal duke was the sort of fantasy that filled his reverie. Edith had a gut understanding of this and intended to exercise the full weight of her privilege on this weakness to force his hand.

"I do hope you'll be comfortable in these rooms. They were King George and the Queen's favorites—they used them quite a lot during the war."

The sitting room she had shown them into was circular, with the palest blue and white paneling, which fused with the Scottish sky through the big curved windows that overlooked the park.

"The bedroom is through there." She gestured to where two footmen had disappeared with their cases.

"Oh, it's simply splendid, isn't it, dearest?" Elizabeth replied with genuine admiration.

"Yes, dear, and the countess seems to have tamed the Scottish climate."

"I wish I could take credit for the weather. Alas. But if I could, fine days like these wouldn't be so few and far between."

The footman bowed their way out of the room and closed the door. Edith turned to the Harkonians in earnest.

"I apologize for the sham performance, but it would seem awfully odd to everyone if I invited total strangers to shoot on the most important day of the year."

Edith's manipulation of Nubar was artful. In one sentence she had put Harkonian in his place, clearly beneath hers, while in the next breath taking him on as an intimate, a confidant, and a co-conspirator.

Elizabeth Harkonian could no longer control herself. Her face revealed the undeniable strain she was under.

"Countess, we were told rather brutally by a perfect stranger using Stedman Wright's name that my daughter had been kidnapped and was in grave danger, and that only by coming here could we help her, but now it appears that Steddy and Thea have been playing a very ugly joke at our expense, and that we've really been brought here for a shooting party. I assure you we would have been delighted to come without these melodramatic cloak-and-dagger shenanigans and—''

Edith warmed to Elizabeth.

"My dear, I wish I could put your mind at ease. I've become very fond of Theadora while she's been with us, and I can't tell you how worried we all are."

Elizabeth's eyes grew larger and glistened. She seemed to shrink visibly under her cape as she crumpled into the huge overstuffed chair by the chimney, which had the effect of making her look even smaller, more childlike and vulnerable. Edith sat on the arm of the chair and took her hand.

"Now, my dear, tears won't—''

Nubar strode over to them. His wife's tears had brought him back to the reality of the situation.

"This whole thing is absurd. I demand to know exactly what's going on."

There was a knock at the door. Edith was glad for an excuse to ignore Harkonian's rude manner.

"Come."

Karesin entered the room, having changed back into the charcoal-gray jacket he wore in the house.

"Yes, Karesin, what is it?"

He eyed the Harkonians suspiciously, hesitant to speak in their presence.

"Come, come, what is it?" she repeated.

"There's a gentleman from the police to see you, milady."

"Can't you see this is no time to entertain the local constabulary? Send him away." She turned her back to Karesin and faced the Harkonians.

"But, milady, he's not a local, and the only thing Scottish about him is that he's from Scotland Yard—and he asked for Mr. Wright."

"God, it must be that awful Allso, or whatever his name is," Harkonian interrupted.

"Allsloe, I believe, sir," Karesin replied, proffering a card. Harkonian groaned.

"What did you tell him?" Edith asked.

"I said that we didn't know a Mr. Wright, and then he said 'Stedman Wright.' Well, I said we knew him, right enough, but that we hadn't seen him in some time. Well, milady, then he asked to see you, or if you weren't available, Mr. Travis. Everyone in the hall was getting curious like, so I put him in the library and came up to fetch you, milady."

"You did the right thing, Karesin. Now go back down and tell him I'll be along directly," Edith said nervously, glancing at the clock on the chimney.

"We've never started a shoot a minute late, and today will not be the first time. I had better go down and see to this policeman."

"Would you like me to come with you?" Nubar volunteered without enthusiasm.

"No, thank you. Why don't you both relax for a bit, and I'll let you—"

"But what about Thea?" Elizabeth exclaimed. "And where's Steddy? Is it true he's not here?"

"My dear, I will send Steddy to you the moment I've got rid of this Scotland Yard man. Now, do try to calm yourself and order some tea." She pulled the bell cord for a maid as she left the room.

Wiley was waiting for her at the landing.

"I gather that bloody Allsloe is here."

"Yes, I'm just going down to see him. They must have followed you when you came up."

"I really don't think so." Wiley defended himself. "But they seem to know that Steddy's here as well."

"I think he's bluffing, otherwise they would have paid us a visit long before now. Now, you go through my room and tell Steddy that the Harkonians have arrived but that he has got to stay hidden until the inspector goes—and make sure no one sees you."

"Will do."

They parted to carry out their individual missions.

* * *

Edith was surprised by the appearance of the person she found waiting for her in the library. For a moment she thought Karesin had been mistaken about where he had put the inspector, for the man whose dull gaze greeted her as she entered the room was certainly not cast in the mold of a chief inspector of Scotland Yard, at least not in the mold that the BBC would have used.

Here was a simple gentleman, not undistinguished, with thinning ginger hair and startlingly red bushy eyebrows that could have marked him as a Scot. His clothes didn't give him away either. Wearing a well-worn tweed suit and clean but not polished brogues, he could have been one of her guests for the shoot, or at the very least one of her gentleman tenant farmers.

"Comfortable" was the only description she could think of. He did look rather comfortable—like almost any one of her old friends.

She straightened her back and approached him to introduce herself as one of the footmen in the hall closed the door behind her. She had the oddest feeling that she was intruding on *him* in *his* library—she forced it from her mind.

"I'm Lady Lynde. How may I help you?"

"Good morning, Lady Lynde. I'm Inspector—"

"Yes, I know." She interrupted him, holding his card out for him to see. "Can't whatever it is wait till another day? It is the twelfth of August, and my shoot starts in twenty minutes. As you can see, I haven't dressed yet."

"I'm sorry to incommode you and don't wish to make you late, but I'm here on a very grave matter."

"Have no fear of making me late. I don't intend to allow it. This shoot has never begun late in over a hundred years, and today will be no exception."

"If you'll just take me to see Mr. Wright, then you can get on with your shooting—you certainly have a lovely day for it."

"My man told me you were looking for Mr. Wright, and that he told you he is not here. I'll save you the trouble of asking again—he is not here." Edith felt better that at least half of what she had told him was the truth.

"I may as well tell you at the start that I have a search warrant."

"And how could that possibly affect what I say?"

"Let's leave that for the moment—"

"Yes, let's do," she said, her tone chastising him for questioning her veracity. He seemed not to notice.

"And Mr. Wiley Travis is not here either?"

"Mr. Travis is one of my guests. Would you like to see him?"

"That would be most helpful."

Edith started toward the door. "I'll have Karesin try to find him for you, but now I really must change. Will you look after yourself till he comes? There are some books over there that might interest you—my husband collected mysteries." And then, at the door: "Would you like some coffee?"

"That would be very nice, thank you."

"I'll look in on you before we leave." She closed the door behind her, gave instructions about the inspector's coffee, and raced up the stairs with Karesin at her heels.

Karesin had trouble keeping up with Edith as she hurried up the stone stairs with her peignoir trailing behind her.

"I want them all out of the house, Karesin—do you hear me? I will not be caught out lying to the police. And can you imagine the cheek—bringing a search warrant!"

"Yes, milady."

"Now, go down to Steddy and get him into some clothes so he looks like a loader—he can load for Harkonian— and I'll go and get them into something suitable for the field."

They reached the top of the landing.

"And be quick about it." Then, as an afterthought: "And *damn*! You had better get one of the men to set the courtyard clock back half an hour, and be sure no one sees him. I will not start this shoot late."

She charged into the Harkonian's sitting room without knocking and found them in the same positions as she had left them.

"Now, there is very little time, and you must do exactly as I say. I'm arranging for you to meet with Steddy, but that policeman has had the nerve to bring a search warrant, and I can't have you found in the house, especially as you say he knows who you are. Now please follow me."

She wheeled and left the room before they had a chance to question her. They followed her down the hall to where a small mahogany door led off a vestibule. She addressed Nubar over her shoulder as she opened the door.

"This was my late husband's dressing room. He was about your size, and you will find everything you need to wear in the field in the cupboards."

"Not this bloody shooting again. Can't you see my wife is half mad from all these charades?"

"Please do as I say. There is no time to explain except to say that Steddy will be your loader and you'll have plenty of time between drives to talk in complete privacy. You can shoot, can't you?"

"Yes, of course I can shoot, but—"

"Then please be quick getting dressed. Here, wear this." She threw a tweed suit from one of the cupboards at him and said to Elizabeth, "You come with me."

Elizabeth walked meekly behind her through a connecting door into Edith's adjacent dressing room, where her clothes were laid out on a chaise and her maid was awaiting her.

"Harriet, I shall dress myself. You help the baroness find a skirt and a sweater and some more appropriate shoes. If she can't wear mine, get her some Wellies from the boot room, but do hurry."

There was a knock from the wall behind her that hid the secret door to the keep. Young Harriet, her lady's maid, looked very puzzled. Edith barked at her, "Go on, quick, quick, down to the boot room with you." Harriet scurried from the room, totally confused but too frightened to question her mistress's orders when she was clearly in a state. When she heard the bedroom door close behind her maid, Edith exhaled a deep sigh.

"Oh, God, what can it be now?"

Elizabeth watched her in total bewilderment as she sprung open the panel to reveal a red-faced, out-of-breath Wiley Travis.

"I hope I did the right thing coming this way, but Karesin told me that Scotland Yard was still in the hall."

"Not in the hall, but in the library waiting for you."

"You can't be serious. What did you tell him?"

"Aside from perjuring myself left, right, and center, the only true thing I told him was that you were here. Not that he didn't seem to know it already."

"But what shall I say to him?"

"Frankly, Wiley, I couldn't give a damn! I've got a shoot to run. You're CIA, I'm sure you'll think of something, but he seems to have an awful lot to say himself. Why don't you just try listening to him?"

Nubar came in through the adjoining door without knocking and immediately spotted Wiley.

"Wiley, my boy, what do you know about all this?"

"Wiley has to go straight down to the inspector before he comes looking for him, and if you don't mind, you're in a lady's boudoir and most unwelcome. We'll fetch you when we're dressed, which will never happen if you don't both leave—*now!*"

Karesin was enjoying reeducating Steddy on his duties as a loader while he dressed him in an odd assortment of borrowed tweeds, a worn tattersall shirt, and a wool tie. Fortunately, with plus fours, there was no need to make allowances for Steddy's height—they simply became plus twos. Steddy was a little put out by Karesin's patronizing attitude.

"You know very well that I had to load for my father for years before I was ever allowed to shoot," he said, defending himself.

"That's not to say you remember. We can't have that foreigner shooting up the local gentry on the first day out—give the shoot a bad name."

"Don't worry, I'll keep an eye on him. He's a pretty good shot, but I'm not sure if he's ever killed grouse before. But he must have—he tries to be more English than the English."

"If he never shot grouse, it might as well be the first time he ever shot a gun, as you well know. Still, I drew a pair of Bosses from the gun room for him. Kinear has them; he'll give them to you in the courtyard.''

"I guess I'll have to go out with the rest of the loaders and the beaters?'' Steddy asked.

"You'll be going with the other loaders and Duncan—he's one of the new underkeepers. The beaters are long gone—they have to get on the ground early. They're beating the tops at Buchowrie for the first drive. But you'll know some of the loaders. I told Kinear to tell them not to let on to their guns that they know you—said you were playing a practical joke on the foreigner.''

"They must have thought that was a little odd?''

"When it comes to foreigners, they don't think nothing's odd. They're all good chaps. They'll play along with it.''

Karesin sneaked Steddy out to the courtyard through the big kitchens, where there was such a flurry of activity getting breakfast out and preparing the lunch to be served in the field that no one gave him a second glance.

Kinear, the head keeper, gave Steddy as big a hello as a Scotsman ever does and handed him the pair of Bosses in their sleeves and the cartridge bags he would need, while Karesin teased the man unmercifully. There was always a friendly rivalry between the indoor and outdoor servants, and Karesin and the rest of the staff in the house never tired of calling the head keeper "the poacher," always careful to grin when they said it.

The last to arrive, Steddy was piled into the back of a long-wheelbase Land Rover with the eight other loaders. He sat next to Donald, a local man employed on the estate, who had loaded for him often over the years.

"Having a bit of sport at a foreigner's expense, we heard. Must be an important fellow for her ladyship to give up her gun on the first day.''

"He's a tycoon, but he likes his shooting and isn't a bad shot.''

"Well, I'll mind to keep my head down if we draw the butt next to you," Donald said without a great deal of humor. "You know, in my granddaddy's day—that was when the seventh earl was still alive—he told me they had a foreign gentleman once, and were shooting the west moor, you know, where the blackface sheep still graze.'' Steddy nodded that he remembered. ''Well, anyway, after the drive, the old earl asked him how many grouse he had killed, and the bugger answered that the grouse were too quick for him, but that he had got five of the ''wild sheep.''

Steddy and the other loaders roared with laughter, even though they had all heard the story many times before. One of the other loaders piped in.

''Tell him about the American general who was here as a guest a few years back, Donald.''

Donald looked sheepishly at Steddy and said, ''I don't like to say.'' But Steddy insisted and said, ''Go on, and I'll tell you one about a Scotsman.''

''Well, we had one of the best drives of the day, but he couldn't hit a thing and blamed it all on the way Kinear deployed the beaters—said he was so mad at him he could shoot him. Well, her ladyship overheard and just said to him, very quiet like but so's we all could hear, ''I don't believe you could!''

Steddy enjoyed the company and the drive through the heather so much that he almost forgot that he had a more serious mission to accomplish than a day of sport on the moors.

Nubar and Elizabeth were at Edith's heels when she corrected the duke, who suggested that they were starting a bit late, and took him by the arm to lead the whole party out to the courtyard. He changed his watch when he saw that the clock over the stables read nine twenty-five. She took from the pocket of her tweed jacket a worn leather slipcase that held the nine numbered ivory counters that would be drawn for position.

''All right, everybody, please draw a number.'' The nine men who were shooting crowded round her and each drew one of the small staves from the pocket that concealed its number.

''Now, we'll be shooting Buchowrie for the first beat— they're driving the tops now. There are a lot of canny old cocks up there that I want killed, so let's see your best shooting. Oh, and for those of you who've never shot with me before, please advance two numbers after each drive. We'll have three drives before lunch and two after. Now, who's drawn five?'' The duke raised his hand and said, ''Here.''

''Oh, grand, Beaky, you've got the hot seat. Now, do your best—those old birds played havoc with my breeding this spring.''

''I'll try not to let any of them by, old girl.''

Edith had kept her thumb over the end counter till everyone had drawn but Nubar and then offered it to him. It was number nine and would be the last butt at the top of the ridge—where he could do the least harm and would have the fewest shots.

Karesin held the door of the tan Bentley shooting brake open for his mistress, and at precisely nine-thirty, she and her guests climbed into the two matching vehicles that would take them out on the moors.

Elizabeth was sitting in the back seat of Edith's car between Nubar and the duke.

''Has your husband done much grouse shooting?'' the duke asked with that curious mixture of genuine curiosity, courtesy, and enthusiasm that royals display.

Nubar answered for himself.

''No, sir, I've never shot grouse before, but I do a fair amount of shooting—mostly in Austria and Czechoslovakia.''

''I used to shoot Czechoslovakia every year with my cousin, but those damn reds finally got the better of me. You know, the political officer always spouting slogans, and of course I was usually the object of his zeal. But you know, my cousin Ferdinand—he's spoken of you often—says your woods are riddled with game.''

''Yes, of course I do, sir. The prince comes to shoot with me often in Austria.''

''Well, grouse shouldn't give you too much trouble. They're a lot faster than pheasant, but there isn't much wind this early in the season. You've got to really watch these old birds on the first drive, though—they haven't lived this long because they're stupid, and they'll jink if they spot you. The best advice I can give you is to keep as still as possible and take your time." He then turned to Elizabeth. "Well, Baroness, you're in for a treat. Edith doesn't usually allow observers in the butts. You must be greatly in her favor."

"I've always wanted to see a grouse shoot," she replied.

"Just remember to get right down behind the wall and stay down if you feel you're being peppered—you'll be all right."

"Thank you for the advice. I'll certainly heed it. I'm only staying out for the first drive, but I'll join you in the field for lunch later."

"That will be a great pleasure," he said, smiling warmly at her. Then he asked Nubar, "What number did you draw?"

"Nine."

"Well, that's good for your first time out. You won't get much action, but at least you'll get a chance to get the hang of it. Couldn't be more perfect if it were planned that way," he said, grinning at Edith in the front seat, who smiled sweetly back at him, full of innocence.

It was a beautiful day, and the drive across the moor—purple with heather and dotted with sparkling brooks and streams—was exhilarating. After about fifteen minutes, Karesin pulled the car up alongside some scrub and pinewood, where the pony men in kilts held their animals, which were laden with large panniers to hold the bag after the drive. The loaders were already at their butts, as Kinear had radioed the draw ahead.

Everyone regrouped by the cars, and Edith said to Nubar, "Baron, you had better start hiking. It's a long, steep climb, and you'll need a few minutes' rest before the drive reaches us. Freddie, will you show them the way? You're number eight, aren't you?" she said to a tall man of about sixty named Colonel Blake-Williams.

The red-faced colonel jovially took them both in hand and led them over the plank bridge to cross the deep burn that ran alongside the road. They followed the rude, stoney path cut through the heather and bracken, and climbed the steep hill to the ridge at the top, passing the seven other butts along the way and listening to the colonel's shooting stories. He was a neighbor and had shot every opening day since the war, and it appeared that he had a tale for each butt. He wished them good luck as he joined his loader in number eight and they continued the grueling climb till they reached number nine, which was dug into a hollow below the ridge, and like the other butts, was built of stones and sod. A grim-faced Steddy—looking very much the local—awaited them.

If Wiley could have fled from the house, he would have, but as things stood, he had little choice but to follow Edith's orders and present himself to the inspector in the library. He had no idea what to say. I'll just have to wing it, he thought with little conviction, as he shut the library door behind him.

The inspector was standing across the room looking out the window and did not turn at the sound of Wiley's entry.

"Hello, inspector. What brings you to Scotland?" Wiley said as casually as he could.

Allsloe answered without turning.

"Mr. Travis, you know very well why I'm here, and as time is not on our side, I think nothing will be gained by beating about the bush." He turned slowly to face Wiley. "I know Mr. Wright is with you, and I know that Miss Boulton is missing." He paused for effect, but the gaze that Wiley returned was as blank as his own. He continued, "Please bring Mr. Wright to me immediately. Nothing will be gained by searching the house and disturbing Lady Lynde any further."

Wiley was floored to think that Allsloe knew about Thea. Where was the leak? Was the phone in the keep tapped?

"I'm afraid I don't know what you mean."

"That simply won't do, Mr. Travis. I have the authority to take you all into custody if you don't cooperate with me to my satisfaction—and that includes Lady Lynde and all her guests, if need be. Now, once more, where is Mr. Wright?"

"I can honestly say that he's not here," Wiley said, still trying to stall.

"Look here, young man, I know that you're doing what you think is right, but you have no idea of the gravity—life-threatening gravity—of the situation in which Miss Boulton and the rest of you have become involved."

"I only know that none of this would have happened in the first place if you hadn't set Steddy up and then pinned Omar's murder on him."

Now it was Allsloe's turn to be taken aback. How could Travis have drawn that conclusion, or even guessed at it, if he really was what he seemed? Allsloe feigned ignorance.

"Whatever do you mean?"

"You know very well that you either murdered Omar or planted the body in Steddy's room—which probably means that either way you murdered him—just so Steddy would lead you to Rockford." Wiley realized that in mentioning Rockford he had probably said too much and silently cursed himself.

"Now where would you get an idea like that?"

Wiley decided to take the offensive.

"Look here, Inspector. I thought you said that there wasn't any more time left for playing games?"

"So I did."

"Well, then, why don't you play straight with us and we'll play straight with you. But just remember that *our* only interest is in getting Thea back safely and putting an end to this whole mess."

"And what makes you think that my motives differ from yours?"

"Because you're after the damn plan and don't give a shit about Thea, or any of us, for that matter."

He had said it and felt better for having done so, even though he knew it meant his head back in Washington. He had made Steddy a promise, and Steddy was right; Thea's life and their trust was more important than some damn top-secret plan that in a year's time would end up covered in dust in a file in Virginia that no one would probably ever look at. He knew that it was not supposed to be up to him to decide what was or was not important, but it looked as though he just had.

"Maybe we had better sit down," Allsloe said, looking markedly older than when Wiley had entered the room.

Steddy and his fellow loaders climbed down from the Land Rover at Buchowrie, the first drive, where the narrow road cut the line of butts between numbers one and two. Number one was on the left of the road, facing the drive, and on the right, numbers two through nine crossed the moor and were staggered in a straight line up the steep rise that defined it, carefully placed under the stoney striations to a point just below the top of the ridge. Each of the men carried a matched pair of twelve-gauge shotguns that belonged to the gentleman they would be loading for, and all were the product of Britain's finest gunsmiths—Holland & Holland, Purdey, or Boss—and had a cumulative value of close to a million dollars. Casually they leaned them in their protective canvas-and-leather sleeves against the low stone wall that separated the road from the deep burn that ran parallel to it and resumed trading shooting stories until Donald, the underkeeper, got their butt assignments from Kinear over the walkie-talkie.

Steddy had the longest climb to reach the number-nine position, so he and the loader for number eight set out first to allow plenty of time for the ascent. One of their duties was to make sure that the keepers had put the butts back in good order after the winter, and if they hadn't, it would be up to them to police them so that all was in readiness for the guns when they arrived.

Steddy had not rehearsed the dialogue he would have with Nubar—so much had transpired all morning, especially with the inspector showing up, that there just hadn't been time. He hadn't been alone for a second. He bid his companion good luck when they reached number eight and concentrated on climbing the treacherous, stoney track to number nine.

Number nine, when he reached it, didn't seem in such bad shape at all—perhaps its position near the top had protected it from the flocks that grazed the lower stretches of the moor. Even the planked wood floor had survived the winter intact.

He leaned the pair of Bosses against the front wall of the butt, put his cartridge bags on the low stool in the corner that was fashioned of sod, and while evening out the top of the front wall with extra sod that was left outside the butt for that purpose, his thoughts turned to what he would say to Nubar. No one really knew for a fact that he was hiding Rollo, and from everything Wiley had told him, it seemed that even the CIA was guessing—just as all their friends in London were guessing. Nobody really knew anything; Nubar was simply the prime candidate. After all, he was the only one in their group with the means—planes, houses, and business connections all over the world—to be able to help Rollo, if he wanted to, and Steddy thought that he probably would have helped Rollo if he could. He always had—at least with money. Steddy recalled that when the rumors originally had started, he'd concluded that if Nubar was going to help Rollo, he would have got him the best lawyer in England and told him to turn himself in. After all, there was more than an even chance that the whole thing would be perceived as an accident and Rollo would get off. . . . But then there was this other thing that complicated matters—the documents. Everyone and his uncle seemed to know about them—but did Nubar? Nubar would never let himself get involved in anything like that; he valued his British passport and his growing position in the establishment too much ever to take such a chance—he even bragged that he was proud to pay his taxes!

The sun was getting high in the sky, and Steddy was sweating in his tweeds as he bent to the work of arranging the sods around the butt. Below him, he could just make out the shooting party arriving in the brakes and setting out across the moor. He redoubled his efforts to analyze the situation: of course, there was more than mere gossip; there were a lot of very serious people who believed that Rollo was still alive. The Israelis had even gone so far as to kidnap an American in Britain, and the CIA was also operating clandestinely under the nose of a friendly power. What about them? What about the British? It seemed almost a fact that they were the ones who had set Steddy up in the first place—maybe they knew something that the others didn't. After all, they had been responsible for the operation to find Rollo's body. Maybe they knew for a fact that he wasn't dead and were withholding the information to keep the others off the track.

Steddy was beginning to get a headache from running all the convoluted possibilities through his head. He shook it hard, as if to clear his mind of all of them, and thought, it's all nothing but speculation. And then, unbidden, from his youth, his grandmother's voice came to him: "Where there's smoke, there's fire." Well, there certainly is a lot of smoke, he thought, as he took his position in the butt and awaited Nubar's arrival, no longer mesmerized by the beauty of the day and the glory of the moor, but once again fully a part of the nightmare he'd been living, grimly determined to make an end of it today, to clear away the smoke, find Thea, and get her back—whatever it took.

It was that grimly resolved countenance that greeted Nubar and Elizabeth when they reached the top of a great flat stone and saw Steddy slightly below them through the opening of the butt.

Nubar slipped on the wind-and-rain-polished surface and almost tumbled headlong into the enclosure, while Elizabeth gingerly picked her way around it and entered the butt composed and frowning in the bright sunshine. Nubar was winded from the climb and tossed the cartridge bags to the floor so that he could collapse on the sod bench and catch his breath. Elizabeth started to question Steddy almost immediately, but Nubar, still unable to speak, flagged at her with his hand to be quiet until he was ready.

"I'm very grateful that you could come so quickly," Steddy said, looking at Elizabeth.

"We had no choice, the way that man spoke to us," Elizabeth said.

"I'm sorry if he was rough, but I assure you it—"

Nubar interrupted. "Where is Thea?" he gasped.

"She's been kidnapped by a very dangerous foreign agent," Steddy answered, not sure how much detail he should go into.

It was Elizabeth's turn to gasp, she did so by sharply

inhaling through her teeth. "But what do you mean? Why would a foreign—?"

"Leave this to me," Nubar snapped, recovering a bit from his exertion but still not enough to take his feet.

"She's my daughter," Elizabeth said, unwilling to be brushed aside so easily.

"And haven't I looked after her as though she were my own since she was twelve? Leave this for Steddy and me to handle." Turning to Steddy, Nubar said, "Now, tell me exactly what has happened, how much money he wants and when and where he wants it."

"It isn't a question of money—"

"Not money. But then what can he want?"

"He wants—and I might add that he's not the only person who's after them—certain top-secret documents that Rollo got hold of before he disappeared."

"Rollo is dead," Nubar almost barked. "This is absurd. What would any of us know about top-secret documents anyway?"

"Israeli, American, and British intelligence don't seem to think he's dead," Steddy answered, watching Nubar's face intently for any sign or reaction.

"Well, then, why don't they find him if it's so important? What could Thea possibly have to do with this? She hardly even knew Rollo."

Steddy decided on his course of action—it seemed so clear to him now, he wondered why it had eluded him before.

"Because they know that you're hiding him, and I've been picked out to play middleman in the exchange," Steddy lied bluntly.

Nubar's face regained the intense shade of red that had only just begun to fade after his climb.

"That's preposterous!" The *r* rolled slightly as he spoke, a sure sign that he was angry—or nervous. "I haven't any idea where he is!"

"Then you admit that you do know he's still alive?" Steddy jumped in like a first-rate cross-examiner.

"Of course I don't. I thought he was dead, like everybody else," Nubar answered defensively. "And I don't know *now* that he isn't," he added, regaining some control and standing up, albeit leaning against the front wall of the butt.

Behind Nubar, on a distant ridge, Steddy saw a flash of crimson and white sparkling in the sun. One of the beaters flags, he thought. The drive was beginning to reach them. Nubar turned around to see what had captured Steddy's interest.

"It's the drive," Steddy said, and as he said it, they could just hear the far-off calling of the beaters and the whacks of their sticks against the heather and bracken echoing hollowly in the valley. Automatically, Steddy methodically broke and loaded the Bosses and leaned them back against the butt. "The birds won't be coming for a while yet, but keep well down so they don't spot you."

"The hell with the birds!" Elizabeth Harkonian said in a radical departure from her normally composed, ladylike demeanor. "What about Thea?"

"He won't give her back except in exchange for the documents. And if Nubar doesn't tell us how to find Rollo, we've got no chance at all," Steddy replied, as though he had heard none of Nubar's denials.

A small pack of birds had risen, flown toward the center of the line, and then settled in the heavy cover of the moor—way out of range of the middle guns. Nubar watched them settle and then turned back to Steddy.

"You evidently haven't heard a word I've been saying," he said, his composure fully regained. "I know nothing more about Rollo than you do. Now let's leave that and discuss what measures we can take to get Thea back. Have you *tried* offering him money?"

The noise of the beaters became louder, and now all the gillies' flags could be seen describing a horseshoe far in front of the line, driving the grouse up and over the batteries to their natural alighting ground, which lay behind them. There was a crack from one of the guns that was out of sight below them. "Here they come," Steddy said softly, handling Nubar one of the guns. "Now, keep a sharp lookout. If we get any up here, they'll be crossing fast in front of you, trying to double back to the higher ground at the top, where they like to hide. Keep very still. They can spot movement long before they're in range.''

Once Steddy had Nubar in position, he crouched behind him, holding the number-two gun ready to pass over his shoulder when both barrels of the first were expended. While they waited, Steddy answered Nubar's question. He spoke very quietly, whether in deference to the birds or the gravity of the subject, one couldn't tell, but Elizabeth could hear clearly what he said over the sporadic, distant popping of gunfire.

"Believe me, I tried offering him money. He wants the documents, and if he doesn't get them, he will kill her. It is not a threat. I have personally witnessed him dispatch one of his victims. According to the CIA, he's one of the most ruthless operatives in the Western world, and I don't intend to stand by and watch Thea become another page in his dossier."

Nubar neither moved nor said a word. For all the world, he was intently watching for birds. Suddenly there were three coming quickly toward them with the wind at their tails.

"Someone down the line must have poked at them and made them jink," Steddy whispered. An old cock was in the lead, hugging the rippling terrain, with the other two lagging behind. "Take the first with one barrel—shoot well ahead of him—then I'll pass you a full gun so you can get the other two with a right and a left," Steddy said, caught up by the sight of the birds.

Nubar killed the first one stone-dead in the air and exchanged guns with Steddy rather smoothly, considering they had never worked as a team before. The second two, either spotting their movement or seeing the first bird fall in front of them, jinked into the wind as if to alight and almost floated in place, right in front of Nubar's gun. He took them easily with a right and a left, just as Steddy had orchestrated.

When Steddy moved to exchange the freshly loaded gun for the now empty one that Nubar held, it was wrenched from his hands, but not by Nubar—by Elizabeth.

Her face was a frightening mask of hatred as she jammed the gun into the small of Nubar's back and held him thus against the front wall of the butt. The birds were in full flight now, and the noise from the guns down the line was terrific.

"You bastard," she seethed. "You are going to tell Steddy exactly how to find Rollo, and you're going to do it right this minute—"

"But, dearest, I haven't the slightest—"

"I said right this minute," she repeated, twisting the barrel of the gun and working it down his spine, so that there was never any lack of pressure again him, until it was firmly lodged between his legs. "I have just removed the safety." There was no reaction from Nubar.

"No one will give it a second thought," she said, jamming the barrel into him and twisting it. "Just another shooting accident, and what's more common on a grouse moor? Why, I don't think even your loader will say anything other than that it was an accident, will you Steddy?"

Steddy's response to the quick glance she shot him was indifference. He was more shocked by the open-mouth, bared-teeth expression on her face than by what she was about to do to Nubar. In a way, he admired her. She turned out to have more balls then either of them, and if she had her way, certainly more than Nubar. Steddy could never have gone this far without knowing for sure that Nubar did know where Rollo was. Elizabeth's renewed invective brought his attention back to what she was saying.

"You rotten bastard! Using me and my family as social stepping stones for your pompous, inflated ego, and now, when my daughter needs you—when I need you—putting your twopenny social fantasies before us." Then, turning to Steddy, almost conversationally; "Only yesterday he bragged to me that next year, after waiting only five years, his name would come up on the list for White's. Who the hell do you think put him up? My uncle, that's who!" Turning back to Nubar: "A member of White's, ha! If you don't help now, when I get finished with you, you'll be lucky if they let you into the men's room at the Automobile Club!"

The threat of losing his member seemed to have less effect on Nubar than the thought of losing his membership to White's. She had found his Achilles' heel, and he succumbed.

"All right, all right. I'll tell you. I didn't know anything about all this, but I would have handled it myself—got the papers back and worked out the transfer without you knowing a thing about it. I would never have involved you in any of this, had I known, but how could I have known—"

"Oh, shut up and tell Steddy where he is," Elizabeth said, white and shaking now, but still holding the gun firmly at Nubar's spine. He looked at her over his shoulder, his flabby jowls twisted by his position and by the too-tight collar of the shirt Edith had lent him. When he answered, he was almost blubbering.

"He's in the Vumba," he said softly.

"Vumba?" she roared back.

"Where the hell's that?" Steddy questioned as he took the gun from Elizabeth's trembling hands and reset the safety.

"It's on the border of Rhodesia and Mozambique."

"You mean Zimbabwe?" Steddy asked.

"That's right, Zimbabwe. I keep forgetting." He was facing them now, and looked as though he didn't know what to do with his hands. "Near a town called Umtali."

"Is that in Zimbabwe or Mozambique?" Steddy asked.

"Zimbabwe. I own a coffee plantation there. Had it since the war. It was the idea of an old war buddy of mine called Bentley who was from Rho—I mean Zimbabwe. He saved my life on Sicily when we were there with Monte, so I bought it for him."

"No wonder no one could find him," Steddy said. "But how did you get him out of—" His words were interrupted by the nearing whistles of the pickup boys working their dogs. None of them had noticed that the firing had long since stopped.

Steddy walked out on the moor and retrieved the three grouse Nubar had killed and placed them outside the butt, where they would be found. Then he reached into one of the cartridge bags and withdrew a walkie-talkie. He and Wiley had set a pair of them on yet a third channel, so that Wiley could warn him if there was trouble.

"Is that you, Steddy?" Wiley answered the beep of the machine on standby.

"It's me all right, and we've found out what we need to know. We're coming in right away—be prepared to travel."

"I'm afraid I've got a surprise for you, too, old boy."

"What's the matter, shouldn't I come back?" Steddy asked, his elation transformed to concern.

"Yeah, yeah, come ahead as quickly as you can. Over and out."

They followed the track down the steep incline, passing the pony men with their charges, whose panniers were bursting with grouse. It wasn't necessary to make excuses when they reached the group already gathered at the road. Edith saw the state Elizabeth was in and said, "My dear, whatever is the matter?"

Nubar, in full control of himself once again, said that she had been taken ill and that the sooner they got her home, the better.

They piled into the waiting brake after brief good-byes and a royal expression of concern, and with a knowing wink from Karesin, were soon on their way.

When Steddy got back to the castle, he learned that Wiley had had no choice but to come clean with Allsloe, the alternative being the arrest of the entire household. Allsloe had agreed, in exchange for Wiley's cooperation, to withdraw all his men save Peter Holbrook, who would stay on to make sure that Wiley and Steddy complied and gave him accurate and continual updates. But Steddy's news that Rollo was in Zimbabwe set off a new round of negotiations, with Allsloe and Holbrook conferring in the library while Wiley filled in Register, who blew his top when he heard what had transpired but eventually agreed that there was little else Wiley could have done under the circumstances.

The upshot was that the two men—Allsloe and Register— met at the castle. No accusations of improprieties were made at the meeting by either party—too many had been committed by both sides to make it a worthwhile exercise. The rules of the sophisticated game they both played left no room for displays of indignation, and in this case it was a wash anyway.

The Harkonians kept to the bargain that Steddy had sworn them to and refused to reveal the exact location of Rollo's hideout to either Register or Allsloe. This was the only leverage Steddy had to force them to keep him in the picture, the only way he could protect Thea's safety. He hadn't even told Wiley. The two department heads had little choice but to let Steddy and Wiley handle the exchange, if they wanted to avoid a scandal and still have the slightest chance of attaining their own goal.

They were all convened in the study when Steddy made his next scheduled radio contact with Chelak, who consented to meet in an hour at the old keep. Steddy set out for the rendezvous, leaving Wiley behind to work out the details of their trip.

Elizabeth insisted they use Nubar's plane to save time, and a chastened Nubar instructed the pilot to be ready for takeoff at four PM.

Steddy didn't get back until well after four. Chelak had kept him waiting a considerable time after he dropped the bomb that Rollo was in Africa. He evidently had to consult with others before consenting to Steddy's making the trip and outlining his own terms and conditions.

It was six in the evening when the *Flying Cloud* touched down to refuel and discharge passengers at the private terminal outside Dublin. The plane would follow a flight plan not unlike the one it had flown just a few months before, when Lord Rockford had been the sole passenger. The Harkonians deplaned in Dublin after Elizabeth had wished them a strained farewell and Nubar had once again pleaded his innocence of any knowledge of top-secret documents. Stedman and Wiley stayed on board during the refueling, as had Rockford—this was only the first leg of the long flight to Zimbabwe.

Part IV
To the Bridge

43

Flying Cloud was still the luxurious leather womb that Steddy recalled from his two previous flights, but absent were the stewards and the crisp linen, the crystal and the smoked salmon, the old port and the waft of Havanas. She was stripped to her bare essentials to increase her range. Her only crew was the same pilot who had flown Rollo out to Africa, one of Nubar's most trusted employees; he would have to handle the entire fourteen-hour flight, including paperwork and refueling, unassisted.

When the aircraft reached its cruising altitude after takeoff from Dublin, Wiley could contain himself no longer.

"Well, what the fuck did the bastard say?"

"Which particular bastard do you mean? We're involved with quite a few on this outing—Register, Allsloe, Nubar . . ."

"Cut it out, Steddy. You know I meant Chelak."

Steddy dropped the sarcasm. "He said that we were to go to the Victoria Falls Hotel when we had the documents. He would contact us there, and that's where the transfer would take place."

"You mean Victoria Falls as in Niagara Falls?"

"How do I know, I've never been there. He wasn't exactly overflowing with information. I just listened and agreed."

"Well, is it near where Rollo is?"

"Wiley, I don't even know if it's in Zimbabwe. I only know that he's as anxious to get the papers as we are to get Thea, so I imagine it shouldn't be too hard to find. It is one of the wonders of the world, I think. Anyway, Stanley or Livingstone found it, so I guess we can. What did Register say?"

"He was furious that I wouldn't tell him where Rockford was hiding out."

"Didn't you tell him you didn't know?"

"Yeah, but after everything that's happened, you don't really think he believed me?"

Steddy unfastened his seat belt and got up to make them a drink.

"Might as well relax; it's gonna be a long flight." He poured out two whiskies with some ice and a little water and handed one to Wiley as he sank back into the deep leather club chair. "So what did he say when he calmed down?"

"He didn't calm down, but he did say that they'd fly someone in from Johannesburg to back us up. He'll contact us at Meikles Hotel in Salisbury tomorrow."

"That's fucking marvelous. Now we not only have to contend with Scotland Yard—or whoever the hell those fucking Brits really are—we've got the CIA to look out for as well. How the hell are we gonna shake an army like that and get to Rockford without their following us? Answer me that. I hope you learned a few tricks from your employers!"

"I told you, they don't employ me, I'm a volunteer. Or maybe I should say *was* a volunteer," Wiley said with some indignation.

"Great! I'm surrounded by spies, and the only one on my team is a fucking amateur."

Wiley ignored the remark and changed the subject.

"But Nubar said his friend Bentley from the plantation would fly down in a plane to pick us up."

"Don't you think these guys have planes, too? No, we're gonna have to lose them somehow."

After a few more drinks, they slept and weren't even aware of the stopover in Rome. Steddy had no qualms about his passport giving him away—anyone looking for him had already found him. At ten in the morning, local time, they landed in Nairobi to refuel and were forced by the authorities to deplane and wait in a minuscule, fly-filled, un-air-conditioned transit lounge, where the politely curious Kenya Airways people who ran it plied them with warm orange squash and the heat of Africa suddenly enveloped them in its breathless embrace.

When the procedure took overly long and the pilot reported that they would not be able to take off until after lunch—a delay of almost four hours—Steddy became suspicious.

"Well, do you think it's the long arm of Uncle Sam, John Bull, or a vengeful God that's engineered this convenient delay to catch up with us?" he asked Wiley, not really interested in the answer.

"You could be right, but they do break for lunch in countries like this. You know, only "mad dogs and Englishmen..." He stopped when he saw that Steddy wasn't paying attention, but had drifted off and was attempting to charm a stewardess into getting him a large gin and tonic, "preferably with ice, but without it will do...."

When finally the plane was allowed to depart, he bid good-bye to the stewardess who had been his supplier and promised to call her when next he returned. As they left the lounge for the waiting aircraft, Wiley had the distinct impression that she thought that would be soon.

Tired of Wiley's occasional disapproving glances, Steddy took the copilot's seat during takeoff while Wiley rummaged in the space-age galley and somehow managed to produce a pot of black coffee to keep the pilot airborne and Steddy from getting any higher.

The first sign that they were approaching Salisbury was not the glint in the sun of tall buildings, but rather what appeared to be a lavender-blue cloud that had settled on the verdant plateau in the distance. It wasn't until they were much closer that one could tell it was composed of acres and acres of flowering jacaranda trees that lined the avenues of the residential section of the capital, but by then the glass and granite skyscrapers of the modern African city dominated the horizon.

Customs was a breeze. The former Rhodesians were anxious to make a good impression on visiting Americans, and as they had virtually no luggage, they were soon in a tiny cab, speeding down the broad Samora Machel Avenue toward the center of town.

Steddy had never in his life got off a private jet and had the pilot ask him if he wanted him to wait, but he was too tired to savor the new experience and merely told him to check into Meikles when he had secured the plane.

It was six o'clock when they pulled up in front of Meikles Hotel. They both were impressed by the size and tastefulness of the building—so far, nothing seemed like Africa, it was all too tame and civilized. They ordered two double rooms for themselves and one for the pilot, handed in their passports, and filled in the forms while a tall, attractive redhead, dressed and coiffed in a style that hadn't been seen in Europe or the States since the sixties, extolled the virtues of the five bars and the pool on the roof. Steddy perked up when he heard about the pool.

"That's exactly what I need. How about you, Wiley?"

"Yeah, sure. But I wonder if there's any place we could buy some clothes? I don't think tweeds were really designed for the African bush."

"There's quite a good men's shop across the lobby, sir," the girl at the desk said. "But you'll have to hurry, it will be closing soon." She spoke with the curious formality that colonials impart to their mother tongue in an effort to get it right.

They bought a few shirts, trousers, and swim suits— Steddy dug into his money belt to pay for it all. When they parted in the corridor by their rooms, they agreed to meet at the pool. At least for the moment, nothing seemed so important as getting into that pool.

The hotel had three wings. The oldest had replaced the original structure that dated from the founding of Salisbury, when Mr. Meikles had manned the supply wagon of the Pioneer Column, Cecil Rhodes's private army that had claimed the rich land for Queen and Empire; while the most modern wing, where Steddy's and Wiley's rooms were, had

just been completed and was handsomely fashioned of rich
Rhodesian woods, granite, and marble that had been joined
with European technology to offer every modern convenience.

Wiley found Steddy wet from the pool and sprawled on
a chaise on the roof of the new wing. It was open to the air
and incongruously constructed of white marble to resemble
a colonnaded Roman pavilion, with breathtaking views of
the plain upon which Salisbury was built. As he approached,
a black servant uniformed in white and wearing a fez
brought Steddy a long drink that looked as though a bush of
mint was growing from it. Steddy looked up and noticed
Wiley as he signed the chit.

"Could you bring another for the gentleman, please,"
he instructed the waiter. "Wiley, this is really a paradise. I
can't imagine there was ever any trouble here. No wonder
Ian Smith held out for so long."

"Steddy, don't you think we should make some plans?"

"Not a word until you've had a swim and a Mizilkasi
or kamikase—whatever this is called," he said, holding up
his drink. "I've already done some thinking. . . but have a
swim and clear away the trip first. We can't do anything till
tomorrow anyway."

Whether out of inclination, resignation, or frustration,
Wiley complied and jumped into the pool.

"We're going to have to hang on to the *Flying Cloud*
for a bit, I think," Steddy said to Wiley after waiting for
him to settle down in the chaise next to him and carefully
observing him as he took a sip from his drink.

"I heard you say that to Jellicoe at the airport, but I
don't remember that being part of the deal."

"I couldn't care less, as long as Jellicoe seems willing
to go along with us. Anyway, he has to stay at least a day
after that *tour de force*. I'm pooped, and I had some sleep."

"But we're supposed to call Nubar's friend to pick us
up in his plane."

"That's O-U-T, out, now that we've lost our lead with
that convenient delay in Nairobi. I checked; the flight from
London got in at eight forty-five this morning, eight hours
before we did, and there are lots of ways to connect through

Johannesburg from anywhere in Europe or the States. We can't risk Chelak following us to Rollo—or the Brits or the CIA, for that matter. We'd have no way of being sure we'd get Thea back once they had what they wanted, any of them!''

"So you want to use the *Flying Cloud* to get us up there?"

"Jellicoe flew Rollo in; he must know the procedure.''

"But no one was following him. If they're really tailing us, they can track us on radar or just get our destination from the flight plan. I'm sure we'd have to file one before takeoff.''

"I don't know, but there must be some way to fiddle it. We'll have to level with Jellicoe—I'm sure he'll help. He's a good guy.''

"Yeah, but don't forget he's Nubar's man first and foremost.''

"And don't forget that Thea is Nubar's daughter—for all intents and purposes. I know he'll help us. I had a long talk with him while you were sleeping between Rome and Nairobi and—''

"Did he say he'd do it?''

"Hold on, I didn't ask him. We were in good shape with the time then. By now, I'll bet that before we could hang up the phone after calling the estate, one of those bastards would be on his way up there to pinch Rollo before this Bentley fellow could even get his plane warmed up.''

"Well, then, what *did* he say?''

"Nothing in particular. Only that he started as a bush pilot in Australia and then came to Europe with Qantas. Then he got into some sort of a jam—he didn't say what—and they fired him. That's when Nubar hired him, and I get the feeling that he'd do anything for Nubar. He's devot—Well, speak of the devil. We were just talking about you. Come sit down and let us buy you a very well deserved drink!''

Peter Jellicoe, a stocky, sandy-haired, athletic fellow, who normally looked younger than his forty years, now appeared considerably older than his age, after fourteen hours of straight flying and God knows how many hours without sleep. He hadn't even gone to his room when he checked in, but had simply taken his swimsuit from his bag and come straight to the roof. In spite of his fatigue, he greeted them with a broad smile that showed up dozens of white lines in his deeply tanned and weathered face.

"See you chaps have the right idea," he said. "Don't mind telling you, I wouldn't like to repeat that trip for at least twenty-four hours," he joked, grinning. "Guess I'm not as young as I used to be. Ten years ago, I could have flown twice that long and still hit the town when I landed."

Steddy summoned the waiter.

"Have one of these, won't you? Don't know what they're called, but they do work wonders on the old—"

"Just a beer, if you don't mind," Jellicoe said before jumping in the water.

While the pilot was in the pool, a banging gong called Wiley's attention to a young page carrying a blackboard with his name written on it—there was a phone call for him.

"Probably the CIA," Steddy said. "They're so discreet."

Wiley took the call in his room, and by the time he returned to the roof, Steddy had already laid out their problem to Jellicoe.

"So you see, anything you can do would be greatly appreciated," he finished.

"I only flew Lord Rockford to Salisbury. Colonel Bentley picked him up in the Cessna. There is a grass strip on the property, though—I flew the boss up there once in a rented twin Beech—but it isn't exactly a jet strip. Oh, it would probably do for length, but did you ever happen to notice the size of the nose wheel on the *Flying Cloud*?"

"Very small, isn't it?"

"Small isn't the word! It'd suit a baby carriage sooner than a jet aircraft—one good-sized rut or hole would flip her."

"What about the airport in Umtali?" Wiley asked.

"That's no good," Steddy answered. "A foreign jet drops out of the blue unannounced, and the first thing they'd do is get Salisbury on the radio."

"Wouldn't they pick us up on radar, even if we landed on the property?"

"That can be finessed," Jellicoe said. "Radar isn't exactly the all-seeing genie it's cracked up to be. Sure, if you're looking for something to happen, you'll see it when it does, but a lot can happen on a radar screen without anyone noticing it. Those mountains in the Vumba are very steep and crowded together. If you fly low, between them, the radar can't pick you up."

"You mean we could land at the plantation without being monitored?" Steddy asked.

"Theoretically. Of course, it would be better if we flew out to sea, beyond the range of their radar, and then came back in low. Trouble is, that would mean crossing Mozambiquean airspace unannounced—and with the raids South Africa's been launching against the ANC, there, we could get shot down."

"That sounds a little too risky. We don't want to start a war," Steddy commented.

"Listen, why don't you guys leave the flying to me? That's what I get paid for."

"You mean you'll do it?"

"Hell, why not?"

"What about the wheel?"

"That Mystere's very sensitive to the controls. If the wind is steady and not gusting across the strip, I can keep her nose up almost until we stop. . . . So when do we leave?"

Steddy looked at Wiley for his accord, and when he got the nod, said, "First thing in the morning?"

"Okay by me," Wiley said.

"What's 'first thing' to you?" Jellicoe asked.

"About six."

"Suits me," Jellicoe said. "I'd better get back out to the airport and file a flight plan so we don't have any delays in the morning."

"Won't that be like announcing in advance where we're going?" Wiley asked.

"Yeah," Steddy said. "How do we do that without giving away the whole thing?"

"I told you to leave it to me, but what I'll probably do

is file a flight plan for Durban or some town down the coast of South Africa—I've got to check my maps first. If I leave it till the morning, there's no way of telling how long we'll get held up."

"Okay, you're the boss. Will you have dinner with us when you get back?"

"Thanks, but if I'm gonna get any sleep at all, I'd better spend the night on board."

"You sure?" Wiley asked.

"Yeah, I need the sleep a lot more than three or four trips to and from the airport. Right, then I'll see you gents in the morning."

"Okay, and thanks again. We both really appreciate what you're doing." They both stood and shook hands with him. When he'd gone, Steddy asked Wiley, "Who was that on the phone?"

"'Fraid you were right."

"Good God—no wonder we lost Iran."

"I told him we'd meet him in the bar at eight."

"Will he be wearing a white sport coat and a pink carnation?"

"No, but you're close—a bush jacket and a black mustache."

"That would just about describe half the people I saw in the lobby."

"Somehow, I don't think we'll have any trouble recognizing him," Wiley said, grinning conspiratorially.

44

They didn't need the chloroform they had brought with them when they took Thea—she was still unconscious. Unfortunately they had a backup vehicle, or Karesin would have found them when he went looking for her. As it was, they just had time to use the other car to push the combined wrecks into the deep burn that ran parallel to the road and replace the piled stones where the crash had pierced the wall. The rain took care of the rest of the cosmetics.

Apart from a black eye, Thea appeared to be uninjured. Her breathing, though labored, seemed normal. She started to come to as they drove from the scene, which was when they administered the first sedative by injection. Since then she had been kept under just enough constant sedation so that she wasn't sure if she remembered what had actually happened since or only remembered what she had dreamed.

The first thing that she was truly conscious of was a not unattractive sloe-eyed girl wearing glasses, who force-fed her coffee and gave her a capsule to swallow. Within half an hour, she was aware of her surroundings and reasonably alert.

The room was cheerful, like a young girl's room, and very French. The walls were covered in the same pale pink toile de Jouy that the curtains were made of, and the bed was recessed in an alcove formed by cupboards at either end. The sloe-eyed girl was sitting on the bed.

Periodically, a gruff-looking man with a gun stuffed into the top of his trousers would open the door and survey the scene as if checking on her. She had a French accent.

"We are going to take a plane trip in a few hours. You must be awake and cooperate if you wish to see your friends again."

"Where are we?" Thea asked, sitting up and for the first time feeling the pain in her chest where she had been crushed into the steering wheel.

"That is not important, nor do you need to know who we are or why you are here. All you need to know is that if you behave yourself, there will be no trouble and you will be back with your friends in a few days. The tablet I gave you was an amphetamine to counteract the sedative we have been giving you."

"Where are we going?"

"We are meeting your friends in Africa. If they keep their part of the bargain, you will be re-united with them in a few days. Do not worry. You are so pretty, I am sure that he would do nothing that could endanger your life. Now please get up. We have to get you dressed."

Her head was awake, but her legs hadn't got the message yet. They felt as though they were being controlled by a different guidance system from the rest of her.

"May I go to the bathroom please?"

"But of course—only please leave the door open." She nodded her head toward the man, who had re-entered the room. "My friend would not like it if I leave you alone." She spoke sweetly, but her sloe eyes behind thick lenses told a different story.

When Thea had finished in the bathroom, the woman pointed at a chair in the corner.

"I have laid out some clothes for you to wear; they will be more suitable for the trip than what you had on when you came to us. But first you must please use this."

She unsnapped a small plastic case like a thermometer box and took out what looked like a tampon. She held it out to Thea.

"What is it?" Thea asked.

"It is like the Tampax, for the period."

"But I don't need one," Thea protested, still a little groggy and confused by the suggestion.

"It is not a request. You will use it or my friend will do it for you."

"But I . . ."

"I will call him now?" she asked with the sweet manner she had used before, like a stage maid in a French farce.

Thea shook her head, took the small cotton tampon from her, and turned toward the bathroom.

"No, no—you will do it here, in front of me, so that I can see that it is done correctly."

She sat on the bench by the bed and inserted the tampon. The string, she noticed, felt stiff and wiry. When she had finished to her keeper's satisfaction, she asked, "But I don't understand? Why . . . ?"

"It is not the usual thing. It contains an explosive charge that can be detonated from this transmitter." She held up a small object that looked like a lighter and withdrew a two-inch antenna from the top. "It is only a precaution that you cooperate while we are traveling. It would be most unpleasant—But I'm sure you will cause no trouble, no?"

Thea shivered and slowly nodded her head.

"We will get dressed now, please. There is very little time to make the plane."

45

The *Flying Cloud* took off at dawn as scheduled. Steddy and Wiley arrived ten minutes before by a circuitous route that began with their slipping out of the hotel while it was still dark, crossing Cecil Square, where the park paths were laid out in the pattern of a Union Jack, and making their way north to the Monomatapa Hotel on Samora Machel Avenue, where they were able to find a taxi. It was still dark, and as far as they could tell, no one was following them. By the time they reached the airport, the great African sun had risen.

"Is this going to be a one-cigarette flight, or do I have time to log a few zees?" Steddy asked Jellicoe when they had leveled off.

"Normally, you'd barely have time to light up, but with the route we're flying, I'd say you could have a good hour's kip—that is, if you don't mind missing the fun during the last half hour or so."

"Dare I ask where you've logged us to?"

"Antananarivo."

"Say again?"

"It's the capital of Madagascar—never been there?"

"Madagascar!" Wiley piped in from the copilot's seat. He had just removed the headset he was using to listen to the tower.

"Don't get excited; we're not going there. But filing

our flight plan to there puts us far enough out to sea to drop off the Zimbabwean and Mozambiquean radar without anyone noticing or caring.''

"What then? Or do I really want to know?" Steddy said.

"We develop a little trouble with the cabin pressure, drop down to equalize it, and head back low, toward the coast of Mozambique."

"What's low about five thousand feet?" Wiley asked.

"Try about thirty."

"But you usually fly at thirty thousand feet," Steddy said.

"Not thirty thousand, man, thirty—thirty feet."

"Holy shit!" Steddy said, exhaling. Wiley just let out a low whistle.

"Isn't that kind of dangerous?" they echoed.

"Well, say thirty to ninety feet—depends on the swell."

"Christ! I guess you really know you're moving at that altitude," Steddy said.

"Too right. But there's really nothing to it—if you know what you're doing, that is."

"And presumably you do?" Wiley said, smiling wanly.

"Yeah, done it a million times. See, there's what's called a surface effect from the sea—puts a lot of static on the receiver. Once they tune that out, they've tuned us out, too, as long as we stay within it."

"Listen, I don't think I want to know any more about this than I need to, or I might develop a surface effect that would require a thorough cleaning of the rear cabin. I'm gonna lie down. Wake me up when it's over." Steddy left the cockpit and headed aft to try to sleep.

"What's the matter with him?" Jellicoe asked Wiley, who remained forward.

"He gave his liver to science last night. All in a good cause, mind you, but he must be feeling like warmed-over death."

"What did you guys get up to then?"

"Let's just say that we had to put someone out of action who could have got in our way today."

Steddy had really cleaned his clock, Wiley thought as

he sat in the co-pilot seat, staring at the sun that was directly in their flight path. They had met the CIA man at the hotel's Can Can Bar. Steddy poked Wiley in the ribs when he singled out, "our man in Salisbury," as he put it. His name was Hegner, and he stood at least a foot taller than anyone else there. Wiley greeted him like an old friend and introduced him to Steddy, who was jokingly watching to see if they used a secret handshake or anything as a recognition signal. They ordered drinks from the bar and took them to a low cocktail table in a red-plush-draped window alcove. The whole place was lined in red plush with gilt-wood trim and looked like a Hollywood version of a turn-of-the-century bordello. The hotel was amazing in that the general impression was conservative, while the bars and the roof were like a hodgepodge of exotic, cast-off film sets.

When Steddy saw that Hegner was drinking a martini, he ordered the same, giving the fellow a fraternal wink as he did so. Before they had finished the ones they had, he went to the bar and signed for the next round. When Hegner excused himself and went to the men's room, Wiley said: "Hell, Steddy, take it easy. We've got to keep our wits about us."

"Listen, Wiley, I know what I'm doing. This guy's a boozer if I ever saw one, and I've seen plenty. Just leave him to me. I'll fix him so he doesn't get up before tomorrow afternoon."

"I hope you do know what you're doing. He's probably trying to do the same thing to you so you'll let something slip."

"We've got to play it real cozy, like we're all part of the same team—get him off guard and relaxed."

Hegner returned to the table.

"Are you guys free for dinner?"

"Sure are," Steddy answered for both of them. "We can't do anything but bide our time."

"I'd like to talk to you about that, but it can wait till we get to the restaurant."

"Is there a good one here?" Wiley asked.

"Hell, yes, one of the best steak houses I've ever been to, bar none. It's not far from here."

"Well, let's have one for the road. It's early yet," Steddy volunteered.

They had two for the road and then piled into Hegner's small rented car and headed for the outskirts of town, where the restaurant turned out to be everything he promised. It was called Wombles and consisted of a series of joined, thatched rondavels.

He ordered the biggest steaks on the menu, which were at least two pounds each, and when Steddy said that nothing went better with a charred and bloody steak than a cold, dry martini, Hegner agreed, and they continued to drink them throughout dinner.

Hegner did think he was being clever and waited until Steddy had put away three martinis at the restaurant before he thought him sufficiently well oiled to bring up the subject of the mission.

"We won't know a thing until the guy who owns the place Rockford's staying at calls us. There isn't any phone there, so until he gets the cable that was sent from England, there's nothing we can do but wait," Steddy said with the most sincere expression he could muster.

"Well, he must have had it by now," Hegner commented casually.

"I don't think so. We were told that it takes three days to get a wire to him where he is," Wiley answered, trying to sound as much "official CIA" as possible.

"Didn't they give you any idea what part of the country he was in?"

"Nope."

The waitress came and asked them if they wanted any coffee. Steddy was inspired and turned to Hegner.

"Ever have a mulata?"

"What's that?"

"Just the only way to drink coffee, that's all. Once you've had one, you'll never drink it any other way. I'll see to it."

He rose from the table and headed to the bar in the adjacent rondavel.

A mulata was a drink of Steddy's own concoction that consisted of a quadruple measure of light Bacardi rum, iced coffee, and just enough heavy cream to turn it the color of its name, or, more aptly, the color of the girl it was named after. It was served in the biggest glass available, preferably a cocktail shaker, and tasted like a coffee frosted. It was lethal. They had three of them and ended up singing "You're a grand old flag" and "I'm a yankee doodle dandy" at the top of their lungs all the way back to town. Then, on Hegner's suggestion—he had finally gone over the top as Steddy had predicted—they went to a Greek discotheque on Baker Avenue, where they started drinking Black Russians. It seemed appropriate and humorous at the time. Hegner found a girl who was, as he must have said a hundred times, "Like I like my coffee—hot, sweet, and black." They left him there in the wee hours of the morning. Steddy threw up violently in Cecil Square on the way back to the hotel. Mission accomplished.

They noted Hegner's key was still in his box when they crept out of the hotel across the darkened lobby a few hours later on their way to the airport—but for Steddy it was a Pyrrhic victory.

When Wiley finished describing the high points of Steddy's sacrifice to Jellicoe, Jellicoe said, "Man, I'm glad I didn't come to dinner with you. Do you have any idea what a trembling hand can do when you're flying thirty feet over the drink at five hundred miles per hour?"

Wiley was glad he hadn't been with them, too.

The change in altitude when it came was so swift that Steddy woke up trying to force his stomach into the same rate of descent as the rest of him. The whisper of the jet engines had changed to a shriek, and through the port of the steeply banking aircraft, the water looked close enough to touch. When they leveled off, he made his way forward to the cockpit, where the sea racing under them looked like an arcade game gone mad.

Jellicoe was flushed and grinning, obviously enjoying himself, while Wiley, in contrast, was pressed to the back of his seat, his face drained of color.

"I thought you were sleeping," Jellicoe said to Steddy.

"I was until you pulled that inverted arabesque. Was the aerobatic display for my benefit?"

"Nah, just the only way to do it. Listen, would one of you get my radar detector out of that bag on the deck?" He nodded his head in the direction of his feet. "I don't like to take my hands off the controls, if you know what I mean. It's about the size of a transistor radio."

Steddy saw that there was no way Wiley was going to release his death grip on the arm rests or lower his unblinking eyes from the horizon, so he crouched down and retrieved the small metal instrument from the bag at Jellicoe's feet and examined it.

"But this is just an automobile radar detector," he said, surprised.

"It's a trick I learned from some American air force boys. They use them when they're flying war games. The old jets they fly don't have sophisticated radar detectors, but they tell me that these are more reliable than the built-in ones on the new ships anyway."

"You mean you've never used it before?"

"Yeah, well, I've tried it out waiting for clearance to land, and it screamed like a banshee."

"But how can a little thing like this have the range to pick up coastal radar?"

"It doesn't need range. All it has to do is detect radar that's reaching us. If it starts screaming, that means they've locked on to us."

"Then what happens?"

"Let's get it going first. Now turn it on, and then tune the control on the right until it squeals." Steddy did so—the high-pitched whistle was very shrill. "Now ease back on the control, very gently, until it stops."

"Now what?" Steddy asked.

"Nothing, just sit tight and pray it doesn't go off."

"But what if it does?"

"Well, they'd probably try to raise us on the radio, but I've got that shut down, and my radar as well—they could pick that up in a second. The Mozambiqueans aren't very well organized. In the time it would take them to scramble their MiG 17s we'll be out of their airspace and over

Rhodesia. Mozambique's only about a hundred miles wide where we cross—shouldn't be in their airspace for more than ten or twelve minutes max. Those MiGs of theirs are ground fighters anyway—no air-to-air missiles, just radar-homing ones. That's one of the reasons our radar's shut down. Still, a twenty-three millimeter cannon can do a real number on one of these babies—she's not exactly armored," he said. "It's the Rhodesians we've got to look out for. If they get a visual on us, we'll have to follow them in to their base. Their Hunters are armed with Sidewinders. If they let one of those fly at us, we wouldn't even be dust in the sky."

"Not very encouraging," Steddy said. Wiley was still rigid.

"I'm not really worried about the Rho's. By the time we're in their airspace, we'll be in the mountains. As long as we stay below the peaks, we'll be hidden from their radar in the ground clutter."

Steddy stopped talking to Jellicoe. They were flying so close to the water that every time Jellicoe turned around to see if Steddy had heard what he was saying over the scream of the engines that reverberated off the sea, Steddy swallowed to keep his stomach down and had to restrain himself from shouting, "Keep your eyes front, damn you!"

The coast was under them almost before he realized they were nearing it. Jellicoe was rhythmically adjusting his altitude to match the gentle rise and fall of the blurred brown terrain. There was a brief squeal from the box in Steddy's hand—his guts went to jelly.

"Don't start worrying. If it doesn't become continuous, we're just part of the ground clutter," Jellicoe said, trying to reassure them.

The blur turned from brown to a pale green, and Steddy could see the pointed peaks of what Jellicoe identified as the Vumba looming in front of them in the distance.

"Not long now," Jellicoe said, but every second was an excruciating eternity on a roller coaster for Steddy and his rigid companion.

Low hills were rising up on either side of them, and the sun glinted off scattered pans of water that sparsely dotted the plain only feet beneath them. As the channel between the hills grew narrower, Jellicoe gained some altitude.

"That's the Burma Valley," Jellicoe said. "When we pass those high rocky outcroppings ahead of us, we'll be in Rhodes—I keep forgetting. I mean Zimbabwe."

By the time Steddy was able to spot them, they had jerked up and overflown them.

The box in his hand started to scream. Steddy's concentration on the terrain had been so intense that he dropped it, but it didn't stop this time. The valley had widened out again and exposed them. The wail continued until they had gained the mountains and the shelter of their peaks. When it stopped, Jellicoe said, "We're not five minutes from the plantation now; if the strip's clear and we can get down on the first pass, we'll be all right."

Steddy didn't answer him. All three of them were flying the plane now. Jellicoe had had to throttle back to maneuver between the peaks. The house was the first thing Steddy saw of the coffee farm.

"Is that it?"

"That's 'Witches' Wood' all right," Jellicoe answered between clenched teeth, obviously no happier than they were about the prospect of taking a Sidewinder up the bum.

They flew so low over the house that Steddy was sure he could have read the headlines of a newspaper had anyone been reading on the terrace. Jellicoe had to climb steeply to gain room to turn and come back. At the top of the turn, the box squealed again for a moment. He throttled back a bit more as they started their descent and said, "Okay, this is it—hang on." It was only the parked Cessna at the edge of the plateau that enabled Steddy to distinguish the grass runway from the rest of the green at the back of the house—they seemed to be diving straight for it. Every muscle in Wiley's face showed in sharp relief. Steddy's knuckles were now white, too, from gripping the back of Wiley's seat and the jamb of the cockpit's door. Just when he thought they were going to hit the ground like a javelin, Jellicoe pulled up the nose, so they couldn't see anything but sky, and cut the power. When they hit, Steddy's grip was wrenched free by the force of the impact, and he was sent flying back into the cabin. The angle was so steep that he couldn't regain his feet. Then the engines let out an unholy wail that sounded as though they would explode any second, and it was over. The nose fell level with a bang, and they came to a stop. Steddy lay there on the thick carpet of the cabin, savoring the moment.

"Right, everybody out and give me a hand—on the double!" Jellicoe shouted.

He was standing by the hatchway, a bunch of chocks for the wheels slung over his shoulder, as the softly whining motor lowered the stair to the ground. Steddy pulled himself together, and when he reached Jellicoe's side, saw that behind the pilot, Wiley had rejoined the land of the living, and some color had returned to his cheeks.

"You never told me to fasten my seat belt!" Steddy said.

"Can it! We've got to secure the plane and try to cover her somehow," Jellicoe replied.

The pilot scrambled down the gangway before it was completely extended. Steddy was right behind him. A slight man with snow-white hair and blue eyes that sparkled from his tanned, smiling face was waiting for them. Behind him, keeping their distance, three black servants stood ogling the unfamiliar airplane and its occupants.

"You gave us quite a turn just then. Thought you'd take the roof off the house, Jellicoe." He grasped the pilot's hand and pumped it enthusiastically, exuding the spry, robust health typical of a certain brand of Englishman who thrives on colonial life in the sun, served up with copious amounts of pink gin. "Bentley's the name," he said, exercising Steddy's arm with equal gusto. Steddy had only said his name when Jellicoe interrupted him.

"No time for that now. Got to find some way to camouflage the plane. We may have visitors any minute. Can you get some of your boys to help us?" he asked.

"You can have the old camouflage netting we used during the war—it's still stored in the shed."

He shouted an order to the two black men who were hanging back by the house with the maids. They took off for the shed at a graceful African lope and soon returned dragging a corpse-shaped bundle of netting between them.

"It won't be big enough by a long shot, but it should do the job. Had it made to protect the Cessna from the ZANLA raids."

Wiley joined them, and together the five men manhandled the cover across the wings of the plane and most of the fuselage. While securing the netting to the outboard wing, Steddy was almost suspended over the edge of the plateau. From the air, he blessedly hadn't appreciated how sheer the drop was—it fell away very steeply into the Burma Valley, which formed the channel they had flown up between the Mountains of the Mist, as they were known, and the plain of Mozambique bordering the Indian Ocean, which he could actually see from his perch on the wing. The *Flying Cloud* had come to a stop only a few yards from the edge.

"That's the best we can do. We'd better get into the house and out of sight, and keep our fingers crossed," Jellicoe said.

"We were quite a target here during the troubles. They used to take pot shots at us from those mountains over there with rockets and anything else they could get their hands on. Fortunately for us, they were lousy marksmen. We did lose the stable and some beautiful beasts, though," Bentley said as he led them into the hall.

The house was cool and big. Made of stone and covered for the most part with ivy, it evoked no particular style. It just seemed to belong there. From the hall, he led them down three or four steps into a large sunken living room that followed the fall of the land to an enormous, many-paned window that dominated the far end of the room like a proscenium arch, framing the spectacular view of the Burma Valley, the plain of Mozambique, and the distant ocean. The steps were flanked by a pair of elephant tusks that Steddy noted were taller than Jellicoe. Another pair, equally tall, symmetrically flanked the window opposite. Big chintz overstuffed chairs were scattered over the highly polished floor, which was paved with matching round slices of wood hewn from gum trees indigenous to the forests of the Vumba.

Everyone collapsed in a grouping of chairs by the immense fireplace.

"Where's Nubar?" their host asked Jellicoe.

"He's not with us this trip, but these chaps are friends of his come out to see Lord Rockford."

Bentley looked around furtively and then said in a lowered voice to Steddy, "You gave me quite a turn when you introduced yourself."

"How's that?" Steddy asked.

"Well, the name he goes under here is Stedman Wright. Guess he didn't expect you to come calling."

"Where is he?" Steddy asked, and then, noticing that the man hesitated: "Perhaps you should read this before we go on."

Bentley took the envelope that Steddy handed him and walked over to the big desk that stood before the wall of glass panes. He rustled through some papers until he found a pair of half glasses, put them on the end of his nose, and perched on the edge of the desk to read the letter Nubar had penned aboard the *Flying Cloud*, over the Irish Sea. When he had finished, he removed the glasses as though they were somehow culpable for the news he'd just read and ambled back to where they were seated.

"It's a nasty business," was all he said.

"Very, and the sooner it's over with the better," Wiley said, uttering his first words in more than two hours.

"Well, he won't be back for some time yet." And then, noticing the houseboy standing at his elbow, Bentley said, "What am I thinking? I haven't offered you a drink. You must think we're completely lacking in hospitality up here. What can I give you?"

Jellicoe asked for a beer. Wiley and Steddy declined drinks but said they hadn't had any breakfast, if it wasn't too much trouble.

"Certainly not. I think I must still be rattled from your surprising—or should I say spectacular—arrival." He told the boy to have a full breakfast for three laid out on the terrace and to bring Jellicoe a beer and himself his usual. With the prospect of food to come, Steddy asked for a beer as well. "And my friend could use a brandy."

"I'll have a beer, too, if the offer's still open," Wiley corrected.

While they were feasting on a breakfast of mealie—the African's staple, a porridge made from white maize—and pan-fried steaks with grilled tomatoes, Jellicoe was the first to identify the unmistakable power-mower sound of a helicopter.

"Must be one of their Hawks, out of Umtali," he said. "That's the worst possible luck. If they spot the *Flying Cloud,* they can just come right down for a closer look and catch us red-handed."

It was a single-engine British Aerospace Hawk, armed with Sidewinder missiles and a thirty millimeter gun. None of them could continue with their breakfast while it poked around between the peaks of the Vumba that surrounded them. When at last it moved on and its drone had died away, Jellicoe said, "That was close. But hell, we weren't on their screen long enough for them to be sure we were an aircraft."

"They patrol around here pretty regularly. Might not be looking for you at all," Bentley said.

"Don't bloody bet on it," Jellicoe commented, frowning.

"Where is Rollo?" Steddy asked again.

"He tells me that he goes off camping, but I'm pretty sure he's involved with the South Africans in something."

"How do you mean?" Wiley asked.

"Well, it's only guessing, don't you know, but there's an ANC base somewhere across the frontier in Mozambique, and I think he's spotting it for the South African Air Force or doing something like that."

"What's the ANC?" Steddy asked.

"African National Congress—outlaw group of South African blacks fighting Pretoria. Mozambique gives them sanctuary. It kills the South Africans that Samora Machel helps them right across their border—but mind you, that doesn't stop the South Africans from using Maputo as a major port. Machel's delighted to have them even though their air force fly raids into Mozambique to bomb the ANC compounds whenever they can locate them."

"And you think Rollo's spotting for them?" Wiley asked.

"He's in the perfect location to do it," Jellicoe piped in.

"Yeah, but how in hell would he have got in touch with the South Africans?" Steddy asked.

"Oh, that's not so hard to figure out," Bentley answered. "A lot of South Africans come up here to Leopard's Rock for their holiday. It's a hotel about a mile from here, built by Italian prisoners during World War II. Funny when you think I had to leave here to fight them in Italy, and while I was gone, a whole flock of them was down here picking the coffee and tending the roses till we got back—upside down sort of world sometimes, isn't it?" He noticed that Steddy was not interested in his digression and returned to the subject. "Anyway, I've seen him at the bar there, chatting them up more than once."

Jellicoe announced that he was going to have a nap and strode into the house. The colonel suggested that they finish their coffee inside, as the terrace was getting very warm and the bees had discovered the remains of breakfast. They were seated in the big chairs by the empty fireplace again— Steddy was facing the window—when Rollo came in. He stood on the landing where he couldn't see Wiley or Steddy, who were sunk deep in their chairs with their backs to him.

"Where the hell are you, Nubar, you silly bastard? I long for the sight of your ugly mug—nearly killed myself running up the valley when I saw the plane come in!"

Steddy rose and faced him, and was surprised by what he saw. There was nothing of the pallid fugitive about Rollo. He had lost twenty pounds and his mustache, and with them twenty years. He was wearing khaki shorts and a bush jacket with the sleeves rolled up, and had a rifle slung over his shoulder, looking every bit the Hollywood version of an African white hunter.

"Christ Almighty! What the hell are you doing here?" And when Wiley rose as well: "My God, the troops have landed; now we'll have some real fun." He noticed their serious expressions, and as he descended the stairs and strode toward them, he added, "If you've come to talk me into going back, don't even try. I wouldn't leave here if my father kicked the bucket and the Queen granted me a full pardon.''

"Not much chance of that," was the first thing Steddy said.

Rollo looked about the room and said, "Where is Nubar anyway?"

"He couldn't make it this trip," Steddy said.

"Don't tell me you're here for the sport? I bagged a leopard the other day that was six pounds under the record—the world record—not fifty miles from here. This place is a bloody paradise.''

Steddy turned to Bentley and said, "Is there someplace I could talk with Rollo alone, sir?"

"Call me Derek, young man. You can use my study—Stedman knows . . . Oh, dear, this is awkward having two Stedmans about the place.''

"I wouldn't worry, this one isn't planning to be around very long.''

Steddy made for the door, but Rollo stopped him.

"Half a minute. I've been out in the bush for two days and just ran up the bloody mountain. You wouldn't begrudge a condemned man a drink?''

Steddy didn't comment, or say anything, for that matter, as Rollo ordered a Pimm's from the servant, who seemed always to wait just beyond the door. It was very awkward facing him after everything that had passed—like running into your best friend, who'd been thrown out of school for cheating, and not knowing what to say. Wiley didn't seem to know what to say either, and when Bentley offered to show him round the coffee plantation, he seemed relieved for once to let Steddy carry the ball.

Rollo's initial joviality had been dampened by Steddy's attitude, and they both became painfully aware of the silence between them as they waited for the boy to finish serving the drink and leave. When at last he did, Steddy was the first to speak. He had rehearsed the angry scene he would have with Rollo so often in his mind—lying in a bed of pain after almost being killed in Aberdeen, buried in sand to escape a trained killer, and, most recently, every waking moment since Thea had been taken—but now it wouldn't come.

"I don't know where to begin, Rollo." It was a poor start.

"Steddy, old boy, you don't think for a minute that I killed her on purpose, do you?"

"Hell, no. I couldn't give less of a shit about your unmourned wife. I hope for your sake that you did do it on purpose. But no, I don't think you did. That's not why I'm here."

"Well, then, what the hell is this all about? I can tell something's bothering you. Tell me what it is!"

"It's a little complicated, but essentially it has to do with the fact that you stole some top-secret Israeli war plans and the fact that Thea's been kidnapped."

None of the color left his well-tanned face, and he barely seemed to notice the mention of secret documents. He moved eagerly to the edge of his seat, exhibiting his newly won litheness.

"What do you mean Thea's been kidnapped?" His face clouded with genuine concern.

"She was taken four days ago."

"But what have I got to do with it?"

"Rollo, she was taken by an extremely dangerous Israeli agent, who will not give her back until I return the documents you stole from his government."

"I never stole anything from his government or anybody else. They were given to me. But how does he know I'm still alive?"

"That doesn't concern me, because if you don't turn them over to me right now, you won't be alive much longer. And don't say you didn't steal them, because if you didn't steal them from the Israelis, then you stole them from the British—your own people—when you didn't turn them over to them as promised." Steddy could see he had touched a nerve. A flash of anger crossed Rollo's handsome face, and he brushed aside a lock of his no-longer-plastered-down blue-black hair.

"We *have* been talking to a lot of people, haven't we?" he said sarcastically. "I never stole them—I simply haven't turned them over yet. They're a sort of insurance policy. I only got them the afternoon of the accident. I was going to meet with the boys at MI5 the next day, but then you know what happened. I was a little panicked, to put it mildly, and I couldn't just leave them lying around, and then well, I just thought it wouldn't hurt to have a little insurance in case there was any big trouble.''

''The only thing you insured was a pack of trouble for me and now maybe . . . God! If anything happens to Thea, I swear—''

''Steady on, old boy, we'll get this thing straightened out. But how did you get involved anyway? Or are you just acting as a messenger boy for Nubar?''

The anger Steddy had been unable to summon on cue now rose within him of its own volition. Rollo's self-assured arrogance left no room for compassion where other people's welfare was concerned.

''God damn it, *old boy*, we will get this thing straightened out right this minute. Hand those papers over to me *now!*''

''Can't do it, I'm afraid.''

''What the hell do you mean?''

''Give me a chance to—''

''You've had nothing *but* chances. If you don't turn them over right now, I'll turn you over to the Israelis, and the Americans, and the British and let them pull you to pieces. I've only come here in person to give you a chance and to prevent Thea from being—''

''Hold your horses, old boy. You'll get your ruddy papers, but I just can't do it now. You—''

''It's got to be now, or Thea won't—''

''Let me finish! They're in the safe at Leopard's Rock. It's a hotel near—''

''I know all about it. That's where you hang out with your South African friends.''

''Who told you that?'' Rollo asked angrily.

''Never mind that. You can start another Zulu war and then fight the Boers all over again, for all I care. All I want are the papers!''

''Look, Steddy, the safe over there is open from eight

in the morning till nine and then from six in the evening until ten. So you see," he said, looking at his watch, "it doesn't re-open for eight hours."

"If you're stalling, so help me . . ."

"Calm down, Steddy. There's no way to get hold of Jock till he comes in in the evening. Oh, he might wander in sometime after five, if he finishes one sector of the coffee early, but not usually, and he's the only person with the key."

Steddy got up from his chair and stood in front of Rollo with his fists clenched, looking as though he would kill him. Rollo tried to mollify him.

"Look, Steddy, there's just nothing we can do now, so let's make the best of it. Why don't you go up and have a shower and a rest, and then we'll play a little backgammon before lunch. I haven't played since Austria, and you owe me a game. Then we'll—"

Steddy grabbed the rifle that was leaning against Rollo's chair and with both arms made as if to bash him with it. At the last moment, with the swing and the strength of a two-hundred-yard drive, he propelled it into the fireplace, where, simultaneously, the stock broke and it went off with a terrific report in the confined space of the chimney. Rollo cowered in the chair. Steddy looked down at him and said, "Fuck you, Rollo, you son of a bitch!" turned his back to him, and strode from the room.

When Steddy found the bedroom where Jellicoe was resting, he outlined the situation for him.

"We'd still have enough light after six, but the later it gets, the easier it is for the radar to pick us up. I'd say we'd do best to make an early start of it in the morning," Jellicoe said.

"Can you get us into Victoria Falls directly?" Steddy asked.

"That's no problem. They've got a customs and immigration there—they get a lot of direct tourist flights from South Africa. I'll have to radio ahead once we enter Zimbabwean airspace legally, but I don't think they'll make us go through Salisbury. I keep forgetting to call it Harare now—it's not easy keeping up with African place names these days.''

"How long will it take us?"

"Well, if we leave at seven, and I wouldn't like to leave any earlier because of the radar, and if we go out the same way we came in, which we'll have to do in order to re-enter legally, we should get into Vic Falls by nine or nine-thirty.''

"Okay, let's plan on doing that." Steddy started to leave the room and then turned back. "Have you got enough room out there to take off?"

'I told you to leave the flying to me. Lucky I used to fly off an aircraft carrier. What we lack in runway length, we pick up in altitude. The drop from the plateau to the plain is almost four thousand feet—we'll make it." And then he added jokingly, "But this time I think your friend Wiley ought to take a seat in the rear.''

Steddy slept through lunch—Wiley told them not to wake him—but he came down just in time to feast on an enormous tea that was laid on the sofa table in the living room. By the time he had finished, it was almost five, and Rollo sheepishly suggested they set out for Leopard's Rock.

They walked over back roads that were still deeply rutted from the rainy season, through broken security fences topped with barbed wire that were no longer needed, and stepping out of a stand of gum trees, came upon the hotel as if by accident—without the advantage of perspective. In front of them lay the green of the eighteenth hole, where six native boys on their knees were weeding by hand. Beyond the green and an ornamental pond filled with white geese was the hotel at the top of the hill. Like Witches' Wood, it was built of weathered stone covered here and there with moss and ivy. It was two stories high with a slate-shingled roof. The ground floor had tall French doors with rounded tops that pierced the four romantic turrets. The overall effect was that of a nineteenth-century French chateau, not a grand chateau, but the kind that is more associated with a working estate or a vineyard. Nevertheless, it was very impressive, finding it there in the middle of the primeval forest commanding the highest point in the Vumba.

"It must have been very grand once upon a time," Rollo commented as they climbed the hill. "Even the Queen stayed here as a princess with her mother and sister, just after the war. Just goes to show what can be accomplished with the unlimited use of slave labor—talented Italian slave labor at that, prisoners of war, you know. Must have had a few stonemasons among them. Pity about the hits it took during the war."

As they drew nearer, Steddy could see the great pits in the stonework that Rollo had referred to. Leopard's Rock was the highest point in the area, and rockets in the hands of the ZANLA forces had found their mark in the stone turrets and outer wings of the hotel.

"The troubles" had been, for seven bloody years, an out-and-out civil war between the white Rhodesians and the blacks. Moreover, the blacks were divided among themselves into warring factions by historic tribal feuds that had begun long before the white settlers ever drew a boundary line around their tribes and formed the nation called Rhodesia and no doubt will continue long after the white man is gone, or until one tribe succeeds in annihilating or enslaving the other.

The ZANLA forces—Zimbabwe African National Liberation Army—, the military wing of the ZANU-(PF) —Zimbabwe African National Union—(Popular Front) which had done the damage to the hotel, consisted in the main of Shona tribesmen, based in Mozambique, supplied by the Chinese and led by Robert Mugabe. The other faction was the ZAPU—Zimbabwe African People's Union—mostly of the Matabele tribe, historically warriors. They were based in Zambia, supplied by the Russians and led by Joshua Nkomo.

The whites were curiously out of the fray since the Lancaster House Agreement had ended white rule, and now those who remained sat on the sidelines and watched the resumption of the age-old tribal wars.

Mugabe, now president, fearing that his country would fall into the same state of economic and agricultural collapse that Zambia and Mozambique had suffered after the departure of the whites, had passed a law forbidding Zimbabweans to emigrate with more than a thousand dollars, no matter how much property they owned. Some whites had left, and some—who had nowhere else to go or who loved the land too much to bear leaving it—had stayed. Many with young children had left because there was no longer any room for white children in the schools.

The young men, who had known nothing but fighting all their adult lives, could get no work with the new government's "hire blacks first" policy. They felt betrayed—it was their country, too. Many of their families had settled the land almost a hundred years before. Disillusioned, they literally drank themselves senseless in city bars till they killed themselves or one another, or emigrated to South Africa with nothing but the shirts on their backs, where they joined the South African forces to do the only thing they knew how—fight—fight guerrillas.

There had been a golden opportunity for the blacks and whites to work together. Rhodesia had never had legal apartheid, and there was little antagonism between black man and white man. But the political pressure on Mugabe had been too great, and he had been forced to fill the government jobs, the army posts, and the schools with only black candidates, leaving no hope for the whites who wanted to stay and rebuild the country. There was little chance that Zimbabwe could now avoid the abyss that her sisters, Zambia and Mozambique, had fallen into.

All this Steddy learned from Rollo as they made their way from Witches' Wood to Leopard's Rock. Rollo had been swept up—fifty years too late—in the great saga of the white man's role in Africa, as it drew to its inevitable close. The heroic ideals and sympathies that overflowed from him belonged in the Victorian era and the age of Cecil Rhodes.

Steddy felt sorry for his friend, who had spent his life as a wayfarer, searching for his place in the world, and now, when he thought he had found it, it was in a world that no longer existed.

Jock the manager of the hotel, had not returned when they checked at the small counter in the circular hall that served as the desk, so Rollo steered Steddy into the bar, where he poured them each a pink gin and filled out a chit that was left on the counter of the bar for the use of guests and local planters, on the honor system. They had the place to themselves and sat down on leopard skin covered stools at the bar.

The gin bottle looked exactly like Gordon's—it was the identical shape and bore the identical label—but on close examination, Steddy noticed that the name was written "Garden's," instead of "Gordon's," and the bitters bottle, that he had taken to be Angostura, on closer examination turned out to be Angus Stewart. He asked Rollo to explain.

"We had U.N. sanctions here for eight years." (Steddy noted that although Rollo had only been in Zimbabwe for a few months, he was already referring to himself as a Zimbabwean.) "It wasn't easy. The only thing they could get from outside was arms from South Africa. The intrepid bloody Rhodesians really rose to the challenge, produced everything right here. Ersatz, mind you, but you can't tell the difference, down to the wrapping on candy bars—really incredible."

"But the U.N. lifted the sanctions a few years ago, didn't they?" Steddy asked, drawn into the story.

"Right, but there wasn't any surplus foreign exchange for anything but necessities."

"You mean like all those brand new Mercedes-Benz that I saw all the government types driving around in in Salisbury?" Steddy asked sarcastically.

"They get those by the dozens through aid programs— the same for the squadrons of BMW motorcycle escorts. The funny thing is that they don't know how to drive them, and when they strip the gears or bend a fender, rather than use foreign exchange to order spare parts, they just order up a new fleet of limos or motorcycles. It's revolting really; there are yards full of perfectly good equipment that is left to rust for want of a spare part. Even the airline's going bust."

"I thought it was the best in Africa, next to South Africa's?"

"It is, but the bloody ministers think nothing of commandeering a whole plane to go to some meeting in

Paris or Havana that they don't need to attend, and never think of paying the company back for the loss of revenue. The one way they could get the foreign exchange to pay for all their shenanigans is to sell their crops abroad—they've got the best crops and beef in Africa.''

"Then why don't they?'' Steddy asked.

"Because Mugabe feels a debt to Samora Machel in Mozambique and Kaunda in Zambia for the help they gave him during the war—he wants to be the great statesman and benefactor of black Africa. He's giving them his surpluses to feed their people and shore up their own governments. When you think that before Machel and Kaunda forced the whites out of their countries, they produced as much as Zimbabwe—it just makes you sick. And now it's the beginning of the same cycle here. Soon they won't have the foreign exchange to buy seed, then there won't be any crops, and then they'll be in the same boat as the rest of Africa—on the dole!''

They talked for a while longer like the old friends they had been. Steddy was impressed at how quickly Rollo had grasped the political and economic situation in present-day Zimbabwe. He seemed to have a mission and appeared to be genuinely happy for the first time in all the years Steddy had known him.

"Of course, I'll miss the boys. It would be grand to have them out here with me—raise them here in the country . . .''

"Well, couldn't you do that?'' Steddy said, warming.

"Apart from the fact that I'm a wanted man with no visible means of support, father would never let them out of his sight as long as he lives, and to be perfectly honest, I haven't set them a very good example,'' he said morosely.

"They're still very young. They won't remember any of this, and if everything works out with the documents and all, I'll have a word with Allsloe—the chap from Scotland Yard. I'm sure that when I tell them that you turned over the papers to me without any problem, they won't want to prosecute you for that. Then, if you'd just face the music about Jackie . . . well, we'd all testify that it was an accident, and I can't imagine that they'd hold you.''

"You don't know my father. They wouldn't let me off if he had anything to say about it. Oh, there's Jock now."

A stout, red-faced man with curly blond hair and a beard made his way to the table, where he clapped Rollo on the shoulder and shook Steddy's hand when Rollo introduced him.

"Here to do some shooting with your friend?" he asked Steddy. "He got a marvelous leopard the other day."

"Not this trip unfortunately, but I hope so next time."

"He's just here for the day on business, but now that he's seen it here, we'll get him back. I need those papers I gave you to lock up for me, Jock—something in them I've got to return to him."

"Surely he's got time for me to join you for a beer first?"

"By all means," Steddy answered.

Jock drank his beer, and in between telling Steddy about the great variety of game in the area, asked dozens of questions about America and how Zimbabwe was being perceived there. Like all the local whites, he seemed starved for news. When he had finished his drink, he left the bar and returned a few minutes later with a brown paper accordion file tied with string, which he handed to Rollo, then excused himself to go and "wash up."

Rollo untied the string, and lifting the flap, rummaged through the few possessions he had managed to gather before his hasty departure from England. He withdrew a flat, pale yellow, eight-by-ten envelope that couldn't have held more than a few sheets of paper and handed it to Steddy. It had no title on the front but was sealed on the back with three blobs of sky-blue sealing wax that were incised with a clear impression of a seven-light candelabrum surrounded by branches—the arms of the state of Israel. Steddy marveled at how so small a thing could be the cause of so much trouble and pain. Then he examined the seals closely, for as Chelak had explained, Thea's survival depended on their condition.

"Never touched it," Rollo said when he noticed Steddy's scrutiny. "I figured that if the seals were broken, no one would believe I hadn't peddled a copy or two."

"Thank God for once you figured right," Steddy said, breathing a sigh of relief. "I can't tell you what holding this intact in my hands means to me."

"I'm glad to do it. I'm only desperately sorry that you—and Thea, too, of course—got involved in all of this in the first place. I had no idea . . ."

Steddy let out a gasp of frustration. "Rollo, do you know the story about the fellow at a London club who posted a notice on the board that said, 'Would the peer who stole my umbrella please have the decency to return it'?" Rollo shook his head. "Well, a friend of his passed, and after reading it, asked, 'How do you know it was a peer who took it?' The chap replied, 'No *gentleman* would ever do a thing like that!'"

Rollo started to laugh, but then hung his head sheepishly.

"You know, Rollo, I realize that you didn't mean to involve us, but you can't blame me for having cursed you on a daily basis for the last month. If only you had stayed in London and faced the music."

"I wonder. I was on a suicide course, living in Europe. Something had to give, and if I hadn't run, I never would have come here. At least I'm doing something useful now, something I believe in. It makes a world of difference, you know." And then, on the verge of proselytizing to Steddy like a true convert, he stopped, as though he had already said too much, and flashing one of his movie-star smiles, changed the subject.

They had one more drink, and as they did, the bar started to fill with an assortment of men who were dressed like Rollo and all seemed to know him well. Steddy couldn't help but feel that he was an intruder and the cause of their reticent behavior. They all seemed bursting to discuss something but reluctant to do so in front of him. When he suggested to Rollo that they get back to the house so that he could make plans for the following day, Rollo seemed happy to go, but when the other men pressed him to stay, and Steddy said he could follow the track back to the house without any trouble by himself, Rollo agreed immediately and walked Steddy to the clump of gum trees where the trail began.

"Tell Derek and Pamela I'll be back in time for dinner," he said as he saluted Steddy in farewell. "We'll have a good old jaw; I've got a lot of catching up to do. And then maybe you'll give me a few games of backgammon after dinner—you owe me a few you know!"

"My pleasure," Steddy called back to him as he set out on the track. He had mixed emotions about what Rollo was up to with the South Africans and didn't want to know about it, but he couldn't dislike Rollo for what had happened or even blame him. Anyway, with a little luck, it would all be over in twenty-four hours.

Steddy made up his mind to lose at least twenty-five thousand dollars of Omar's money to him before leaving.

Steddy was in the copilot's seat for the takeoff this time. Jellicoe had spent the early morning hours examining the length of the strip with a fine-tooth comb, and with the help of two African boys, had filled every furrow and pothole they could find. With Wiley safely in the aft cabin, he carefully maneuvered the aircraft to the farthest extremity of the runway and then, with the brakes locked, ran her up to full power.

"It's lucky we don't have to try this with a full load of fuel!" he commented dryly.

"Have we got enough to get to Victoria Falls?" Steddy asked.

"That and then some," Jellicoe said as he eased off the brakes.

It took only a few yards before it felt to Steddy as though they were being ejected from a cannon. The ground sped by at a terrific rate as they bumped and lurched over the uneven surface toward the end of the runway—the edge of the plateau.

"We just passed the point of no return," Jellicoe said through clenched teeth, adding little to Steddy's confidence.

When they crossed the edge, the plane bellied out sickeningly as Jellicoe fought to hold the nose up into the updraft off the mountains, but it soon became evident that they were holding their own and were airborne.

The radar detector that Steddy held never went off

once, though it was of little consolation to him, with Jellicoe continuing to cling to the sides of the sloping hills to avoid contact as they swept down the valley, maneuvering the slalom course between the mountains that led to the plain of Mozambique and the Indian Ocean. Eventually Steddy relaxed; Jellicoe was clearly the master of his airplane, gently effecting the banking turns to the right and left with only the deftest movement of his strong, rough hands which held the controls with the delicacy a diamond cutter uses to hold his wedge.

When they passed over the shoreline, tearing across the open sea causing the water to boil, Jellicoe's face relaxed, and he said: "Piece of cake."

"Maybe so, but not one I'd like to cut with anyone else at the helm, thank you very much. You know, that was really fun. I took up flying once. Nothing fancy, just single-engine Cessnas to learn how. But it was so boring; there was no sensation of speed. This was really exciting— makes me want to take it up all over again."

"Don't get too excited; you won't get many opportunities to play with a six-million-dollar aircraft the way we just did."

They reached approximately the same point in the open ocean where they had dropped off the radar the previous day, made a low-level turn back toward the African coast, and ascended to thirty thousand feet.

When they crossed over Beira on the Mozambique coast, Jellicoe was on the radio to them announcing his destination as Victoria Falls. The Umtali tower in Zimbabwe picked them up five minutes later; he repeated the same procedure, giving them an approximate ETA of eleven hundred hours.

"Sorry we're gonna be a little late, but I had to make sure about the runway. Taking a chance with it once was risky, but twice would have been plain crazy—especially at full power," Jellicoe said.

"Don't sweat it. Listen, I never thought we'd get what we needed so quickly—we're in good shape."

Steddy still couldn't get over the ease with which Rollo had turned over the documents. He seemed so changed, so purposeful, Steddy thought, not at all the man pursued by demons he had come to know over the last few years when gambling and feminine conquest had lost their pleasure for him and become a habit he was driven to feed no longer for quality, but for quantity.

Steddy was awakened by Jellicoe's poking him in the ribs. Wiley was standing between them, leaning on the backs of their two seats.

"Christ, Steddy, wake up! You can't miss this!" Wiley almost shouted at him.

About five miles ahead of them in the middle of the lush green, deeply channeled plateau was a tremendous column of smoke that looked like a brush fire extending in a line about a mile wide.

"What is it?" Steddy asked.

"The smoke that thunders," Jellicoe intoned in an accent imitative of the local Africans.

"Of course, the Falls. I never thought . . . I mean I knew we were going to Victoria Falls, but I guess I wasn't thinking. Christ, you could put half a dozen Niagaras in there."

"That's the spray the Falls throw up—it's about a thousand feet high. Want to go in for a closer look?"

"Never mind that!" Wiley cut in. "I've done enough low-level flying to last me a lifetime."

Peter Jellicoe and Steddy laughed as the plane began its descent through a right-hand banking turn in preparation to land at the small airport of Victoria Falls, not far from where David Livingstone had landed in a very different manner some hundred twenty-five years before.

46

Thea had walked through the last two and a half days in a more or less trancelike state, not so much due to the periodic doses of Valium her captives were giving her as to the difficulty she was having in grasping the reality of her situation. She was vaguely aware that they had taken off from one of the Paris airports and that they had subsequently changed planes in Rome for a seemingly endless flight that she passed in a half-sleeping, half-waking state filled with grotesque nightmares made all the worse by the utter confusion of her emotions. She loved Steddy, or did she? Where was he? How could he allow this to happen to her? If it hadn't been for him she would never have got into this mess at all. But then he *had* tried to stop her, he *had* warned her not to even come to Scotland. . . . The plan had been entirely her idea, and she knew it was only right that she suffer the consequences. But where was he *now!* The words screamed through the cotton wool in her brain. The battle of her conflicting emotions—logic, irrationality, and just plain fear— waged back and forth continually, contributing more to her helpless state than the injections.

She read the name of the airport as they descended the gangway into the hot, steamy climate of subequatorial Africa. The sign over the terminal read ''Lusaka,'' but for the life of her she couldn't match the name of the city to a country.

They were separated from the line of people at passport control and escorted—politely, she thought—to a small waiting room that was decorated with flags and pictures of a black leader flanked by Marx and Engels. She remembered thinking it odd at the time, but she couldn't think why it was.

After a brief wait, they were taken to a small twin-engine plane that had a black pilot. No one said a word during the flight, which lasted a little over an hour.

They landed at a small field in the middle of what looked like a residential development gone to seed, where the roads had been put in, but no one had ever built any houses. The signs were mostly so weather-beaten that they were illegible. The only things that she remembered for sure were that just before they landed, she saw the smoke of what must have been a tremendous bush fire, and then, as they got out of the car in front of the hotel that proved to be their destination, she noticed a low, rumbling, roaring noise that never altered in either volume or resonance but bespoke some great force, like an active volcano or a giant dynamo.

Ironically, the hotel was an American Inter-Continental, although it more closely resembled a series of bungalows that appeared to be deserted, so that Thea was surprised when they were greeted at the door by a blue-black, giant King Kong of a man dressed, in spite of the appalling heat and humidity, in an American-cut tuxedo with shawl lapels that must have been put together from the cannibalized parts of at least two suits of normal size. "Cannibal" was the operative word—all he lacked to be a casting agent's dream was a bone in his nose, a leopardskin loincloth, and a giant caldron.

She was confused by everything. She thought she must be in a Marxist country from the pictures and flags at the airport, but then what was an Inter-Continental hotel doing there? And since when did Marxists extend airport courtesies to Israeli agents. She remembered only too well the Israeli raid into Uganda. The man who greeted them looked like Idi Amin's double.

When they were installed in the sparsely furnished bungalow that passed as a suite, she learned from the paraphernalia on the desk that they were in Livingstone—on the Zambian side of Victoria Falls. The two countries—Zambia and Zimbabwe (formerly Northern Rhodesia and Southern Rhodesia)—were divided by the great Zambezi River, with half the falls in Livingstone and half in the town of Victoria Falls.

Why the hell have they brought me here? she wondered. Zambia was surely Marxist. It didn't make any sense.

"Can I take out that thing now?" she asked the woman, while her other keeper, the man with the gun, checked out the bedrooms.

"Yes, of course you may, only put it in some tissue and return it to me. We wouldn't want to lose it."

They had not let her go to the lavatory on the airplanes for fear that she would get rid of the horrible device, and when they had let her go in the airports in Rome and Lusaka, the woman had accompanied her right into the cubicle, watching her closely so that she could not tamper with it.

"Just behave yourself, my dear. It won't be long now," the woman said to her after she had checked out the bathroom before letting her enter. "And leave the door open, won't you?"

47

The room was cool but small, and the constant wheeze of the ancient freestanding air conditioner was almost as bad as if there hadn't been one at all—but not quite. The temperature was well into the nineties, much warmer than up in the Vumba.

The Victoria Falls Hotel was the usual cream-colored colonial pile that one finds, in various states of disrepair, scattered throughout Queen Victoria's former empire. Except for one thing—it was perched on a rise not a thousand feet from the edge of the Zambezi Gorge, where the millions of gallons of water that poured every minute over the mile-wide Falls converged and were compressed into the narrow three-hundred-fifty-foot-deep channel, where, still "boiling," they raced by the hotel on their way to the Kariba Dam, three hundred miles away.

Wiley and Steddy had not seen any of these wonders, nor could they hear the continuous great roar of the Falls over the clatter of the antediluvian cooler. They had arrived an hour before and found only one message awaiting them—it was from Thea. They had missed her call by just ten minutes. The message was that she would call again at six. They didn't know whether she had got free or whether, more probably, Chelak was simply using her to make the call. They would have to wait to find out in the only room available, a small double on the fourth floor.

"What the hell are we supposed to do, sit here all day and wait?" Steddy said, pacing the small room like an animal while Wiley reclined on the bed.

"What the hell do you want to do? I told you to go for a swim, and I'll hold the fort here," Wiley replied, not terribly interested whether he did or didn't.

"Fuck this! The message said six, and six is what they meant. If Thea were free, she would have come here or said she was free."

"Sure! 'Would you kindly leave a message for Mr. Wright that I've got away from the men who were holding me at gunpoint.' I can just imagine," Wiley answered sarcastically.

"Well, I'm not going to sit in this fucking room for five fucking hours. I'll go fucking nuts!"

"Do what you like," Wiley said, leafing casually through a guide to the Falls.

"The way you're acting, you'd think she was your fucking girl."

"I'm very fond of Thea," Wiley answered somewhat defensively.

"How do you think I feel about her?"

"I really don't know. Your amorous behavior can be a little erratic at times, to put it mildly."

"Listen, you son of a bitch!" Steddy paused and looked out the window for a time, then turned to his friend. "I'm sorry, Wiley. We've been on top of each other a lot the past few days, under a lot of pressure—if Chelak said he'd call again at six, you can bet he'll call at six, not five to or five after. What say we take a look at the Falls and grab something to eat? We'll leave a message that we'll be back by five, just in case. That way, at least we'll have a chance to calm down, clear our heads. We'll need all our wits about us if we're gonna pull this one off on our own."

Wiley saw the sense in what Steddy said. He knew that he wouldn't go without him, and he also knew that after five more hours cooped up like this, they might kill each other and would certainly be in no shape to manipulate the delicate exchange to the outcome they wanted. He agreed to go, and the minute he did, Steddy visibly relaxed. He was like a destroyer or a terrier—not designed to operate at slow speed or lie about the fire. Perhaps that was why he was good at games; he always had to be worrying about something, whether a game, a girl, or a puzzle. Wiley saw that it didn't really matter which—as long as he was doing something.

Neither of them wanted to face the fact that Thea had come between them, so, in a way, the compromise to see the Falls was a silent accord to put off the inevitable confrontation until after she was safely returned.

They told the desk that they'd be back at five, and following the clerk's instructions, left the hotel through the big French doors that led to the terrace. The sight that awaited them was a surprise—they hadn't realized that they were literally within spitting distance of the Falls. Following the lawned terraces down to the edge of the gorge, they could see the bridge that spanned it, shrouded in glistening technicolor mists that rose from the "Boiling Pot," where the waters converged; beyond that, all that was discernible of the Falls were the great clouds of spray that hung above them and the deep rumble that resonated in their belly.

They followed the narrow dirt path along the edge of the gorge, which, aside from the discreet wooden arrows marking the trail, was devoid of the more obvious signs of civilization, i.e., concrete and Coke bottles. In fact, apart from the narrow track, little had changed since Livingstone's day.

" 'The midstream of the Zambezi is the border between Zambia and Rhodesia,' " Wiley commented, reading from the guidebook. "I wonder which side the crossing point is on?"

As they continued along the path, nearing the Falls, the trees and undergrowth thickened, and the moisture that hung in the air turned into an English mist that little by little increased into a fine shower until, when they reached a small clearing where there was a simple but larger-than-life-size bronze statue of Livingstone, they were in a veritable deluge that fell from a clear blue sky.

Soaked to the skin, they took off their shirts. Wiley used his to protect the guidebook.

"That's the 'Devil's Cataract' he said, pointing in the direction of Livingstone's imperious gaze.

They scrambled down the crude, steep steps cut from the stone side of the cliff until they were just a few yards from where tons of sun-white water raged past them in great, tangible, foaming clumps to the shadowy bottom of the narrow cut, which was hidden in the mist. The flimsy wooden rail offered little protection against sliding from the wet, muddy ledge into the staggering vortex beneath them. Steddy clung to one of the woody creepers that grew along the face of the cliff and tried to peer out along the length of the Falls. The roar of the water was deafening, and when he shook his head to clear the water from his eyes, he noticed that a family of baboons had followed them down halfway and seemed to be screaming at them, but their shrieks couldn't reach them. There was a moment when he lost his footing and thought, this isn't supposed to be happening in one of the world's greatest tourist attractions. But that was the wonder of the place: for a brief moment, he was the discoverer of the Falls—there was no one else. The moment was quickly over, but the memory lingered long after they had regained Livingstone's statue with the baboons scampering in front of them.

"I guess we'll have to buy some more clothes," he said to Wiley.

"I guess so. I lost my shirt climbing up, but I managed to salvage this," he said, holding the sodden guidebook aloft. He was standing by the statue trying to get a bearing on the map in the book. When the baboons saw that Steddy and Wiley were soaked and almost as naked as they were— with no possibility of any food to offer—they took their leave.

"I just want to get to the 'Danger Point,' " Wiley said, indicating a place on the map. "If we make our way through the rain forest along the south cliff for about half a mile . . ."

"You mean there's something more dangerous than this?" Steddy shouted to be heard. "I almost bought it down there."

"It's at the point where all the water from both sides rejoins at the Boiling Pot and becomes the Zambezi again.

We should be able to see the bridge from this side from there.''

"I don't imagine it's any different on this side than on the side we can see from the hotel,'' Steddy said good-naturedly.

"Come on, there's something I want to check out.'' Wiley took off his soggy shoes and set out purposefully down the winding track. Steddy, who wore no socks, took his off as well and followed him.

They followed the trail around the corner of the Devil's Cataract and then along the top of the cliff at the edge of the rain forest that ran parallel to the Falls, two hundred yards across the cut. Even so, the Falls were not always visible through the clouds of spray, but when they were, the sight of them, in all their breadth, was staggering.

During the entire walk along the opposite cliff to the Falls—about three-quarters of a mile—they passed not one tourist, only a few African women, and they, like Wiley and Steddy, had taken off their tops, putting them under their skirts to protect them from the heavy rain of spray. Their brilliant smiles and slippery, naked breasts added to the time warp of Steddy's fantasy that they were the first white men there.

At Danger Point, the rain forest thinned to grassland, and across it they could see the bridge, shrouded in spray and rainbows, spanning the narrow gorge three hundred fifty feet above the Boiling Pot.

"That's where he'll do it, I'd bet anything.''

"What are you talking about?'' Steddy shouted back at Wiley.

"The exchange. That's where he'll make it.''

"Isn't that a little dramatic?''

"Listen, I do know a little bit about this sort of thing, and I'm telling you that that is where he'll orchestrate the exchange.''

"But why the hell do it on the bridge? Steddy asked, humoring Wiley.

"Come on, I'll show you,'' he said, cutting across the grassland of the point toward the bridge. "It's the frontier; that has to be it.''

"What do you mean?" Steddy asked, hurrying to keep up with him.

"It's in the guidebook. 'The midstream of the Zambezi is the frontier between Zambia and Rhodesia.'"

"Zimbabwe," Steddy corrected him.

"It's an old guidebook. Anyway, the frontier is on the bridge—it's a natural. Why else would he drag us to Victoria Falls if it wasn't so that he could have a bolt-hole across the frontier into Zambia at his back? The only thing I can't figure is that Zambia is Marxist and no friend of Israel. . . ."

When they reached the narrow approaches to the bridge, they were back in civilization. A line of trucks and smaller vehicles crawled in the lane toward the Zambia side, and a line of Africans carrying bulging bundles clogged the footpath.

"They come over here to buy. Zambia's bankrupt of food and everything else you can think of," Wiley said.

"How do you know that?" Steddy asked.

"I read the papers." Wiley smirked. "Not everything's classified, you know."

They crossed the railroad track and joined the line of Africans, interspersed with a few tourists, and shuffled toward the customs and police control that was housed in a small single-story building constructed about ten yards along the six-hundred-foot span. Wiley had given Steddy his passport to put with his in his money belt to keep it dry.

"I've got the passports. Do you want to go across?" Steddy asked him. "We could see the Falls on the Zambia side."

"It might be a good idea to check out the control points," Wiley said, still thinking about the frontier. "Let's see how the line goes."

The rain of spray from the Boiling Pot got stronger as they neared the span, so that Wiley had to put the guidebook, which he had been reading as they shuffled along, in his hip pocket.

"It says that Cecil Rhodes personally picked the location of the bridge, so that people crossing on the train could see and hear the Falls and feel the spray. Must have been quite an engineering feat seventy-five years ago."

When they reached the building and entered through the "In" door, they found themselves in a typical British bureaucratic office, painted the same pale hospital-green that one would find if applying for a driver's license in London or Delhi—only in Zimbabwe, they seemed to have run out of paint, and it was peeling.

There was a special place at the counter for tourists, and with only a family from Belgium and a couple from Germany ahead of them, it didn't take long for them to get exit stamps on their passports.

The five hundred feet of the span between checkpoints was no-man's land, and one was free to cross at one's own pace, presumably because it was one of the best views of the Falls. When they got to the midpoint, they crossed the railroad track that bracketed the roadway on either side and climbed onto the big electrical conduit pipes to reach the railing for the view.

"Don't you see he has to do it here?" Wiley shouted at Steddy, who was looking straight ahead at the Falls, shielding his eyes from the spray.

"You mean in no-man's land? But what's the advantage to him?"

"Maybe he's made some sort of arrangement so he can slip back across the border and be away before we could get across."

"But even if you're right, I don't have any interest in catching him. All I want is to get Thea back safely."

"But you know the man is homicidal. If she's got a look at him, and I think we have to assume that she has, he'll kill her. With all this noise from the Falls, you could shoot someone and no one would even hear it."

"Someone would see the body if he shot someone."

"Yeah, but not right away. And even if they did, you could yell your head off and nobody'd hear you—at least he'd have enough time to get clear. I'm not saying that the only reason he set it up this way is so he can kill one or all of us, but you can see he's left himself the option, and at the very least a way to escape."

"But not before he gets the file," Steddy interrupted.

"You're right—at least I hope so. But don't you see? If

the exchange is made here, he'll be able to get the file and then take a shot at her before she reaches us.''

''If you're right, what the hell can we do about it?''

''Forewarned is forearmed.''

''But we're not armed at all!'' Steddy cut him off.

''Come on, let's see what the control is like on the Zambia side.''

They continued across the bridge, still barefoot and naked to the waist.

The Zambia checkpoint was embellished with a lot of Marxist trappings, but the paint job was no better. There was no special line for tourists, and Wiley and Steddy had to stand in line for some time before they were given visa application forms. When they had filled them out, they were told to wait, until, eventually, they were sent into a small office, where a black man in uniform sat at a desk.

''You should have applied for a visa in advance, you know,'' he said, frowning over their forms.

They were embarrassed to sit down in their sodden state so stood in front of him, making puddles on the raw concrete floor.

''We're just here for a few days and want to see the Falls from your side and have lunch. We've heard they're much more impressive on the Zambia side,'' Steddy lied.

''Oh, yes, much bigger, much bigger.''

''We have money for the fee and to buy lunch,'' Steddy said. ''That is, if it's all right to pay in American dollars?'' he continued, having a sneaking suspicion that it would be.

''How much money are you bringing across with you?''

''Only two hundred dollars,'' Steddy volunteered, ''but we would like to come back again tomorrow if we could get a visa that would be good for two days.'' Steddy pulled the two hundred-dollar bills from his pocket, careful not to push his trousers down and, in so doing, reveal the money belt that was tied at his waist. He put the wet but negotiable bills on the desk.

''The fee is twenty-five dollars per person. It would have been less if you had made arrangements in advance.''

"That's all right. We're sorry to have caused the inconvenience."

"That's twenty-five dollars per person, per day," he added, trying to get as much of the money as he could. "How many days will you wish to cross?"

"Just today and tomorrow would be fine," Steddy answered.

The officer filled out two flimsy slips of paper from a pad, stamped each of them twice, and handed them to Steddy. Reluctantly he pushed one of the hundred-dollar bills toward him; it left a trail of wet on the linoleum top of his desk.

"Enjoy the Falls," he said, unsmiling.

"Can you recommend anyplace within walking distance where we could have lunch?" Steddy asked.

"Inter-Continental Hotel. Very good, very American." He grinned for the first time, showing at least thirty-eight white teeth. "Just follow the road—you won't miss it."

"Christ, Steddy, that was clever of you to get a pass for tomorrow, too," Wiley said admiringly. "You handled that really well."

"I'm not a double-dyed idiot, and I do listen occasionally," Steddy replied as they walked barefoot off the bridge into Zambia.

48

The marriage of Pete Register of the CIA and Allsloe of Scotland Yard, seconded to British Intelligence, was not made in heaven. It was more on the order of a shotgun wedding, a marriage of convenience. Once they realized what they were up against, they had come clean with each other in Scotland and decided to pool their resources and any information they eventually got. The issue was entirely too hot politically for them not to cooperate. Apart from the very real intelligence value of the material at stake, the British had set up an American citizen and put his life and his American girl friend's in jeopardy, and the Americans had been caught hands down with CIA operatives actively pursuing their craft on British soil. It was a first-class mess, and neither country wanted any of it to see the light of day.

Register and Allsloe, with Holbrook in tow, took the direct flight to Zimbabwe the day after Steddy and Wiley left on the *Flying Cloud*. Allsloe had arranged with his opposite number in Nairobi to hold up their plane so that Register's man in Johannesburg would have time to get to Harare (Salisbury) before Steddy and Wiley arrived.

When they got there to find that "the idiots," as they were now referring to them, had given Register's man the slip, they were both incensed—Register doubly so, as Wiley was supposed to be one of his men. The chief inspector refrained from comment while Register read his bleary-eyed assistant the riot act and sent him back to South Africa. They decided that Holbrook, Allsloe's assistant, would be all the help they needed if they ever succeeded in locating their quarry again.

Their break came the next day, when the *Flying Cloud* was spotted landing at Harare airport. (Steddy had sent Jellicoe back there after he dropped them off at the Falls, thinking the plane would be less conspicuous in a big airport.) Allsloe had no trouble finding out from the tower that it had come in from Victoria Falls, and during a few minutes of private conversation with Jellicoe, he was able to "persuade" him to fly them back.

It was only a twenty-minute flight in the *Flying Cloud*. The Victoria Falls Hotel was the first place they went from the airport. The man on duty at the desk was very helpful and told them that Steddy and Wiley had gone out to see the Falls and would be back by five. "Are you the gentlemen they're expecting to hear from?"

"That's right, but don't say we've been by—we want to surprise them," Allsloe told the man. And then quietly to Register, he said, "That must mean that we're in time and they haven't made contact yet."

The clerk said he was sorry but there were no rooms available and directed them down the road, where they checked in to the Elephant Hills Country Club, left their things, and set out on the trail to the Falls to try to find "the idiots" before they could get in contact with Chelak.

They were even less prepared for the wet than Steddy and Wiley had been, and it wasn't long before they were sliding around in the mud in their city shoes and weighed down by their soggy tweeds. After an unsuccessful hour, they were about to give up and go back to the hotel to wait, when they came upon the bridge, the first place Allsloe could act like a policeman and ask someone if he'd seen them. He strode ahead of the line into the checkpoint and showed a limp picture of Steddy to the man on duty at the tourist desk. He recognized him and volunteered that he had been in the company of a blond man, equally as tall.

Halfway across the bridge, looking like survivors of the wreck of the *African Queen*, they ran into Wiley and Steddy on their way back. They were bare-chested and barefoot, had rolled up their trousers *à la* Huckleberry Finn, and looked a great deal more comfortable than the three men who confronted them. Allsloe kept trying to wipe his glasses to see clearly, but there was nothing dry to wipe them on, and Register's gabardine Brooks Brothers suit was glued to him, showing off all the bulges in his pockets. Holbrook, who always looked very slicked down, looked surprisingly together. The noise from the Falls played to "the idiots'" advantage in the conversation that followed.

"You bloody idiots!" was all Register could manage to splutter.

"What's that?" Steddy yelled at him, one hand cupped at his mouth and the other around his ear.

"You were supposed to stay in touch with Hegner, not get him silly-assed drunk! We had a deal!" Register bellowed.

"We couldn't find him the morning after we had dinner, and we had to leave," Steddy yelled back.

"Did you get the documents?" Allsloe asked.

The rough timbre of his voice boomed out clearly. Nevertheless, Wiley answered, "Can't hear you. Better wait till we get back," gesturing toward the Zimbabwe side of the bridge. Allsloe gave up for the moment. He could see they weren't hiding any documents about their persons.

They made their way in a group back to the Zimbabwe outpost, and entering from the other side of the building, found themselves on the opposite side of the counter that they had so recently been processed out from. Without talking, Register prodded Steddy and Wiley to go first at the opening marked "Tourists." After a brief examination of their papers, the official stamped them and reached for the three passports Register slid across the counter. He examined them a little more carefully than he had Wiley's and Steddy's and then looked up and addressed Register.

"I do not find your exit stamp from Zambia. As a matter of fact, I do not find your entrance stamp to Zambia," he said seriously.

"That's because we haven't been to Zambia," Register replied politely. "We changed our minds."

"But I am not permitted to enter you into Zimbabwe unless you have legally exited another country."

"But we did legally exit Zimbabwe," Register said, pointing to the Zimbabwean exit stamp and beginning to get annoyed.

"But that does not tell me where you have been in the meantime."

"It was only stamped five minutes ago." Register was red-faced and steaming now.

"I cannot help that. You must have a legal stamp from another country—we must follow the rules."

Register was apoplectic. It was the last straw after a generally unsatisfactory, uncomfortable day. Allsloe saw that he was about to explode and grabbed him firmly by the elbow, muttering under his breath, "We don't need any trouble here just now." He maneuvered Register from in front of the window and said to the clerk, "If we were to enter Zambia and exit it with a stamp, would that be all right?"

"Oh, perfectly, sir," the man said, smiling.

"Then that is what we'll do. Thank you very much," Allsloe said politely.

"Oh, thank you, sir—and have a nice trip."

Steddy and Wiley were standing off in a corner roaring with laughter—the CIA and Scotland Yard had met their match at the hands of an African bureaucrat, who had probably been trained by the British in the first place. They called to the sodden threesome from the door that exited into Zimbabwe, "We'll see you back at the hotel. We've just got to get into some dry clothes." They laughed most of the way along the paved road to town, where they bought some rather bizarre-looking shirts and trousers—all that was available—before returning to the hotel to await the call from Chelak.

Steddy and Wiley were unaware that as they ate lunch by the empty pool in the run-down, semi-deserted Inter-Continental Hotel compound, they were just yards away from the bungalow where Thea was being held. They had walked all the way from the bridge. As they left the spray of

the Falls behind them, the heat became terrific, so that by
the time they got there and were ushered to a table by the
same giant in black tie who had greeted Thea and her group,
all they really wanted was a beer. He informed them that
Zambia was out of beer that week.

Steddy said, "You mean the hotel is out of beer?"

"No, sir, the country is out of beer."

What Rollo had told Steddy suddenly hit home. They
ordered the simplest thing on the menu, a croque-monsieur
and the fellow said he would see if there was any cheese.
When it finally came, it did have a sort of cheese on it, but
it looked as though they had simply scraped the clotted top
off six-day sour milk and slathered it on the ham. Steddy
thought it revolting and wouldn't touch it, but Wiley was so
famished that he tried to salvage the bread. In disgust,
Steddy turned his chair into the sun and his back to Wiley,
until he heard Wiley screaming, "Get away! Get away!"
accompanied by outraged shrieks. He turned to see that a
large baboon with bared teeth had jumped on the table and
was having a vicious tug-of-war with Wiley over the last
crust of bread. Poor Wiley—who must have been starving to
even think of eating the revolting thing—lost it, and the
baboon jumped off to join his fellows, who had formed a
sort of rooting section during the fray. It seemed everyone in
Zambia was hungry. "So much for Socialism or Marxism or
whatever," Steddy said, laughing as he paid the outrageous
bill. Wiley was not amused at having lost out to a baboon,
and more importantly, at having lost his lunch, and didn't
say very much until they had a good laugh together after
their encounter with Allsloe and Register on the bridge on
the way back.

It was five when they got to the hotel, and Wiley
announced in the lobby that the first thing he was going to
do was order a sandwich from room service.

"Order me one, too," Steddy said. "I'm going to have
a look around down here, to get the lay of the land, as it
were. And I'll try to find a plastic bag for the documents. If
you're right and we do meet on the bridge, they'll want to
see the envelope, so I'd better get it wrapped in something,
or it'll get soaked."

"Good thinking, but don't be long. He may call any minute."

Steddy was back in the room in less than half an hour.

"You know they've got a casino in the hotel?"

"Well I'm glad you had the fortitude to resist it, for a change."

"Come on, Wiley. I'm very upset about all this—we just react in different ways," he said, picking up half of the ham sandwich Wiley had ordered for him.

"We'd better talk about this, Steddy. You know, it's okay to play cat and mouse with Register and Allsloe, but as you yourself pointed out, when push comes to shove, neither of us is armed, and if Chelak pulls any funny business . . . We may have the visas to follow him back over the bridge—if I'm right, that is—but there's precious little we can do about it. We're going to need the boys in blue."

"Yeah, you're right. But we can't just turn over the documents to them and lose control of the whole thing. You know that's all they care about—Thea's of secondary importance as far as they're concerned."

"I agree with you, but what we'll have to do is play our cards very close to our chests—not tell them about the arrangements until the last minute and hang on to the papers—"

"So how much do we tell them?" Steddy interrupted.

"Let's see what Chelak says first. Then we can—"

The phone rang. They looked at each other. It rang a second time before Wiley uncradled the receiver and handed it to Steddy.

"Hello?" Steddy said.

"Steddy, it's you—" It was Thea, but her words were cut off.

"It's Thea, but—" Steddy started to say to Wiley, when another voice came on the line.

"Mr. Wright." It was a woman's voice with an accent. "I will give you the instructions for tomorrow's meeting on behalf of our mutual friend. Can you hear me clearly?"

"Yes," Steddy replied, the phone half on his ear and half on Wiley's, who was crouched next to him, head to head.

"Good, for I will say this only once. You will be on the bridge over the Zambezi, with the documents, at eleven o'clock. You will stop halfway to admire the view of the Falls, and you will be approached. Please bring your friend, Monsieur Travis, with you, but no one else. Until tomorrow then."

"She rang off as though she were making a date for tea," Steddy said to Wiley after he had hung up the phone. "Well, you sure called that one right," he said, patting Wiley on the shoulder.

"Wouldn't have been able to if you hadn't forced me to go to the Falls today. And they sure were punctual," he said, pointing at his watch. "Two minutes after six."

There was an urgent knock on the door.

"Right on cue, wouldn't you say?" Steddy said as he opened the door and let in the three bedraggled hotshot superspies.

49

Steddy and Wiley set out on foot for the bridge, fifteen minutes ahead of Register and Allsloe. Holbrook was already in position somewhere on the span. They took the footpath again at the back of the hotel and looked as though they had gone native, dressed in the local shirts and trousers they had bought the day before. Register and Allsloe had managed to procure disposable Hong Kong raincoats and walked by the main road to the bridge from the Elephant Hills Country Club. They had all synchronized their watches at dinner in the vast dining room of the Victoria Falls Hotel, which could hold a thousand people, while being serenaded by a "continental" orchestra that alternated with a chamber music group throughout the meal.

Steddy adamantly refused even to let them have a look at the envelope that contained the documents. Wiley backed him up all the way. A serious argument followed, but when Allsloe and Register realized that further efforts to sway him were futile, they agreed to give him backup on the exchange. They had little choice given the predicament they were in, and they didn't want to miss their opportunity to be in at the kill.

Wiley went straight to bed after dinner, but Steddy had a nightcap at the bar with Register, Allsloe, and Holbrook, and when, at ten o'clock, Allsloe expressed a desire to retire, Register agreed to look in on the casino with Steddy for a few hands of blackjack. The casino was small and, it turned out, temporary, as the big one had been destroyed during the war, by rockets fired by the ZIPRA forces from Zambia across the Zambezi. The crowd consisted mostly of white Rhodesians, who, it appeared, were wild gamblers, probably partially due to the fact that they couldn't take any funds out of the country and didn't know how long they would be allowed to keep what they had.

They played a few hands but couldn't really get into the game as their minds were elsewhere, so they quit and had one for the ditch at the small bar in the gaming room. Register again tried to persuade him to be more cooperative.

"Don't you see that leveling with us is the best thing for the girl? We can't be really effective if we're dancing in the dark."

"I just can't take the chance. I'm responsible for getting her into this in the first place—and none of it would have happened at all if it hadn't been for that limey bastard setting me up. In spite of the fact that you're a nice guy, you're both cut from the same mold, and our priorities in this thing are in no way the same. Nothing you could say or do will change my mind."

"You're just too damn close to the situation—"

"What the fuck should I be?" Steddy interrupted.

"Look, I do understand, but you don't. You don't have any idea what you're up against, and there's no way I can convince you. It might have been different if you were working for me . . ."

"Say again?"

"Just that, in spite of our differences, I have to say that for an amateur you've really been thinking on your feet—given all of us a merry chase. I think Allsloe would agree with me. We all underestimated you."

"Flattery will get you nowhere."

"No, I mean it. If you weren't involved with this girl, I think you could have been a big help. As it is . . . well, if you'd ever like to do something useful for your Uncle Sam when this is over . . ."

"Gosh, there's no limit to how far you people will go to—"

"No, I mean it, but let it be. We'll play it your way tomorrow."

They parted in the lobby at the foot of the stairs from the casino. Steddy went to his darkened room to join Wiley in pretending to sleep, and Register walked down the road to his hotel to do whatever a seasoned spy does before an operation.

It was quarter to eleven when Wiley and Steddy cleared customs on the Zimbabwe side and set out on the footpath to cross the bridge. When they reached midspan, they traversed the railroad track, climbed up on the big conduit pipe, and leaned over the rail—for all the world, tourists hypnotized by the panorama of the Falls. They were already soaked to the skin, but the broad-brim, woven-hemp native hats they had bought protected their vision from the warm downpour. The documents were safely encased in the clear plastic bag Steddy had got from the desk, and were tucked in his belt, under his shirt. Holbrook, they noticed, was stationed on the same rail, about forty yards farther along toward the Zambia side. They alternated straining to see in either direction for any sign of Thea, and Steddy spotted Register and Allsloe—equipped with cameras—as they entered the passport hut on the Zimbabwe side. It was almost eleven, and there was still no sign of Thea or her captors.

By ten minutes past, Steddy was getting agitated.

"You don't suppose they've spotted those assholes, do you?" he asked Wiley.

"I doubt it. Try to relax; he's probably just checking the terrain."

"I don't like it. He's always done everything he said he would do almost to the second."

"Just relax, Steddy!" Wiley answered, revealing the state of his own nerves. "We're here, unfortunately, at his convenience, not vice versa. Relax!"

"Yes, Mr. Wright, you must listen to your friend and relax. This will be quite painless if we all keep our heads."

The voice came from Steddy's left elbow. It startled him, as he had not noticed anyone approaching him, so intent was his gaze to the right toward the Zambia frontier. When he spun around, he saw a small, wiry black man wearing a hat similar to his that was, like the rest of his clothes, verging on rags—but there could be no mistaking the voice. It was Chelak. He could never forget the tone of that voice from the first time he had heard it on the Scottish moors.

"Do not stare at me but continue to observe the Falls. They are most majestic, are they not?"

Steddy poked Wiley in the ribs so hard with his elbow that he almost doubled over; the roar of the Falls had prevented him from hearing Chelak's words, and he was still staring off to the right. Wiley swore at Steddy, but Steddy cut him short with a stage whisper that could have been heard at the Victoria Falls Hotel, had it not been for the vortex of rushing water in the Boiling Pot below them.

"It's him, it's him!" he said fiercely.

"Have you got the documents with you?" Chelak asked.

For some reason, in his nervousness, Steddy fumbled in his trouser pockets.

"I believe you'll find them under your shirt," Chelak said politely. "And I already know my disguise is most effective; please ask your friend not to stare at me. Just act normally—as if you're showing me a map to ask a question."

"Don't look at him, Wiley," Steddy breathed at him as he unbuttoned his shirt to get at the envelope.

"It isn't necessary to disrobe," Chelak said in the same even, lilting voice. His remark made Steddy realize how rattled he was, and he tried to pull himself together.

"Where is Thea? I don't see her."

"First I will examine the seals on the documents, and if all is in order, I will signal for her to be brought into view. Then the exchange can be made."

"I will want her to be safely in the hands of my friend

before I turn them over to you," Steddy said, repeating the plans they had rehearsed the night before.

"That is agreeable. But come, come—the documents."

Steddy removed the plastic sheath from under his belt, and holding it firmly in two hands, showed it to Chelak in the manner he had suggested, as though they were consulting over a map. When Chelak made a move to hold the envelope, Steddy withdrew it and cautioned him.

"You may look—but don't touch," he said unemotionally, more in control of himself now.

Chelak bent over the envelope, studying the seals through the plastic, periodically wiping the rain from it with his hand. Steddy let him, as he was unwilling to loosen the death grip with which he held it in both hands.

"Not the best conditions for the sort of examination required, would you say? You will have to be patient and bear with me," he said, noticing Steddy's trembling white knuckles. "Clever of you to think of the plastic wrapper. Have you been here before?" His conversation was casual, but his eyes furtively caressed the seals on the back of the envelope.

"We had a look around yesterday while we were waiting for your call."

"Well, at lest you've had some pleasure from your journey. Please turn it over."

Steddy brought the plastic to his chest to execute the reversal, wiped it off on his shirt, and then returned it to its position under Chelak's nose. He examined the blank side of the envelope with as much care as he had the side with the seals, and then closely eyed the edges.

"Come on, let's get on with this. It's not in my interest to have fiddled with the damn thing. All I want is Thea back—now!"

"Just the last edge, Mr. Wright." He continued eyeing it as he spoke, until his straightened shoulders indicated that he had finished to his satisfaction, and then he said, "If you will just watch by the customs house on the Zambia side, please."

Steddy replaced the envelope under his belt but continued to hold it to him with one hand as he turned to his right and peered at the crowd of people coming toward them from the Zambia customs building. Chelak bent over as if to pick up something he had dropped. It must be a signal, Steddy thought. He noticed a heavyset European peel off the opposite rail and head toward the building. A few minutes later he re-appeared with a smallish European woman—Thea was in between them. It had to be Thea. She towered over both of them, and even with her hair hidden under a scarf and wearing an unfamiliar cotton dress that was glued to her in the rain, there could be no mistaking her. Steddy instinctively moved to go to her, but Chelak held him back.

"That would be very unwise. We must do this as planned."

"All right. All right!" he said, turning back toward the wiry little man.

"Your friend will cross to the pedestrian way on the other side of the bridge, where Miss Boulton will advance to meet him. When they are together, you will turn the documents over to me. It is very simple, but don't think you can try anything. She will be killed instantly if you make one false step before I am safely back over the Zambian frontier," he said, the casualness gone from his voice, replaced by a savage quality that Steddy knew to be more genuinely representative of his character.

Steddy turned to Wiley and repeated Chelak's instructions with a few of his own.

"He means business—for God's sake don't get any patriotic notions about absolving your sins in the eyes of your employer," Steddy hissed at him.

"Fuck you, Steddy—I love her too!" It was out and he didn't care, as he strode across the tracks and the roadway to the footpath on the other side—to Thea, who was advancing on her own, slowly but with determination, to meet him.

Steddy stood with his back to the Falls, counting each footstep that brought Wiley and Thea closer together. He didn't have the time or inclination to wrestle with Wiley's confession—he didn't even allow it to enter his consciousness. That was already filled with thoughts of Chelak—what he would and could do—and visions of Thea with her face blown away by a silent gunshot.

Wiley reached the point on the footpath opposite them and stood, still as a stone, waiting for Thea to reach him. She did, and he put an arm around her. She seemed to go limp against him and shrink to someone half her stature.

"All right, Mr. Wright, the documents please," Chelak said at his elbow.

Steddy pulled them from where they rested against his belly, never for an instant taking his eyes from Thea's pathetic form.

All of a sudden, all hell broke loose. In the corner of the frame of his vision, Steddy saw Holbrook running toward Wiley and Thea. At the same moment, Chelak tried to wrest the envelope from his grip. He struggled with him, and as he did so, noticed Register and Allsloe racing toward them from behind Chelak's back—but someone was closer. Thea started screaming, a piercing wail that could be heard over the rush of the Falls, and Holbrook was on one knee, holding a gun in front of him with both hands, firing at the man and woman who were running toward Thea. Steddy was holding off Chelak's arm with one hand when he noticed the deathly glint of white metal flash dully in Chelak's free hand and had to drop the envelope in order to try to fight off the hideous platinum spike that he knew by reputation. His purchase on that arm was awkward as he had stepped off the pipe, and Chelak had the advantage of height over him. He felt the thing scratch the back of his neck and knew he couldn't hold him off much longer, when suddenly Chelak went limp in his arms and collapsed in a heap at his feet. There was a figure behind him, but to Steddy it was just a blur as he whipped around to see Thea, who was still screaming, still evidently whole. He was just in time to see the man fall dead under Holbrook's gun—the woman already lay writhing on the ground. Thea pushed Wiley away from her with a violence that two minutes before he wouldn't have thought her capable of. She hiked up her skirt and squatted on the path for a moment as though defecating, then vaulted the tracks and pitched something out over the water. There was a flash of light and then a pressure in his eardrums that he felt more than heard. He started to run to her when a hand restrained him. When he looked around, it was a perfect stranger—the man he owed his life to.

"Could I just trouble you for the envelope, please, Mr. Wright?" he said with the greatest courtesy.

"Who the devil are you?" Steddy asked, still registering shock and surprise. ,

"The man who saved your life. Wouldn't you say that's enough of an introduction?"

Steddy was very confused. Too much had happened too quickly for his brain to compute it all, and on top of that he saw Register and Allsloe casually strolling back toward the Zimbabwe control point and Holbrook running for his life in the same direction.

"I must have dropped it when we were fighting," Steddy said to the swarthy, stocky man in the raincoat who faced him. Out of the corner of his eye, he saw Wiley supporting Thea on the other side of the bridge—walking slowly toward Zimbabwe.

Steddy looked down at the ground to find the envelope, and for the first time focused on Chelak. He was lying on his back, contorted spastically. His lips were drawn back from his teeth, and his shirtfront had torn open, revealing a green-white, hairless chest that contrasted sharply with the dyed black skin of his arms and face.

There was no sign of the envelope. The stranger stood over him motionless, watching. Steddy gingerly tried to shift the body to see if it was under him, but the weight was more than he would have guessed, and he had to get down on his hands and knees to move it. The envelope lay in the pool of blood that had formed from the deep knife wound in Chelak's back. Steddy grasped it between two fingers and tugged it out from under the lifeless form—it was slathered with blood. He rose to his feet and thought, why should I give this to a perfect stranger?

"It's a bit messy, I'm afraid." He addressed the man as he held it up into the rain, over the rail, to get the full benefit of the spray from the Boiling Pot.

"Be careful, Mr. Wright."

He knows my name, Steddy thought, and noted his harsh but unidentifiable accent.

It was the man's preposterous accent that decided Steddy. Holding the plastic sheath by its edge and shaking—ostensibly to wash away the blood—he allowed the pale yellow envelope to slide from it into the Boiling Pot, three hundred fifty feet below them.

The man made a move to grab for it, but then threw up his hands and smiled. "It doesn't matter—the original is in safe keeping. You have done my government a great service, Mr. Wright."

Now Steddy was completely baffled.

"But it was an Israeli document, wasn't it? I saw the seals myself!"

"That is correct. But I haven't introduced myself—the name's Lev Ginsberg, Israeli State Security."

"But you killed him," Steddy said, pointing at Chelak's body.

"He was a traitor, a fanatic working for the Syrians. We've known for some time. It would have been very bad if they'd got hold of that," he said, pointing down to the river. "But he was good at his work, and I know that if he was willing to accept the exchange, then the seals were not broken and—how do you say?—we have a happy ending, no?"

"Happy ending" brought Thea to Steddy's mind, and he looked back to where she had been, but she and Wiley were gone. They must have got back into Zimbabwe, he thought. There was a big showrie going on over the two bodies, with frontier police from both sides and crowds of people gathered round. The sound of an ambulance could be heard getting nearer. Lev interrupted his thoughts.

"We'd better be getting out of here before they notice there are three bodies on this bridge."

Steddy concurred. He didn't fancy being held indefinitely in an African lockup while they tried to sort out the mess.

They walked together from the bridge, into the customs hut and out the door on the other side, into Zimbabwe. There was so much confusion that no one even bothered to stamp their passports. They just waved them through.

At the fork in the road, Ginsberg shook Steddy's hand heartily, as if to make up for the words he couldn't express in his poor English.

"I say good-bye, my work is done. Thank you, thank you."

"Thank you," Steddy said, a sense of light-headed elation creeping over him. They waved again as Ginsberg turned to take the road to town and Steddy, the road to the hotel.

50

Allsloe and Register were huddled in the lobby when Steddy arrived at the hotel. They separated and bracketed him on either side.

"Where's Thea—is she all right?" was the first thing Steddy asked them.

"She's in your room, the doctor's with her." And then, seeing the concern scribed on Steddy's face: "She's all right, just very badly shaken."

"Where's Wiley?" Steddy growled.

"He took the doctor up, but don't go now. He's giving her an injection; she'll sleep for quite a while. The doc's one of ours—had him on call, just in case."

"Just in case! Just in case! It's only sheer fucking luck that we weren't all killed with the stunt that asshole pulled. Where is that son of a bitch Holbrook?"

"He's in custody for the moment, but not for very long. We should have him out in a day or two. The new government here is more cooperative with her Majesty's government than the newspapers would lead one to believe," Allsloe said.

"Don't go off half-cocked about Holbrook, Stedman," Register interjected. "Those people on the bridge were about to detonate a bomb that was wired to Thea. Allsloe will explain it—I have to make a call."

Register left them to telephone from the booth by the

desk. Steddy and Allsloe wandered into the bar, where the Englishman explained in some detail how Thea had been booby-trapped and how only the quick action by Holbrook had saved her and Wiley's lives.

"I hope you will bear that in mind if you're thinking about making any trouble for her Majesty's government."

"Don't bring the Queen into this—she didn't have a fucking thing to do with the way you set me up!" Steddy replied angrily.

"Certainly not, just a figure of speech," Allsloe countered, taking Steddy at his word. "We never planned it to go this far, but I'm afraid I rather misjudged your—how shall I say?—resourcefulness."

"What the hell did you expect me to do?"

"That, in essence, was the problem—you never did what we expected you to do. Are you sure that you've never had a run-in with the law before?" Allsloe said, half in jest, trying to heal the situation with a little humor.

"Now you're making me angrier," Steddy said, and then cut off Allsloe's objections with: "What will happen to Rollo now?"

"Ah, yes, Lord Rockford." He sighed. "Well, now that we know at least what country he's in, it shouldn't be much of a job finding him. Of course, if you'd like to cooperate . . ."

"Fuck that! What'll you do to him once you get him? His wife's death was accidental; you won't be able to hang that on him."

"His wife's death is the least of his problems. He's seriously breached the Official Secrets Act, and I'm not sure that he isn't guilty of high treason."

"You mean, 'hanged by the neck until dead' on the old silk cord?"

"Hanging peers by a silk cord was voted out by the House of Lords ten or twenty years ago."

"You know what I mean," Steddy insisted.

"I should think he'll be sent away for quite a time."

"He didn't really do anything. He told me that he was going to turn the documents over to you the next day, but then the accident happened, and I guess he got scared and ran. He was drunk and thought that he might be able to buy his way out of the mess with the documents.''

"I doubt if they would have helped, but they are no longer an issue. You saw to that!"

"Just one fucking minute. That guy you let follow me around for a month was a fucking Syrian agent—he would have killed me on the bridge if it hadn't been for the Israeli. And where were you guys, by the way? My protection, ha!"

"We saw that Mr. Ginsberg had matters well in hand and thought it best to withdraw."

"Would you rather have had the Syrians get the papers?"

"None of this is any longer germane, I'm afraid. I don't see where all this is leading."

"Then I'll tell you. If you don't let Rollo off, I'm going to scream bloody murder, all over your lousy British tabloids."

"I don't see how that would help you, and if you think it could make the slightest difference in a case where a peer has committed high treason, you're very much mistaken," Allsloe said, rising in his chair indignantly, feathers ruffled.

"Well, if you'll wait here just a minute, I'll show you something that might make a difference." Without waiting for an answer, Steddy strode from the bar, through the big hall, and out into the lobby. Register was still on the phone in the booth as Steddy passed on his way to the desk. He took a small silver key from his trouser pocket and flashed it at the clerk as he walked behind him into the vault where the safe-deposit boxes were located. The clerk followed him in, took his key, found the corresponding box, and with Steddy's key and the one that he had on a chain, opened it, then left the room.

"Let me know when you're finished."

Steddy lifted the lid, pushed his money belt aside, and took out one of the two envelopes that lay beneath it. He reclosed the box and turned the lock that still had his key in it, put it in his pocket, and told the chap at the desk that he'd already locked his side, as he passed him on the way back to the bar.

Allsloe was still sipping his whiskey and soda when

Steddy returned. He took his seat, undid the fastener at the back of the envelope, and withdrew a copy of the four sheets of paper that had caused so much trouble. He held the first sheet that bore the shield with the candelabrum under Allsloe's nose and gloated at the reaction it produced. The bright red, permanently surprised eyebrows turned into circumflex accent marks, and the tiny red mouth opened, forming a perfect *O*.

When he had regained enough of his composure to speak, he said, "Mr. Wright, you do amaze me. But this a Xerox copy; how did you get it? Chelak examined the seals!"

"I never broke the seals. I cut the envelop open from the back with a razor blade and made the copy for fifty pence at the desk—they let me do it myself. As for Chelak noticing—well, through the plastic cover and with all that spray, and sometimes even seasoned spies see only what they want to, wouldn't you agree?"

"Touché," was all that Allsloe could say in response. "I assume you intend to exact your pound of flesh for those," he said, pointing at the papers, which still remained in Steddy's hand.

"You bet your British ass I do," Steddy said, restacking the papers and relaxing back into the big, comfortable chair.

"And what would that be?"

"Withdraw all charges against Rollo. In effect, think of me as his messenger, delivering your ill-gotten goods as promised."

"And if not?" Allsloe asked, with little hope of being given quarter.

"If not, I'll release them to the papers—and the United Nations—and raise the most unholy diplomatic stink that's been seen since the Zimmermann telegram."

"Say no more—you have a deal." Allsloe paused pensively and continued, "I doubt if Lord Rockford deserves your loyalty...." He looked up from under his startling eyebrows. "On the other hand, perhaps you deserve each other!" He took the papers from Steddy's extended hand and left him to ponder his words.

*   *   *

The room was darkened when Steddy was finally allowed in to see Thea at ten o'clock that evening. At first all he saw were her enormous eyes in the pale light that reflected into the room through the bathroom door, which was ajar. She didn't say anything as he approached the bed, so he didn't either. He didn't know what he could say. He was overwhelmed by the horror of what had happened to her; the hideous violation of her body was an invasion of her free spirit.

He gently lowered himself to the bed beside her and took her hand, which lay lifeless on top of the sheet.

"I'm so very sorry, darling," he said tenderly.

She didn't open her mouth, but the corners wrinkled up a bit, acknowledging what he had said.

"I guess you don't want to talk about it?"

Her head moved slightly to the right and then to the left.

"Would you rather rest some more?" he asked.

She squinted her eyes and moved her head up and down. He bent over and kissed her tenderly on the nose.

The nurse was standing out in the hall talking in hushed tones with Wiley. Steddy must have looked crestfallen, for she volunteered, "I wouldn't worry, sir. The doctor gave her a very strong sedative, and I'm just going to give her another injection now. Sleep's what she needs. Mark my word, by tomorrow she'll be fit as a fiddle."

Her accent was pure British, and Steddy wondered what branch of the service Allsloe had drawn her from. They seemed better prepared for the mopping up than for the actual dirty work.

Wiley followed Steddy, who took the stairs down rather than waiting for the lift. Steddy was depressed, and he didn't know why. Certainly he was worried and upset over Thea, but the source of his depression eluded him. Wiley, on the other hand, was walking on air, in spite of the dressing down Register had given him before dinner. But he sensed Steddy's mood and said, "Want to have a drink?"

"Sure, why not?" Steddy answered, without enthusiasm.

"Oh, by the way, Allsloe's got us a room at the Elephant Hills. He couldn't send our things over, 'cause we don't have any," Wiley said, trying to raise Steddy's spirits, or at least get a reaction out of him.

"Bully," was all he got in return.

They were on their second drinks. Wiley was carrying on a one-sided conversation, Steddy's only remarks being an occasional "uh-huh," when Steddy asked him, "What's going to happen between you and Register?"

"Not much. You can't fire someone who was never on the payroll," he said, trying to make light of his breach with the Company.

"Come on, Wiley, don't tell me you don't care about it—just a little?"

"Well, I guess I do. I've been working with him a long time, and now, well, I blew the first real operation I've ever been involved in—at least in their eyes, anyway."

"Well, not in mine!" Steddy affirmed. "I owe you one. You really stood by me when it counted."

"Don't be so morose, Steddy. You sound like Napoleon saying farewell to his generals—it's not really a big deal."

"Yes, it is, and I know what it means to you in spite of what you say. If I hadn't made you stick by me, you probably would have ended up a hero. Here," Steddy said, tossing the small key to the vault over the table. "This should go a long way toward fixing things up."

"What is it?" Wiley asked, perplexed.

"The key to my safe-deposit box at the desk."

"I don't want any money, Steddy," Wiley said, insult instantly creeping into his tone at the thought.

"It's not money, but you should find it of much greater value. But don't go get it if Allsloe and Register are still around."

"They've gone back to the Elephant Hills," Wiley answered, still puzzled.

"Then go and get it, and bring my money belt back while you're at it. Maybe I'll stop in at the casino before we move out of here."

Wiley returned with the opened envelope in his hand while Steddy was paying the bill.

"Steddy, I don't know what to say. How could you have taken a chance like that with Thea's life at stake?"

"Isn't that what you wanted from the beginning?"

"Well, yes, but not—"

"Oh, can it, Wiley," Steddy said, moving to leave.

Wiley answered with a trace of bitterness.

"Maybe you're the one who should give this to Register—you obviously have more of a stomach for this sort of work than I do."

"Oh, just keep it and shut up!" Steddy told him, stuffing the papers in Wiley's breast pocket. "Maybe tomorrow everything will look a little different," Steddy said, as he strode from the bar toward the casino.

"And maybe it won't, Steddy, maybe it won't," Wiley intoned under his breath.

The holding lounge at Nairobi airport was as hot and fly-ridden as it had been when Stedman was stuck there with Wiley on the way down, only now, perhaps because it was Sunday, there was no stewardess serving up iced gins—not that anything would have lightened the weight of confused emotions he carried with him.

They had treated their love carelessly, the way some people treat their clothes, taking for granted it would be there when they needed it.

He needed her but could think of no dialogue that would bring them together.

She needed him but felt violated and blamed him against her will.

The twangy tones of Peter Jellicoe's Australian accent cut through the heat and the flies and the haze of his self-centered mental meanderings. He was speaking to the flight attendant at the door of the lounge.

"If Mr. Wright's in here, would you tell him that we're ready to take off whenever he is."

"What the hell are you doing here?" Steddy called across the room. "I'm booked on Air Zimbabwe!"

Jellicoe, spotting Steddy for the first time, replied, "Well, I'm still responsible for getting you back in one piece, and I don't appreciate having to chase you down all over Africa."

Steddy's initial anger melted. The man had gone beyond the bounds of his duties for them, and Steddy realized that he'd never even thanked him.

"I'm sorry. I guess it all finally got to me," Steddy said when he reached him.

"What's that then—a week's vacation in sunny Zimbabwe?"

Steddy was unable to suppress the smile that came to his face.

"My flight to London's due to be called any minute."

"Your flight is ready whenever you are. I don't like losing passengers, even if they try to lose me."

"I've got my ticket," Steddy said lamely, holding out his boarding pass as proof.

"You don't need one to fly with me."

"But . . ."

"Hey, we came together, we'll go back the same way, if it's all the same to you. I don't like ten-hour solo legs anymore, and besides, I've got used to your lousy coffee."

Steddy laughed, and symbolically tearing his boarding pass in two, followed Jellicoe out onto the steamy tarmac, where the water puddles from the earlier rain hissed and boiled in the hot sun.

She was at the foot of the *Flying Cloud*'s stair and broke into a run when she saw him, stopping halfway while a Cessna taxied between them.

Even from afar, the impact of seeing her hit him with the force of a physical blow that took the wind out of him, and when he glanced accusingly at the pilot, he realized there were tears in his eyes and quickly turned away—back toward Thea.

The Cessna had broken her stride. When it had passed, she closed the gap between them more slowly, until she saw the sun glint off the wetness on his cheeks and began to run again. They were both laughing by the time their tears mingled and her body molded to his with a perfection that told the world they'd been made for each other.

He'd got a full pardon at the last minute. Life and joy

overfilled him, and he had to keep laughing to relieve the pressure.

"Let's go home," he said as they walked toward the plane in an awkward tangle.

"Where's that?" she laughed.

"Wherever you are."

They never even heard Jellicoe start the engines.

Mystery . . . Intrigue
. . . Suspense

By the year 2000, 2 out of 3 Americans could be illiterate.

It's true.

Today, 75 million adults… about one American in three, can't read adequately. And by the year 2000, U.S. News & World Report envisions an America with a literacy rate of only 30%.

Before that America comes to be, you can stop it… by joining the fight against illiteracy today.

Call the Coalition for Literacy at toll-free **1-800-228-8813** and volunteer.

Volunteer Against Illiteracy. The only degree you need is a degree of caring.

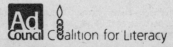

Ad Council Coalition for Literacy

Warner Books is proud to be an active supporter of the Coalition for Literacy.